OTHER BOOKS BY

SHERWOOD ANDERSON

WINDY McPHERSON'S SON
MARCHING MEN
MID-AMERICAN CHANTS
WINESBURG, OHIO
POOR WHITE
TRIUMPH OF THE EGG
MANY MARRIAGES
HORSES AND MEN
A STORY-TELLER'S STORY
THE MODERN WRITER
DARK LAUGHTER
SHERWOOD ANDERSON'S NOTE-BOOK
TAR
A NEW TESTAMENT
HELLO TOWNS
PERHAPS WOMEN

BEYOND DESIRE

BEYOND DESIRE

SHERWOOD ANDERSON

With an Introduction by

WALTER B. RIDEOUT

LIVERIGHT PUBLISHING CORPORATION

New York

BLACK AND GOLD EDITION

Library of Congress Catalog Card Number : 61-18088

TO ELENORE

INTRODUCTION

After Sherwood Anderson's first popular success, *Dark Laughter,* it was seven years before he published another novel. In many ways these were seven lean years and he went through months of what he called "just plain damn unspeakable gloom." He was working dispiritedly on a novel called at first *No God* and then *Beyond Desire,* but he finally admitted to his publisher, Horace Liveright, that he would never finish it. "I'm through," he wrote Liveright, "with the ordinary problem of middle-class people in love." Instead, he continued, he had a new interest; he was going to write about "working people in the mills, particularly the working people, the poor whites, in the mills in the South."

Anderson's impulse "to go where working men were" had come from talks with Eleanor Copenhaver, who had grown up in his adopted home town of Marion, Virginia, and who was later to become his wife. At her urging he began to travel through the South in the first months of the Depression Decade, going inside the mills, particularly textile mills, to observe the machines and the men and women who tended them. Having been appalled by the dirt and racket of factories in his Chicago days, he was surprised to discover the "complex beauty" of high-speed machinery, but he became more convinced than ever that "the whole tendency of modern industry has been rather to dehumanize people." The workers themselves were defeated, he felt, and his own months of frustration and despondency helped him go out to them in an immediate act of identification. In their lives, economically and emotionally impoverished, yet basically honest and poten-

tially creative, he saw the material he needed for fiction. Trans-
ferring the old title to a new narrative, he wrote *Beyond
Desire* during the Depression years of 1931 and 1932.

Since *Beyond Desire* comes to its climax in a direct clash
between striking workers and National Guard troops, it has
been customary to view the book as being primarily concerned
with the industrial strife of the times. To be sure, Anderson
draws on actual fact for the setting and situation in the fourth
and last section of the novel. His is one of four "proletarian"
novels published in 1932 that deal in some way with the textile
strike led three years before in Gastonia, North Carolina, by
Communist organizers, a strike in which bitter violence flared
repeatedly between the strikers on one side and the police and
vigilante groups on the other. But *Beyond Desire* is only in a
limited sense one of the strike novels of the Angry Thirties.
Its central theme is wider and more complex. *What Anderson
is primarily concerned with is the effect of industrialism, not
only on workers, but on the whole human community in
microcosm.* A dozen years earlier he had shown in *Poor White*
what happens to an Ohio town when it enters the machine
age. Now he examines the impact of industrialization on two
towns in the South. Just as in *Poor White,* labor strife is only
one result of the forces embodied in the machine. Much more
important consequences, as Anderson sees it, are the corrup-
tion of old values, greater discrepancy between the community's ideals and its reality, more and more emotional isolation
of the individual, and further disruption of understanding
between men and women. Conversely, however, the author
sees the tentative birth, particularly among his working-class
characters, of new values, new relationships, new possibilities for human communication and understanding.

Whereas Anderson the Midwesterner had from birth been
assimilating the experience that became *Poor White,* he was
limited in his knowledge of the South by temperamental dis-
like for some of its traditions and by the fact of his being, however sympathetic, from the North. Yet although he was always

a "Grant man" rather than a "Lee man," he had lived in the South for a number of years by choice and had observed its folkways both as a country newspaper editor and as a creative writer. *Beyond Desire* shows him sensitively aware of the peculiar intimacies and antagonisms, the totems and taboos, of a Southern community. In the hot little town of Langdon, Georgia, where the larger part of the action is set, a "great deal is made of family," the physical closeness of whites and Negroes proceeds under rigid, intricate (and ambivalent) codes of conduct, and white women are reverently guarded as much as possible from the realities. Such attitudes have long antedated industrialization, as Anderson knew, but the spirit of "Northern" commercialism that the machine brings in has intensified and multiplied latent hypocrisies and hostilities. The absolute cleavage between the citizen of the town and the textile worker in the adjoining mill village is one sign of a reduction in the total fund of human sympathy. Nowhere is the perversion of values more obvious, Anderson insists, than in the changed content of Christianity, to the forms of which people still intensely adhere. Early in the book, for example, the author describes a typical alliance between a future mill owner and a revivalist, who in all sincerity goes about preaching to yearning congregations the new gospel of material wealth.

"Yes, God," someone in the audience said fervently.
"I want that. I want it. I want it," a woman's voice cried.
It was a sharp plaintive voice.

It is a measure of Anderson's own humanity that he sees these confused, hungry people as pathetic rather than foolish or vicious. Yet if the purity of the religious impulse is preserved at all, he suggests in Book Four of the novel, it may be preserved in the spirit of unity engendered among the striking workers.

Without being schematic about it, Anderson makes the

three major male characters of *Beyond Desire* represent three different responses to this confusion of values attendant on industrialization. Willard Long, the father of Ethel Long, the "heroine" of the book, is a Southern gentleman, scrupulously faithful to traditional ideals and entirely obtuse about actual human relationships. Tom Riddle, a tough-minded, realistic lawyer, does not "care for the respectable standards of others." More "Northern than Southern," he laughs both at "church-going people like Ethel's father" and at the Ku Klux Klan, asserts that "it is money that rules," and believes that, "Some men are meant to be slaves, some masters." Anderson is remarkably fair in his presentation of both these men, but he is clearly much more sympathetic with Red Oliver, the most important person in the book.

Red is one of Anderson's young men who question life. Confused and groping—Anderson was less offended by these words and mental states than were his critics—Red is nevertheless honestly searching for the reality beneath the social mask. If the conflict between his life-denying mother and the life-affirming Negro woman who cared for him as a child seems too much a borrowing from *Dark Laughter,* the reader must admire the skill with which at every point Anderson places his hero between two worlds, one dying, one struggling to be born. Nowhere does Red fully belong. The son of estranged parents, he attends college but at home in the summer takes an unskilled job in the mill. He sides with the workers both by playing on the mill baseball team, rather than the town one, and by fighting against the townsmen during a strike in Langdon; yet his teammates are not at ease with him, and the townspeople mistakenly assume that he has supported them in a strike riot. He falls in love with Ethel Long, who is considerably older than he, has lived in Chicago as well as Langdon, and honestly recognizes the muddled understanding between men and women; but she ruthlessly uses young Red to clarify her own problems and coldly enters into a marriage contract with Tom Riddle. Even in the concluding section of the book when Red joins the strikers in Birchfield (Gastonia), he is mistaken for a Communist organizer and, though still undecided about the virtues of Communism, sacrifices himself in an impulsive effort to get "beyond desire," beyond the fever of personal concerns into the tranquillity of an unexpressed, because unexpressible, sense of human unity.

To Anderson, apparently, Red represents the young American in catastrophic times—puzzled, alienated, but committed to a search for new values and loyalties. He is also a kind of projection of the writer's own feelings; for Anderson himself felt alienated from industrialized America, he sought for alternative loyalties that might end this alienation, and he remained tentative and inconclusive in his own affirmations. It was better, he felt, to be honestly puzzled than glibly certain. Even Red's reservations about Communism reflected his creator's. He had already for years distrusted businessmen, and his sympathies were with the underdog. Quite honestly he preferred the worker to the bourgeois because he felt that the poverty and obscurity of the former had protected him from the latter's corrupting desire for status and possessions.

Because of his reservations about Communism, Anderson does not let *Beyond Desire* become a sterile exercise in ideology; because of his sympathies, he is at his best in the book when he is describing the lives of the mill workers. Certainly the finest single section of the novel is Book Two, "Mill Girls." Here his material is most fully mastered under strict but unobtrusive technical control. What he is after is not the realistic surface, any more than he was after it years before in the stories of *Winesburg, Ohio*. Rather he uses oblique methods to penetrate imaginatively the lives of four girls, but particularly the strong, tender Doris Hoffman, and make the reader aware of the inner quality of those lives. His major device for achieving this purpose is a subtly shifting dual time scheme. The present event of the two chapters that comprise Book Two is the visit of the girls to a fair on Saturday afternoon, the day reserved by unspoken agreement in Langdon for mill workers and Negroes. The action of this event is broken into many short passages, which are distributed in more or less chronological sequence throughout the two chapters. Between these passages are placed in non-chronological order quick scenes, narrative, and author's comment concerned with everyday life. There are glimpses of the spinning-room in the mill where Doris and her friends work at top speed in the wet heat. These flow into brief pictures of the girls at home in the cheap, identical company houses; of Doris nursing her baby; of Doris rubbing the mill weariness from the body of her husband, who talks of organizing the workers, or from the body of her less robust friend, Grace, who describes the waterfalls on the farm where she grew up in the hills to the north of town. Then the reader is taken back briefly from the "prison" of everyday life to the moments of gaiety at the fair.

The fragments of experience within this constantly shifting time scheme, as one reads on, soon begin to relate complexly to each other and enrich each other's meaning. The little "fair of shows," with its stands, its games, its ferris wheel, is gimcrack and tawdry; but for Doris it is a release into a world "outside the cotton mill where she worked and the cotton-mill village where she lived with her husband." Near the end of Book Two, Doris and Grace have a ride on the ferris wheel, from the top of which Doris sees for the first time in her life all of the tree-shaded town of Langdon, the yellow river bending around it, hills far away to the north under a blue sky. She recognizes them as the hills where Grace had once lived, "Where the waterfalls were"; and the reader, too, recalling Grace's nostalgic dreams of youthful freedom, feels Doris's sudden surge of emotional expansion. Working thus fluidly backward and forward in time, Anderson succeeds in getting the reader into the consciousness of a poor-white girl in a Southern textile town and in creating the illusion that the whole of her life exists simultaneously in his own consciousness. "Mill Girls," it can be said without exaggeration, is one of the achievements in Anderson's career as a writer.

Admittedly *Beyond Desire* is an uneven work. It was probably a mistake to give so much space to the experiences of Ethel Long, though in various ways her story carries out the book's theme. (One of Anderson's most effective touches is the symbolic contrast between the Blanche-Ethel rlationship and the Doris-Grace one.) There are passages, too, where the short sentences, exactly right for "Mill Girls," become exasperatingly choppy, flat, and repetitive. Still one long remembers from the book part after part like that, to take a final example, in which Willard Long takes his daughter on a drive to visit a Negro school. Here again the delicately shifting time sequences, the events that dissolve into other events and then reëstablish themselves, the subtly complementary and contradictory echoes among all these events and the present natural setting—all these together give the reader the illusion, necessary for any successful fiction, that he is watching total human personalities react with other total personalities at a certain point in time. *Beyond Desire* on the whole measures up to Anderson's rather defiant assertion to a friend: "For myself, I know well enough that the book is sound, and I believe it will take its definite place in the story of our American civilization. . . ."

WALTER B. RIDEOUT

Northwestern University
July 21, 1961

CONTENTS

CONTENTS

BOOK ONE

YOUTH

1

NEIL BRADLEY wrote letters to his friend Red Oliver. Neil said he was going to marry a woman in Kansas City. She was a revolutionist and Neil did not know when he first met her whether he was quite one or not. He said:

"It's like this, Red. You remember the empty feeling we had when we were in school together. I don't think you had it much when you were out here, but I did. I had it all the time I was in college and after I came home. I can't talk to Father and Mother about it much. They wouldn't understand. It would hurt them.

"I guess," Neil said, "that all of us younger men and women with any life in us have it now."

Neil spoke in his letter of God. That was a bit strange, Red thought, coming from Neil. He must have got that from his woman. "We can't hear His voice or feel Him in the land," he said. He thought perhaps the earlier men and women in America had something he and Red had missed. They had "God," whatever that had meant to them. The early New Englanders, who had been so intellectually dominant and who had influenced so much the thought of the whole country must have thought they had God really.

If they had, what they had, it had come down to Neil and Red in some way pretty much weakened and washed out. Neil thought that. Religion, he said, was now an old gown, grown thin and with all the colors washed out of it. People still wore the old gown but it did not warm them any more.

People needed warmth, Neil thought, they needed ro-

3

mance and, most of all, the romance of feeling, of thinking they were trying to go somewhere.

People, he said, needed to hear voices coming from outside themselves.

Science also had raised hell and the cheap sort of popular knowledge ... or what was called knowledge ... spread about everywhere now had raised even more hell.

There was, he said in one of his letters, too much emptiness in affairs, in the churches, in government.

The Bradley farm wasn't far from Kansas City, and Neil went often to the city. He had met a woman he was going to marry. He tried to describe her to Red but didn't succeed very well. He described her as full of energy. She was a school teacher and had begun reading books. She had become first a socialist and then a communist. She had ideas.

One was that she and Neil should live together for a time before they decided about marriage. She thought they ought to sleep together, get used to each other. So, Neil, a young farmer living on his father's Kansas farm, began to live with her secretly. She was small and dark, Red gathered. "It seems a little unfair to her to be talking about her with you, another man ... you may meet her some day and be thinking of my words," he said in one of his letters. "But I feel I must," he said. Neil was one of the outgoing kind. He could be more frank and outgoing in letters than Red and was less embarrassed about telling of his feelings.

He spoke of everything. The woman he had met boarded in a certain house belonging to very respectable people, fairly well-to-do people in the city. The man was the treasurer of a small manufacturing company. They had taken the school teacher in to live with them. She was staying there for the summer, while there was no school. She said, "The first two or three years ought to tell." She wanted to go through them with Neil without marriage.

"We can't sleep together there of course," Neil said, meaning the house where she lived. When he came into town, into Kansas City—his father's farm was close enough so that he could drive into the city in an hour—Neil went to the house of the treasurer. There was something like a laugh in Neil's letters telling about such evenings.

There was the woman, small and dark, really a revolutionist, in that house. She was like Neil, the farmer's son who had been East to college, and like Red Oliver. She came from a respectable church-going family of a little Kansas town. She had gone through high school and had then gone to a normal school. Most young women of that sort were dull enough, Neil said, but this one wasn't. She had felt from the first that she had a social problem to face as well as an individual woman's problem. Red gathered, from Neil's letters, that she was alert and intense. "She has a beautiful little body," he said, writing to Red. "I admit," he said, "that when I write such words to another man they mean nothing."

He said he supposed that any woman's body became beautiful to the man who loved her. He began touching her body and she let him. Modern girls sometimes went pretty far with young men. It was a way of getting education. Hands on their bodies. It was everywhere almost an accepted fact, even among the older, more frightened fathers and mothers, that such things went on. A young man tried it out with a young woman and then quit her perhaps, and she also perhaps tried several.

Neil went to the house where the school teacher boarded in Kansas City. The house was out near the edge of the city, so that Neil, in driving in to see his woman, did not have to pass through the city. The four people, he and the school teacher with the treasurer and his wife, sat for a time on the porch of the house.

On rainy nights they sat and played cards or talked, the treasurer of his affairs and Neil of farming. The treasurer was rather an intellectual man ... "of the old sort," Neil said. That kind could even be liberal, very liberal ... in their minds, not in fact. If they knew that, after they went to bed, sometimes ... on the porch of the house or inside, on a couch. "She sits on the edge of the low porch and I kneel on the grass at the edge of the porch. ... She is like a flower opening."

She said to Neil, "I can't begin to live and think and know what I want beyond a man until I have my man." Red gathered that the little dark school teacher Neil had found was of some new world he himself wanted to get into. Neil's letters about her ... in spite of their being so very personal sometimes ... Neil even tried to describe the feeling in his fingers when he touched her body, the warmth of her flesh, the sweetness of it to him. Red himself hungered with all his being to find such a woman for himself but never did. Neil's letters made him also. hungry for some relationship with life that was sensual and fleshly but beyond just flesh. Neil was trying to express that in the letters he wrote to his friend.

Red had had other men friends. Men had come to him, sometimes before, pouring themselves out to him. He thought, at the end, that he himself never did get a woman, not really.

There was Neil out there on the Kansas farm, or in the evening gone to town to see his woman. He seemed full of life, rich with life. He worked on his father's farm. The father was getting old. He would die or retire presently and the farm would belong to Neil. It was a pleasant farm in a rich pleasant country. Farmers, such as Neil's father had been and as Neil would be, didn't make much money but they lived well. The father had manged to send Neil East to college where he had met Red Oliver. The two had played ball on the same college baseball team, Neil at second base and Red at short-stop. Oliver to Bradley to Smith. Zip! They had been a good double-play pair together.

Red had gone out to the Kansas farm and had stayed there for a few weeks. It was before Neil met the school teacher in the city.

Neil was a radical then. He had radical thoughts. Red had asked him once, "You are going to be a farmer, like your

father?" "Yes." "Would you give up ownership of this?" Red
had asked. They were standing at the edge of a cornfield
that day. Such magnificent corn they raised on that farm.
Neil's father kept cattle. He raised corn and put it in great
cribs in the fall. Then he went West and bought steers which
he brought to the farm to be fattened during the winter. The
corn wasn't hauled away from the farm to be sold but was
fed to the cattle and the rich manure that accumulated all
through the winter was then hauled out and spread over the
land. "Would you give up ownership of all this?" "Yes, I
guess," Neil had said. He laughed, "It's true they might have
to take it from me," he said.

Even then Neil had got notions into his head. He
wouldn't, at that time, have called himself frankly a communist as he did afterwards in letters, under the influence
of the woman.

It wasn't that he would have been afraid.

But yes, he was afraid. Even after he met the school
teacher and wrote the letters to Red, he was afraid of hurting
his father and mother. Red did not blame him for that. He
remembered Neil's¹ father and mother as good people, honest
people, kind people. Neil had one sister, older than himself,
who had married a young neighboring farmer. She was a
big strong good woman like her mother and very fond of
Neil and proud of him. When Red was in Kansas that summer she came once with her husband to spend the week-end
at home and talked to Red of Neil. "I am glad he has been
to college and is educated," she said. She was also glad that
her brother, in spite of his education, was willing to come
back home and be a simple farmer like the rest of them. She
thought Neil was smarter than all the rest of them, broader
in his mind, she said.

Neil said, speaking of the farm he would some day in-
herit, "Yes, I guess I'd give it up that way," he said. "I
think I am going to be a good farmer. I like farming."
He said that he dreamed of his father's fields at night

sometimes. "I am always planning and planning," he said. What he would do with every field was planned, he said, years in advance. "I'd give it up because I can't give it up," he said. "Men can never go away from the land." He meant that he intended to make of himself a very capable farmer. "What difference will it make to such men as myself if the land finally belongs to the state? They will need such men as I intend to make of myself."

There were other farmers in that neighborhood not so capable as he was. What difference did that make? "It would be glorious to spread myself out," Neil said. "I wouldn't ask any pay if they would let me do that. All I'd ask would be a living."

"They wouldn't let you do it, though," Red said.

"And we'll have to make them let us some day," Neil answered. Neil was probably a communist then and didn't quite know it.

Evidently the woman he had found had made him know something. They had got at something together. Neil, in his letters about her and his relations with her, told of things they did. Sometimes the woman told lies to the treasurer and his wife with whom she lived. She told Neil that she wanted to spend the night with him.

Then she got up a cock and bull story about going home for the night to her own Kansas town. She packed her bag and met Neil in the city, getting into his car, and they drove off to some town. They registered at the same little hotel as husband and wife. They had not married yet, Neil said, because they both wanted to be sure. "I don't want it to make you feel like settling down and I don't want to settle down myself," she said to Neil. She was afraid he might become contented with being just a fairly prosperous Middle-Western farmer ... no better than a merchant ... no better than a banker or any money-hungry man, she said. She told Neil she had tried two other men before she came to him. "All the way?" he had asked her. "Sure," she said. "If," she said, "a man became absorbed just in the happiness of possessing a woman he loved, or she gave herself just to him and to having children..."

She had become a sincere Red. She thought there was something beyond desire, but that you had to satisfy desire and understand and appreciate the wonders of desire first. You had to see whether or not it could conquer you, make you forget everything else.

First, though, you had to find it sweet and know that it was sweet. If you could not bear the sweetness of it and go on, you were no good.

There had to be exceptional people. The woman kept telling Neil that. She thought a new time had come. The world was waiting for new people, a new kind of people. She did not want Neil and herself to be big people. The world, she told him, wanted now big little people, plenty of them. There always had been such people, she said, but they had to begin to speak out now, to assert themselves.

She gave herself to Neil and watched him and, Red gathered, he was doing something of the sort with her. Red got that out of Neil's letters. They went off to little hotels to lie in each other's arms. When their bodies were quiet they talked. "I guess we'll marry," Neil said in a letter to Red Oliver. "Why not?" he asked. He said people had to begin to prepare themselves. The revolution was coming. When it came it was going to demand strong and quiet people willing to work, not just noisy ill-prepared people. He thought that every woman ought to begin by finding her man, at any cost, and that every man ought to make the search for his woman.

It was to be done in a new way, Neil thought, more fearlessly than the old way. The new men and women who had to begin to appear, if the world were ever to be made sweet again, had first of all to learn to be fearless and even reckless. They had to be life lovers who would throw even life itself into the game.

*

THE machinery in the cotton mill at Langdon, Georgia, made a low singing sound. Young Red Oliver was working there. All week the sound never stopped, night or day. At night the mill was brightly lighted. There was the town of Langdon above the little plateau on which the mill stood and it was a rather shabby town. It wasn't shabby as it had been once, before the mill came, when Red Oliver was a small boy, but a boy hardly knows when a town is shabby.

How is he to know? If he is a town boy, the town is his world. He has known no other world, has made no comparisons. Red Oliver had been a rather lonely lad. His father had been a doctor in Langdon and his grandfather before him had also been a doctor there, but Red's father had not done very well. He had faded out, gone rather stale, when he was still a young man. At that time it wasn't so difficult to become a doctor as it became later. Red's father got through his studies and began his practice. He practiced with his father and lived with him. When the father died—doctors also die— he lived in the old doctor's place, inherited it, a rather flamboyant old frame house with a wide porch in front. The porch was supported by tall wooden pillars made originally to look like stone. They did not look like stone in Red's day. There were great cracks in the old wood and the house had long been unpainted. There was what in the South is called "a dog run" through the house and, standing in the street at front, you could, on a summer, spring or fall day, look directly through the house, and across hot still cotton fields to Georgia hills, seen in the distance.

The old doctor had a small frame office in a corner of the yard near the street but it had been discarded as an office by the young doctor. He had got an office upstairs in one of

the buildings on Main Street. Now the old office was overgrown by vines and had fallen into decay. It was unused and
the door had been taken off. An old chair, with the bottom
out, stood in there. You could see it from the street, sitting
in there in the dusky light behind the vines.

Red had come for the summer to Langdon from a school
he had been attending in the North. He had known at school
the young man Neil Bradley, who later wrote him the letters.
He worked as a common laborer in the mill that summer.

His father was dead, had died during the winter while
Red was a freshman in the Northern college.

At the time of his death Red's father was no longer
young. He had not married until he had reached middle life
and then had married a nurse. It was said in the town, whispered about the town, that the woman the doctor had married,
Red's mother, was not from a very good family. She was
from Atlanta and had come to Langdon, where she met Doctor Oliver, on an important case. At that time there were no
trained nurses in Langdon. A man, the president of the local
bank, the man who later became president of the Langdon
Cotton Mill Company, at that time a young man, got seriously
ill. The nurse was sent for and came. Doctor Oliver was on
the case. It wasn't his case but he had been called in consul-
tation. There were only four doctors in the county then and
they were all called.

Doctor Oliver met the nurse and they got married. People of the town raised their eyebrows. "Was it necessary?"
they asked. Evidently it was not. Young Red Oliver was not
born until three years later. It turned out that he was to be
the only child of the marriage. There were, however, rumors
in the town. "She must have made him think it was necessary." Such tales are whispered about the streets and in the
houses in Southern towns as well as in the towns of the East,
the Middle West and the Far West.

There are always other whispers going about in streets
and houses of Southern towns. A great deal is made of fam-

ily. "What sort of family has she, or he?" There has never been much immigration into Southern States, into the old American slave States, as every one knows. Families have just gone on and on.

A good many families have decayed, gone to pieces. In a surprising number of old Southern communities, where no industry has come in, as it came to Langdon and has come to many other Southern towns in the last twenty-five or thirty years, there are no men left. Very likely you will find, in such a family, no one left but two or three queer fussy old women. A few years ago they would have been talking constantly of Civil War days or of the days before the Civil War, the good old days when the South really was something. They would have told you tales of Northern generals who carried away their silver spoons and were in other ways brutal and cruel to them. That kind of old Southern woman has pretty much died out now. Those who are left live somewhere in town or in the country in an old house. It has once been a grand house, or at any rate a house that in the South in the old days was thought grand. There are wooden pillars supporting a porch across the front as at the front of the Oliver house. Two or three old women live there. No doubt, after the Civil War, much the same thing happened to the South that happened to New England. The more energetic young men lit out. After the Civil War the men in power in the North, the men who came into power with the death of Lincoln and after Andrew Johnson was got out of the way, were afraid of losing their power. They passed laws giving the vote to Negroes, expecting to control them. For a time they did control. There was a so-called reconstruction period, that was in reality a time of destruction more bitter even than the war years.

But every one who has read about American history now knows about that. Nations have lives like people. It is perhaps best not to inquire too closely into most people's lives. Even Andrew Johnson is now looked upon with favor by the historians. In Knoxville, Tennessee, where he was once hated and derided, there is now a big hotel named for him. He is no longer thought of as merely a drunken traitor, elected by accident and staggering through a few years as President until a real President could be named.

In the South also, in spite of the rather amusing idea of Greek culture, no doubt taken up because both the Greek and the Southern cultures were founded upon slavery, a culture that, in the South, never flamed into art as in old Greece but remained merely an empty claim on the lips of certain solemn long-coated Southerners, and the notion of a peculiar chivalry, inherent in the Southerner, got probably, as Mark Twain once declared, from reading too much Sir Walter Scott . . . in spite of these things tongues wagged and do wag in the South. Little knife thrusts are made. It is a civilization, as suggested, where much emphasis is placed upon family, so that is a vulnerable point. "In such and such a family there is a touch of the tar pot." Heads wagging.

They had wagged over young Doctor Oliver and later over the middle-aged Doctor Oliver who suddenly married a nurse. There had been a certain colored woman, living alone in Langdon, who had insisted on having children. The younger Oliver was her doctor. He went often, over a period covering several years, to her house, a small cabin on a country road beyond the Oliver place. The Oliver house had once stood on the best street in Langdon. It was the last house before the cotton fields began, but later, after the cotton mill was built, after new people began to come in, after new buildings and new stores were put up on Main Street, the best people began building at another end of the town.

The colored woman, a tall straight yellow woman with fine shoulders and an erect head, did no work. She was a Negro's Negro, not a white man's Negro, people said. She had once been married to a young Negro man but he had disappeared. She may have driven him off.

The doctor went often to her little house. She did not

work. She lived simply but she lived. The doctor's car was occasionally seen standing in the road before her house even quite late at night.

Was she ill? People smiled. Southerners do not much fancy talking of such things, particularly when there are outsiders about. Among themselves ... "Well, you know." Words passed about. One of the yellow woman's children was almost white. That was a boy who disappeared later, after the time of which we are now writing, when Red Oliver was also a young boy. Of all of these earlier head-waggings, both male and female head-waggings, whispers on summer nights, the doctor seen driving out that way, even after he got himself a wife and had a son ... of all these innuendoes, knife-thrusts against his father in the town of Langdon, Red Oliver knew nothing.

Perhaps Doctor Oliver's wife, Red's mother, knew. She may have decided to say nothing. She had a brother in Atlanta who, in the year after she married Doctor Oliver, got into trouble. He was working in a bank and stole some money and lit out with a married woman. They got him later. His name and picture were in the Atlanta papers that circulated in Langdon. To be sure, the sister's name was not mentioned. If Doctor Oliver saw the item he said nothing and she said nothing. She was by nature a rather silent woman and, after her marriage, became even more quiet and reserved.

Then suddenly she began going regularly to church. She got converted. One evening, when Red was a high school boy, she went off alone to church. There was a revivalist in town, a Methodist revivalist. Red always remembered that evening.

It was an evening in the late fall and Red was to graduate from the town high school the next spring. He was invited to a party that evening and was to escort a young woman. He dressed early and went for her. His relation with that particular young woman was a passing thing, never amounting to anything. His father was away from home. After his marriage, he had begun drinking.

He was one of the sort of men who drink alone. He did not get helplessly drunk but having drunk until he was a little incoherent and inclined to stumble when he walked, he carried a bottle with him, taking drinks in secret, and often stayed in that condition for a week at a time. He had been, when younger, on the whole, a rather talkative man, careless about his dress, liked as a person but not too much respected as a doctor, a man of science ... who, to be really successful should always perhaps be a trifle solemn in appearance and a trifle dull ... doctors, to be really successful, should adopt early in life a certain attitude toward laymen ... they should appear always a bit mysterious, not talk too much ... people like to be bullied a bit by doctors. ... Doctor Oliver had not done these things. Let us say there was a case about which he was a bit mystified. He went to see a sick man or woman. He went in to her.

When he came out there were the sick woman's relatives. There was something wrong down inside. She was in pain and had a high fever. Her people were anxious and upset. Heaven knows what they hoped. They might have hoped she would get well and, on the other hand ...

No use going into that. People are people. They gathered about the doctor. "What is it, doctor? Will she get well? Is she very bad?"

"Yes. Yes." Doctor Oliver perhaps smiled. He was puzzled. "I don't know what is wrong with the woman. How the devil am I to know?"

Sometimes he even laughed in the very faces of the anxious people standing about. That was because he was slightly embarrassed. He was always laughing or frowning at the wrong moment. After he married and began to drink, he even sometimes giggled in the very presence of the sick people. He did not want to. The doctor wasn't a fool. For example, when talking to laymen, he did not call diseases by the names commonly used by outsiders. He managed to remember names, even for the most common sort of diseases, every one did not know. There are always long difficult names, derived usually from Latin. He remembered them. He had got them at school.

But even with Doctor Oliver there were certain people with whom he got along very well. He was understood by a few people in Langdon. After he grew more and more unsuccessful and was more often half drunk there were a few men and women who stuck to him. They were, however, likely to be very poor people and they were usually queer. There were even a few men and older women to whom he spoke of his own failure. "I'm no good. I don't see why any one employs me," he said. When he said it he tried to laugh but wasn't successful. "Lord God Almighty, did you see that? I almost broke into tears. I am becoming sentimental about myself. I am getting full of self-pity," he said to himself sometimes, when having been with some one with whom he felt sympathetic; he had in this way rather let go.

On the evening when young Red Oliver, then a high school boy, went to the party, escorting a young high school girl, a pretty girl with a long slender young body ... she had soft blond hair and breasts just beginning to bud, breasts just seen, pushing out the soft clinging summer dress she wore ... her hips were very slender, like a boy's hips ... on that evening he had come down out of his room upstairs in the Oliver house and there was his mother dressed all in black. He had never before seen her dressed like that. It was a new dress.

There were sometimes days when Red's mother, a tall strong-looking woman with a long sad face, scarcely spoke to her son or to her husband. She had a certain air. It was as though she had said aloud, "Well, I have got into this. I came to this town, not expecting to stay here and I met this doctor. He was much older than I am. I married him.

"My people may not be so much. I had a brother who got into trouble and went to prison. Now I have a son.

"I have got into this and now I will do my job as best

I can. I will try to stand on my own feet. I ask nothing of any one."

The yard of the Oliver house had a rather sandy soil and few things would grow in it, but after Doctor Oliver's wife came there to live with him she was always trying to raise flowers. Every year she failed, but with the coming of a new year she tried again.

The old Doctor Oliver had always belonged to the Presbyterian church in Langdon and although the younger one, Red's father, never went to church, he would have called himself, if asked regarding his church connections, a Presbyterian.

"Are you going out, Mother?" Red had asked her that evening, coming down from upstairs and seeing her dressed like that. "Yes," she said, "I'm going to church." She did not ask him to go with her, nor did she ask where he was going. She had seen him dressed as for an occasion. If she was curious she suppressed her curiosity.

That evening she went alone to the Methodist church where the revival was going on. Red walked down past the church with the young woman he was taking to the party. She was a daughter of one of the so-called "real families" of town, a slender young woman and rather enticing, as has already been suggested. Red was excited, just being with her. He wasn't in love and, in fact, was never with that young woman after that evening. However, he felt something within himself, a matter of little fleeting thoughts, half desires, awakening hungers. Afterwards, when he came back from college to work in the cotton mill in Langdon as a common laborer, after his father died and the fortunes of the Oliver family were at a low ebb, then Red would hardly have expected to be asked to escort that particular young woman to a party. She was, by chance, the daughter of the same man whose illness had brought his mother to Langdon, the same man who was later president of the Langdon Mill, where Red became a workman. He walked along with her that night, going to the party, having waited for a half hour on the steps before her father's house while she did certain last-minute feminine primpings, and they passed the Methodist church where the revival meeting was being held. There was a preacher in there, a stranger in town, brought to town for the revival, a rather vulgar-looking man with a bald head and a large black mustache, and he had already begun to preach. He really shouted. The Methodists in Langdon did that. They shouted. "Like Negroes," the girl he was with said to Red that evening. She did not say that. "Like niggers," was what she said. "Listen to them," she said. There was scorn in her voice. She did not go to the high school in Langdon but attended a young ladies' seminary somewhere near Atlanta. She was at home on a visit because her mother had been ill. Red did not know why he had been asked to escort her to the party. He thought, "I suppose I might have asked Father to let me have his car." He never had asked for it. The doctor's car was a cheap one and was pretty old.

White people in a little frame church on a side street listening to a preacher shout, "Get God, I tell you, you are lost unless you get God.

"It is your chance. Don't put it off.

"You are miserable. If you haven't got God you are lost. What are you getting out of life? Get God, I tell you."

The voice rang in Red's ears that night. He always afterwards, for some obscure reason, remembered the little street of the Southern town and the walk toward the house where a party was being held on that evening he took the young woman to the party and afterwards escorted her home. He later remembered passing with relief out of the little street in which the Methodist church stood. On that evening there were no services being held in any other church in town. His own mother must have gone in there.

Most of the Methodists, of that particular Methodist church in Langdon, were poor whites. People who worked in the cotton mill went to church there. There was no church

in the cotton mill village itself, but the church stood on property belonging to the mill, although it lay outside the mill
village and quite near the home of the mill president. The
mill had contributed most of the money for the building of
the church, but people of the town were quite free to go to
it. The mill even paid half of the salary of the regular
preacher. Red went past the church with the girl and through
Main Street. People spoke to Red. Men he met bowed with
rather over-elaborate ceremony to the young girl he was with.

Red, already a tall boy and still growing fast then, had
on a new hat and a new suit. He felt awkward and a little
ashamed of something. This he remembered afterwards as
being mixed in him with a feeling of being ashamed that
he was ashamed. He kept passing people he knew. There
was a man riding a mule under the bright lights through Main
Street. "Hello, Red," he called. "How absurd," Red thought.
"I don't even know the man. I suppose it is some smarty who
has seen me playing baseball."

He was shy and raised his hat to people shyly. His hair
was fiery red and he had let it grow too long. "I should have
got a hair cut," he thought. There were large freckles on his
nose and cheeks, such freckles as red-haired young men fre-
quently have.

Really Red was popular in the town, more popular than
he knew. He was then on the high school baseball team, the
best player on the team. He liked playing baseball but hated,
as he always afterwards did, the fuss made about baseball
by people who did not play. When he was playing baseball
and had made a long hit, perhaps reaching third base, there
would be people, commonly quiet enough people who would
be running up and down the base lines and shouting. He stood
on third base and men even came and slapped him on the
shoulder. "The damn fools," he thought. He liked the fuss
being made over him and hated it too.

Just as he liked being with that girl and at the same
time would have liked not being with her. There was an un-

comfortable feeling that really lasted all evening and until he had got her home from the party and safely in her own house. If a man could touch a girl like that. Red had at that time never done such a thing.

Why had his mother suddenly taken it into her head to go to that church? The girl he was with had contempt for people who went to the church. "They shout like niggers, don't they," she had said. They did too. He could hear that preacher's voice clear into Main Street. A boy was put into an odd position. He couldn't have contempt for his own mother. It was queer her suddenly making up her mind to go to that church. Perhaps, he thought, she had merely gone out of curiosity or because she had suddenly become lonely.

*

SHE hadn't. Red knew it later that evening. He had at last got that young woman home from the party. It was held at the house of a minor official of the mill, who also had sons and daughters in the town's high school. Red took the young woman home and they stood together for a moment by the front door of the house of the man who had once been a banker and was now a prosperous mill president. It was the most imposing house in Langdon.

There was a large yard, shaded by trees and planted with shrubs. The young woman he was with had really been pleased with him but he didn't know that. She had thought he was the best-looking young man at the party. He was large and strong.

She, however, was not serious about him. She had practiced on him a little, as young women do; even his embarrassment, being with her, was nice, she thought. She had used her eyes. There are certain little subtle things a young woman can do with her body. It is permitted. She knows how. You do not have to teach her the art.

Red walked into the yard of her father's house and stood

with her for a moment trying to say good night. At last he got off an awkward speech. Her eyes were looking at him. They grew soft.

"That's nonsense. She wouldn't be interested in me," he thought. She wasn't particularly interested. There was a way she stood, on the lower step of her father's house, her head a little thrown back, then the head being lowered, her glance meeting his. The little undeveloped breasts stood forth. Red rubbed his trousers legs with his fingers. His hands were large and strong, they could grasp a baseball. They could put a sharp curve on the ball. He would have liked ... with her ... just then ...

No use of thinking that. "Good night. I had a hot time," he said. What a word to have used! He hadn't had a good time at all. He went home.

He got home and had got into bed, when something happened. Although he did not know it, his father had not yet come home.

Red had gone softly into the house and upstairs and had undressed, thinking of that girl. He never did think about her after that night. Afterwards other girls and women came to do to him what she had done. She hadn't, at least not very consciously, intended to do anything to him.

He was lying in bed and suddenly drew the fingers of his rather large hands together, making a fist. He squirmed in bed. "Jesus, I'd like ... Who wouldn't ..."

She was such a willowy, really undeveloped creature, that girl. A man could take such a one.

"Suppose a man could make a woman of her. How is that done?

"How absurd really. Who am I to call myself a man?" No doubt Red did not have any such definite thoughts as are here set down. He was lying in bed, rather tense, being male, being young, having been with the young female with the slim figure in the soft dress ... the eyes that could suddenly become soft . . . the little hard breasts thrusting themselves forth.

Red heard his mother's voice. There had never been such a sound in the Oliver house. She was praying, making a little sobbing sound. Red heard words.

Getting out of bed, he went softly to the stairs that led to the floor below, to the floor on which his father and mother slept. They had slept together down there ever since he could remember anything at all. Their doing so stopped after that night. Afterwards Red's father slept, as he did, in a room upstairs. Whether or not his mother said to his father, after that night, "Go away. I do not want to sleep with you any more," Red of course did not know.

He went part way down the stairs and listened to the voice from below. There was no doubt it was his mother's voice. She was crying, even sobbing. She was praying. Words came from her. The words ran through the quiet house. "He's right. Life is as he says. A woman gets nothing. I won't go on.

"I don't care what they say. I'll join with them. They are my people.

"God, You help me. Help me God. Jesus, You help me."

There was Red Oliver's mother using such words. She had been to that church and had got religion.

She had been ashamed to let them know at the church how much she was moved. Now she was safely at home in her own house. She knew her husband had not come home and did not know of Red's arrival, had not heard him come in. As people do, when they are excited and religion has gripped them, she used words remembered from her girlhood in Atlanta, where, with her brothers, she had gone to Sunday School. "Jesus," she said, in a low strained voice, "I know about You. They say You sat down with publicans and sinners. Sit down with me."

In reality there was something a little suggestive of niggers in the way Red's mother talked so familiarly to God·

"Come and sit here with me. I want You, Jesus." The sentences were broken by groans and sobs. She kept it up a long time and her son sat in the darkness on the stairs and listened. He wasn't particularly touched by her words and was even ashamed thinking, "If she wanted to get like that, why didn't she go to the Presbyterians?" But over and above that feeling there was another. He was filled with boyish sorrow and forgot the young woman who, but a few minutes before, had absorbed his thoughts. He thought only of his mother, suddenly loving her. He would have liked to go to her.

As Red sat bare-footed, in his pajamas, on the steps that night he heard his father's car stop in the street before the house. He left the car like that every night, standing in the street. He came toward the house. Red could not see him in the darkness, but he could hear. The doctor was probably a little drunk. He stumbled on the steps that led up to the porch.

If Red's mother was to get religion she would be as she was about raising flowers in the sandy soil of the Olivers' front yard. She might not get Jesus to come and sit with her as she demanded, but she would keep on trying. She was a determined woman. That was really the way it turned out. The revivalist preacher afterwards came to the house and prayed with her but when that happened Red had got out of the way. He had seen the man coming.

That night he sat for long minutes in the darkness on the stairs, listening. Shivers ran through his body. His father opened the door that led in from the street and stood with the knob in his hand. He also listened; minutes seemed to pass more and more slowly. The husband must have been surprised and shocked as was the son. When he had opened the door partially a little light came in from the street. Red could see his father's figure, dimly outlined down there. Then, after what seemed a long time, the door closed softly. He heard the low sound of his father's feet on the porch. The doctor must have fallen when he tried to step down off the porch and into the yard. "God damn," he said. Red heard the words very distinctly. His mother kept on with her prayers. He heard his father's car start. He was going away somewhere for the night. "God, this is too much for me," he was perhaps thinking. Red did not know about that. He sat listening for a time, his body trembling, and then the voice from his mother's room grew silent. He went silently up the stairs again and into his own room and got into bed. His bare feet had made no sound. He did not think any more of the girl he had been with during the evening. He thought instead of his mother. There she was down there, alone, as he was. There was a queer tender feeling in him. He had never felt that way before. He really wanted to cry like a small child, but instead merely lay in the bed staring into the darkness of his room in the Oliver house.

2

RED OLIVER had got a new sympathy with his mother and perhaps a new understanding of her. Working that first time in the mill may have helped. His mother was, without doubt, rather looked down on by the people who were called "the best people" of Langdon and, after she got religion and joined the church to which the mill workers went, the shouting Methodists, the groaning Methodists, the Georgia Crackers who now worked in the mill and who lived in the rows of rather meaningless little houses on the lower plateau below the town, her stock did not go up.

Red had begun work as a common laborer in the mill. When he went to the mill president, to apply for the job, the man had seemed pleased. "That's right. Don't be afraid to begin at the bottom," he said. He called in the mill superintendent. "Give this young man a place," he said. The superintendent protested a little. "But we do not need any men."

"I know. You find a place for him. You take him on."

The mill president got off a little speech. "After all, bear this in mind; he is, after all, a Southern boy." The mill superintendent, a tall stoop-shouldered man who had come to Langdon from a New England state, did not quite catch the significance of that. He might even have been saying to himself, "Well, what of that?" Northern men coming into the South to live become fed-up on Southern talk. "He is a Southern boy. What the hell? What difference does that make? I am running a shop. A man is a man. He does his

25

work to suit me or he does not. What do I give a damn who his parents were or where he was born?

"In New England, where I came from, we do not say, 'be careful of this tender little sprout. He is a New Englander.'

"They do not get off that sort of thing in the Middle West either. 'His grandfather was so and so or his grandmother was so and so.'

"To hell with his grandfather or his grandmother.

"You are asking me to get results. I notice that you Southerners, for all your big talk, want results. You want profits. You be careful. Don't you go throwing any of your Southern cousins or other poor relatives off on me.

"If you want to employ them, keep them in your damn office here."

The superintendent of the Langdon shop, that time when Red first got a job there, may have been thinking something like that. As you, the reader, may have guessed, he said nothing of the sort aloud. He was a man with a rather impersonal face and filled with his own kind of enthusiasm. He loved machinery, loved it almost tenderly. There are a growing number of that sort of men in America.

The man had eyes of a peculiar, rather faded blue, much like the blue of corn flowers that grow in masses beside country roads in many of our Middle-Western American states. When on duty in the mill he walked about with his long legs slightly bent and with his head thrust forward. He did not smile and never raised his voice. Afterwards, when Red had begun working in the mill, he was interested in the man and a bit frightened by him. You have seen a robin standing on a green lawn after rain. Watch him. His head is turned slightly to one side. Suddenly he hops forward. He has thrust his bill quickly into the soft ground. Out comes an angleworm.

Did he hear the angleworm moving about down there, underneath the surface of the ground? It seems impossible.

The angleworm is such a soft damp slithery thing. Perhaps the movements of the worm underground disturbed slightly some few grains of the surface soil.

In the shop at Langdon the mill superintendent moved here and there. He was in one of the warehouses—now he was watching cotton being unloaded at the mill door—now in the spinning-room—now in the weaving-room. He was standing at a window that looked down toward the river that flowed below the mill. Suddenly his head turned. How like the robin he was now. He darted to some part of the room. Some minute part had gone a bit wrong in some machine. He knew. He flew there.

For him, people were apparently of no account. "Here, you. What's your name?" he would say to a workman or a workwoman, or to a child. A good many children were at work in that mill. He never noticed. He asked the same workman his name several times during one week. Sometimes he fired a man or a woman. "Here, you. You are not wanted here any more. Get out." The mill worker knew what that meant. Word had been whispered about the mill often enough. The worker went quickly away. He hid himself. Others helped. Soon he was back at his old place. The superintendent did not notice, or if he did notice he said nothing.

At night, when his work was done for the day he went home. He lived in the largest house in the mill village. Visitors seldom came there. He sat in a chair, and, putting his stockinged feet in another chair, spoke to his wife. "Where's the paper?" he asked. His wife got it. This would be after dining and in a few minutes he was asleep. He got up and went to bed. His mind was still in the mill. It was running. "I wonder what is going on down there," he was thinking. His wife and children were also afraid of him, although he seldom spoke unkindly to them. He seldom spoke at all. "Why be wasting words?" he perhaps thought.

The president of the mill had an idea in his head, at

least he thought he had. At that time he was remembering Red's father and grandfather. Red's grandfather had been the family doctor for his family when he was a child. He thought, "There aren't many young Southern men with any family at all who would do as this boy has done. He is a good boy." Red had simply come into the mill office. "May I have a job, Mr. Shaw?" he had said to the president of the mill, having been, after waiting some ten minutes, admitted to Mr. Shaw.

"May I have a job?"

There was a little smile on the mill president's face. Who wouldn't like to be a mill president? He can give jobs.

In every situation there are these shades. Red's father, so well known after all to the mill president, hadn't made good. He had been a doctor. Like other men who set forth in life he had his chance. So he hadn't tended to his practice, had begun drinking instead. There had been whispers about his morals. There was that yellow woman in the country. The mill president also had heard whispers about that.

And then it was said he had married a woman who was beneath him. That was what people in Langdon said. They said she came from rather low-class people. Her father, it was said, amounted to nothing. He kept a little general store in a workingman's suburb in Atlanta and a brother of hers had been sent to prison for stealing.

"Just the same, there's no use blaming this boy for all that," the mill president thought. How kindly and fair he felt, thinking that. He smiled. "What do you want to do, young man?" he asked.

"I don't care. I'll do anything I can get to do." That was the way to talk. All of this took place on a hot day in June, as had been suggested after Red's first year at school in the North. Red had suddenly come to a resolution. "I'll just see if I can get a job," he had thought. He had consulted no one. He knew that the mill president, Thomas Shaw, had known his father. Red's father had, at that time, been dead but a short time. He had walked down to the offices of the mill on a hot morning. The air was heavy and still on Main Street when he passed through. Such moments are pregnant to a boy or to a young man. He is going to work for the first time. Look out now, boy. You start. How, when and where will you stop? This moment may have as much significance in your life as a birth, a marriage or a death. There were merchants and clerks standing inside the doors of stores on Langdon's main street. Most of them were in their shirt sleeves. A good many of the shirts did not look too clean.

In the summer the men in Langdon wore light linen clothes. Such clothes, when soiled, had to be sent to a laundry. In Georgia, in summer, the days were so hot that men moving about were soon wringing wet with sweat. The linen suits they wore soon sagged at the elbows and knees. They became soiled quickly.

It did not seem to matter to a good many of the men of Langdon. Some of them went on wearing such a soiled suit for weeks.

There was a sharp contrast coming from the scene on Main Street to the mill office. The office of the mill at Langdon was not in the mill proper but stood off by itself. It was in a new-looking brick building, with a green watered lawn in front and with flowering bushes by the front door.

The mill was quite modern. One of the reasons so many of the Southern mills had succeeded, rapidly replacing New England mills, so that, after the rise of the South industrially, there was a sharp industrial slump in New England, was that the Southern mills, being newly built, had put in the very latest machinery. In America, when it came to machinery ... a machine could be the very latest thing, the most efficient, and then ... five, ten or, at the latest, twenty years later ...

To be sure, Red did not know about such things. He knew something vaguely. He had been a child when the mill in Langdon was built. It had been almost a semi-religious occasion. Suddenly there was talk everywhere along the main street of the little sleepy Southern town. The talk was heard on the streets, in the churches, and even in the schools. When that happened Red was a small child in one of the lower grades in the town school. He remembered it all, but vaguely. The man who was now president of the mill and who was at that time cashier of the little local bank ... his father, John Shaw, being president ... the young cashier had started it all.

He was at that time, physically, a rather small young man with a delicate body. He was, however, capable of enthusiasms and of stirring others. What had happened in the North and in particular in the great American Middle West, even during the very years when the Civil War was being fought had begun to happen in the South. Young Tom Shaw began running about the little Southern town and talking. "Look," he said, "what's happening everywhere, all over the South. Look at North Carolina and at South Carolina." It was true things had happened. At that time there was a man in Atlanta, an editor on the staff of the *Daily Constitution* there, a man named Grady, who had suddenly become the South's new Moses. He went about making speeches, both in the North and in the South. He wrote editorials. The South still remembers the man. His statue stands in a public street near the offices of the *Constitution* in Atlanta. He also, if the statue is to be believed, was a rather small man with a somewhat delicate body and, like Tom Shaw, with a round chubby face.

Young Shaw had read his Henry Grady. He had begun talking. He had at once enlisted the churches in his cause. "It isn't only a matter of money," he kept saying to people. "Let's forget for the time about money.

"The South is ruined," he declared. It had happened that just at that time, when men in Langdon began talking of building a cotton mill as other towns all over the South were doing, a revivalist preacher came to Langdon. Like the revivalist, who was afterwards to convert Red Oliver's mother, he was a Methodist.

He was a man with power as a preacher. Like the later revivalist, who came when Red was a high school boy, he was a large man with a mustache and a great booming voice. Tow Shaw went to see him. The two men talked. That whole section of Georgia raised practically nothing but cotton. The fields had been worked for cotton before the Civil War and were still so worked. They were rapidly becoming worn out. "Now, you look at it," Tom Shaw said, talking to the preacher, "our people are getting poorer and poorer with every passing year."

Tom Shaw had been in the North, he had gone to school in the North. It happened that the revivalist to whom he talked that time . . . the two men spending several afternoons together closeted in a little room in the Langdon Savings Bank, the bank then housed precariously in an old frame building on Main Street . . . the revivalist preacher to whom he talked was a man without education. He could scarcely read, but Tom Shaw had taken it for granted that he wanted what Tom called a full life. "I tell you," he said that time to the preacher, his face flushed, a kind of holy enthusiasm running through him, "I tell you . . .

"Have you ever been in the North or in the East?"

The preacher said that he had not. He was the son of a poor farmer, really a Georgia Cracker himself. He told Tom Shaw so. "I'm just a Cracker," he said. "I'm not ashamed of it." He had been inclined to get off the subject.

At first he suspected Tom Shaw. "These old Southerners. These aristocrats," he thought. What did the banker want of him? The banker asked him if he had children. Well, he had. He had been married early in life and his wife had given birth to a new child almost every year since. He was now a man of thirty-five. He hardly knew how many children he had. There was a troop of them, thin-legged children living in a little old frame house in another Georgia town

very like Langdon, a run-down town, it was. He said so.
The takings of a preacher, going about as he did, a revivalist, were meager enough. "I've got a good many children,"
he said.

He did not say how many, and Tom Shaw did not press
the point.

He was driving at something. "We, of the South, have
all got to get to work," he continually said in those days.
"Let's have an end to all of this mourning about the old
South. Let's get to work."

If a man, such a man as that preacher, a common enough
man ... Almost any man, if he had children ...

"We have to think of the children of the South," Tom
was always saying. Sometimes he mixed things up a bit. "In
the children of the South lies the womb of the future," he
said.

A man, such as that preacher, might not have any very
lofty personal ambitions. He might be satisfied, just going
about, shouting at a lot of poor whites about God ... still ...
if a man had children ... The preacher's wife had come from
a family of poor Southern whites as he had himself. She had
already grown thin and yellow.

There was one thing rather nice about this being a revivalist preacher. A man did not always have to stay at home.
He went places. Women crowded about him. Some of the
Methodist women were nice. There were some good-lookers
among them. He was a big man among them.

He knelt beside such a one in prayer. What fervor he
put into his prayers!

Tom Shaw and the preacher had got together. There
had been a new kind of revival in town and in the country
communities about Langdon. Presently the revivalist dropped
everything else and, instead of talking about a life after
death, talked only of the present ... of a new glowing kind
of life, already lived in many Eastern and Middle-Western
towns and that, he said, might as well be lived in the South,

in Langdon. As a somewhat cynical citizen of Langdon, who later remembered those days, said, "You would have thought the preacher had been a traveler all his life, and he hasn't been out of a half-dozen Georgia counties." The preacher began to wear better clothes and to spend more and more time talking to Tom Shaw. "We Southerners have got to arouse ourselves," he cried. He described towns of the East and of the Middle West. "Citizens," he cried, "you should pay a visit up there." Now he was describing a town in Ohio. It had been a small no-account sleepy place, as Langdon, Georgia, still was. It was merely a little crossroads town. A few poor farmers came in there to trade as they did to Langdon.

Then there had been a railroad built and presently a factory came. Other factories followed. Things began to change with incredible rapidity. "We Southerners do not know what such a life is like," the preacher declared.

He went all over the county making speeches; he talked in the court house in Langdon and in all of the town churches. In the North and in the East, he declared, towns had been transformed. A town in the North, in the East, or in the Middle West was a little sleepy place and then suddenly the factories came. People who had been out of work, many people who had never had a cent to their names, suddenly began to get wages.

How rapidly everything changed! "You ought to see it," the preacher cried. He was carried away. Enthusiasm shook his big body. He pounded pulpits. When he had come to town, but a few weeks earlier, he had been able to arouse but a feeble enthusiasm among a few poor Methodists. Now every one came to listen. There was a good deal of confusion. Although the preacher had got a new theme, was speaking now of a new Heaven men might enter, did not have to wait until death to enter, he still used the tone of a man delivering a sermon and, as he talked, often pounding some pulpit and running up and down before his audience, the audience be-

came confused. There were shouts and groans at the mill
meetings as there had been at the religious meeting. "Yes,
God, that's true," a voice shouted. The preacher said that,
because of the wonderful new life, brought into so many
Eastern and Middle-Western towns by the factories, every
one had suddenly become prosperous. Life was filled with
new joys. Now, in such towns any man could own an automobile. "You ought to see how people are living up there. I
do not mean rich people, but poor people like me."

"Yes, God," some one in the audience said fervently.

"I want that. I want it. I want it," a woman's voice cried.
It was a sharp plaintive voice.

In the Northern and Western towns the preacher was
describing, all people, he said, had phonographs; they had
automobiles. They could hear the best music in the world.
Their houses were filled day and night with music. . . .

"Streets of gold," a voice cried. A stranger, coming into
Langdon, when the preliminary work for selling stock in the
new cotton mill was being done, might have thought that the
voices of the people, responding to that of the preacher, were
really making fun of him. He would have been mistaken. It
is true there were a few people of the town, a few old
Southern women and one or two old men who said, "We do
not want any of this Yankee nonsense," they said, but such
voices were for the most part unheard.

"They are building new houses and new stores. There
are bathrooms in all of the houses.

"There are people, common people like me, not rich
people, mind you, who walk about on floors of stone."

A voice: "Did you say, bathroom?"

"Amen!"

"It is the new life. We must build a cotton mill here in
Langdon. The South has been dead too long.

"There are too many poor people. Our farmers are
making no money. What do we poor people of the South
get?"

"Amen. Bless God."

"Every man and every woman must go down deep into his pocket now. If you have a little property go to the bank and borrow some money on it. Buy stock in the mill."

"Yes, God. Save us, God."

"Your children are half starved. They have got the rickets. There are no schools for them. They grow up ignorant."

The preacher at Langdon sometimes grew humble as he talked. "Look at me," he said to the people. He remembered his wife at home, the woman who had, but so short a time ago, been a fair young girl. She was a toothless worn-out old woman now. It was no fun to be with her, to be near her. She was always too tired out.

At night, when a man went to her . . .

It was better to be out preaching. "I am myself an ignorant man," he said humbly. "God has, however, called me to do this work. My people were once proud people here in the South.

"Now I have many children. I cannot educate them. I cannot feed them as they should be fed. Gladly would I put them into a cotton mill."

"Yes, God. It's true. It's true, God."

The campaign made by the revivalist preacher in Langdon had been successful. As the preacher talked publicly, Tom Shaw was quietly and energetically at work. Money was got in. The mill in Langdon was built.

It is true some capital had to be borrowed in the North; machinery had to be bought on credit; there were dark years when it looked as though the mill would fail. Presently the people no longer prayed for its success.

Better years, however, came.

The mill village at Langdon had been hurriedly thrown up. Cheap lumber was used. Before the World War the houses in the mill village had been left unpainted. There were rows of little frame houses to which the working people came to live. For the most part they were poor people off little worn-out Georgia farms. They had come swarming in when the mill was first built. At first four or five times as many people came as could be employed. There were not too many houses built. Money was at first wanted for the building of better houses. The houses were crowded with people.

A man, such as that preacher had been, who had many children, could, however, do very well. In Georgia there were few enough laws concerning children at work. The mill ran night and day when it did run. Children of twelve, thirteen and fourteen went to work in the mill. It was easy to lie about your age. Small children in the mill village at Langdon had nearly all of them two ages. "How old are you, my child?"

"What do you mean, my real age or my mill age?"

"For God's sake, be careful, child. What do you mean, talking like that? We people of the mills, we lint-heads ... they call us that, the people of the town, you know they do ... don't be gabbling like that." For some queer reason the streets of gold, the fair lives of work people pictured by the preacher before the mill in Langdon was built hadn't materialized. The houses remained as they had been built, small sheds really, hot in summer and bitterly cold in winter. No grass grew in the little lawns before the houses. There were rows of half-fallen-down privies at the back of houses.

However, a man who had children could do fairly well. Often he did not have to work. Before the days of the World War and the great boom, there were enough mill daddies, men not unlike that revivalist preacher, in the cotton mill village at Langdon.

*

THE mill at Langdon closed on Saturday afternoons and on Sundays. It started again at midnight on Sunday and ran steadily, night and day, until the next Saturday noon.

After he became an employee of the mill, Red went

down there once on a Sunday afternoon. He walked down
through Langdon's main street to the mill village.

In Langdon the main street was dead and silent. Red
had stayed a long time in bed that morning. A Negro woman
who had been in the house since Red was a babe brought his
breakfast upstairs. She had grown middle-aged and was now
a big brown woman with great hips and breasts. She took
a motherly attitude toward Red. He could talk more freely
with her than with his mother. "What you want to work
down there in that mill for?" she asked, when he went to
work. "You ain't no poor white," she said. Red laughed at
her. "Your father wouldn't have liked you doing what you
are doing," she said. In bed Red lay reading one of the books
he had brought home from college. A young English professor, who had been attracted to him, had filled an old grip
with books and had suggested his reading his way through
them during the summer. He did not dress until after his
mother left the house for church.

Then he strolled out. His walk took him past the little
church his mother attended, down at the edge of the mill
village. He heard singing in there and had heard singing in
other churches as he came through town. How dull, dragging
and heavy the singing was! Evidently the people in Langdon
didn't much enjoy their God. They did not give themselves
to God with joy as did the Negroes. In Main Street the stores
were all closed. Even the drug stores, where Coca Cola, that
universal drink of the South, could be had, were closed. The
men of the town would get their cokes after church. The drug
stores would open then to let them coke up. Red had passed
the town jail, standing back of the court house. There were
some young moonshiners from the North Georgia hills lodged
in there and they were also singing. They sang a ballad:

> *Don't you know I'm a traveling man?*
> *God knows I'm a traveling man.*

Fresh young voices singing with delight in the song. In the mill village that lay just outside the corporation limits, a few young men and women walked about or sat in groups in the little porches before the houses. They were dressed in their Sunday best, the girls in bright colors. Although he was working in the mill, they all knew Red was not one of themselves. There was the mill village and then the mill, with its mill yard. There was a high wire fence about the mill yard. You went in, from the village, through a gate.

There was always a man at the gate, an old man with a lame foot who recognized Red but would not let him into the mill yard. "What do you want in there for?" he asked. Red did not know. "Oh, I don't know," he said. "I was just looking." He had just come out for a walk. Was he becoming fascinated by the mill? Like other young men, he hated the peculiar deadness of American towns on Sundays. He wished the mill team he had joined had a ball game on for the afternoon, but he knew also that Tom Shaw would not have permitted it. The mill, when it was running, all the machinery flying, was something. The man at the gate looked at Red without smiling and he walked away. He followed a high wire fence around the mill yard and got down to the river bank. The railroad that came to Langdon followed the river and there was a spur running into the mill yard. Red did not know why he was there. It may have been that he had left home because he knew that when his mother returned from church he would feel guilty for not having gone with her.

There were a few poor white families in town, families of laborers, who went to the same church his mother did. There was another Methodist church in the upper end of the town and there was a Negro Methodist church. Tom Shaw, president of the mill, was a Presbyterian.

There was a Presbyterian church and a Baptist church. There were Negro churches, little sects of Negroes too. There were no Catholics in Langdon. After the World War the Ku Klux Klan was strong there.

Some of the mill boys at Langdon had organized a baseball team. The question had come up in town: "Is Red Oliver going to play with them?" There was a town team. It was made up of young men of the town, a clerk in a store, a man who worked in the post office, a young doctor and others. The young doctor came to Red. "I see," he said, "that you have got a job in the mill. Are you going to play on the mill team?" He had smiled when he said that. "I suppose you'll have to if you want to hold your job, eh?" He didn't say that. There was a new preacher, a young Presbyterian preacher, just come to town, who, if it came to a pinch, could take Red's place on the town team. The mill team and the town team did not play each other. The mill team played other mill teams from other Georgia and South Carolina towns where there were mills and the team of the town played town teams from nearby towns. For the town team to have played the mill boys would have been almost like playing niggers. They wouldn't have said that, but they felt it. There was a way in which they got across to Red what they felt. He knew.

That young preacher could take Red's place on the town team. He seemed a bright alert young fellow. He was prematurely bald. He had played baseball in college.

Such a young fellow, coming to a town, to be a preacher. Red was curious about him. He wasn't much like the revivalist who had converted Red's mother or like the one who had once helped Tom Shaw sell stock in the mill. This one was more like Red himself. He had been to college and had read books. It was his aim to be a cultured young man.

Red didn't know whether or not he wanted that. At that time he did not know what he did want. He had always felt a bit lonely and apart in Langdon, perhaps because of the attitude of the town toward his mother and his father; and after he went to work in the mill, the feeling grew.

The young preacher was a man intent on getting into the life of Langdon. Although he did not approve of the Ku Klux Klan he said nothing publicly against it. None of the preachers in Langdon did. It was said some of the prominent men of the town, prominent in the churches, were in the Klan. The young preacher spoke against it in private, to two or three men he knew well. "I believe a man should give himself to service not to violence," he said. "That's what I want to do." He had joined an organization in Langdon called the "Kivanis Club." Tom Shaw belonged to it although he seldom went. At Christmas time, when presents had to be found for children of poor families of the town, the young preacher raced about, getting the presents. There had been something rather ugly in town, during the first year Red was in the North, while he was away at college. There was a man in town who was suspected.

He was a young salesman who took subscriptions for a Southern woman's magazine.

It was said that he . . .

There was a young white girl of the town, a regular slut, people said.

The young subscription solicitor, like Red's father, was given to drink. When he had been drinking he became quarrelsome. First it was said that he beat his wife when he was drunk. People heard her crying in her house in the night. Then he was said to have been seen going to the house of that woman. The woman, who had got such a bad reputation, lived with her mother in a little frame house, just off Main Street, in the lower end of town, the end of town where the cheaper stores and the stores patronized by Negroes were located. It was said her mother sold drinks.

The young solicitor was seen going in and out of the place. He had three children. He went there and then went home to beat his wife. Some men in masks went and got him one night. They got also the young girl he was with and they

were both taken to a lonely road, some miles from town, and
tied to trees. They were lashed with whips. The woman had
been taken, clad only in a thin gown, and when the two
people had been thoroughly whipped, the man was turned
loose, to make his way as best he could to town. The woman,
almost naked now, her thin dress torn and shredded, herself
white and silent, had been taken to the front door of her
mother's house and pushed out of a car. How she had
screamed! "The bitch!" The man had taken it in grim
silence. There was some fear the girl might die but she got
well. There had been an effort made to find and whip the
mother also, but she had disappeared. Afterwards she reappeared and continued to sell drinks to the men of the town
and her daughter continued to see men. It was said that
more men than ever went there. The young subscription
solicitor, who had a car, got his wife and children and drove
away. He did not even return to get his furniture and was
never seen again in Langdon. When this event had occurred,
the young Presbyterian preacher had just arrived in town.
There was an Atlanta newspaper that took the matter up.
A reporter came to Langdon to interview several prominent
men. Among others he went to the young preacher.

He spoke to him in the street in front of a drug store
and there were several men standing about. "They got what
they deserved," most of the Langdon men said. "I wasn't
there but I wish I had been," the druggist said. Some one
in the crowd whispered, "There are other men in this town
who should long ago have had that happen to them."

"What about George Ricard and that woman of his . . .
you know the one I mean." The reporter for the Atlanta
paper did not hear the words. He kept boring away at the
young preacher. "What do you think?" he asked. "What do
you think?"

"I think that none of the better men of the town could
have been in it at all," the preacher said.

"But what do you think of the idea back of it? What do you think of that?"

"You wait a minute," the young preacher said. "I'll be right back," he said. He went into the drug store but did not come out. He was unmarried and kept his car in a garage in an alleyway. He got into his car and drove out of town. That evening he phoned to the house at which he boarded. "I won't be at home to-night," he said. He said he was with a sick woman and was afraid the sick woman might die in the night. "She might need a spiritual adviser," he said. He thought he had better stay for the night.

It was a little strange, Red Oliver thought, to find the mill at Langdon so silent on Sunday. It did not seem like the same mill. That Sunday when he went down there, he had been working in the mill for some weeks. The young Presbyterian preacher had also asked him about playing on the mill team. That had happened shortly after Red went to the mill to work. The preacher knew about Red's mother going to the church where mostly mill people went. He felt sorry for Red. His own father, in another Southern town, hadn't been counted among the best people. He had kept a little store where Negroes traded. The preacher had worked his own way through school. "I'm nothing beside you as a player," he said to Red. He asked a question, "Have you affiliated with any church?" Red said he hadn't. "Well, you are welcome to come and worship with us."

The mill boys did not mention the matter of Red's playing with them for a week or two after he went to the mill to work, and then, as he knew Red had quit playing on the town team, a young foreman spoke to him. "Are you going to play on the team here at the mill?" he asked. The question was asked tentatively. Some of the members of the team had spoken to the foreman. He was a young mill man, from a mill family, who had begun to work his way up. It may be that such a one, who works his way up, must always have respect in him. That one had great respect for the better people of Langdon. After all, if Red's father hadn't been such a big man in town, his grandfather had. Every one respected him.

Old Doctor Oliver had been a surgeon in the Confederate Army during the Civil War. It was said he was a relative of that Alexander Stevenson who was Vice-President of the Southern Confederacy. "The boys don't play very well," the foreman said to Red. Red had been a star player on the town's high school and had already attracted notice on the freshman team in college.

"Our boys don't play very well."

The young foreman, although Red was just a common workman in the shop under him . . . Red had begun work in the mill by being a sweeper . . . he swept floors . . . the young foreman was certainly respectful enough. "If you would like to play. . . . The boys would be grateful to you. They'd appreciate it." It was as though he had said: "You'll be doing them a kindness." For some reason something in the man's voice made Red squirm.

"Sure," he said.

Just the same . . . that time Red took the walk on Sunday and visited the silent mill, walking through the mill village . . . it was in the late morning . . . people would be out of church soon . . . they would be going to Sunday dinners.

To be on a baseball team, with the men of the mill, was one thing. Going to that church with his mother was another.

He had gone to church with his mother several times. After all, he went few enough places with her. Since that time, after her conversion, when he heard her praying in the house, he had continually wanted something for her she did not seem to have, never had got out of life.

Did she get something out of religion? After her first excitement, the revivalist preacher coming to the Oliver house to pray with her, Red had not heard her praying aloud any more. She went determinedly to church twice every Sunday and to prayer meetings during the week. In the church she sat always in one place. She sat alone. The members of the church often got excited during the ceremonies. There were low muttered words coming from them. This happened particularly during prayers. The minister, a small man with a red face, stood up before the people and closed his eyes. He prayed loudly. "Oh, Lord, give us contrite hearts. Keep us humble."

Nearly all the people of the congregation were older mill people. Red thought they were surely humble enough ... "Yes, Lord. Amen. Help us, Lord," low voices said. The voices came from the audience. Sometimes a member of the church was asked to lead in the prayer. Red's mother wasn't asked. No words came from her. She bowed her shoulders and kept looking at the floor. Red, who had come to church with her, not because he wanted to come but because he had felt guilty, seeing her always going off to church alone, thought he saw her shoulders tremble. As for himself, he did not know what to do. The first time he went with his mother, and when the time of prayer came, he bowed his head as she did and the next time he sat with head held straight up. "I've no right to pretend I am feeling humble or being religious when I'm not," he thought.

Red went down past the mill and sat on the railroad tracks. There was a steep bank leading down to the river and some trees grew at the river's edge. Two Negro men were fishing, having hid out of sight under the steep bank to fish on Sunday. They paid no attention to Red, perhaps did not see him. There was a small tree between him and the fishermen. He sat on the projecting end of a railroad tie.

He did not go home to dinner that day. He had got into a queer position in the town and had begun to feel it sharply, half separated from the life of the other young men of his own age, among whom he had once been quite popular, and he was not admitted really to the lives of the workers in the mill. Did he want admission among them?

The mill boys with whom he played baseball were nice enough. All of the workers in the mill treated him all right, as for that matter did the people of the town. "What am I kicking about?" he asked himself that Sunday. Sometimes the team from the mill went in a bus on a Saturday afternoon to play at another town with another mill team and Red went with them. When he made a good play or got a good hit the young men of his own team clapped their hands and shouted with delight. "Good," they cried. There was no doubt his presence had strengthened the team.

Just the same, when after the game they were driving home . . . they left Red sitting alone at one end of the bus, hired for the occasion, as his mother sat alone in her church, and did not address him directly. Occasionally, when he was walking down to the mill in the early morning or was leaving it at night, he walked as far as the mill village with some man or with a little group of men. They had been talking freely until he had joined them and then, suddenly, the talk stopped. Words seemed to freeze on the men's lips.

With the girls in the mill it was, Red thought, somewhat better. Now and then one of the girls gave him the eye. He did not talk much with them that first summer. "I wonder if my going to the mill to work is something like mother's joining the church?" he thought. He might have asked for a job in the mill office. Most of the people of the town who worked in the mill did work in the office. When there was a ball game they came to see it but did not play. Red hadn't wanted such a job. He didn't know why.

Had there always been something in the attitude of the town toward him, because of his mother?

There had been that mystery about his father. Red did not know that story. When he was playing ball on the high school team, during his last year in high school he had slid into second base and had accidentally cut a player of the opposing team with his spikes. He was a high school player from a nearby town. He grew angry. "That's nigger stuff," he said angrily to Red. He had started toward Red as if he wanted to fight. Red had tried to apologize. "What do you mean 'nigger stuff'?" he asked.

"Oh, I guess you know," the boy said. That was all. There had been nothing more said. Some other players came rushing up. The incident was forgotten. Once, standing in a store, he had overheard some men talking of his father. "He's that kind," a voice said, speaking of Doctor Oliver.

"He likes the low-grade ones, the low-grade whites and the black ones." That had been all. Red was a young boy then. The men had not seen him standing in the store and he had gone out without being seen. On the Sunday when he was sitting on the railroad tracks, lost in thought, he remembered the chance remark heard long ago. He remembered how angry he had been. What had they meant in speaking thus of his father? He had been thoughtful and rather upset when he went to bed on the night after the incident, but later he had forgotten it. Now it came back.

Perhaps Red was merely having a fit of the blues. Young men have the blues as well as older men. He hated going home. A freight train came along and he went to lie on some long grass on the incline leading down to the stream. He was quite hidden now. The Negro fishermen went away and, during the afternoon, some young men from the mill village came down to the river to swim. Two of them played about for a long time. They dressed and went away.

It was growing late in the afternoon. What a queer day it had been for Red! A group of young girls, also from the mill village, walked along the tracks. They were laughing and talking. Two of them were quite pretty girls, Red thought. Many of the older people, who had been working in the mill for years, were not very strong and a good many of the children were delicate and sickly. People in town said it was because they did not know how to take care of themselves. "The mothers do not know how to take care of their babies. They are ignorant," the people of Langdon said.

They were always speaking of the ignorance and stupidity of the mill people. The mill girls Red saw that day did not look stupid. He liked them. They walked along the track and stopped near where he was lying in the tall grass. Among them was one girl Red had noticed in the mill. She was one of the girls who had, he thought, given him the eye. She was a little thing with a short body and a big head, and Red thought she had nice eyes. She had thick lips, almost like a nigger's lips.

She was evidently a leader among the mill girls. They gathered about her. They had stopped but a few feet from where Red lay. "Come on now. You teach us that new song you got," one of them said to the thick-lipped girl.

"Clara says you got a new one," one of the girls urged. "She says it's hot stuff." The thick-lipped girl prepared to sing. "You all got to help. You all got to join in the chorus," she said.

"It's about the water-house," she said. Red smiled, lying hidden in the grass. He knew that in the mill the girls called the toilets water-houses.

The foreman in the spinning-room in the mill, the same young man who had asked Red about playing with the mill ball team, was named Lewis.

In the mill, during the hot afternoons, a man from the town was permitted to pass through the mill with a little cart. He sold bottles of Coca Cola and cheap candies. There was one kind of cheap candy, a great soft chunk of cheap candy that was called "Milky Way."

The song the girls were singing concerned the life in the mill. Red suddenly remembered that he had heard Lewis and other foremen complaining that the girls went too often to the toilets. When they grew tired, in the long hot afternoons, they went in there to rest. The girl on the track was singing about that.

"You can hear those doggone clean-up hands say," she sang, throwing her head back.

Give me Coca Cola and a Milky Way.
Give me Coca Cola and a Milky Way.
Twicet a day.
Give me Coca Cola and a Milky Way.

The other girls sang with her. They laughed.

Give me Coca Cola and a Milky Way.
We're going down the room four by four,
Faces toward the water-house door.
Give me Coca Cola and a Milky Way.
Old Lewis swear, old Lewis knock,
I'd like to hit him with a rock.

The girls went off down the tracks. They were shouting with laughter. Red could hear them for a long time singing as they went.

Coca Cola and a Milky Way.
Pilin' into the water-house.
Outa the water-house.
Into the water-house door.

Evidently there was a life in the mill at Langdon of which Red Oliver knew nothing. With what gusto that thick-lipped girl had sung her song of life in the mill. What feeling she had managed to put into the crude words. In Langdon there was always talk going on about the attitude of the mill hands toward Tom Shaw. "Look what he has done for them," people said. Red had heard such talk in the streets of Langdon all his life.

It was thought the mill people were grateful. Why shouldn't they be? Many of them couldn't read and write when they came to the mill. Hadn't some of the finest women of the town gone down to the mill village at night to teach them to read and write?

They were living in better houses than they had known when they were back on the Georgia plains and in the hills. They lived in such shacks then.

Now they had medical attention. They had everything.

Evidently they were not satisfied. There was something wrong. Red lay in the grass, thinking of what he had heard. He stayed there, on the incline by the river, back of the mill and the railroad tracks, until darkness came.

> *Old Lewis swear, old Lewis knock,*
> *I'd like to hit him with a rock.*

That must have been Lewis, foreman of the spinning room, knocking on the toilet-room doors, trying to herd the girls back to their work. There had been venom in the voices of the girls as they sang the crude lines. "I wonder," Red thought, "I wonder if that Lewis really has the nerve to do that." Lewis had been so respectful when he spoke to Red about playing ball on the team with the mill boys.

*

The long rows of spindles in the spinning-room of the mill flew at terrific speed. How clean and orderly it was in the big rooms! It was so all through the mill. All of the machines, that moved at such speed, doing their work with such accuracy, were kept bright and shining. The superintendent saw to that. His eyes were forever on the machines. The ceilings, the walls and the floors of the rooms were clean. The mill was in sharp contrast to the life of the town of Langdon, to the life in houses, on the streets and in stores. Everything was orderly, everything moved with orderly speed toward one end—the making of cloth.

The machines knew what they had to do. You did not have to tell them. They did not stop or hesitate. All day they went singing and humming to their tasks.

Fingers of steel moved. There were in the mill hundreds of thousands of tiny steel fingers handling thread, handling cotton to make thread, handling thread to weave it into cloth. There were, in the great loom-room of the mill, threads of many colors. Little steel fingers picked up just the right-colored thread to make the design of the cloth. Red felt a kind of exaltation in the rooms. He felt it in the spinning-rooms. There was thread dancing in the air in there; here were spoolers and warpers in a nearby room. There were great drums. The warping machines fascinated him. Thread came from hundreds of spools onto a great roll of thread, each thread in its place. It would be harnessed into the looms from the great rolls.

In the mill, as never before in his young life, Red got a sense of the human mind doing something definite and in an orderly way. There were the great machines that handled the cotton as it came from the cleaners. These were combing and caressing the tiny fibers of the cotton, laying them in straight parallel lines, to be twisted into thread. The cotton came white from the huge machines ... in a thin broad veil.

There was something exultant in Red, working in that place. On some days all the nerves in his body seemed to dance and run with the machines. Without knowing what was happening to him he had fallen into the path of the American genius. For generations before his day, the best brains of America had gone into the making of such machines as he found in the mill.

There were other marvelous, almost superhuman machines in great automobile plants, in steel plants, in plants where food was put up in tins, in plants where steel was fabricated. Red was glad he had not applied for a job in the office of the mill. Who would want to be a keeper of books, a buyer or a seller? Without quite realizing it, Red had struck upon America at its best, at its finest.

Oh, the great light rooms, the singing machines, the shouting dancing machines!

Look at them against the sky in cities! See the machines running in a thousand mills!

Red had borne, within him, a great admiration for the

day superintendent in the mill, that man who knew every machine in the plant, knew just what it should do, who watched his machines so closely. Why was it that, as his admiration for that man grew, he grew also to have a kind of contempt for Tom Shaw and the men of the mill office? He did not know Tom Shaw well, but did know that, in some way, he was always bragging. He thought he had himself made what Red now, for the first time, saw. What he saw must really have been made by workmen, men like that superintendent. There were machine tenders in the mill too, men who cleaned the machines, who repaired machines that got out of order. In the streets of the town men were always bragging. Each man seemed to be trying to make himself appear bigger than some other man. There was no such bragging in the mill. Red knew that the tall stoop-shouldered mill superintendent would never be a braggart. How could a man be in the presence of such machines and be a braggart, a man who sensed the machines?

It must be that men like Tom Shaw ... Red did not see Tom Shaw often after he got the job ... he came seldom into the mill. "Why do I think about him?" Red asked himself. He was in that great light clean place. He helped to keep it clean. He had become a sweeper.

It was true there was lint in the air. It hung in the air like fine white dust, scarcely visible. Overhead, against the ceiling, there were flat disks from which came a fine white spray. Sometimes the spray was blue. Red thought it must have appeared blue because there were certain heavy cross beams in the ceiling that had been painted blue. The walls of the room were white. There was even a touch of red. Two of the young girls working in the spinning-room wore red cotton dresses.

There was life in the mill. The girls in the spinning-room were all young. You had to be quick in there. They chewed gum. Some of them chewed snuff. It made dark, discolored little places at the corners of the mouth. There was the girl with the large mouth and big nose, the one Red had seen with other girls walking on the railroad tracks, the one who had made the songs. She looked at Red. There was something provocative in her eyes. They challenged. Red couldn't think why. She was not pretty. When he went near her a thrill ran through him and he dreamed of her afterwards at night.

They were a young man's woman dreams. "Why does one of them set me off like that while another doesn't?" That one was a laughing talkative girl. If there was ever labor trouble among the women in that mill she would be a leader. Like the others, she ran up and down between the long rows of machines tying broken thread. For that purpose she wore on her hand an ingenious little tying machine. Red watched the hands of all the girls. "How nice working people's hands are," he thought. The hands of the girls did the little job of tying broken threads so rapidly the eye could not follow. Sometimes the girls walked slowly up and down and sometimes they ran. No wonder they grew tired and went off to the water-houses to rest. Red dreamed he was running up and down between rows of machines after the big-mouthed girl. She kept running to other girls and whispering to them. She dogged about, laughing at him. She had a strong little body with a long waist. He could see her firm young breasts, their forms showing through the thin dress she wore. When, in his dreams, he pursued her, she was like a bird in her quickness. Her hands were like wings. He never could catch her.

There was even, Red thought, a certain affinity between the girls in the spinning-room and the machines they tended. They seemed at times to become all one thing. The young girls, almost children, who attended the flying machines, seemed like little mothers. The machines were children who needed constant attention. In the summer the air in the room was stifling hot. The air was kept damp by the floating spray from above. Dark stains showed on the surface of the thin dresses. The girls ran restlessly up and down all day long. Toward the end of the first summer of Red's experience as a workman he was put on the night shift. In the daytime he could get some relief from the feeling of tenseness that always pervaded the mill, a feeling of something flying, flying, flying, a tenseness in the air. There were windows through which he could look. He could see into the mill village or, from another side of the room, the river and the railroad tracks. Occasionally a train passed. There was another kind of life outside. There were forests and rivers. Children were playing in the bare streets of the nearby mill village.

At night everything was different. The walls of the mill closed in on Red. He felt himself sinking, sinking, down, down—into what? He was sunk utterly in the strange world of lights and movement. Little fingers seemed always playing on his nerves. How long the nights were! He grew at times utterly tired. It wasn't that he was tired physically. His body was strong. The tiredness came from just watching the never-ceasing speed of the machines and the movements of those who attended the machines. There was a young man in that room who played third base on the mill ball team and who was a doffer. He took bobbins loaded with thread out of the machines and put in bare bobbins. He moved so rapidly that at times, just to watch him, tired Red terribly and at the same time frightened him a little.

Queer little moments of fright came. He was going about his work. Suddenly he stopped. He stood staring at some machine. How incredibly fast it ran! There were thousands of spindles at work in the same room. There were men who went about to tend the machines. The superintendent moved silently through the rooms. He was younger than the day man and this one also came from the North.

It was difficult to sleep in the daytime, after a night in the mill. Red kept waking suddenly. He sat up in bed. He slept again and in dreams sank away into the world of movement. In dreams also there were the flying belts, the looms danced, making a clattering sound as they danced. Tiny steel fingers were dancing as they danced in the looms. Bobbins were flying as they flew in the spinning-room. Tiny fingers of steel were picking at Red's hair. They were weaving that also into cloth. Often by the time Red grew really quiet it was time to get up and go again to the mill.

How was it with the girls and women and the young boys who worked all the year, many of whom would work all their lives in the mill? Was it so with them? Red wished he could ask. He was still shy with them, as they were with him.

There was a foreman in each room of the mill. In the rooms where the cotton first began to move forward in its journey toward becoming cloth, the rooms near a platform where the baled cotton was taken from cars, burly Negro men handling the bales, where it was broken up and cleaned, the dust in the air was thick. Huge machines handled the cotton in that room. They broke it out of the bales, rolling and tumbling it. Negro men and women tended the machines. It passed from one huge machine to another. The dust became a cloud. The kinkly hair of the men and women working in that room became gray. The faces were gray. Some one told Red that many of the Negro cotton-mill workers died young of tuberculosis. They were Negroes. The man who told Red laughed. "What does it matter? So many less niggers," he said. In all of the other rooms the workers were white.

Red became acquainted with the superintendent of the night shift. In some way he found out that Red was not of the mill village but of the town, that he had been to a Northern college during the summer before and was going back to college. The night superintendent was a young man of twenty-seven or -eight with a small body and an extraordinarily large head covered with fine yellow hair cropped close. He had come to the mill out of a technical school of the North.

He felt lonesome in Langdon. The South puzzled him. The Southern civilization is complex. There are all sorts of cross-currents. Southerners say, "No Northerner can understand. How can he?" There is the queer fact of Negro life, so intimately connected with white life, so drawn away from it. Little quibbles come up and become vastly important. "You must not call a Negro man mister or a Negro woman Mrs. Even the newspapers, wanting Negro circulation, have to be careful. All sorts of queer subterfuges are used. Life between the browns and the whites becomes unexpectedly intimate. It draws sharply apart over the most unexpected details of everyday life. There is confusion. In these late years, industry coming in, the poor whites being brought suddenly, sharply and suddenly, into modern industrial life...

The machine makes no distinctions.

A white clerk can kneel before a colored woman in a shoe store, to sell her a pair of shoes. It's all right. If he were to say, "Miss Grayson, do you like the shoes?" He has used the word "Miss." A Southern white says: "I'd cut my arm off before I'd do that."

Money makes no distinction. There are shoes to be sold. Men live by selling shoes.

There are the more intimate relations between men and women. Better keep quiet about that.

If a man could cut down through everything, get at the quality of life.... The young mill superintendent Red met asked him questions. He was a new kind of man to Red. He lived at a hotel in town.

He walked away from the mill at the same hour Red did. When Red began to work at night they left the mill at the same hour in the morning.

"So you are working as a common laborer?" He took it for granted that what Red was doing was just a temporary thing. "While your vacation lasts, eh?" he said. Red didn't know. "Yes, I guess," he said. He asked Red what he was

going to do in life and Red couldn't answer. "I don't know,"
he said, and the young man stared. One day he invited Red
to come to his room at the hotel. "Come this afternoon, when
you get through sleeping," he said.

He was like the day superintendent in that machines
were the important thing in his life. "What do they mean
here in the South when they say so and so? What are they
driving at?"

He had felt, even in the president of the mill, Tom
Shaw, a kind of queer self-consciousness about the working
people. "Why," the young Northern man asked, "is he always talking about 'my people'? In what way are they 'his
people'? They are men and women, aren't they? They do
their work all right or they don't.

"Why do they use colored working people in one room
and whites in another?" The young man was like the day
superintendent. He was a machine man. When Red was in his
room that day he got out a catalog issued by a machine maker
of the North. There was a machine he was trying to get the
mill to introduce. The man had small and rather delicate
white fingers. His hair was thin and was of a pale sandy
yellow. It was hot in the little Southern hotel room and he
was in his shirt sleeves.

He had laid the catalog upon his bed and was showing
it to Red. The white fingers opened the pages reverently.
"See," he exclaimed. He had come to the Southern mill at
about the time Red got his job, having replaced another man
who had died suddenly, and since he had come, there had been
a threat of trouble among the workers. Red had known little
of that. None of the men with whom he played ball or saw
in the mill had talked of it to him. There had been a ten
per-cent cut in wages and there was grumbling. The mill
superintendent knew. Foreman in the mill had told him.
There were even among the mill employees a few amateur
agitators.

The superintendent showed Red the picture of a huge

and complex machine. His fingers fairly trembled with delight pointing to it, and trying to explain its workings. "Look," he said. "It does the work twenty or thirty people are now doing and does it automatically."

One morning Red was walking from the mill toward town with the young man from the North. They had come through the village. The men and women of the day shift were already in the mill and those of the night shift were coming out. Red and the superintendent walked among them. He used words Red couldn't understand. They got out into a road. As they walked along, the superintendent spoke of the mill people. "They are pretty stupid, aren't they?" he asked. He may have thought Red was also stupid. Stopping in the road, he pointed back toward the mill. "It isn't half what it will be," he said. He went talking along the road. The mill president, he said, had consented to buy the new machine, the picture of which he had shown Red. It was, he said, a type of automatic machines that were rapidly being introduced into the best mills. "Machinery is going to become more and more automatic," he said.

Again he spoke of the labor trouble brewing in the mill, of which Red had heard nothing. There was an effort being made, he said, to unionize the Southern mills. "They'd better drop that," he said.

"Pretty soon they'll be lucky if any of them are employed.

"We are going to run the mills with fewer and fewer people, with more and more automatic machinery. The time will come when all mills will be automatic." He assumed that Red had his point of view. "You are working in the mill, but you are one of us," his voice and manner implied. The mill people were nothing to him. He spoke of Northern mills in which he had worked. Some of his friends, young technicians like himself, were working in other kinds of mills, in automobile factories and in steel mills.

"In the North," he said, "in the mills in the North, they

know how to handle labor." Since automatic machinery was being introduced there was always more and more surplus labor. "The thing to do," he said, "is to keep plenty of surplus labor about. Then you can cut wages when you choose. You can do what you want to," he said.

3

IN the mill there was always a sense of order, of things moving forward to an orderly end, and then there was the life in the Oliver house.

The big old Oliver house had gone to decay now. It had been built by Red's grandfather, the Confederate surgeon, and his father had lived and died there. Great people of the old South built generously. The house was too large for Red and his mother. There were many empty rooms. Just behind the house and attached to it by a covered passageway was a large kitchen. It was large enough for the kitchen of a hotel. A fat old Negro woman cooked for the Olivers.

In Red's childhood there was another Negro woman who made the beds and swept the floors of the house. She had taken care of Red when he was a small child and her mother had been a slave, belonging to old Doctor Oliver.

The old doctor had been, for his day, a great reader. There were rows of old books in glass-fronted and now dilapidated bookcases in the parlor of the house downstairs and boxes of books in one of the empty rooms. Red's own father had never opened a book. For years, after he became a doctor, he took a medical journal, but rarely took it out of its wrapper. A little pile of these journals had been thrown on the floor upstairs in one of the empty rooms.

Red's mother had tried to do something with the old house after she had married the young doctor, but had made little progress. The doctor was not interested in her efforts and what she tried to do had been a bother to the servants.

59

She made new curtains for some of the windows. Old chairs that had become broken or out of which seats had fallen and that had been standing about unnoticed in corners ever since the old doctor's death were dragged out and repaired. There was not much money to be spent, but Mrs. Oliver hired an ingenious young Negro of the town to help. He came with nails and a hammer. She began trying to drive her servants. In the end not much was accomplished.

The Negro woman, already employed in the house when the young doctor married, did not like his wife. They were both still young then, although the cook had married. Her husband disappeared later and she grew enormously fat. She slept in a small room off the kitchen. The two Negro women had contempt for the new white woman. They did not want, did not dare to say to her: "No. I will not do that." That was not the Negro's way with the whites.

"Yes, indeed. Yes, Miss Susan. Yes, indeed, Miss Susan," they said. A struggle that went on for years began between the two colored women and the white woman. The doctor's wife was not directly crossed. She could not say, "This was done to defeat my purpose." Chairs that had been mended became broken again.

A chair had been mended and put into the parlor. In some mysterious way it got into the front hall and the doctor, coming home late at night, stumbled over it and fell. The chair was again broken. When the white woman complained to her husband he smiled. He was fond of Negroes, liked them about. "They were here when Mama was alive. Their people belonged to us before the war," he said. Even the child in the house knew later that there was something going on. When the white woman had, for some reason, left the house the whole atmosphere changed. Negro laughter ran through the house. When he was a child Red liked it most when his mother was not at home. The Negro women were laughing at Red's mother. He did not know that, was

too young to know. When his mother was out of the house
other Negro servants from neighboring houses slipped in.
Red's mother did her own marketing. She was one of the
few white women, of the better class, who did that. She went
through the streets sometimes with a basket of groceries on
her arm. The Negro women gathered in the kitchen. "Where
is Miss Susan? Where has she gone?" one of the women
asked. The woman speaking had seen Mrs. Oliver leave.
She knew. "Isn't she the grand lady," she said. "Young
Doctor Oliver has sure done well, hasn't he, now?"

"She is gone to market. She went to the store."

The woman who was Red's nurse, the upstairs girl, got a
basket and walked across the kitchen floor. Red's mother
always had something defiant in her walk. She held her head
rigidly poised. She frowned slightly and there was a tight
line about her mouth.

The Negro girl could imitate the walk. All the visiting
Negro women shook with laughter and even the child
laughed as the young Negro woman with the basket on her
arm and her head held so rigidly walked up and down. Red,
the child, did not know why he laughed. He laughed because
the others did. He crowed with delight.

To the two Negro women Mrs. Oliver was something.
. . . She was Poor White. She was Poor White Trash. The
women did not say so in the presence of the child. Red's
mother had put new white curtains at some of the windows
downstairs. One of the curtains was burned.

It was being ironed, after washing, and the hot iron was
left standing on it. It was one of the kind of things that
kept happening. There was a great hole burned. It was no
one's fault. Red had been left alone on the floor in the hall
of the house. A dog appeared and he cried. The cook, who
was doing the ironing, ran to him. It was a perfect explanation of what had happened. The curtain was one of three
bought for the dining-room of the house. When Red's mother

went to get cloth to make a new one to take its place all of that kind of cloth had been sold.

Sometimes, as a small child, Red cried in the night. There was some childish ailment. His tummy hurt. His mother came running upstairs, but before she could get to the child the colored woman was standing with Red held against her breasts. "He's all right now," she said. She did not offer the child to its mother and the mother hesitated. Her breasts ached to be holding the child and comforting it. The two colored women in the house were always speaking of how things were run in the house when the old doctor and his wife were alive. To be sure, they were themselves children. Still they remembered. There was something implied. "A real Southern woman, a lady, does so and so." Mrs. Oliver went out of the room and back to her bed without touching her child.

The child nestled against warm brown breasts. His small hands reached up and felt warm brown breasts. With his father before him it might have been like that. Women of the South, of the old South, in the old Doctor Oliver's day, were ladies. The Southern white men, of the slave-owning class, made great talk of that. "I do not want my wife to soil her hands." The women of the old South were to remain always the white spotless ones.

The strong brown woman who was Red's nurse when he was small threw back the covering of her bed. She got the child and took it into her own bed. She bared her breasts. There was no milk, but she let the child suckle her breasts. Her large warm lips kissed the white body of a white child. There was more of that than the white woman knew.

There was much Susan Oliver never knew. When Red was small his father was often called out at night. After his father's death, he had, for a time, quite a large practice. He rode a horse and there were three horses kept in the stable back of the house, the stable that afterwards became a garage. There was a young Negro man who took care of the horses. He slept in the stable.

Clear hot Georgia summer nights came. There were no screens at the windows or doors of the Oliver house. The front door of the old house was left open, as was the back door. There was a hallway directly through the house, the "dog run," it was called. The doors were left open to get the breeze ... when there was a breeze.

Stray dogs did actually trot through the house at night. Cats trotted through. Occasionally there was a rush of strange, startling sounds. "What's that?" Red's mother, in her room downstairs, sat up in bed. The words popped out of her. They rang through the house.

The Negro cook, already beginning to grow fat, was in her room off the kitchen. She lay on her back in her bed and laughed. Her room and the kitchen were separated from the main house, but there was a covered passage, leading into the dining-room, so that, in winter or when there were rains, food could be brought in without getting wet. The doors were open between the main house and the cook's room. "What's that?" Red's mother was nervous. She was a nervous woman. The cook had a booming voice. "It's only a dog, Miss Susan. It's only a dog. He was after a cat." The white woman wanted to go upstairs and get her child, but for some reason hadn't the courage. Why did it take courage to go get her own child? She often asked herself that question but could not answer. She had been reassured but was still nervous and lay awake for hours hearing strange noises, imagining things. She kept questioning herself about the child. "It's my child. I want it. Why shouldn't I go for it?" She said the words aloud so that the two listening Negro women often heard the soft murmured words from her room. "It's my child. Why don't I?" She said over and over.

The Negress upstairs had taken possession of the child. The white woman was afraid of her and of the cook. She was afraid of her husband, of the white people of the town of Langdon, who had known her husband before his marriage, and her husband's father. She never admitted to herself that she was afraid. On many nights, when Red was a small child, his mother lay in bed trembling as the child slept. She cried softly. Red never knew about that. His father hadn't known.

There was, in the hot Georgia summer nights, the song of insects outside and inside the house. The song rose and fell. Huge night moths came into the rooms. The house was the last one on the street and beyond it the fields began. Some one walked on a country road and shouted suddenly. A dog barked. There was the sound of horses' hoofs trotting in dust. Red's crib was covered with white mosquito netting. All the beds in the house were so covered. The beds for grown people had posts and canopies and the white mosquito netting hung down like curtains.

There were no closets built in the house. Nearly all of the older Southern houses were built without closets and in each sleeping-room there was a large mahogany armoire standing against a wall. The armoire was huge and went up to the ceiling.

Moonlight night came. There was an outside back stairs leading up to the second story of the house. Sometimes, when Red was a small child and when his father had been called out in the night, his horse having gone clattering away down the street, the young brown man from the stable came barefooted up the stairs.

He came into the room where the young brown woman and the babe were lying. He crept under the white canopy to the brown woman. There were sounds in there. There was a tussle. The brown woman giggled softly. On two occasions Red's mother almost caught the young man in the room.

She came into the room without warning. She had made up her mind to take the child to her own room downstairs and, walking in, lifted Red out of his crib. He began to cry. He kept on crying.

The brown woman got out of her bed, her lover lying in silence. He was hidden under the sheets. The child kept crying until the brown woman took him from the mother and then he became silent. The white woman went away.

The next time Red's mother came the Negro had got out of the bed but did not have time to get to the door that led to an outside stairway. He stepped into the armoire. It was high enough to let him stand upright and he pulled the door softly shut. He was almost nude and some of his clothes were lying on the floor of the room. Red's mother did not notice.

The Negro man was a strong man with broad shoulders. He was the one who taught Red to ride a horse. One night when he was in bed with the brown woman a notion came into his head. He got out of bed and took the child into the bed with himself and the woman. Red was quite small then. Afterwards he remembered dimly. It was a clear still moonlit night. The Negro man had thrown back the white netting separating the bed from an open window and the moonlight streaming in fell across his body and across the body of the woman. Red remembered that night.

The two brown people were playing with the white child. The brown man tossed Red into the air and caught him as he fell. He laughed softly. The Negro took hold of Red's small white hands and with his own huge black hands made him walk up the broad flat brown belly. He let him walk over the woman's body.

The two people began pitching the child back and forth. Red loved the game. He kept begging for it to go on. It seemed glorious to him. When they had tired of playing, he crawled over the two bodies, over the broad brown shoulders of the man and over the breasts of the brown woman. His lips sought the rounded upstanding breasts of the woman. He went to sleep on her breasts.

Red remembered these nights as one remembers a fragment caught and held out of a dream. He remembered the laughter of the two brown people in the moonlight as they played with him, the soft laughter that could not be heard outside the room. They were laughing at his mother. It may have been they were laughing at the white race. There are times when Negroes do something like that.

BOOK TWO

MILL GIRLS

1

DORIS HOFFMAN, who worked in the spinning-room at the Langdon Cotton Mill, Langdon, Georgia, had a dim but ever-present consciousness of a world outside the cotton mill where she worked and the cotton-mill village where she lived with her husband, Ed Hoffman. She was conscious of automobiles, of passenger trains seen now and then through windows as they went whirling past the mill (don't be wasting time now at windows, time wasters get fired in these times), of movies, of swell clothes a woman might own, of voices coming over radios. There wasn't any radio in the Hoffman house. They hadn't got one. She was very conscious of people. In the mill sometimes she felt like playing the devil. She would have liked playing with the other girls in the spinning-room, dancing with them, singing with them. Come on, now, let's sing. Let's dance. She was young. She made up songs sometimes. She was a smart fast workwoman. She liked men. Her husband, Ed Hoffman, wasn't a very strong man. She would have liked a strong young man.

Just the same she wouldn't have gone back on Ed Hoffman, not she. She knew that and Ed knew it.

On some days you couldn't touch Doris. Ed couldn't have touched her. She was closed up, quiet and warm. She was like a tree or like a hill lying still in warm sunlight. She worked quite automatically in the big light spinning-room of the Langdon Cotton Mill, the room with the lights, the flying machines, the subtle changing flying forms—you couldn't touch her on such days, but she did her work all right. She could always do more than her share of work.

One Saturday, in the fall, there was a fair in Langdon. It wasn't right by the cotton mill nor in the town. It was in an empty field by the river out beyond the cotton mill and the cotton-mill town. People from Langdon, if they went out there, went mostly in cars. The fair was there all week and a good many people from Langdon went out. They had the field lighted with electric lights so they could have shows at night.

It wasn't a horse fair. It was a fair of shows. There was a ferris wheel and a merry-go-round and stands for selling things and places to ring canes and a free show on a plat-form. There were places for dancing, one for whites and one for Negroes. Saturday, the last day of the fair, was a day for mill hands and for poor white farmers and for Negroes mostly. Hardly any of the town people went on that day. There were hardly any fights or drunks or anything. To get the mill people it was arranged that the mill baseball team should play a game with a mill team from Wilford, Georgia. The mill at Wilford was a small one, just a little yarn mill. It was pretty sure that the Langdon mill team would have it easy. They would be almost dead sure to win.

Doris Hoffman had consciousness of the fair all week. All the girls in her room at the mill had consciousness of it. The mill at Langdon ran night and day. You put in five ten-hour shifts and one five-hour shift. You had it off from Sat-urday noon until Sunday night at twelve, when the night shift started the new week.

Doris was strong. She could go places and do things her husband Ed couldn't do and go. He was always feeling done up and had to lie down. She went to the fair with three mill girls named Grace and Nell and Fanny. It would have been easier and a shorter way round to go by the railroad track, but Nell, who was also a strong girl, like Doris, said, "Let's go through town," so they all did. It wasn't so nice for Grace, who was weak, going the long way, but she never said a thing. They came back the short way, by the railroad tracks that followed the winding of the river. They went to Langdon Main Street and turned to the right. Then they went through nice streets. Then it was a long way on a dirt road. It was pretty dusty.

The river that went below the mill and the railroad tracks wound around. You could go to Main Street, in Langdon, and turn to the right and get into a road that went on out to the fair. You walked through a street of nice houses, not all alike, as in a mill village, but each one different, with yards and grass and flowers and girls sitting on the porch, no older than Doris herself, but not married, not with a man and kid and a sick mother-in-law, and you got to a flat place by the same river that went past the mill.

Grace would eat her supper quickly after her day in the mill and she would clean up quickly. You get to eating quickly when you eat alone. You don't care what you eat. She would clean up and do the dishes quickly. She was tired. She hurried. Then she went out on the porch and took off her shoes. She liked to lie on her back.

There wasn't any street lamp along there. That was a good thing. It took Doris longer to clean up, and then, besides, she had to nurse her baby and get it to sleep. It was lucky it was a healthy kid and slept well. It was like Doris. It was naturally strong. Doris spoke to Grace about her mother-in-law. She always called her "Mrs. Hoffman." She said, "Mrs. Hoffman's worse to-day," or, "she's better," or, "she bled a little."

She didn't like to put her baby in the front room of the four-room house, where all four of the Hoffmans ate and sat on Sundays and where Mrs. Hoffman lay when she lay down, but she didn't want Mrs. Hoffman to know that she didn't want that. It would hurt her feelings. Ed had built his mother a kind of low couch to lie on. He was handy. She could lie down easily and get up easily. Doris didn't like to put her baby in there. She was afraid the baby would get it. She told Grace that. "I'm afraid all the time he'll get it," she told Grace. She put her baby, after it was nursed and ready to go to sleep, in the bed where she and Ed slept, in another room. Ed had been sleeping, during the day, in the same bed, but when he got up in the afternoon he made the bed up fresh for Doris. Ed was that way. He was nice that way.

Ed was almost like a girl in some things.

Doris had big breasts but Grace hadn't hardly any at all. That might have been because Doris had had a kid. No, it wasn't. She had big breasts before that, before she ever even got married.

Doris went out to Grace nights. In the mill she and Grace worked in the same big light long spinning-room between the rows of bobbins. They ran up and down or walked up and down or stopped a minute to talk. When you work with some one that way all day every day, you can't help getting to like her. You get to love her. It's like being married almost. You know when she is tired because you are tired. If your feet ache you know hers do. You can't tell, just walking through a place and seeing people working, like Doris and Grace did. You don't know. You don't feel it.

There was a man came through the spinning-room in the middle of the morning and in the middle of the afternoon selling things. They let him. He sold a big chunk of soft candy, called "Milky Way," and he sold Coca Cola. They let him. You blew in ten cents. It hurt to blow it in but you did. You got the habit and you did. It braced you. Grace could hardly wait when she was working. She wanted her "Milky Way," she wanted her coke. She was laid off by the time she and Doris and Fanny and Nell went to the fair. There were hard times. A lot were laid off.

They always took the weaker ones, of course. They knew all right. They didn't say to a girl, "Do you need it?" They said, "We won't need you now for a while." Grace needed it, but not as badly as some. She had Tom Musgrave and her mother working.

So they had laid her off. It was tight times, not flush times. It was harder work. They made Doris' side longer. They'd be laying off Ed next. It was hard enough without that.

They had cut Ed's pay and Tom Musgrave's and his mother's pay.

They charged just as much for house rent and everything. You had to pay just about as much for things. They said you didn't but you did. There was a little flame of anger always in Doris at about the time she went to the fair with Grace and Fanny and Nell. She went most of all because she wanted Grace to go and have some fun and forget it and get it off her mind. Grace wouldn't have gone if Doris hadn't gone. She would go anywhere Doris did. They hadn't laid Nell and Fanny off yet.

When Doris went out to Grace, when they were both working yet, before the tight times came so bad, before they made Doris' side so much longer and gave Ed and Tom and Ma Musgrave so many more looms ... Ed said it kept him on the jump now so he couldn't think ... he said it tired him out worse than ever keeping up; and he looked it ... Doris herself kept up by working, she said, almost twice as fast ... before all that happened, in the good times yet, she used to go out like that to Grace at night.

Grace was so tired, lying on the porch. Particularly on hot nights she was so tired. There would maybe be some people, just mill people like themselves, in the mill village street, but not many. There wasn't any street lamp right near the Musgrave-Hoffman house.

They could lie in darkness beside each other. Grace was like Ed, Doris' husband. She hardly ever spoke in the daytime but at night, when it was all dark and hot she would talk. Ed was that way. Grace wasn't like Doris, raised in a mill town. She and her brother Tom and her pa and ma had been raised on a farm in the North Georgia hills. It wasn't much of a farm, Grace said. You could hardly raise a thing, Grace said, but it was nice. She said they would have stayed there maybe, only her father died. They owed some money and the farm had to be sold and Tom couldn't get work; so they came to Langdon.

There was a kind of waterfall near their farm when they had a farm. It wasn't exactly a waterfall, Grace said. This would be at night, before Grace got laid off, when she was so tired at night and was lying on the porch. Doris would come to her and would sit down by her or lie down and would not talk loud but whisper.

Grace would have her shoes off. She would have her dress open wide all down the neck. "Take your stockings off, Grace," Doris would whisper.

There was a fair. It was in October, 1930. The mill closed at noon. Doris' husband was lying down at home. She had left her baby with her mother-in-law. She saw things, a-plenty. There was the ferris wheel and a long street-like place with banners up and pictures on . . . a fat woman and a woman with snakes around her neck and a two-headed man and a woman in a tree with fuzzy hair and, Nell said, "God knows what else," and a man on a box, talking about it all. There were some girls in tights, not very clean. They and the men all yelled together, "Yea, yea, yea," to get the people to come.

There were niggers there a-plenty, it seemed, town niggers and country niggers, thousands of them, it seemed.

There were country people a-plenty, white people. They had come mostly in rickety wagons drawn by mules. The fair had been going on all week, but Saturday was the big day. In the big field, where the fair was held, the grass was all worn away. All that part of Georgia, when there wasn't any grass, was red. It was as red as blood. Ordinarily that place, away out there, nearly a mile from Langdon's main street, a mile and a half, no less, from the Langdon cotton-mill village, where Doris, Nell, Grace and Fanny all worked and lived, was filled with tall weeds and grass. Whoever owned it couldn't plant cotton on it because, when the river came up, it got flooded. It might get flooded any time after rains in the hills north of Langdon.

The ground was rich. Weeds and grass grew tall and thick there. Whoever owned the ground had rented it to the fair people. They came in trucks to bring the fair there. There was a night show and a day show.

You didn't pay anything to get in. There was a free baseball game on the day when Doris went to the fair with Nell and Grace and Fanny and there was to be a free show by performers on a platform in the middle of the fair. Doris felt a little guilty going when her husband Ed couldn't go, didn't feel like it, but he had kept on saying, "Go on, Doris, Go with the girls. Go on with the girls."

Fanny and Nell kept saying, "Ah, come on." Grace didn't say anything. She never did.

Doris felt motherly toward Grace. Grace was always so tired after a day in the mill. After a day in the mill, when night came, Grace said, "I'm so tired." She had dark circles under her eyes. Doris' husband, Ed Hoffman, worked in the mill nights . . . a pretty smart man but not strong.

So, on ordinary nights, when Doris came home from the mill and when her husband Ed had gone to work, he worked nights and she worked days, so they were only together on Saturday afternoons and nights and Sunday and Sunday night until twelve . . . they usually went to church on Sunday nights, taking Ed's mother with them . . . she'd go to church when she couldn't get up strength to go anywhere else. . . .

On just ordinary nights, when the long day in the mill was at an end, when Doris had done what housework at home there was left to do and had nursed the baby and it had gone to sleep and her mother-in-law was lying down, she went outside. The mother-in-law got the supper for Ed and then he left and Doris came and ate and there were the dishes to do. "You're tired," the mother-in-law said, "I'll do them." "No you won't," Doris said. She had a way of saying things so people minded what she said. They did what she told them to do.

There would be Grace waiting for Doris outside. She would be lying on the porch if it was a hot night.

The Hoffman house wasn't really the Hoffman house at all. It was a mill-village house. It was a double house. There were forty houses just like it in that street in the mill village. Doris and Ed and Ed's mother, Ma Hoffman, who had tuberculosis and couldn't work any more, lived on one side and Grace Musgrave and her brother Tom and their mother, Ma Musgrave, lived on the other. Tom wasn't married. There was just a thin wall between them. There were two front doors but there was just one porch, a narrow one running clear across the front of the house. Tom Musgrave and Ma Musgrave, like Ed, worked nights. Grace was alone in her side of the house at night. She wasn't afraid. She said to Doris, "I'm not afraid. You're so near." Ma Musgrave got the supper in that house and then she and Tom Musgrave left. They left enough for Grace. She washed the dishes like Doris did. They left at the same time Ed Hoffman did. They went together.

You had to go in time to check in and get ready. When you worked days you had to stay right on the job until quitting time and then clean up. Doris and Grace both worked in the spinning-room at the mill and Ed and Tom Musgrave were loom-fixers. Ma Musgrave was a weaver.

At night, when Doris had got her work done and had nursed her kid and it had gone to sleep and Grace had her work done Doris went out to Grace. Grace was one of the kind that will work and work and won't give up, and so was Doris.

Only Grace wasn't strong like Doris. She was frail and had black hair and dark brown eyes that looked unnaturally big in her thin small face and she had a small mouth. Doris had a big mouth and nose and a big head. Her body was long but her legs were short. They were strong though. Grace's legs were round and nice. They were like a man likes a girl's legs to be and she had pretty small feet but they weren't strong. They couldn't stand the racket. "I don't wonder," Doris said, "they're so little and so pretty." After a day in the mill . . . on your feet all day, running up and down a body's feet hurt. Doris' feet smarted but not like Grace's. "They hurt so," Grace said. She always meant her feet when she said that. "Take off your stockings."

"No, you wait. I'll take them off for you."
Doris took them off for Grace.
"Now you lie still."

She'd rub Grace all over. She didn't exactly feel her. Every one said that knew that Doris had good rubbing hands. She had strong quick hands. They were alive hands. What she did to Grace she did also to Ed, her husband, when he was off on Saturday night and they slept together. He needed it all right. She rubbed Grace's feet and her legs and her shoulders and her neck and everywhere. She began at the top and then began at the bottom. "Now turn over," she said. She rubbed her back a long time. She did that to Ed too. It was nice, she thought, to feel people and to rub them, hard but not too hard.

It was nice if the people you rubbed were nice. Grace was nice and Ed Hoffman was nice. They didn't feel the same. "I guess no two people's bodies feel the same," Grace thought. Grace's body was softer, not so stringy as Ed's.

You rubbed her awhile and then she talked. She began talking. Ed always began talking when Doris rubbed him that way. They didn't talk about the same things. Ed was a man of ideas. He could read and write and Doris and Grace couldn't. When he had time to read he read both newspapers and books. Grace couldn't read or write any more than Doris could. They hadn't been brought up to it. Ed had wanted to be a preacher but he hadn't made it. He'd have made it if he hadn't been so shy he couldn't stand up before people and talk.

If his father had lived he might have got up nerve and made it. His father, when he was alive, wanted him to. He saved and sent him to school. Doris could write her name and could spell out a few words if she tried but Grace couldn't do even that much. When Doris rubbed Ed with her strong hands that never did seem to get tired, he talked of ideas. He had got it into his head he would like to be a man to get up a union.

He had got it into his head mill people might get up a union and strike. He talked about it. Sometimes, when Doris had been rubbing him a long time he got to laughing and laughed at himself.

He said, "I talk about myself getting up a union." Once, before Doris knew him, he had worked at a mill in another town where they had a union. They had a strike too and got licked. Ed said he didn't care. He said it was good times. He was just a young kid then. That was before Doris met and married him, before he came to Langdon. His father was alive then. He laughed and said, "I got ideas but no nerve. I'd like to get up a union here and I ain't got the nerve." He laughed at himself that way.

Grace, when Doris rubbed her at night when Grace was so tired, when her body began to feel softer and softer, nicer and nicer under Doris' hands, she never did talk about ideas.

She liked to describe places. There was a little waterfall, in a little creek, with some bushes, near the farm where

she lived before her father died and she and her brother Tom
and her mother moved to Langdon and got to be mill people.
There wasn't just one waterfall, a big one. There was one
over rocks and then another and another and another. There
was coolness, a shady place with rocks and bushes. There
was water, Grace said, acting as though it was alive. It
seemed to whisper and then it talked, she said. If you went
a little way it was like horses trotting. There was a little pool
beneath each fall, she said.

She used to go there when she was a child. There were
fish in the pools but if you kept still, after awhile, they paid
no attention. Grace's father died when she and her brother
Tom were children yet, but they didn't have to sell the farm
right away, not for a year or two; so they went there all
the time.

It was near their house.

It was wonderful to hear Grace talk of it. Doris thought
that on a hot night, when she was tired herself and her own
feet smarted, it was the nicest thing she ever knew. In the
hot cotton-mill town, in Georgia, where the nights are so
still and hot, when Doris had got her baby to sleep at last
and had rubbed Grace and had rubbed her, until Grace said
the tiredness had all gone out of her feet and her arms and
her legs and the smarting and the tenseness and all . . .

You'd never have thought that Grace's brother, Tom
Musgrave, who was such a homely tall-like man and had never
married and whose teeth were all so black and who had such
a big Adam's apple . . . you'd never have thought a man like
that, when he was a small boy, would have been so nice to
his little sister.

Taking her to pools and waterfalls and fishing.

He was so homely you'd never have thought he could
be Grace's brother at all.

You'd never have thought a girl like Grace, who was
always getting tired so easily and who was ordinarily so
silent and who was always looking, when she had her job in

the mill yet, as though she was going to faint or something—
you'd never have thought, when you rubbed her and rubbed
her, as Doris did, so patiently and nice, liking to, you'd never
have thought she could talk as she did about places and
things.

2

THE fair at Langdon, Georgia, fed Doris Hoffman's consciousness of worlds outside her own mill-bound world. That was a world of Grace and Ed and Mrs. Hoffman and Nell and thread being made and flying machinery and wages and talk of the new stretch-out system that had been put in at the mill and always wages and hours and things like that. It wasn't varied enough. It was too much always the same. Doris couldn't read. The fair was something to tell Ed about afterwards at night in bed. It was nice also for Grace to go. She didn't seem to get so tired. The fair was crowded and your shoes got dusty and the shows were shabby and noisy but Doris didn't know that.

The shows and the merry-go-round and the ferris wheel came from some far outside world. There were show people shouting in front of tents and girls in tights who maybe never had been in any mill but had traveled everywhere. There were men selling jewelry, sharp-eyed men who had the nerve to say anything to a body. Perhaps they and the shows had been up North and out West, where the cowboys were and on Broadway in New York and everywhere. Doris knew about all of these things because she had been to the movies quite a lot.

Being just a mill hand, born one, was like being always a prisoner. You couldn't get out of knowing that. You were housed in, shut up. People, outside people, not mill hands, thought you were different. They looked down on you. They couldn't help it. They couldn't know how you got sometimes, wanting to explode, hating every one and everything. When you got that way you had to hold on tight and shut up. It was the best way.

The show people went places. They were in Langdon, Georgia, for a week and then they disappeared. Nell and Fanny and Doris all thought the same thing that day when they first got to the fair and began to look around but they didn't talk about it. Maybe Grace didn't feel what the rest felt. She was gentler and more tired. She would have been a home body if some man had married her. Doris didn't understand why some man hadn't. It might be that the show girls, at the hoola-hoola tent, weren't so nice, in their tights and showing their legs, but they weren't mill hands anyway. Nell in particular was in rebellion. She almost always was. Nell could swear like a man. She didn't give a damn. "God, I'd like to try it myself," she was thinking that day when the four first got to the fair.

Before she had her kid, Doris and Ed, her husband, used to go to the movies a lot. It was fun, something to talk about; she liked it, particularly Charlie Chaplin and westerns. She liked movies about crooks and people getting in tight places and fighting and shooting. It made her nerves tingle. There were pictures about rich people, how they lived, etc. They wore wonderful dresses.

They went to parties and dances. There were young girls and they were ruined. You saw a scene, in the movies, in a garden. There was a high stone fence with vines on it. There was a moon.

There were nice grass and flower beds and little houses with vines and with seats inside.

A young girl came out of a house, out at a side door, with a man, older than she was, a lot. She was beautifully dressed. She had on a low-neck dress. That was what you wore at parties among swells. He talked to her. He took her into his arms and kissed her. He had a gray mustache. He led her away to a seat in a little open house in the yard.

There was a poor young man who wanted to marry her. He didn't have any money. The rich man got her. He betrayed her. He ruined her. Such plays, in the movies, gave Doris a queer feeling inside. She walked home with Ed to the mill house in the mill village where they lived and they didn't talk. It would be funny if Ed wished, just for awhile, that he was rich and could live in a house like that and ruin such a young girl. If he did, he didn't say so. Doris was wishing something. After seeing such a show sometimes, she wished some rich wicked man would come and ruin her just once, not for keeps but just once, in such a garden, back of such a house . . . so quiet and the moonlight shining . . . you knowing you didn't have to get up and get breakfast and hurry off to the mill at half-past five, rain or snow, winter and summer . . . if you had swell underwear and were beautiful.

Westerns were nice. There were men always riding horses and they had guns and shot each other. They were always fighting about some woman. "Not my kind," Doris thought. Even a cowboy wouldn't be such a fool about a mill girl. Doris was curious, something in her always running out to places and people, alert. "Even if I had the money and the clothes and the underwear and the silk stockings to wear every day I guess I wouldn't be any swell," she thought. She was short of body and firm-breasted. Her head was big and so was her mouth. She had a big nose and strong white teeth. Most of the mill girls had bad teeth. If there was always a lurking sense of beauty, following her sturdy little figure like a shadow, going every day to the mill with her, coming home, going with her when she went somewhere with other mill girls, it wasn't very obvious. Not many people saw it.

Things got suddenly ridiculous and funny to her. It might happen any time. She wanted to scream and dance. She had to hang onto herself. If you get too gay in a mill, out you go. Then where are you?

There was Tom Shaw, who was the president of the Langdon mill, the big gun there. He didn't come into the mill often—he stayed in the office—but now and then he did come. He walked through, looking, or he brought some visitors through. He was such a funny self-important little man that Doris wanted to laugh at him but she didn't. When he came past her side, or walked through, or the foreman or the superintendent came, before Grace got laid off, she was always scared. Mostly about Grace. Grace hardly ever had her side up.

If you didn't keep your side right up, if some one came along and too many of your bobbins were stopped...

Thread was wound on bobbins in the spinning-room of a mill. A side was one side of a long narrow hallway between rows of flying bobbins. Thousands of separate threads came down from up above somewhere to be wound, each thread on its own bobbin, and if it broke the bobbin stopped. You could tell how many had stopped at one time by just looking. The bobbin stood still. It was waiting for you to come quickly and tie the broken thread in again. There might be four bobbins stopped at one end of your side, and at the same time, at the other end, a long walk, there might be three more stopped. The thread, coming to feed the bobbins, so they could go to the loom-room, kept coming and coming. "If it would only stop, just for an hour," Doris thought sometimes, not often. If a girl only didn't have to see it coming and coming all day long, or if she was on the night shift, all night long. It kept coming all day long, all night long. It was wound onto bobbins that were to go into the loom-room where Ed and Tom Musgrave and Ma Musgrave all worked. When the bobbins on your side were full, a man, who was called a "doffer," came and took the full bobbins away. He took out the full bobbins and put in empty ones. He pushed a little cart along before him and it was taken away filled with the loaded bobbins.

There were millions and millions of bobbins to be filled.

They never ran out of empty bobbins. It seemed there must be hundreds of millions of them, like stars, or like drops of water in a river or grains of sand in a field. The thing about getting out now and then to a place like that fair, where there were shows and people you had never seen and talking and niggers laughing and hundreds of other mill hands, like herself and Grace and Nell and Fanny, not in the mill now but outside, was a great relief. Thread and bobbins got out of your head for awhile anyway.

They didn't go on so much in Doris' head when she was not in the mill at work. They did in Grace's head. Doris didn't know so well how it was with Fanny and Nell.

At the fair there was a man performed free on the trapeze. He was funny. Even Grace laughed at him. Nell and Fanny laughed hard and so did Doris. Nell, since Grace had been laid off, had taken Grace's place in the mill next to Doris. She hadn't taken Grace's place purposely. She couldn't help it. She was a tall girl with yellow hair and long legs. Men fell for her. She could put the bee on men. She was on the square just the same.

Men liked her. The foreman in the spinning-room, a young man but with a bald head and married, would have liked to get Nell. He wasn't the only one. Even at the fair the show men and others, who didn't know the four girls, looked at her most. They made cracks at her. They got too smart. Nell could swear like a man. She went to church, but she swore. She didn't care what she said. When Grace got laid off, when the tight times came, Nell, who was put on her side with Doris, said:

"The dirty skunks, they laid Grace off." She came in there where Doris was, at work, with her head up. She always carried it up.... "It's damn lucky she's got Tom and her mother working," she said to Doris. "Maybe she can make it go with Tom and her mother working, if they don't get laid off," she said.

"She oughtn't to be at work in here nohow. Don't you

think so?" Doris did think so. She liked and admired Nell but not as she did Grace. She liked the to-hell-with-everything about Nell. "I wish I had it," she thought sometimes. Nell would goddam the foreman and the super when they weren't around but when they came around ... of course she wasn't a fool. She gave them the eye. They liked it. Her eyes seemed to be saying to men, "Ain't you splendid?" She didn't mean it. Her eyes always seemed to be saying something to men. "All right. Get me if you can," they said. "I'm getable," they said. "If you're man enough."

Nell wasn't married but there were a dozen men in the mill, married and unmarried, who had tried to make her. The young unmarried ones meant marriage. Nell said, "You got to work 'em. You got to keep them guessing, but don't give in to 'em unless they make you. Make 'em think you think they're swell," she said.

"God damn their souls," she said sometimes.

The young man, unmarried, who was doffer on their side, the side Grace and Doris had been on and then Nell and Doris, after Grace got laid off, used not to say much when he came around when Grace was there. He was sorry for Grace. Grace never could quite keep up her side. Doris was always having to leave her side and work Grace's side so Grace wouldn't be shown up. He knew it. He used to whisper sometimes to Doris, "The poor kid," he said. "If Jim Lewis gets onto her she'll get laid off." Jim Lewis was the room foreman. He was the one who was hot on Nell. He was a bald man, about thirty, with a wife and two kids. When Nell took Grace's side the young fellow who was doffer there changed.

He was always kidding with Nell, trying to date her up. He called her "legs." "Hello, legs," he said. "What about it? What about a date? What about the movies to-night?" The nerve of him.

"Come on," he said, "I'll take you."

"Not to-night," she said. "We'll think it over," she said. She kept giving him the eye, keeping him on it.

"Not to-night. I'm busy to-night." You'd have thought she had a man dated up for almost every night in the week. She didn't. She never went out alone with men, didn't walk with them or talk with them outside the mill. She stuck to the other girls. "I like 'em better," she told Doris. "Some of 'em, a lot of 'em, are cats but they got more spunk in 'em than the men." She talked rough enough about the young doffer when he had to leave their side and go to the next side. "The damn little skate," she said. "He thinks he can date me up." She laughed, but it wasn't a very pleasant laugh.

At the fair there was an open space, right in the center of the field, where all the ten-cent side shows were and there was a free show. There was a man and woman who danced on roller skates and did tricks and a little girl in tights who danced and two men who tumbled over each other and over chairs and tables and everything. There was a man kept coming out on the platform. He had a megaphone. "Professor Mathews. Where's Professor Mathews?" he kept calling through the megaphone.

"Professor Mathews. Professor Mathews."

Professor Mathews was to be the trapeze performer. He was to be the best thing in the free show. The hand-bills they had put out said so.

There was a long wait. It was Saturday and there weren't many town people from Langdon at the fair, hardly any, maybe none... Doris didn't think she saw any that looked like that. If they had been there, they had come earlier in the week. It was niggers' day. It was a day for mill hands and for a lot of poor farmers with mules and their families.

The niggers kept pretty much off to themselves. They generally did. There were separate stands for them to eat at. You could hear them laughing and talking everywhere. There were fat old Negro women with their Negro men and young Negro girls in bright-colored dresses and the young bucks after them.

It was a hot day in the fall. There was a jam of people. The four girls kept off by themselves. It was a hot day.

The field had been all overgrown with weeds and with tall grass, but now it was all trampled down. There was hardly any. There was mostly dust and bare places coming and it was all red. Doris had got into one of her moods. She was in a "don't-touch-me" mood. She had got silent.

Grace clung to her. She stayed right close. She didn't much like Nell and Fanny being there. Fanny was short and fat and had little short fat fingers.

Nell said of her—not at the fair but before that, in the mill—she said, "Fanny's lucky. She's got a man and no kids." Doris didn't know exactly how she did feel about her own kid. It was at home with her mother-in-law, Ed's mother.

Ed was lying up. He would lie up the whole afternoon. "You go on," he had said to Doris, when the girls came for her. He would get a newspaper or a book and lie up all afternoon on the bed. He would take his shirt and shoes off. The Hoffmans didn't have any books except a Bible and some children's books Ed had left over from his boyhood, but he could get books from the library. There was a branch of the Langdon town library in the mill village.

There was a man called, "a welfare worker," employed by the Langdon mills. He had a house on the best street of houses in the village, the street in which the day superintendent and some of the other higher-ups lived. Some of the foremen lived over there. The foreman of the spinning-room did.

The night superintendent was a young man from the North and unmarried. He lived in a hotel up in Langdon. Doris had never seen him.

The welfare worker's name was Mr. Smith. The front room of his house had been made into a branch library. His wife kept it. Ed would put on his good clothes, after Doris left, and go get a book. He would take back the book he got the week before and get another. The welfare worker's wife would be nice to him. She'd think, "He's nice. He cares for higher things." He liked stories about men, men who had actually lived and had been big men. He had read about big men like Napoleon Bonaparte and General Lee and Lord Wellington and Disraeli. He read in the books in the afternoon all week, after he woke up. He had told Doris about them.

After Doris got in the don't-touch-me mood that day at the fair and was that way a little while, the others noticed how she was. Grace noticed first but didn't say anything. "What the hell's the matter?" Nell said. "I got the woozies," Doris said. She didn't have any woozies at all. She didn't have the blues. It wasn't that.

Sometimes with a person it's this way: the place you are in is there, but it isn't there. If you are at a fair it's that way. If you are at work in the mill it's that way.

You hear things. You touch things. You don't.

You do and you don't. You can't explain. Doris might even be in bed with Ed. They liked to lie awake a long time on Saturday night. It was the only night they had. They could sleep in the morning. You were there and you weren't there. Doris wasn't the only one who was that way sometimes. Ed was sometimes. You spoke to him and he answered but he was away off somewhere. It might have been the books with Ed. He might be somewhere with Napoleon Bonaparte or with Lord Wellington or some one like that. He might be a big-bug himself instead of just a mill hand. You couldn't tell what he was being.

You could smell it; you could taste it; you could see it. It didn't touch you.

There was a ferris wheel at the fair ... ten cents. There was a merry-go-round ... ten cents. Stands were selling hot dogs and Coca Cola and lemonade and "Milky Ways" at the fair.

There were little wheels you could gamble on. A mill hand from the Langdon mill, that day Doris went with Grace and Nell and Fanny, lost twenty-seven dollars. He had saved it up. The girls didn't hear about it until Monday at the mill. "The damn fool," Nell said to Doris, "don't the damn fool know you can't beat them at their own game? If they weren't out to get you what would they be there for?" she asked. There was a little bright shining wheel with an arrow that went around. It stopped on numbers. The mill hand lost a dollar and then another. He got excited. He plunked down ten dollars. He thought, "I'll keep up till I get even." "The damn fool," Nell said to Doris.

Nell felt about a game like that, she felt: "You can't beat it." She felt about men: "You can't beat it." Doris liked Nell. She thought about her. "If she ever gives up she'll give up hard," she thought. It wouldn't be exactly like herself and her husband Ed, she thought. Ed asking her. Her thinking, "I might as well, I guess. A woman might as well have herself a man." If Nell ever gave in to a man it would be a cave-in.

*

"PROFESSOR MATHEWS. Professor Mathews. Professor Mathews."

He wasn't there. They couldn't find him. It was Saturday. Perhaps he had got drunk. "I'll bet he's off somewhere drunk," Fanny said to Nell. Fanny was standing beside Nell. Grace stayed right close to Doris all that day. Not saying a word hardly. She was little and pale. As Nell and Fanny walked toward the place where the free show was to be, a man laughed at them. He laughed at Nell and Fanny walk-

ing together. He was a showman. "Hello," he said to another man, "there's the long and short of it." The other man
laughed. "Go to hell," Nell said. The four girls stood close
together to watch the trapeze performance. "They advertise
a trapeze performance free and then they don't have it,"
Nell said. "He's off drunk," Fanny said. There was a man
who was tanked up. He came forward out of the crowd.
He was a man who looked like a farmer. He had red hair
and no hat. He came forward out of the crowd. He reeled.
He could hardly stand up. He had on blue overalls. He had
a big Adam's apple. "Ain't your Professor Mathews here?"
he managed to ask the man on the platform, the one who
had the megaphone. "I'm a trapeze performer," he said. The
man who was on the platform laughed. He put the megaphone under his arm.

The sky above the fair grounds at Langdon, Georgia,
that day was blue. It was a clear light blue. It was hot. All
the girls in Doris' gang had on thin dresses. The sky that
day was the bluest she had ever seen, Doris thought.

The drunken man said, "If you can't find your Professor Mathews, I can do it."

"You can?" The eyes of the man on the platform registered surprise, amusement, doubt.

"You're damn right I can. I'm a Yank, I am."

The man had to hold onto the edge of the platform. He
almost fell. He fell back and fell forward. He could just
stand.

"You can?"

"Yes, I can."

"Where'd you learn?"

"I learned up North. I'm a Yank. I learned on an apple
tree limb up North."

"Yankee Doodle," the man shouted. He opened his
mouth wide and shouted, "Yankee Doodle."

So that was what a Yank was like. Doris had never seen

a Yank before—not to know he was a Yank! Nell and Fanny laughed.

Crowds of niggers laughed. Crowds of mill hands standing and looking laughed. The man on the platform had fairly to lift the drunken man up. He got him almost up once and then let him fall, just to make a fool of him. The next try he got him up. "Like a fool. Just like a fool man," Nell said.

The man performed well after all. He didn't at first. He fell and fell. He'd get up on the trapeze and then he'd fall on the platform. He fell on his face, on his neck, on his head, on his back.

The people laughed and laughed. Afterwards, Nell said, "I cracked my damn sides laughing at the damn fool." Fanny laughed hard too. Even Grace laughed a little. Doris didn't. It wasn't her laughing day. She felt all right but it wasn't her laughing day. The man on the trapeze fell and fell and then he seemed to get sober. He performed all right. He performed well.

The girls had a Coca Cola. They had a "Milky Way." They had a ride on the ferris wheel. There were little seats so you could sit two by two. Grace sat with Doris and Nell with Fanny. Nell would rather have been with Doris. She let Grace be. Grace didn't set 'em up like the others did, one a Coca Cola, one a "Milky Way" and one a ferris-wheel ride, the way the others did. She couldn't. She was broke. She was laid off.

*

THERE are days when nothing can touch you. If you are just a mill girl in a Southern cotton mill it doesn't matter. Something lives inside you that looks and sees. What does anything matter to you? It is queer about such days. The machinery in the mill gets on your nerves terribly some days, but on such days it doesn't. On such days you are far away from people, it's odd, sometimes then you are most attractive to them. They all want to crowd up close. "Give. Give me. Give me."

"Give what?"

You haven't got a thing. You are just that way. "Here I am. You can't touch me."

Doris was in the ferris wheel with Grace. Grace was scared. She hadn't wanted to go up in it, but when she saw Doris was going, she got in. She clung to Doris.

The wheel went up and up and then down and down ... a great circle. There was a town, a great circle. Doris could see the town of Langdon, the court house and some office buildings and the Presbyterian church. She could see, around a shoulder of hill, the smoke-stack of the mill. She couldn't see the mill village.

She could see trees where the town was, a lot of trees. There were shade trees before houses in town, before the houses of people who didn't work in any mill but in stores or offices. Or who were doctors or lawyers or maybe judges. Not having any use for mill people. She could see the river stretching away in a great bend around the town of Langdon. The river was always yellow. It never seemed to get clear. It was golden yellow. It was golden yellow against a blue sky. It was against trees and bushes. It was a sluggish river.

The town of Langdon wasn't on a hill. It was just on high ground. The river didn't go all around. It went on the south side.

On the north side, far away, were hills.... It was far far away up where Grace used to live when she was a little girl. Where the waterfalls were.

Doris could see people, looking down on them from above. She could see lots of people. Their legs went in a funny way. They were walking about the fair grounds.

The river that went past Langdon had catfish in it.

Niggers fished for them. They liked to. Hardly any one else did. Whites hardly ever did.

In Langdon, right in the busiest parts, not far from where the best stores were, there were nigger streets. No one but niggers went there. If you were white you didn't go. White people ran the stores in the nigger streets but whites didn't go there.

Doris would have liked to see the streets of her mill village from up there. She couldn't. A shoulder of land made it impossible. The ferris wheel went down. She thought, "I'd like to see where I live, from high up there."

You couldn't rightly say that people like Doris, Nell, Grace and Fanny lived in their houses. They lived in the mill. All week nearly all of their waking hours were in the mill.

In the winter they went when it was dark. They came away at night when it was dark. Their lives were walled in, shut in. How could any one ever know who hadn't been caught and held from childhood, through young girlhood and on into womanhood. It was the same with the mill men. They were a special people.

Their lives were in rooms. The life of Nell and Doris in the spinning-room of the Langdon mill was in a room. It was a big light room.

It wasn't ugly. It was big and light. It was wonderful.

Their life was in a little narrow hallway inside a big room. The walls of the hallway were machines. Light came from above. A fine soft spray of water, really mist, came from above. That was to keep the flying thread soft and flexible for the machines.

Flying machines. Singing machines. Machines making walls to a little alive hallway in a big room.

The hallway was narrow. Doris hadn't ever measured how wide it was.

You began as a child. You stayed until you were old or

worn out. The machines went up and up. Thread came down and down. It fluttered. You had to keep it damp. It fluttered. If you didn't keep it damp it would be always breaking. In the hot summer the dampness made you sweat more and more. It made you sweat worse. It kept you wringing wet with sweat.

Nell said, "Who gives a damn for us? We're only machines ourselves. Who gives a damn for us?" On some days Nell growled. She swore. She said, "We're making cloth. Who gives a damn? Some whore maybe'll get her a new dress out of some rich man." Nell talked plain. She swore. She hated.

"What difference does it make who gives a damn? Who wants them to give a damn?"

There was lint in the air, fine floating lint. It was what gave some people tuberculosis, some said. It might have given it to Ed's mother, Ma Hoffman, lying on her couch, Ed had made, and coughing. She coughed when Doris was there at night, when Ed was there in the daytime, in the afternoon when he was lying in his bed, when he was reading about General Lee or General Grant or Napoleon Bonaparte. Doris hoped her kid wouldn't get it.

Nell said, "We work from cansee to can'tsee. They got us. They got the bee on us. They know it. They got us hogtied. We work from cansee to can'tsee." Nell was tall, swaggering, profane. Her breasts weren't big, like Doris'—almost too big—or like Fanny's or too little, just nothing, a flat place, like a man, like Grace's. They were just right, not too big or not too little.

If a man ever got Nell he'd get her hard. Doris knew that. She felt it. She didn't know how she knew but she knew. Nell would fight and swear and fight. "No you don't. Damn you. I ain't that kind. You go to hell."

When she gave up she'd cry like a child.

If a man got her, he'd have her. She'd be his. She wouldn't talk about it much, but ... if a man got her she'd be his. Doris almost wished she were a man to try, thinking of Nell.

A girl thought of such things. She had to be thinking about something. All day, every day, thread, thread, thread. Flying, breaking, flying, breaking. Sometimes Doris wished she could swear like Nell. She wished sometimes she were Nell's kind, not her own kind. Grace said, when she was working in the mill on the side where Nell now worked, once at night, after she had come home...a hot night...she said...

Doris was rubbing Grace with her hands, softly, strongly, the way she could rub, not too hard, not too soft. She rubbed her all over. Grace liked it so. She was so tired. She could hardly do her dishes that night. She said, "I got thread in my brain. Rub it there. I got thread in my brain." She kept thanking Doris for rubbing her. "Thank you. Oh, thank you, Doris," she said.

In the ferris wheel, Grace was scared when it went up. She clung to Doris and shut her eyes. Doris kept hers wide open. She didn't want to miss a thing.

Nell would have looked Jesus Christ in the eyes. She would have looked Napoleon Bonaparte in the eyes or Robert E. Lee.

Doris' husband thought Doris was that way too, but she wasn't just the way her husband thought she was. She knew that. Once Ed talked to his mother about Doris. Doris didn't hear it. It was in the afternoon when Ed had wakened and when Doris was at work. He said, "If she had a thought against me she'd tell it. If she had even a thought about another man she'd tell me." It wasn't true. If Doris had heard it, she would have laughed. "He's got me wrong," she would have said.

You could be in a room with Doris and she'd be there and not there. She'd never get on your nerves. Nell said that once to Fanny and it was true.

She didn't say, "Look. Here I am. I'm Doris. Pay attention to me." She didn't care whether you paid attention or
not.

Her husband Ed could be in a room. He could be reading there on a Sunday. Doris could be lying down too, on
the same bed, beside Ed. Ed's mother could be lying on the
front porch on the couch Ed had made for her. Ed would
have put it out there for her so she could get the air.

It could be hot summer.

The baby could be out there playing on the porch. He
could be crawling around. Ed had made a little fence so he
couldn't crawl off the porch. Ed's mother could watch her.
Her cough kept her awake.

Ed could be on the bed beside Doris. He could be thinking about the people in the book he was reading. If he had
been a writer he could have been on the bed beside Doris
writing his books. Nothing in her said, "Look at me. Pay
attention to me." It never did.

Nell said, "She goes toward you. She's warm toward
you." If Nell had been a man she'd have been after Doris.
She said to Fanny once, "I'd be after her. I'd want her."

Doris never hated any one. She never hated anything.

Doris could rub warmth into people. She could rub
relaxation into people with her hands. Sometimes when she
was in the spinning-room at the mill, keeping up her side,
her breasts hurt. After she got Ed and her baby, she nursed
her baby early, when she woke up. Her baby woke up early.
She gave him a little warm drink again before she went off
to work.

She went home and nursed her baby again at noon. In
the night she nursed him. On Saturday nights the baby slept
with her and Ed.

Ed had nice feelings. Before she married him, when
they were going together . . . they both worked in the mill
then too . . . Ed had a day job then . . . Ed used to walk with

her. He used to sit in Doris' mother's and father's house with her at night in the dark.

Doris had been in the mill, in the spinning-room, since she was twelve. So had Ed been. He had been in the loom-room since he was fifteen.

On the day when Doris was in the ferris wheel with Grace ... Grace clinging to her ... Grace with her eyes shut because she was afraid ... Fanny and Nell in the next seat below ... Fanny whooping with laughter ... Nell yelled.

Doris kept seeing things.

She saw two fat Negro women, far off, fishing in the river.

She saw cotton fields, far off.

There was a man driving an automobile in a road between cotton fields. He made a red dust.

She saw some of the buildings of the town of Langdon and the smoke-stack at the cotton mill where she worked.

There was a man selling patent medicine in a field near the one where the fair was being held. Doris saw him. He had only Negroes gathered about him. He was on the back of a truck. He was selling patent medicine to niggers.

She saw a crowd, a surging crowd on the fair grounds, Negroes and whites, lint-heads (cotton mill workers) and niggers. Most of the mill girls hated Negroes. Doris didn't.

She saw a young man she knew. He was a strong-looking red-headed young town man who had got a job in the mill.

He had been there working twice. He came one summer and then the next summer he was back again. He was a sweeper. The girls in the mill said, "I'll bet he's a spy. What else is he? If he wasn't a spy, why would he be here?"

He worked in the mill the first time. Doris wasn't married then. Then he went away and some one said he went to college. Doris got married to Ed the next summer.

Then he came back. It was tight times with people being laid off but he got a job back. They had put in the stretch-out and they were laying people off and there was talk of a union. "Let's have a union."

"Mr. Shaw won't stand for it. The super won't stand for it."

"I don't care. Let's have a union."

Doris didn't get laid off. She had to work a longer side. Ed had to do more. He could hardly do what he did do before. When that young fellow with the red hair . . . they called him "Red" . . . when he came back they all said he must be a spy.

There was a woman, a strange woman, came to town and got hold of Nell and told her whom to write to about a union, and Nell came at night, on a Saturday night, to the Hoffman house and said to Doris, "Can I speak to Ed, Doris?" And Doris said, "Yes." She wanted Ed to write to some people to get a union, to send some one. "A communist one I hope," she said. She had heard that was the worst kind. She wanted the worst. Ed was afraid. He wouldn't at first. "It's hard times," he said, "it's Hoover times." He said he wouldn't at first.

"It's no time," he said. He was scared. "I'll get fired or laid off," he said, but Doris said, "Ah, go ahead," and Nell said, "Ah, go ahead," and he did.

Nell said, "Don't tell a soul. Don't tell a damn soul." It was exciting.

The red-haired young man had come back to work in the mill. His poppy had been a doctor in Langdon and he used to doctor sick mill people but he had died. He was on the square.

His son was just a sweeper in the mill. He played ball on the mill ball team and was a crack player. That day, when Doris was at the fair, in the ferris wheel, she saw him. The mill ball team usually played ball on the ball field the mill owned, right by the mill, but that day they were playing right near the fair. It was a big day for mill people.

There was to be a dance that night at the fair on a big platform—ten cents. There were two platforms, one for niggers, one for whites, not very near. Grace and Nell and Doris didn't intend to stay. Doris couldn't. Fanny stayed. Her husband came and she stayed.

There was to be a greased pig caught after the baseball game. They didn't stay for that. They went on home after the ferris-wheel ride.

Nell said, speaking of that young red-haired man from town who played on the mill ball team, "I'll bet he's a spy," she said. "The damn rat," she said, "the skunk. I'll bet he's a spy."

They were having the union formed. Ed got letters. He was afraid they'd get onto him every time he got a letter. "What's in it?" Doris asked. It was exciting. He got cards to be signed up to join the union. There was a man coming. There was to be a big union meeting to come out in the open as soon as they had enough signed up. It wasn't communist. Nell had been wrong about that. It was just a union, not the worst kind. Nell said to Ed, "They can't fire you for that."

"Yes, they can. The hell they can't." He was scared. Nell said she bet young Red Oliver was a damn spy. Ed said, "I'll bet he is."

Doris knew he wasn't. She said he wasn't.

"How do you know?"

"I just know."

When she was in the spinning-room of the mill at work she could just see, in the daytime, down the long passageway, lined with the flying bobbins on both sides, a little piece of sky. There was a little piece of tree, the limb of a tree, somewhere far off, over by the river maybe—you couldn't see it always, only when a wind blew. A wind blew and swayed it, and then, if you looked up just then, you saw it. She had been seeing it since she was twelve. Lots of times she had thought, "When I get outside sometime I'm going to look and see where that tree is," but when she got outside she couldn't tell. She had been seeing it since she was twelve. She was eighteen now. There weren't any threads in her head. There weren't any threads in her legs from standing so long where thread was made.

That young man, that red-haired young man used to give her the eye. Grace, when he was there first, didn't know and Nell didn't know. She wasn't married to Ed the first time. Ed didn't know.

He got around that way when he could. He came and looked at her. She looked at him, like that.

When she was going with Ed she and Ed didn't do anything they would be ashamed of afterwards.

She used to let him touch places, in the dark. She let him.

After she got married to him and had her baby he didn't do it any more. He might have thought it wouldn't be nice. He didn't say.

Doris' breasts hurt in the late afternoon when she was in the mill. They began hurting steadily before quitting time, when she had her baby and hadn't weaned him yet. She was weaning him but hadn't got him weaned. When she was in the mill, before she married Ed and when that red-haired young man came around and looked at her, she felt funny. Her breasts hurt then, a little. That day, when she was in the ferris wheel and saw Red Oliver playing baseball with the mill team and was looking at him he was at bat and he hit a ball hard and ran.

It was nice to see him run. He was young and strong. He didn't see her of course. Her breasts began to hurt. When the ferris-wheel ride was over and they came down and had got out she told the others she guessed she'd have to be getting along back home. "I got to go home," she said. "Got to nurse my kid."

Nell and Grace went with her. They came home by the railroad tracks. It was a shorter way. Fanny started with them but she met her husband and he said, "Let's stay," and so she stayed.

BOOK THREE

ETHEL

1

ETHEL LONG, of Langdon, Georgia, was surely not a
true Southern woman. She wasn't in the true Southern-
woman tradition, at least not the old tradition. Her people
were entirely respectable, her father very respectable. Surely
her father had expected his daughter to be something she
wasn't. She knew that. She smiled, knowing it, although the
smile was not intended to be seen by her father. At least he
didn't know. She wouldn't for anything have upset him any
more than he was already upset. "Poor old Dad." Her father
was having a hard ride, she thought. "Life has been a buck-
ing bronco for him." There was that dream of a spotless
white Southern womanhood. She had herself thoroughly ex-
ploded that myth. Of course he didn't know, wouldn't have
wanted to know. Ethel thought she knew where that spotless
white Southern womanhood dream had come from. She had
been born in Langdon, in Georgia, and at least she thought
she had always had her eyes open. She was cynical about
men and in particular about Southern men. "It's pretty easy
for them to talk about spotless white womanhood, getting
what they want all the time, the way they do get it, usually
from the browns, taking few enough risks.

"I'd like to show one of them.

"But hell, why should I bother?"

Ethel wasn't thinking of her father when she thought
these thoughts. Her father was a good man. She herself
wasn't good. She wasn't moral. She was thinking of the
whole present-day Southern white man's attitude, of the way

puritanism had, after the Civil War, moved south. "The Bible belt," Henry Mencken called it in his *Mercury*. It involved all sorts of ugliness, poor whites, Negroes, upper-class whites, gone a little crazy trying to hang onto something lost.

Industrialism in its ugliest form coming in ... all that mixed up in people with religion ... pretensions, stupidity ... just the same it was physically a gorgeous land.

The whites and the blacks in an almost impossible relation to each other ... men and women lying to themselves.

All of this in a warm sweet land. Ethel wasn't particularly, not consciously, aware of nature in the South ... the red sand clay roads, the piney woods, the Georgia peach orchards in bloom in the spring. She knew clearly that it might have been the sweetest land in all America, and wasn't. The rarest opportunity white men had missed in all their missing fire in America ... the South ... how gorgeous it might have been!

Ethel was a modern. That old talk of a high fine Southern civilization ... making gentlemen, making ladies ... she didn't want to be a lady herself ... "That old stuff doesn't go any more," she told herself sometimes, thinking of her father's standards of life, standards he would have so liked to press down upon her. Perhaps he thought he had pressed them down. Ethel smiled. She had the notion, rather firmly fixed in her mind, that, for a woman like herself, no longer young ... she was twenty-nine ... that she had better try to cultivate, if she could, a certain style in life. It was better even to be somewhat rigid. "Don't give yourself too cheaply, whatever you do," she had grown fond of telling herself. There had been in her, formerly, at times ... the mood might at any time come back ... she was, after all, only twenty-nine, a rather ripe age for an alive woman ... she knew well enough that she was far from out of danger ... formerly there had been in her, at times, a rather wild and mad passion to give.

Herself . . . recklessly to give.

What difference did it make who it was?

The act of giving would itself be something. There is a fence over which you would like to get. What matter what is beyond? Getting over is something.

To live recklessly.

"Wait a minute," Ethel said to herself. She smiled saying it. It wasn't as though she hadn't tried that, that reckless giving. It hadn't worked.

Still she might try again. "If only he would be nice." She felt that, in the future, what she thought of as niceness would be very, very important to her.

It wouldn't, the next time, be giving at all. It would be surrender. That or nothing.

"To what? To a man?" Ethel asked herself. "I presume a woman has to cling to something, to a belief that there is something for her, to be got through a man," she thought. Ethel was twenty-nine. You get into the thirties and then the forties.

Women who do not give themselves utterly dry up. They get dry-lipped, dry inside.

If they give they get sufficiently punished.

"But perhaps we want punishment."

"Beat me. Beat me. Make me nice. Make me beautiful, for a moment, anyway.

"Make me blossom. Make me flower."

Ethel had got interested again that summer. It was rather nice. There were two men, one much younger than herself, one much older. What woman wouldn't be pleased having two men wanting her . . . or for that matter three, or a dozen? She was glad. Life in Langdon, but for the two men wanting her, would be, after all, pretty dull. It was rather too bad that the younger of the two men in whom she had suddenly got interested and who had got interested in her was such a young one, much younger than herself, really immature, but there was no doubt she was interested in him. He stirred her. She wanted him close. "I'd like to . . ."

Thoughts drift. Thoughts excite. Thoughts are dangerous and nice. Sometimes thoughts are like hands touching, where you want to be touched.

"Touch me, thoughts. Come close. Come close."

Thoughts drift. Thoughts excite. Thoughts of women in a man.

"Do we want actuality?"

"If we could decide that we could decide everything."

It may be an age gone blind and mad with actualities—machinery, science. Women like Ethel Long of Langdon, Georgia, who read books and think, or try to think, who dream sometimes of a new freedom, separate from man's freedom.

Man having failed in America, women now trying something. Were they really?

Ethel wasn't, after all, just a product of Langdon, Georgia. She had been to a Northern college, had associated with American intellectuals. She had Southern memories clinging to her.

Sense of brown women and girls about when she was a child and when she was growing up through young girlhood into womanhood.

Southern white women, growing up, always conscious, in some subtle way of brown women about . . . women big of hips, unmoral, broad-breasted women, peasants, brown bodies . . .

They having in them something for men, too, for both brown and white men . . .

Persistent denial of fact . . .

Brown women in fields, working in fields . . . brown women in towns, as servants . . . in houses . . . brown women walking in streets with heavy baskets balanced on their heads . . . hips swaying.

The hot South . . .

Denial. Denial.

"A white woman may be a fool, forever reading or thinking." She cân't help it.

"Why, I haven't done so much of either," Ethel said to herself.

The younger man, in whom she had suddenly got interested, was named Oliver and he had come back to Langdon from the North, where he also had been in college. He did not come at the beginning of the vacation time, but rather late, in late July. The local paper said he had been out West with a school friend and now he had come home. He had begun coming into the Langdon public library, where Ethel worked. She was the librarian of the new public library in Langdon. It had been opened during the past winter.

She thought about young Red Oliver. Without a doubt she was, from the moment she first saw him, when he returned to Langdon that summer, she was excited by him. The excitement took a new turn for her. She had never before felt like that toward a man. "I guess I'm beginning to grow motherly," she thought. It had become a habit with her to analyze her own thoughts and emotions. She liked it. It made her feel mature. "It is a hard time in life for such a young man as that," she thought. At least young Red Oliver did not seem like the other young men of Langdon. He seemed puzzled. And how physically strong he looked! He had been on a Western farm for some weeks. He was brown and healthy-looking. He had come home to Langdon to spend some time with his mother before going off again to school.

"It may be I am interested in him because I am myself a little stale," Ethel thought.

"I am a little greedy. He is like firm fresh fruit I want to bite into."

The young man's mother was, to Ethel's mind, a rather queer woman. She knew about Red's mother. All of the town knew about her. She knew that, when Red had been at home the year before, after his first year in the Northern school and after his father, Doctor Oliver, died, he had worked in the Langdon cotton mills. Ethel's father had known Red's father and had even known Red's grandfather. He spoke of Red's return to town at table at the Long house. "I see that young Oliver's home. I hope he's more like his grandfather than his father or his mother."

In the library, when Red came in there, sometimes in the evening, Ethel looked him over. He was already a strong man. How big his shoulders were! He had a rather large head covered with red hair.

He was obviously a young man who took life rather seriously. Ethel thought she liked that kind.

"Maybe I do, maybe I don't." She had got, that summer, very self-conscious. She didn't like the trait in herself, would have liked rather being more simple, even primitive ... or pagan.

"It may be because I am nearing thirty." She had got it into her head that, for a woman, thirty was the turning point.

That notion might also have come from her reading. George Moore ... or Balzac.

The notion ... "She is ripe now. She is splendid, gorgeous.

"Pluck her. Bite her. Eat her. Hurt her."

That wasn't exactly the way it was put. That notion was involved in it. It implied American men, able to do it, who dared to try doing it.

Unscrupulous men. Daring men. Masculine men.

"It is all this damn reading ... women trying to rise, to take hold of life. Culture, eh?"

The old South, of Ethel's grandfather and Red Oliver's grandfather, hadn't read. They talked about Greece and had Greek books in their houses, but they were safe books. No one read them. Why read when you can ride abroad over

fields and command slaves? You are a prince. Why should
a prince read?

The old South was dead, but it certainly hadn't died a
princely death. Once it had a profound, a princely contempt
for the Northern shop-keepers, money-changers, factory-
owners, but now it was itself all eager for factories, for
money, for shop-keeping.

Hating and imitating. Muddled for sure.

"Am I any better?" Ethel had to ask herself. Evidently,
she thought, thinking of the young man, he has a desire to get
hold of life. "God knows, so have I." After Red Oliver came
home and began coming often to the library and after she
had got acquainted with him—she herself managed that—
she got onto the fact that he sometimes wrote things on bits
of paper. He wrote verses he would have been too shy to
show her had she asked him. She didn't ask. The library was
open in the evening on three evenings of the week and on
such evenings he almost always came in.

He explained, a little awkwardly, that he wanted to
read, but Ethel thought she understood. It was because, like
herself, he didn't feel much a part of the town. In his case
it might be, partly at least, on account of his mother.

"He feels out of it here and so do I," Ethel thought.
She knew about his writing because at night, when he had
come to the library and had got a book from a shelf, he sat
down at a table and, not looking at the book, began to write.
He had brought a writing tablet with him.

Ethel walked about in the little reading-room of the
library. There was a place she could stand, among the shelves
of books, and look over his shoulder. He wrote to a friend
in the West, a man friend. He tried his hand at verses. They
didn't come off much, Ethel thought. She only saw one or
two feeble attempts.

When he had first come home that summer—after his
visit to the Western friend—a fellow who had been in college with him, Red told her—he occasionally talked to her,

shyly, eagerly, with the boyish eagerness of a young man
with a woman in whose presence he is moved but feels young
and inadequate—a fellow who had also played on the college
baseball team. Red had been at work during the early part
of the summer on a farm in Kansas, belonging to that one's
father. . . . He came home to Langdon with his neck and
arms burned by the sun of fields . . . that also pleasing Ethel
. . . when he had first come home he didn't get a job at once.
The weather was very hot but it was cooler in the library.
There was a little toilet in the building. He went in there.
He and Ethel had been alone in the building. She ran and
read what he had been writing.

It was Monday and he had been wandering about alone
on Sunday. He had written a letter. To whom? To no one.
"Dear unknown," he had written, and Ethel read the words
and smiled. There was a little tight feeling about her heart.
"He wants some one, a woman. I presume every man does."

Wh' ' queer ideas men had, that was to say, the nice
ones. There were other kinds a-plenty. Ethel knew about
them too. The young nice kind had yearnings. They were
trying to reach out toward something. Such a one was conscious always of some inner hunger. He hoped some woman
could satisfy it. If he didn't have a woman he tried to create
one, in his own fancy.

Red had tried to do that. "Dear Unknown." He had told
his unknown about his lonely Sunday. Ethel had read
rapidly. To get back from the toilet to which he had gone he
would have to pass along a short hallway. She would hear his
footsteps. She could make her getaway. It was fun thus to
peep into the boy's life. After all he was only a boy.

He had written to his unknown about his day, a lonely
day. Ethel herself hated the Sundays in the Georgia town.
She went to church but hated going. The preacher was stupid,
she thought.

She had thought that all out. "If the people, going to
church on Sundays here were really religious," she had

thought. They weren't. Perhaps her father was. Her father was a Georgia County Judge, and on Sundays he taught a Sunday-school class. On Saturday evenings he was always busy getting his Sunday-school lesson. He went at it like a boy, preparing for an examination in school. Ethel had thought, a hundred times, she had thought, "It gets into the air of the town on Sundays, the fakiness about religion." There was something heavy and frigid in the air of the Georgia town on Sundays, particularly among the whites. She thought maybe the Negroes were all right. Their religion, the American kind of Protestant religion they had taken over from the whites... perhaps they had made something of it.

Not the whites. Whatever the South had once been, it had become—such towns as Langdon, Georgia, had become —with the coming of the cotton mills, Yankee towns. There had been a kind of deal made with God. "All right, we'll give you this one day of the week. We'll go to church. We'll put up enough money to keep the churches going.

"In return for that you give us Heaven when we get through with this life here, this life of running this cotton mill, or this store, or this law office. . . .

"Or being sheriff or deputy sheriff or being in the real-estate business.

"You give us Heaven when we get through with all this and we'll hold up our end."

To Ethel Long something seemed to get into the air of the town on Sundays. It hurt a sensitive person. Ethel thought she was sensitive. "I don't see how it turns out that I still am sensitive, but I believe I am," she thought. A kind of staleness seemed to her to run through the town on Sunday. It got into the walls of buildings. It invaded houses. It hurt Ethel, made her ache.

She had had an experience with her father. Once, when he was a young man, he had been quite eager-minded. He read books and wanted others to read books. Suddenly he had stopped reading. He seemed to have stopped thinking, didn't want to think. It was one of the ways in which the South, although the Southerner would never admit it, had fallen in with the North. Not to think, to read newspapers instead, go to church regularly . . . not being any more truly religious . . . listen to the radio . . . join a civic club . . . boost for growth.

"Don't think. . . . You may begin to think what it really means."

In the meantime letting the Southern land go to pot.

"You Southerners betraying your own Southern fields . . . the old half-savage strange beauty of the land and the towns going.

"Don't think. Don't you dare think.

"Be like the Yanks, newspaper readers, radio listeners.

"Advertise. Don't think."

Ethel's father insisted on Ethel's going to church on Sundays. Why, it wasn't exactly insistence. It was a half pathetic imitation of insistence. "You'd better," he said, with an air of finality. He was always trying to be final. It was because her position as town librarian was a semi-public position. "What will people say if you don't?" That was what her father meant.

"Jesus," she thought. Nevertheless she went.

She had brought home a lot of her own books.

As a younger man, her father might have found an intellectual bond with her. He couldn't now. A thing had happened to him that, she knew, had happened to many American men, perhaps to most American men. There came a certain time, in the life of the American man, when he stopped dead. For some queer reason all intellectuality died in him.

After that he thought only of making money, or of being respectable or, if he happened to be the lustful sort, of getting women or living luxuriously.

Innumerable books written in America were of that

sort, as were most of the plays and the movies. Nearly all of them stated some problem of life, often an interesting problem. They went about so far with it and then stopped dead. They stated a problem they themselves wouldn't face, then suddenly they began crawfishing. They got out of it by suddenly becoming cheerful or optimistic about life, something of that sort.

Ethel's father was pretty sure about Heaven. At least he wanted to be. He was determined to be. Ethel had brought home with her, among her other books, a book by George Moore, called *The Brook Kerith*.

It was a story about the Christ, a moving tender story, she thought. It had touched her.

The Christ ashamed of what he had done. The Christ gone up in the world and then come down. He began life as a poor shepherd boy and after the terrible time when he proclaimed himself God, when he went about leading men astray, when he cried out, "Follow me. Follow in my footsteps," after men had put him up on the cross to die. . . .

In George Moore's beautiful book he did not die. A rich young man loved him and took him down from the cross, still alive but terribly maimed. The man nursed him, brought him back to life. He crept off, away from people and became a shepherd again.

He was ashamed of what he had done. He saw dimly, far into the future. Shame shook him. He saw, looking far into the future, what he had started. He saw Langdon, Georgia, Tom Shaw, the mill owner of Langdon, Georgia . . . he saw wars being fought in His name, commercialized churches, churches, like industry, controlled by money, churches turning away from the lowly, turning their backs on labor. He saw hatred and dullness spring up over the world.

"Because of me. I have given mankind this absurd dream of Heaven, turning their eyes away from earth."

The Christ had gone back to be again a simple unknown

shepherd in the barren hills. He had been a good shepherd. The flocks were run down because there was no good ram and he went to find a ram. To shoot, to flood new life into the old sheep mothers. What an amazingly strong sweet human story it had been. "If my own fancy could but go wide and free like that," Ethel thought. Once, when she had newly come home to her father's house, after two or three years away, and had been rereading the book, Ethel had begun suddenly to speak of it to her father. She had some notion of getting close to him. She had wanted to tell him the story. She tried.

She wouldn't soon forget the experience. Of a sudden he had got the idea. "And the writer says He didn't die on the cross."

"Yes. It seems there is an old story of that sort in the East, told in the East. The writer, George Moore, an Irishman, took it and built upon it."

"He didn't die and was not born again?"

"No, not in the flesh. He was not born again."

Ethel's father had got up from his chair. It was evening and the father and daughter were sitting together on the porch of the house. He had gone white. "Ethel." His voice was sharp.

"Do not ever speak of it again," he said.

"Why?"

"Why? My God," he said. "There is no hope. If the Christ did not rise again in the flesh there is no hope."

He meant . . . of course he had not thought out what he meant . . . this life of mine, I have lived here on this earth, here in this town, is such a strange, sweet healing thing that I cannot bear the thought of its going out, completely and finally, as a candle is blown out.

What staggering egotism and all the more amazing because Ethel's father was not really an egotistical man at all. He was really a humble man, too humble.

And so Red Oliver had had a Sunday. Ethel read what he had written, while he stayed in the toilet in the library. She read it hurriedly. He had merely walked out of town some miles, going out along the railroad that followed the river. Afterwards he had written about it, addressing some purely fanciful woman because he had no woman. He had wanted to tell some woman.

He had felt what she felt on Sunday in Langdon. "I couldn't stand the town," he wrote. "It is better on week days when the people are sincere."

So he was also a rebel.

"When they lie to each other and cheat each other it is better."

He had spoken of the big man of the town, of Tom Shaw, the mill owner. "Mother went to her church and I felt I ought to offer to go with her but I couldn't," he wrote. He had waited in bed until she had left the house and then had cut out alone. He had seen Tom Shaw and his wife going to the Presbyterian church in their big car. It was the church to which Ethel's father belonged, in which he taught the Sunday-school class. "They say Tom Shaw has got rich on the labor of the poor here. It is better to see him scheming to get richer. It is better to see him telling himself lies as to what he does for people than to see him thus, going to church."

At least Ethel's father would never have questioned the new gods of the American scene, of the new industrialized Southern American scene, like that. He wouldn't have dared it, even to himself.

The young man had gone out of town along the railroad track and had turned from the track, some miles out of town and had got into a pine forest. He wrote words about the forest and about the red Georgia land seen beyond the pine forest through trees. It was a simple little chapter of a man, a young man alone with nature on Sunday when all the rest of his town was in church. Ethel had been to church. She wished she had been with Red.

However, if she had been with him . . . Something stirred within her thinking of it. She put down the leaves out of the cheap pencil tablet on which he had written and returned to her desk. Red came out of the toilet. He had been in there for five minutes. If she had been with him in the pine forest, if the unknown woman to whom he had written, the woman who didn't evidently exist in reality, if it had been she herself. She might make it herself. "I might be very, very nice."

Then there might not have been any writing about it. There wasn't any doubt but that he had given, in the scrawled words on the tablet, a kind of real feeling of the place he had been in.

If she had been there with him, lying beside him on the pine needles in the pine forest he might have been touching her with his hands. A little quiver ran through her body thinking of it. "I wonder if I want him?" she asked herself that day. "It seems a little absurd," she told herself. He was back at the table in the writing-room, writing again. He occasionally looked up, in her direction, but her eyes avoided looking at him while he looked. She had her woman's way of managing that. "I am not ready to say anything to you yet. Why, you have been coming in here less than a week."

If she had been with him and had got him, as she already felt she could get him if she decided to try, he wouldn't have been thinking of the trees and the sky and the red fields beyond the trees nor yet of Tom Shaw, the cotton-mill millionaire going to church in his big car, telling himself that he was going there to worship the poor and lowly Christ.

"He would have been thinking of me," Ethel thought. The thought pleased and at the same time, perhaps because he was so much younger than she was, amused her too.

After he had come home that summer Red got a temporary job in a local store. He didn't stay at that long. "I don't want to be a clerk," he told himself. He went back to the mill and, although they did not need men, they took him on again.

It was better there. Perhaps, at the mill, they thought, "In case of trouble he will be on the right side." From the window of the library, housed as it was in an old brick building, just where the region of stores ended, Ethel sometimes saw Red at evening going through Main Street. It was a long walk from the mill to the Oliver house. Ethel had already dined. Red wore overalls. He wore heavy workingmen's shoes. When the mill team was having a ball game she wanted to go. He was, she thought, a queer isolated figure in the town. "Like myself," she thought. He was a part of the town and yet not a part of it.

There was something nice about Red's body. Ethel liked a certain free swing to his body. It remained, even when he was tired, after the day's work. She liked his eyes. She had got into the habit of standing near the library window when, in the evening, he went home from his day's work. Her eyes appraised the young man walking thus along the hot street of the Southern town. Quite frankly she thought of his body in connection with her own woman's body. "It might be the thing I want. If he were only a bit older." There was desire in her. Desire invaded her body. She knew that feeling. "I haven't handled that sort of thing very well in the past," she thought. "Shall I take a chance with him? I can get him if I go after him." She was a bit ashamed of her own rather calculating mind. "If it came to marriage. That sort of thing. He is so much younger than I am. It doesn't work out." It was absurd. He was not more than twenty, a boy, she thought.

He was pretty sure, in the end, to find out what she had done to him. "Just the same I could if I tried." Almost every evening, after his day's work and when the library was open he came there. When he had begun thinking of her, it was when he had been working again in the factory for a week ... he was only to stay in town some six or eight weeks more before he returned to school ... already, although perhaps he was not quite conscious of what had been done to him, he was all afire with thoughts of her.... "If I tried?" It was evident no woman had got him. Such a young lonely man, Ethel knew, is always to be got by a clever woman. She thought herself fairly clever. "I don't know what there is in my past record to make me think I'm clever but I do think so, evidently," she thought, standing thus near the library window as Red Oliver passed, seeing but not seen. "A woman, if she is any good can get any man some other woman has not already marked down." She was half ashamed of her own thoughts concerning a young boy. She was amused by her own thoughts.

2

ETHEL LONG'S eyes were puzzling. They were greenish-blue and hard. Then they were softly blue. She wasn't particularly sensual. She could be brutally cold. She wanted sometimes to be soft and yielding. When you saw her in a room, tall and slender, well formed, her hair seemed brown. When light shone through, it became red. As a young girl she had been of the awkward tom-boy type, a rather excitable, fiery child. As she grew older she developed a passion for clothes. She would have liked always to wear better clothes than she could afford. Sometimes she wished she had gone in for being a designer of clothes. "I could have made a success of that," she thought. Most people were a little afraid of her. If she did not want them to come near, she had her own way of holding them off. Some of the men who had been attracted to her, and who had made no progress, thought of her as something of a serpent. "She has serpent's eyes," they thought. If the man, attracted to her, was at all sensitive, it was easy for her to upset him. That rather annoyed her, too. "I guess I want a brute of a man, one who will pay no attention to my whims," she told herself. Often, that summer, after Red Oliver had got into the habit of going, at every opportunity, to the library and had begun thinking of her in relation to himself, he thought, catching her eyes looking at him, that they invited everything.

He had been in the West, with a young man, a friend, working during the early part of the summer on the farm of the friend's father in Kansas and, as is usual with young men, there had been a good deal of talk of women. Talk of women had been mixed with talk of what the young men were to do with their lives. Both young men had been touched by modern radicalism. They had got that in college.

They had been stirred. There was one young professor—he had taken a special fancy to Red—who had talked a good deal. He had lent him books—Marxian books, anarchist books. He was an admirer of the American anarchist, Emma Goldman. "I saw her once," he said.

He described a meeting in a small Middle-Western industrial town, the local intelligentsia gathered in a little dark hall.

Emma Goldman making a speech. Afterwards Ben Reitman, a large loose-looking noisy man, went through the audience selling books. The audience was a little excited, a little frightened by the woman's bold talk, her bold ideas. There was a dark wooden stairway leading up to the hall and some one carried a brick up there and threw it down.

It went bumping down the stairs—boom, boom, and the audience in the little hall . . .

Men and women in the audience jumping to their feet. There were pale faces, trembling lips. They thought the hall was being blown up. The professor, then a student, had bought one of Emma Goldman's books which he gave to Red.

"They call you 'Red,' eh? It's a significant name. Why don't you be a revolutionist?" he asked. He asked such questions and then laughed.

"Our colleges have already turned out too many young bond-sellers, too many lawyers and doctors." When he was told that Red, during the previous summer, had worked as a common laborer in a Southern cotton mill, he was excited. He thought both young men—Red and his friend, Neil Bradley, the young Western farmer—ought to devote themselves to some kind of effort to remake society, be frankly socialists or even communists, and he wanted Red, when he had finished school, to remain a laborer.

"Don't do it because of any good you think you can do humanity," he said. "There isn't any such thing as humanity. There are only all these millions of individuals in a strange unaccountable situation.

"I tell you to be a radical because being a radical is a little dangerous in America and will grow more dangerous. It is an adventure. Life is too safe here. It is too dull."

He found out that Red had a secret yearning to write. "All right," he said cheerfully, "remain a laborer. That might be the supreme adventure in a great middle-class country, to remain poor, to consciously choose to be a common man, a worker, rather than any kind of a big bug ... a buyer or seller." The young professor, who had made rather a deep impression on the minds of the two young men, was himself almost girlish in appearance. There might have been something girlish in him, but if that was true he concealed it well. He had himself been a poor young man but said he had never been strong enough to be a workman. "I had to be a clerk," he said, "I tried being a worker. One year I got a job digging in a sewer in a Middle-Western city but I couldn't stand it." He had admired Red's body and sometimes, in expressing his admiration, had embarrassed Red. "It's a beauty," he said, touching Red's back. He meant Red's body, the unusual depth and breadth of the chest. He himself was small and slender and had sharp bird-like eyes.

When Red had been on the Western farm, earlier that summer, he and his friend Neil Bradley, also a ball player, sometimes, in the evening, drove into Kansas City. Neil hadn't got his school teacher yet.

Then he got one, the school teacher. He wrote Red letters describing his intimacies with her. He had got Red started thinking about women, wanting a woman as he never had before. He looked at Ethel Long. How nicely her head sat on her shoulders! The shoulders were small but they were well formed. Her neck was long and slender and there was a line, flowing down from her small head along her neck and losing itself under her dress, his hand wanted to follow. She was a trifle taller than he was, as he was inclined to stockiness. Red had broad shoulders. They were, from the point of view of manly beauty, too broad. He did not think of himself in connection with the notion of manly beauty although that college professor, the one who had spoken of the beauty of his body, the one who had made a special point of cultivating him and his friend, Neil Bradley.... He might have been a trifle on the queer side. Neither Red nor Neil ever spoke of that. He always seemed about to caress Red with his hands. When they were alone together he was always asking Red to come to his office in the college building. He drew near. He had been sitting at his desk in a chair, but got up. His eyes that had been so bird-like, sharp and impersonal, became suddenly, strangely, like women's eyes, the eyes of a woman in love. It had given Red a queer uncertain feeling sometimes in the man's presence. Nothing had ever happened. Nothing had ever been said.

Red had begun haunting the library in Langdon. There were many hot still evenings that summer. Sometimes, after he had come from his job in the mill and had bolted his dinner he hurried away to practice on the ball field with the mill team, but the mill boys, after the day's work, were tired and could not keep it up long, and so Red, wearing his baseball uniform, came back into town and went to the library. On three evenings a week the library was open until ten, although there were few enough people coming in. Often the librarian sat alone.

He knew that another man in town, an older man, a lawyer, was after Ethel Long. It worried him, frightened him a little. He thought of the letters Neil Bradley was writing him now. Neil had got in with a woman older than himself, and almost at once an intimacy had begun. "It was something glorious, something to live for," Neil said. Was there a possibility of another such intimacy for himself with this woman?

The thought made Red a little frantic. It also frightened him. Although he did not know it then, Ethel's mother having died and her one sister, older than herself, having married and moved to another Southern town and her father having married a second wife, she, like Red, was not too comfortable at home.

She wished she did not have to live in Langdon, that she had not come back there. She and her father's second wife were almost of the same age.

The step-mother in the Long household was pale, a pale blonde. Although Red Oliver did not know it, Ethel Long was also ready for adventure. As the boy sat sometimes in the evening, in the library, a little tired, pretending to read or write, furtively looking at her, furtively dreaming of possessing her, she was looking at him.

She was weighing the possibilities of an adventure with the young man, little more than a boy to her, against another sort of adventure with a much older and quite different sort of man.

The step-mother, after her marriage, had wanted to have a child of her own and none had come. She blamed her husband, Ethel's father.

She fussed at her husband. Ethel, sometimes at night, lying in her bed, heard her new mother—the thought of her as a mother was absurd—fussing at her father. On some evenings Ethel went into her own room early. There was the man and wife, the woman scolding. She issued orders sharply—"do this . . . do that."

The father was a tall man with black hair, growing gray now. By his first marriage there had been two sons and two daughters, but both of the sons had died, one at home, as a grown man, older than Ethel, and the other, the youngest of his children, as a soldier, an officer in the World War.

The older of the two sons had been sickly. He was a pale sensitive man who wanted to be a scholar, but who, because of illness, never finished college. He died suddenly of heart failure. The younger son was like Ethel, tall and slender. He had been his father's pride. The father had a mustache and a little pointed beard that, like his hair, had begun to get gray, but he kept it colored, usually doing the job of coloring it very well. Sometimes he failed or was careless. People met him on the street one day and the mustache was streaked with gray and the next day, when they met him, it had become black and shiny again.

His wife took it out on him about his age. That was her way. "You have to remember you are getting old," she said sharply. She said it sometimes with an air of kindliness but he knew and she knew that she was not being kindly. "I am wanting something I guess you are too old to give me," she was thinking.

"I want to bloom. Here I am a pale woman, not very well. I want to be spread out, thickened and broadened, if you please, made into a real woman. I guess you can't do it to me, damn you. You aren't man enough."

She didn't say that. The man also wanted something. By his first wife, dead now, he had been made the father of four children, two of whom were sons but both of the sons were now dead. He wanted another son.

He had felt a little frightened when he had brought his new wife home to his house and to his daughter, Ethel's sister, who was not married then. He had told the daughter at home nothing of his plans and she herself was married during the same year. He and the new woman had driven off together one evening, going to another Georgia town, saying nothing to any one of their plans, and, when they were married, he had brought her home. His house, like the Oliver house, was out at the edge of town at the end of a street. There was a large old Southern frame house and there was a sloping meadow beyond the house that belonged to him. He kept a cow in the meadow.

Ethel had been away from home at school when all of this had happened. Then she came home for the summer vacation. A queer drama had begun to play itself out in the house.

Ethel and her father's new wife, the blonde young woman with a sharp voice, so few years older than herself, seemed to have become friends.

The friendship was a sham. It was a game they played. Ethel knew and the new wife knew. The four people went about together. The younger sister, the one who was married soon after it began—thus, Ethel thought, getting out of it— didn't understand. It was as though two factions had been formed in the house: Ethel, the tall sleek-looking, somewhat sophisticated one, and the new pale blonde wife of her father in the one faction and the father and husband, with the younger daughter, in the other.

O love,
Little naked child with the bow and the quiver of
rrows.

More than one wise man had laughed at love. "There isn't any such thing. That is all nonsense." Wise men had said it, conquerors, emperors, kings, artists.

Sometimes the four walked out together. On Sundays sometimes they all went together to the Presbyterian church, walking there together through the hot Sunday morning streets. The Presbyterian preacher at Langdon was a man with stooped shoulders and big hands. His mind was infinitely dull. When, on week days, he walked through the town streets he thrust his head forward and held his hands clasped behind his back. He seemed like a man pushing forward against a heavy wind. There was no wind. He seemed about to fall forward, to be lost in deep thought. His sermons were long and very dull. Later, when there was labor

trouble in Langdon and two of the workers in the mill village at the edge of town were killed by deputy sheriffs, he
said, "No Christian minister should perform the burial ceremony for them. They should be buried like dead mules."
When the Long family went to church, Ethel walked with
the new step-mother and the younger sister walked with
the father. The two women went ahead of the others, talking
busily. "You do so love to go. It pleases your father to have
you go," the blonde woman said.

"After your life in school, in the city, in Chicago . . . to
come home here . . . to be so sweet to all of us."

Ethel smiled. She half liked the pale thin woman, her
father's new wife. "I wonder why father wanted her?" Her
father was still a strong man. He was a big, a tall man.

The new wife was malicious. "What a good little hater
she is," Ethel thought. At any rate, it wasn't dull for Ethel,
being with her. She liked it.

All of this had happened before Red Oliver went off to
school, when he was still a high school boy.

There had been three summers after that, after her
father's marriage, followed by the marriage of her younger
sister, when Ethel did not come home. During two of the
summers she worked, and during the third summer she attended summer school. She had been educated at the University of Chicago.

She had got her A.B. from the university and had then
taken a course in library work. A new Carnegie library had
been secured for the town of Langdon. There had been an
old one but every one said it was too small and unworthy
the town.

The blonde wife, named Blanche, had egged her husband
on about the library.

She kept at her husband, making him go to speak before meetings of the town's civic clubs. Although he no
longer read books he had still the reputation of being an in-

tellectual. There was a Kiwanis Club and a Rotary Club. She herself went to see the editor of the town's weekly newspaper and wrote articles for the paper. Her husband was puzzled. "Why is she so set on it?" he asked himself. He didn't understand and was even ashamed. He knew what she was up to, getting the job as librarian of the new library for his daughter Ethel and her interest in his daughter, almost of her own age, puzzled him. It seemed to him a little strange, even unnatural. Had he dreamed of some sort of quiet home life with his new woman, his old age comforted by her? He had been under the illusion that they would be intellectual companions, that she would understand all of his thoughts, all of his impulses. "We can't do it," he said to her, with a note almost of desperation in his voice.

"We can't do what?" The pale eyes of Blanche could be absolutely impersonal. She spoke to him as to a stranger, or as to a servant.

He had always a way of saying things with an air of finality that wasn't final. It was a bluff at finality, a hope for finality, never achieved with her. "We can't work like this, so openly, so obviously, to get this library put in, asking the town to do its share, asking the tax-payers to pay money to have this larger library and all the time—you understand... you yourself have suggested the idea of turning the job of running it over to Ethel.

"It will look too much like a fixed-up thing."

He wished he had never got into the fight for the new library. "What does it matter to me?" he asked himself. He had been led, pushed into it, by his new wife. It was the first time, since he had married her, that she had shown any interest in the cultural life of the town.

"We can't do it. It will look like a fixed-up thing."

"Why, my dear, it is fixed up." Blanche was laughing at her husband. Her voice had grown sharper after her marriage. She had always been a woman without much color in her face, but before her marriage she used rouge.

After marriage she didn't bother. "What's the use?" she seemed to be saying. She had had a rather sweet mouth, like the mouth of a child, but, after marriage, her lips seemed to go dry. There was something, after her marriage, about her whole being that suggested... it was as though she belonged not to the animal but to the vegetable kingdom. She had been plucked. She had been laid carelessly aside, in the sun and wind. She was drying up. You felt it.

She also felt it. She did not want to be what she was, what she was becoming. She did not want to be disagreeable to her husband. "Do I hate him?" she asked herself. Her husband was a good man with an honorable position in the town and county. He was scrupulously honest, went regularly to church, was a devout believer in God. She had watched other women who had married. She had been a school teacher in Langdon, had come there from another Georgia town to be a teacher. Some of the other school teachers had got husbands. She had gone to visit some of them in their houses after marriage, and had kept in touch with them. They had children and then, after that, their husbands called them "mother." It was a kind of relationship, mother and child, a grown child who slept with you. The man went out and hustled. He made money.

She couldn't do it, couldn't take that attitude toward her husband. He was so much older than herself. She kept declaring her devotion to her husband's daughter, Ethel. She was becoming all the time more and more determined, cold and determined. "What do you think I have been up to about this library, getting this library?" she asked her husband. Her tone frightened and disconcerted him. When she took on that tone, his world always seemed tumbling about his ears. "Oh, I know of what you are thinking," she said. "You are thinking of your honor, of your standing in the eyes of the respectable people of this town. It is because you are Judge Long." He had been thinking of just that.

She grew bitter. "To hell with the town." Before he mar-

ried her, she would never have used such a word in his
presence. Before marriage she had always been very respectful toward him. He had thought her demure, a quiet gentle
little thing. Before marriage he had worried a good deal although he had said nothing to her of what was in his mind.
He had been anxious about his own dignity. He had felt that
his marriage to a woman so much younger than himself
would cause talk. Often he had shivered thinking of it. Men
standing before the drug store in Langdon and talking. He
thought of men of the town, of Ed Graves, Tom McKnight,
Will Fellowcraft. Some one of them might break loose at a
meeting of the Rotary Club, say something publicly. They
were always trying to be jolly, hail-fellows at the club. For
weeks before his marriage he had not dared to go to a meeting of the club.

He wanted a son. There had been two sons and they were
both dead. It might have been the death of his younger son
and the long illness of the older one, an illness that had
begun in childhood that had led to his own deep interest in
children. He had developed a passion for children, particularly for young boys. That had led to his accepting a place
on the county school board. The children of the town, that is
to say, the children of the more respectable whites, and in
particular the sons of such families, all knew and admired
him. He knew dozens of young boys by their first names.
More than one older man, who had been a schoolboy in Langdon, who had grown up and had gone somewhere else to
live, came back to Langdon. Such a man almost always
came to see the judge. They called him "Judge." "Why, hello,
Judge." There was such heartiness, such good will in the
voices. Such a one said to him, "Look here," he said, "I want
to tell you something."

He spoke perhaps of what the judge had done for him.
"After all, a man wants to be an honorable man."

The man spoke of something that had happened, when he

was a schoolboy. "You said so and so to me. I tell you it stuck in my mind."

The judge had perhaps taken an interest in the boy, had, in a time of boyish trouble, sought him out, trying to help. It had been the judge's best side.

"You wouldn't let me be a fool. Do you remember? I was angry with my father and had decided to run away from home. You got it out of me. Do you remember how you talked?"

The judge didn't remember. He had always been interested in boys, had made boys his hobby. The fathers of the town knew it. He had that reputation. When he was a young lawyer, before he became a judge, he had organized a troop of boy scouts. He had been the scout master. He had always been more patient and kind with other men's sons than with his own, had been rather severe with his own sons. He had thought it best.

"Do you remember when George Grey, Tom Eckles and I got drunk? It was night and I stole my father's horse and buggy and we went to Taylorville.

"We had got into a mess. It makes me ashamed yet, thinking of it. We came near getting arrested. We were going to get us some nigger girls. We had got arrested, being drunk and noisy. What young beasts we were!

"Knowing about it all, you didn't go talk to our fathers, as most men would have done. You talked to us. You had us into your office, one by one, and talked to us. For one, I will never forget what you said."

So, he had got them out of it, had hushed it up.

"You made me feel the seriousness of life. I can almost say you were more to me than my father."

*

THE judge had been profoundly bothered and annoyed about the matter of the new library. "What will the town think?"

The question was never off his mind. It had been a point of
honor with him never to push himself or his own family.
"After all," he had thought, "I'm a Southern gentleman
and a Southern gentleman doesn't do such things. These
women!" He thought of his younger daughter, married now,
and of his dead wife. The younger daughter had been a
quiet serious-seeming woman, like his first wife. She was
pretty. After the first wife's death and until he re-married
she had been her father's housekeeper. She had married a
man of the town who had known her in high school and who
had now gone to Atlanta where he had a job in a mercantile
house.

For some reason and although he often looked regret-
fully back to the days with her in his house, the second
daughter had never made much impression on her father.
She was pretty. She was nice. She never got into trouble.
When the judge thought of women he thought of his older
daughter Ethel and of his wife Blanche. Were most women
like that? Were all women at bottom alike? "Here I have
worked and worked, trying to get a library for this town and
now the whole thing has taken this turn." He hadn't thought
of Ethel in connection with the library. That had been his
wife's notion. The whole impulse in himself ... he had been
thinking about it for years. ...

There wasn't enough reading done in the South. He had
known that since he was a young man. He had said so.
There was little intellectual curiosity among most of the
young men and women. In intellectual development the North
seemed far ahead of the South. The judge, although he no
longer read, had faith in books and in reading. "Reading
broadens a man's culture," he kept saying. When the drive
for the new library became more definite he went about talking to merchants and to the professional men of the town. He
spoke at the Rotary Club and got an invitation to speak also
at the Kiwanis Club. The president of the Langdon Mills,

Tom Shaw, helped a lot. There was to be a branch at the mill village.

The whole matter was arranged and the building, a fine old Southern residence, was bought and remodeled. There was Mr. Andrew Carnegie's name over the door.

And there was his own daughter Ethel appointed to be the town librarian. The committee had voted for her. It had been Blanche's idea. Blanche had been the one who had kept at Ethel to prepare herself.

There had, to be sure, been certain whispers about town. "No wonder he was so hot on having a library. It broadens a man's culture, eh? It broadens his pocketbook. Pretty soft, eh? A foxy scheme."

But Judge Willard Long was not foxy. He hated it all and had even begun to hate the library. "I wish I had let the whole matter alone." When his daughter was appointed he wanted to protest. He spoke to Blanche. "I think she had better withdraw her name." Blanche laughed. "You can't be such a fool."

"I won't let her name be put up."

"Yes, you will. If necessary I will go down there and put it up myself."

The queer thing about the whole affair was that he could not think that his daughter Ethel and his new wife Blanche were really fond of each other. Had they simply entered into a conspiracy against himself, to hurt his standing in the town, make him seem to the town something he wasn't, did not want to be?

He grew petulant.

You bring what you hope and think is going to be love into your house and it turns out to be some new queer kind of hate you can't understand. There is something brought into the house that poisons the air. He wanted to speak of the whole matter to his daughter Ethel when she came home to take the new position but she also seemed to have drawn herself away. He wanted to take her aside and plead with her. He couldn't. Nothing was very clear in his head. He could not say to her, "Look here, Ethel, I don't want you here." There was a queer notion in his head. It frightened and alarmed him. While in one moment it seemed the two had conspired against himself, in the next moment they seemed preparing for a kind of battle with each other. Perhaps they sought it. Ethel, although she had never had much money to go on, was a dresser. In spite of Mrs. Tom Shaw, wife of the town's rich mill owner, with all her money... she had grown fat... Ethel was obviously the best-dressed, the most up-to-date and stylish-looking woman in town.

She was twenty-nine, and her father's new wife, Blanche, was thirty-two. Blanche had let herself become a good deal of a frump. She didn't seem to care, wanted perhaps to be a frump. She wasn't even very particular about bathing and when she came to table, sometimes, even her nails were not clean. There were little black streaks under her untrimmed nails.

*

THE father asked the daughter to go with him on a trip into the country. He had long been on the county school board and had to go visit a Negro school, had said he would go.

There was trouble about a Negro woman school teacher. Some one had reported that the woman, who was unmarried, was pregnant. He had to go and find out. It was a good chance for a real talk with his daughter. He might find out something about her and about his wife.

"What has gone wrong? You weren't, formerly, as you are now... so tight... so strange." Perhaps she hadn't changed. He hadn't thought much about Ethel when his first wife and his sons were alive.

Ethel sat beside her father in his car, a cheap roadster. He kept it clean and neat-looking. The daughter was slender and rather finely drawn and she was well groomed. Her eyes told him nothing. Where had she got the money to buy such clothes as she wore? He had sent her off to the city, to the North, to be educated. She must have changed. There she sat beside him now, looking cool and impersonal. "These women," he kept thinking, as they drove along. It was just after the completion of the new library. She had come home to help select the books and to take charge. At once he had felt something wrong in his house. "I am shut out," he thought. "Out of what?" Even if there was a war in his house, it would be better if he knew what it was all about. A man wanted to keep his own dignity. Did a man do wrong, trying to have, living in one house, a daughter and a wife, both so nearly of the same age? If it was wrong why had Blanche been so anxious to have Ethel at home? Although he was almost an old man there was in his eyes the troubled look of a troubled boy, and his daughter was ashamed. "We ought to chuck it," she thought. Something had to be settled between Blanche and herself. "What has he, poor man, to do with it?" Most men were very tiresome. They understood so little. The man sitting beside her in the car that day, driving the car as they rode along red Georgia roads, through clumps of pine trees, over low hills... it was spring and men were in the fields plowing for the next year's cotton crop, white men and brown men driving mules... there was a smell of new-plowed ground and of pine trees... the man sitting beside her, her father, was obviously the one who had done it to the other woman... that woman her mother now... how absurd... that woman taking Ethel's mother's place.

Did her father want her to think of that woman as her mother? "I dare say he doesn't quite know what he wants.

"Men won't face things. How they hate to face things.

"It is impossible to talk to a man, in such a situation, when he is your father."

Her own mother, when she was still alive, had been to Ethel... exactly what had she been? The mother had been rather like Ethel's sister. She had got married when she was a young girl to this man, Ethel's father. She had the four children.

"That fact must be an intense satisfaction to a woman," Ethel thought that day. A queer little tremor ran through her body, thinking of her mother, as a young wife, first feeling in her body the movements of a child. In the mood she was in that day she could think of her mother, now dead, as just another woman. There was something between all women few enough men ever understood. How could a man understand?

"There might be a man. He would need to be a poet."

Her mother must have known, after she had been married to her father for a time, that the man she had married, although he had an honorable position in the life of the town and the county, although he became a judge, he wasn't terribly mature, never would be mature.

He couldn't be mature in a real sense. Ethel did not know exactly what she meant by that. "If I could find a man to whom I could look up, a free-walking man, not afraid of his own thoughts. He might bring me something I need.

"He might penetrate me, color all my thinking, all my feeling. I am this half thing. I want to be made into a real woman." There was the thing in Ethel that was also in the woman Blanche.

But Blanche was married—to Ethel's father.

And she hadn't got it.

What?

There was something to be achieved. Vaguely Ethel had begun to understand what it was. Being at home, in the house with Blanche, had helped.

The two women did not like each other.

They did.

They didn't.

There was a kind of understanding. There will always be something, as between women, no man will ever perhaps quite understand.

And yet, every woman, who is really a woman will, all her life, want that more than anything else in life—real understanding with a man. Had her mother achieved it? Ethel looked sharply at her father that day. He wanted to talk about something and didn't know how to begin. She did nothing to help. Had the conversation he had in mind got started, it would have got nowhere. He would have begun, "You are at home here now, Ethel ... I hope you and Blanche will get along all right. I hope you will like each other."

"Oh, shut up." You can't say that to your father.

As to herself and the woman Blanche ... None of the things Ethel thought that day were said. "As to me and your Blanche ... it is nothing to me that you have married her. That is a thing outside me. You have undertaken to do something to her...."

"Do you know that?"

"You do not know what you have undertaken. Already you have failed."

American men were such fools. There was her father. He was a good, an honorable man. All of his life he had worked hard. A good many Southern men ... Ethel had been born and had grown up in the South ... she knew things ... a good many Southern men, when they were young ... there were brown girls everywhere in the South. It was easy for the Southern boy to find out certain physical things about life.

The mystery penetrated. An open door. "It can't be so easy as all that."

If a woman could find a man, even a brute man, who would stand up. Her father had made a bad guess in the woman he had picked as a second wife. That was obvious. If he hadn't been so unsophisticated it should all have been plain to him before he married. The woman had worked him outrageously. She had decided to get him and so she had begun working along certain lines.

She was getting a little faded and worn-out and so she

perked up. She tried to appear unsophisticated, a soft-speaking, child-like woman.

She wasn't of course anything of the sort. She was a disappointed woman. The chances were that, somewhere, there was some man she had really wanted. She had made a mess of that.

Her father, if he hadn't been such an honorable man. She was quite sure that her father, although he was Southern ... he hadn't fooled about, when he was young, with the brown girls. "It might have been better for him now if he had done that, if he hadn't been such an honorable man."

What his new woman needed was a good beating. "I'd give her one if she were mine," Ethel thought.

There might be a chance, even with her. There was a kind of vitality to Blanche, something hidden away in her, down there under the paleness, under the dirt of her. Ethel's thoughts returned, that day she rode with her father, to her own mother. The ride turned out to be a rather silent one. She managed to get her father to talking of his boyhood. He had been the son of a Southern planter who owned slaves. Some of his father's acres still stood in his name. She managed to make him talk of the days when he was a young country boy, just after the Civil War, of the struggle of whites and blacks to adjust themselves to a new life. He wanted to talk of something else but she wouldn't let him. It was so easy to manage. As he talked she thought of her own mother as a young woman, married to Willard Long. She had got a good man, an honorable man, a man, unlike most of the Southern men about, a man who was interested in books, who seemed intellectually alive. He wasn't really. Her mother must soon have found that out.

For the woman, Ethel's mother, the man she had got must have seemed rather above the average. He didn't tell little lies. He didn't chase off secretly after brown women.

There were brown women everywhere about. Langdon, Georgia, was in the very heart of the old slave-owning

South. The brown women weren't bad. They were unmoral.
They hadn't the white women's problems.

They were going to grow more and more like white
women, facing the same problems, the same difficulties in life
but...

In her father's day, as a young man.

How had he kept so straight? "I would never have done
it," Ethel thought.

Such a man as her father would go ahead and perform
certain functions for a woman. He could be depended upon
for that.

He couldn't give a woman what she really wanted. It
might be no American man could. Ethel had just returned
from Chicago where she had gone to school and where she
had studied to be a librarian. She was thinking of her experiences there... a young woman's attempts to thrust out
into life, what had happened to her in the few adventures
she herself had made to get hold of life.

It was a spring day. In the North, in Chicago, where
she had been living for four or five years it would still be
winter but in Georgia it was already spring. Her ride with
her father to the Negro school building, some miles from the
town, past Georgia peach orchards, past cotton lands, past
little unpainted cabins, scattered so thickly over the land...
the usual cropper's portion was ten acres... past long
stretches of worn-out lands... the ride during which she did
so much thinking about her father in relation to his new wife
...making it a kind of key to her own thoughts of men and
a possible permanent relation to some man of her own—
her ride took place before the two men of the town, one
very young, one almost old, became interested in her. Men
with their mules were plowing the fields. There were brown
men and white men, the brutalized ignorant poor whites of
the South. Not all of the woods in that country were pine
woods. There were stretches of lowland along a river road
they traveled that day. At places red newly plowed land

seemed to go right up the side of a slope into the dark wood. A brown man, driving a team of mules, went right up a slope into a wood. His mules disappeared in the wood. They turned in there and came out. Single pine trees seemed to run out from the mass of trees as though to dance on the fresh newly plowed land. At the river's edge, below the road along which they drove, Ethel's father now quite lost in a tale of his young boyhood on the land, a tale she kept going by asking occasional questions—at the river's edge swamp maples grew. A little earlier the leaves of the swamp maples had been blood-red but they were now turning green. The dogwood was coming into bloom. It gleamed white against the green of the new growth. The peach orchards were almost ready to bloom, soon they would burst forth in a mad riot of bloom. Just at the river's edge, cypress grew. You could see the knees sticking up out of the brown slack water and out of the red mud at the edge of the river.

It was spring. You felt spring in the air. Ethel kept glancing at her father. She was half angry with him. She had to keep him going, keep his mind occupied with thoughts of his boyhood. "What's the use? . . . he will never know, can never know why his Blanche and I hate each other, why at the same time we want to help each other." Her eyes had a way of getting bright, like a serpent's eyes. They were blue and as thoughts came and went they sometimes seemed to grow green. They were really gray when she felt cold, gray when warmth came into her.

The intensity broke. She wanted to chuck it. "I should take him into my arms, as though he were still the boy he is talking about," she thought. No doubt his first wife, Ethel's mother, often did that. There might be a man, who was still a boy, as her father was, who nevertheless knew he was a boy. "I could perhaps make a go of it with such a one," she thought.

Hatred grew in her. It was as a bright-green new spring plant in her that day. The woman Blanche knew she had hatred in her. That was why the two women could both hate and respect each other.

If her father had only known a bit more than he did know, than he could ever know.

"Why couldn't he have got for himself, if he were determined to have another wife, if he felt he needed one?..." She felt vaguely her father's hunger for a son...the World War had taken his last one...and yet he could go on, like the eternal child he was, believing the World War justified . . he had been one of the leaders in his section, whooping it up for the war, helping to sell Liberty Bonds...she remembered a silly speech she had once, before her mother's death, after the son had enlisted, heard her father make. He spoke of the war as a healing thing. "It will bind up old wounds here in our own country, between the North and the South," he said that time...Ethel sitting beside her own mother listening...the mother went a little pale...women surely have to stand for a lot of nonsense from their men...Ethel felt it was rather absurd, the determination of the male about sons ...a vanity that went on and on in men...wanting to reproduce themselves...thinking that so terribly important....

"Why, in God's sweet name, if he wanted another son, did he pick out Blanche?"

"What man would want to be Blanche's son?"

It was all a part of the immaturity of men a woman got so tired of. Now Blanche was tired of it. "Such damn children," Ethel thought. Her father was sixty-five. Her mind leaped to something else. "What do women give a damn whether or not the man who can do to them what they want done is good or not?" She was getting into the habit of swearing, even in her thought. Perhaps she had caught that from Blanche. She thought she had one thing on Blanche. She was less tired. She wasn't tired at all. She thought, sometimes, when she was in the mood she was in that day..."I'm strong," she thought.

"I could hurt a lot of men before I die."

She might have gone in for something—with Blanche. "I could fix her," she thought. "This business of her letting herself go, dirty and shabby-looking as she is . . . It may be a way of keeping him off . . . It wouldn't be my way."

"I could take her, make her live a little. I wonder if she wants me to. I guess she does. I guess that is what she is up to."

Ethel sat in the car beside her father smiling, a hard queer smile. Once her father caught a glimpse of it. It frightened him. She could still smile softly. She knew that.

There he was, the man, her father, perplexed by the two women he had got into his house, his wife and his daughter, wanting to ask his daughter, "What's wrong?" Not daring to ask.

"There are things going on about me I can't understand."

"Yes, boy. You are right about that. Yes, there are things going on."

Two or three times during the drive that day, a flush came to the judge's cheeks. He wanted to lay down certain rules. He wanted to be a law-maker. "Be kind to me and others. Be honorable. Be fair."

"Do unto others as you would have others do unto you."

Ethel's father used to put his foot down hard sometimes when she was a little girl at home. At that time she was half a tom-boy, she was eager, easily excited. At one time she had a mad desire to play with all the bad little boys of town.

She knew which the bad ones were. You could tell them, the bold ones.

They would do things to you, perhaps, that kind.

There was all the terrible talk about pure spotless white womanhood in the South. Better to be a nigger girl.

"For God's sake, come here. Put some spots on me. Don't listen to anything I say. If I become frightened and cry out pay no attention to me. Do it. Do it."

There must have been some sense in the strange, half-mad men of Russia, before the revolution, who went about urging people to commit sin.

"Make God happy. Give Him a lot to forgive."

Some of the bad little white boys of Langdon, Georgia, might have done it. One or two had almost got the chance with Ethel. There was one bad little boy who had come close to her in a barn, another at night in a field, in the field near her father's house, where he kept his cow. She herself had crept out at night to that one. He had told her that afternoon coming home from school to creep out there, in the early evening, just after dark, to the field, and although she had trembled with fright, she had gone. There had been such a strange, half-frightened eager daring look in his young boy's eyes.

She had got out of the house safely, but her father had missed her.

"Damn him. I might have learned something."

There were memories like that in Blanche too. Of course. She being puzzled and puzzled a long, long time, through girlhood, through early womanhood, as Ethel had been, Blanche taking Ethel's father at last, going after him and getting him.

That good, good old boy. O Lord!

Ethel Long was hard, she was glistening, riding with her father as he went one day to pay a visit to a Negro school teacher who had been indiscreet, riding with him and thinking.

Not seeing, on that day, the dogwood shining against the green by a river's edge, not seeing white men and brown men driving mules, plowing the Southern land for another cotton crop. White cotton. Sweet purity.

Her father had come into the field that night and had found her there. She stood in the field trembling. There was a moon. There was too much moon. He didn't see the boy.

The boy had come toward her across the field as she crept out of the house. She had seen him coming.

It would be odd if he were also shy and frightened as she was. What chances people take! Men and women, boys and girls, approaching each other thus... seeking some obscure Heaven, for the moment. "Now! Now! We may at least have this moment's taste of it... if it be Heaven.

"So blunderingly we go. It is better to go blunderingly than not to go."

Perhaps the boy felt that. He had determination. He ran toward her and grabbed at her. He tore her dress at the neck. She trembled. He was of the right sort. She had picked one of the right sort.

Her father hadn't seen the boy. When the father came out at the door of the Long house that night, his heavy feet making a loud sound on wooden steps, the boy dropped to the ground and crawled toward a fence. There were some bushes by the fence and he achieved the bushes.

Queer that her father, seeing nothing, was yet suspicious. He was convinced there had been something wrong, something to him terrible. Were all men, even good men, like Ethel's father, closer to animals than they ever let themselves know? It would be nicer if they did let themselves know. If men dared let themselves know women might live more freely, they might lead sweeter lives. "In the present world of men there is too much thought and not enough thought. Men want courage and, not having it, they make women too much afraid," Ethel thought.

"But why was I given a mind? I am too much woman and not enough woman."

That night in the field her father hadn't seen the boy. If there hadn't been a moon she might have got away from her father and followed the boy into the bushes. There was too much moon. Her father sensed something. "Come here," he said to her harshly that night, advancing toward her across the pasture. She didn't move. She wasn't afraid of him that night. She hated him. "Come here," he kept saying, striding across the field toward her. At that time her father wasn't the meek thing he became after he got Blanche. He had a woman then, Ethel's mother, who was perhaps even afraid of him. She never crossed him. Was she afraid or was she merely patient? It would be nice to know. It would be nice to know whether it had always to be so, the woman either dominating the man or the man the woman. The name of the vulgar little boy she had arranged to meet that night was Ernest and although the father had not seen him on that night, several days later he suddenly said to her, "Do you know a boy named Ernest White?" "No," she lied. "I want you to stay away from him. Don't you dare have a thing to do with him."

So he knew without knowing. He knew all of the little boys of the town, the bad bold ones and the good gentle ones. Ethel, even as a child, had sharp senses. She knew then, or if not then later, that dogs, when there was a female dog that had desires ... the male dog threw his nose into the air. He stood alert, at attention. There was a female dog wanting, perhaps miles away. He ran. Many dogs ran. They gathered in packs, fighting and growling at each other.

After that night in the field Ethel was malicious. She cried and swore that her father had torn her dress. "He attacked me. I wasn't doing anything. He tore my dress. He hurt me."

"You were up to something, creeping out there like that. What were you up to?"

"Nothing."

She kept crying. She went sobbing into the house. Suddenly her father, that good man, had begun talking about his honor. It sounded so senseless. "Honor. A good man."

"I'd rather see a daughter of mine in her grave than not have her be a good girl."

"But what is a good girl?"

Ethel's mother had remained silent. She had gone a little

white, listening to the father talking to the daughter, but she had said nothing. Perhaps she had thought, "That is the way we have to begin. We have to begin to understand men, what they are like." Ethel's mother was a good woman. Not the child, listening to a father's talk about his honor, but the woman the child became, admired and loved the mother. "We women have to learn, too." Sometime there might be a good life on the earth but the time was a long, long way off. It implied some new kind of understanding between men and women, an understanding grown more general among all men and all women, a sense of the oneness of human beings not realized yet.

"I would really like to be like mother," Ethel thought that day after she had come back to Langdon to be the librarian there. She doubted her capacity to be the thing she was thinking of as she rode in the car with her father and afterwards as she sat in the car before a little Negro school, half buried in pine woods. Her father had gone into the school to find out whether or not a woman in there, a Negro woman, had been misbehaving. She wondered whether or not he could ask her, brutally, directly. "Perhaps he can. She is a Negro woman," Ethel thought.

3

THERE was a scene in Ethel's mind.

It came into her mind after her father had visited the Negro school and they were driving homeward in the warm early spring sunlight, riding over the red Georgia roads, riding past fields newly plowed. She saw little enough of the fields and did not ask her father how he had come out with the Negro woman in the school.

The woman had perhaps been indiscreet. She had perhaps got caught. Her father had gone in there, into the little Negro school while she remained in the car outside. He would have got the teacher to one side. He couldn't ask her directly, even though she were a Negro woman. "They say.... Is it true?" The judge was always getting himself into situations. He was presumed to know a lot about handling people. Ethel smiled. She was living in the past. On the ride homeward she got her father back to the subject of his own boyhood. He had hoped to have a serious talk with her, to find out from her, if he could, what was wrong in his own house, but he didn't succeed.

Men were plowing in red fields. Red roads went winding over low Georgia hills. A river, with trees growing along its banks and with white dogwood looking out from amid bright new green leaves, followed the road.

Her father wanted to ask her, "What's up at home? Tell me. What are you and my wife Blanche up to?"

"So, you want to know?"

"Yes. Tell me."

148

"The devil I will. Find out for yourself. You men are so smart. Find out for yourself."

A queer old enmity between men and women. Where did it begin? Was it necessary? Would it always go on?

At one moment that day Ethel wanted to be as her mother had been, patient and kindly with her father, while, in the next moment...

"If you were my man..."

Her mind occupied itself with the drama of her own life, in Chicago, thinking of it, now that it was a thing of the past, trying to understand it. There was one particular adventure. It had happened, at the end of her days as a student there. One evening she had gone to dine with a man. At that time—it was after her father's second marriage, when she had been at home on a visit and had returned to Chicago— the scheme to make her the librarian of the new library at Langdon had already been hatched in Blanche's mind and, falling in with it, Ethel had managed to get a job in the Chicago Public Library. . . . She went to a library school. Another young woman, also working at the library, had gone to dine with Ethel and a certain man, and with a man of her own. She was a small rather plump woman, young and inexperienced in life, whose people—very respectable people as were Ethel's people in Langdon—lived in a Chicago suburb.

The two women were going out to make a night of it, to achieve an adventure, and the men they were with were married men. It had just come about. It had been Ethel who had arranged it. She could not help wondering how much the other woman knew, how innocent she was.

There was the man Ethel was to spend the evening with. He was a queer one all right, a new sort to her. Ethel had met him one evening at a party. He had interested her. In her curiosity about him there was something of Ethel, the girl-child in the field waiting for the bad little small-town boy.

She was at a literary party when she first met the man

and there were a number of men and women present who were prominent in the Chicago literary world. For one, there was Edgar Lee Masters, and Carl Sandburg, the famous Chicago poet, also came. There were a lot of younger writers and some painters. A woman, older than Ethel, who also worked in the public library, had taken Ethel. The party was held in a large apartment, near the lake, over on the North Side. A woman who wrote poetry and who had married a rich man gave the party. There were several large rooms filled with people.

It was easy enough to tell which were the famous ones. The others gathered about, asking questions and listening. The famous ones were nearly all men. A poet named Bodenheim came, smoking a corn-cob pipe. It stank. People kept arriving and presently the large rooms were filled with people.

So this was the higher life, the cultural life.

At the party, Ethel, who was at once forgotten by the woman who had brought her, had wandered rather aimlessly about. She saw several people sitting apart in a small room. They were obviously unknown people like herself and she went in among them and sat down. After all, she couldn't help thinking, "I'm the best-dressed woman here." She had pride in that fact. There were women present wearing more expensive gowns but almost without exception they had missed something. She knew that. She had kept her eyes open since she had come into the apartment. "What a lot of frumps there are among the literary ladies," she thought. That night, although she was out of it, not being known as a writer or painter, being a mere employee in the Chicago Public Library, a student, she was filled with self-confidence. If no one paid her any attention, it was all right. People kept coming, crowding into the apartment. They were being addressed by their given names. "Hello, Carl." "Why, Jim, here you are." "Hello, Sarah." The little room into which Ethel had got faced a hallway by which people entered a larger room, crowded with people. The smaller room began also to fill.

She had, however, got into a little side-current out of the main stream. She watched and listened. A woman seated near her was informing a friend, "There's Mrs. Will Brownlee. She writes poetry. She has had poems in *Scribner's* and in *Harper's* and in a lot of other magazines. She is to publish a book soon. The tall woman with red hair is a sculptress. The little frumpy-looking one writes a column of literary criticism for one of the Chicago dailies."

There were the women and the men. Most of the people at the party were evidently of importance in the Chicago literary world. If they hadn't yet risen to national fame, they had hopes.

There was something a bit queer about the position of such people, the writers, painters, sculptors and musicians in American life. Ethel sensed the position of such people, particularly in Chicago, and was amused and puzzled. So many people wanted to be writers. Why? The writers were always writing books that were reviewed in the newspapers. There was a little flare of enthusiasm or of condemnation that died very quickly. There was really very little intellectual life. The great city sprawled itself out. Distances within the city were immense. For the people who were on the inside, in the intellectual circles of the city, there was both admiration and contempt.

They were in a great commercial city, lost in it. It was an undisciplined city, magnificent but unformed. It was a changing city, always growing, changing, always getting bigger.

On the side of the city, facing Lake Michigan, there was a street on which the main building of the public library stood. It was a street lined with great office buildings and hotels, the lake on one side and there was a long narrow park.

It was a wind-blown street, a glorious street. Some one

had told Ethel that it was the most magnificent street in America and she believed it. On many days it was a sun-washed, a wind-swept street. A river of motors flowed along. There were smart shops and great hotels, and smartly dressed people walked up and down. Ethel loved the street. She liked to put on a smart dress and walk there.

Beyond this street, to the west, there was a network of dark tunnel-like streets, not taking queer and unexpected turns as in New York, Boston, Baltimore and other older American cities, cities which Ethel had visited when she had taken a trip for just that purpose, but streets laid out in a grill, going straight away to the west, going north and south.

Ethel in doing her work had to go out west, to a branch of the Chicago public library. She lived, after she had finished her university life and was studying to be a librarian, in a small room on lower Michigan Avenue, below the Loop, and every day walked up Michigan Avenue to Madison where she took her car.

On the evening when she went to the party and there met the man with whom she afterwards went to dine, and with whom she later had an adventure that had a deep influence upon her outlook on life, she was in a period of revolt. She was always having such periods. They came and went, and after she had passed through one of them she was rather amused at herself. The truth was that she had been in revolt ever since she came to Chicago.

There she was, a tall straight figure of a woman, a trifle mannish. She might so easily grow more or less mannish. She had been in the university for four years and, when not in the university, had been working in the city or had been at home. Her father was far from a rich man. He had inherited some money from his father and his first marriage had brought him some and he owned Southern farm lands but the land did not bring in much income. His salary wasn't large and he had, besides Ethel, other children to take care of.

Ethel was in one of her periods of revolt against men.

At the literary party that night, as she sat rather to one side
...not feeling neglected...she knew only the older woman
who had brought her to the party...why should that woman
bother about her, having got her in there..."having done
me that great favor," she thought...at the party she realized
also that she might long since have had a man of her own,
even an intellectual man.

There had been a man out at the university, a young
instructor, who also wrote and published poetry, an eager
intense young man who had courted her. What a queer performance his courtship had been! She had cared nothing
for him, but she had used him.

At the beginning, having met her, he had begun asking
her if he could come to see her and if he could take her
places and then he had begun helping her with her work.
The help had been needed. Ethel had cared little enough about
some of her studies. They were a bother to her.

You had to select a certain number of studies. The
examinations at the university were stiff. If you got behind,
you were thrown out. If she were thrown out, her father
would be angry and she would have to return to Langdon,
Georgia, to live. The young instructor was a help. "Look
here," he said, when there was to be an examination, "these
will be about the sort of questions the man will ask." He
knew. He prepared answers. "You answer them in this way.
You'll get through all right." Before an examination he
worked with her for hours. What a joke the four years at
the university had been! What a waste of time and money
for such a one as herself!

It was a thing her father had wanted her to do. He had
made sacrifices, had gone without things and had saved
money to enable her to do it. She did not want specially to
be educated, an intellectual woman. More than anything else,
she thought she would have liked being a rich woman. "God,"
she thought, "if I only had a lot of money."

She had an idea...it might very well be absurd...she

might have got it from novel reading ... there seemed to be
rather a fixed idea in most Americans that happiness was to
be got through wealth ... there might be a life in which she
could really function. There might be, for a woman like herself, with a certain undoubted swank, a place. She even
dreamed sometimes, her dreams influenced by her reading,
of a kind of glorious life. In a book about English life she
read of a certain Lady Blessington, in Peel's time in England.
That was when Queen Victoria was still a young girl. Lady
Blessington began life as the daughter of an obscure Irishman who married her off to a rich and disagreeable man.

Then the miracle. She was seen by Lord Blessington,
who was very rich, an English nobleman. There she was, a
real beauty, and no doubt, like Ethel, a woman of style,
hidden away like that. The noble Englishman took her to
England, got her a divorce and married her. They set off for
Italy accompanied by a young French nobleman who became
Lady Blessington's lover. Her noble lord didn't seem to mind.
The young man was brilliant. What the old lord wanted no
doubt was some real decoration to his own life. She gave him
that.

The great difficulty with Ethel was that she was not
quite poor. "I'm middle class," she thought. She had picked
up that word somewhere, perhaps from her admirer, the college instructor. His name was Harold Grey.

There she was, just a middle-class young American
woman, lost in the crowd at an American university, later
lost in the Chicago crowds. She was a woman always wanting
clothes, wanting jewels to wear, wanting to ride in a fine
automobile. No doubt all women were like that, although a
good many would never admit it. That was because they
knew they hadn't a chance. She took *Vogue* and other
women's magazines, filled with pictures of the latest Paris
gowns, gowns draped over the bodies of tall slender women,
much like herself. There were pictures of country houses,
people driving up to the doors of country houses in very

elegant-looking automobiles...perhaps in the advertising
pages of the magazines. How clean and nice and first-class
everything seemed! In the pictures she saw in the magazines,
lying alone sometimes in her bed in a little room...it being
Sunday morning...pictures meaning to suggest a kind of
life quite possible to all Americans...that is to say, if they
were real Americans, not foreign trash...if they were
earnest and hard-working...if they had brains enough to
make money....

"God, but I'd like to marry a rich man," Ethel thought.
"If I had the chance. I wouldn't give a damn what he was."
She didn't quite mean that.

She was always getting into debt, having to scheme and
scheme to get the clothes she thought she needed. "I haven't
a thing to cover my nakedness," she said sometimes to other
women she met at the university. She had even had to bother
to learn to sew and was always having to think about money.
It had resulted in her always living in rather shabby quar-
ters, doing without many simple little luxuries other women
had. She did so much want to make a swank appearance
before the world and in the university, while she was a student. She was a good deal admired. None of the other women
students ever got very close to her.

There had been two or three...rather soft little feminine things they were...who had got crushes on her. They
wrote little notes and sent flowers to her room.

She had a dim notion what they meant. "Not for me,"
she told herself.

There were the magazines she saw, talk she heard, books
she read. Out of occasional fits of boredom she had become
a novel reader and that had been mistaken for an interest
in literature. In the summer, when she went home to Langdon
she took a dozen novels with her. Her reading had put the
idea of her being the town librarian into Blanche's head.

There were these pictures of people, always on glorious
summer days, in places to which only the rich went. There

was the sea to be seen in the distance and a golf course by the sea. There were handsomely dressed young men walking about. "God, I might have been born into such a life." It was always spring or summer in the pictures or, if winter came, tall women in expensive furs were engaged in winter sports, accompanied by handsome young men.

Although Ethel was a born Southerner, she had few illusions about life in the American South. "It's shabby," she thought. Chicago people she met asked her about Southern life. "Isn't there great charm to your life down there? I have always heard about the charm of life in the South."

"Charm, hell!" Ethel did not say that, although she thought it. "There's no use making yourself unnecessarily unpopular," she thought. The life might be quite charming to some people ... people of a certain sort ... not fools by any means, she knew that ... she thought her own mother had found life in the South, with her lawyer husband, who understood so little ... so full he was of his middle-class virtues, believing in his own honesty of mind, his honor, his deeply religious nature ... her mother had managed not to be unhappy.

Her mother would have got some of the charm of Southern life, people of the North like so to prattle about, Negroes always about the house and in the streets ... Negroes usually pretty slick, telling lies, working the whites ... the long hot dull Southern summer days.

Her mother had lived out her life, sunk deep in that life. Ethel and her mother had never really talked. There always had been something, a kind of understanding, as later between her and the blonde step-mother. Ethel's hatred grew and grew. Was it man hatred? It might well be that. "They are such self-satisfied damn stick-in-the-muds," she thought. As for her being specially interested in books, being an intellectual, it was a joke. A lot of the other women she met when she had begun studying to be a librarian seemed interested, even absorbed.

No doubt the people who wrote books thought they were up to something. Some of them really were. Her own favorite author was the Irishman, George Moore. "Writers should create, for those of us whose lives are drab, lives not so drab," she thought. With what joy she had read Moore's *Memoirs of My Dead Life*. Love should be like that, she thought.

There were these lovers of Moore's at the inn at Orelay, their going out at night into the little French provincial town to find the pajamas, the shop-keeper, the room in the inn that was such a disappointment and then the delightful room they later found. No bothering about each other's souls, about sin and the consequences of sin. The writer had liked fine lingerie on his ladies; he liked soft delicate clinging gowns slipping gently off the female form. Such lingerie imparted to the women who wore it something of its own elegance, its own rich softness and firmness. The whole matter of earthiness, in most of the books Ethel read, was, she thought, too much overdone. Who wanted it?

It would be better to be a high-class whore. If a woman could only pick her men, that wouldn't be so bad. Ethel thought that more women than men would ever guess had thought that. She thought that men were, on the whole, fools. "They are children wanting to be nursed through life," she thought. In a Chicago newspaper one day she saw the picture and read the account of the adventures of a woman highwayman, and her heart jumped. She imagined herself walking into a bank and holding it up, getting thereby, in a few minutes, thousands of dollars. "If there was a way of meeting a really first-class highwayman and he'd fall for me, I'd fall for him, all right," she thought. In Ethel's time, when she, by a mere chance, she thought, got herself connected, always on the outer edge, of course, with the literary world, a great many of the writers who were getting most attention just then ... not the really popular ones, the ones she really liked, the ones who had sense enough to write only of the lives of the rich, and the successful ... the only really interesting lives ... a great many of the writers who, just then, had big names, Theodore Dreiser, Sinclair Lewis and others, concerned themselves with such low-grade people.

"Damn them, they write of people just like myself, caught as I am."

Or they tell stories of working people and their lives ... or little farmers on poor little farms in Ohio, Indiana or Iowa, people driving about in Fords, a hired man, in love with some hired girl, going into the woods with her, her sadness and fright afterwards when she discovers she is that way. What difference did it all make?

"I can imagine just how such a hired man would smell," she thought. After she had finished at the university and had got a job at a branch of the Chicago public library ... it was far out on the West Side ... handing out dirty soiled books to dirty soiled people day after day ... having to be cheerful about it and act as though you liked it ... such tired weary faces most of the working people had ... for the most part their women came for the books. ...

Or young boys.

The boys liked to read about crime or about outlaws or cowboys in some vague place known as the "Far West." Ethel didn't blame them. She had to ride home at night on a street car. Rainy nights came. The car ran past the grim walls of factories. There were workingmen crowding into the car. How black and dismal seemed the city streets under the street lights, seen through the car windows, and how far, far away were the people of the advertising pictures seen in *Vogue,* the people with country houses, the sea at the door, the spreading lawns with great avenues of shade trees, those who went, richly gowned, in expensive cars to dine at some big hotel. Some of the workingmen in the car must have been in the same clothes day after day, even month after month. The air was heavy with dampness. The car reeked.

Ethel sat grimly in the car and sometimes grew pale. A workingman, perhaps a young one, stared at her. None of them dared sit very close. They felt dimly that she must belong to some outside world, far removed from their world. "Who's the dame? How did she get here, into this part of town?" they asked themselves. Even the poorest paid workingman had, at some time in his life, walked in certain downtown Chicago streets, even on Michigan Avenue. He had walked, feeling perhaps awkward and out of place, past the entrances to great hotels.

He had seen such women as Ethel seemed, coming out of such places. The pictures they had in their minds of the lives led by the rich and the successful were somewhat different from the picture in Ethel's mind. An older Chicago had expressed that. There had been great saloons, all built of marble, with silver dollars set in the floor. A workingman told another of a certain Chicago house of prostitution he had heard of. A friend had been there once. "You sank in silken carpets to your knees. The women in the place were dressed like queens."

Ethel's picture wasn't that. She wanted elegance, style, a world of color and of movement. A passage read in a book, that afternoon rang in her head. It described a house in London. . . .

"One passed through a drawing-room in gold and ruby, filled with beautiful amber vases which had belonged to the Empress Josephine, to enter the long narrow library with its white walls on which mirrors alternated with panels of richly bound books. Through the tall window at the end could be seen the trees of Hyde Park. Round the room were sofas, ottomans, tables of enamel, covered with bibelots, and in a yellow satin fauteuil Lady Marrow, dressed in a gown of blue satin, cut extremely low. . . ."

"The American writers, who call themselves real writers, writing about this kind of people," Ethel thought, looking

up and down the street car, her eyes surveying a street car
filled with Chicago factory hands, homeward bound as she
was after a day's work...to God only knew what kind of
dreary little crowded apartments...squalling dirty little
children playing on the floor...herself alas going to a place
not so much better...no money in her pockets half the time
...she had often to dine at cheap little cafeterias...herself
having to skimp and grub to get a little money...the writers
concerning themselves with such lives, the loves, the hopes
of such people.

Not that she hated them, the workingmen and the work-
ingwomen she saw in Chicago. She tried not to have them
exist for her. They were like the white people of the mill
village at the edge of her home town of Langdon, they were
as the Negroes had always been to the people of the South,
that is to say, at any rate as the field Negroes had been.

She did in a way have to read the books of the writers
who wrote of such people. She had to keep up. People were
always asking questions. After all, she was planning to be
a librarian.

She picked up such a book sometimes and read it through
to the end. "Well," she said, putting it down, "what of it?
What does it matter about such people?"

*

As for the men who had interested themselves directly in
Ethel, who had thought they wanted her.

The instructor out at the university, Harold Grey, would
do as an example. He wrote letters. That seemed to be his
passion. Several men with whom she had had passing flirta-
tions had been of that sort. They were all intellectuals. She
had something in her attractive, apparently to that sort, and
yet, when she got one, she hated him. They were always trying to delve into her soul or they were fussing about with
their own souls. Harold Grey was just the type. He tried to

psychoanalyze her and had rather watery blue eyes, hidden behind thick glasses, rather thin hair carefully combed, narrow shoulders, not too strong legs. He went absent-mindedly along the street, hurrying along. He always had books under his arm.

If you married such a man ... she tried to imagine herself living with Harold. The truth was, probably, that she was on the look-out for a particular kind of man. It might even be all nonsense about her wanting fine clothes and a certain elegant position in life.

Being one who did not warm easily to others, she was a good deal alone, was alone often even in the presence of others. Her mind was always leaping forward. There was in her a touch of the masculine, meaning only, in her case, a kind of boldness, not very womanly, quick flights of fancy. She could laugh at herself. She was thankful for that. She saw Harold Grey hurrying along the street. He had a room near the university, and to get to his classes did not need to go through the street where, during her university days, she had a room but, after he had begun paying attention to her, he often did. "It's funny, his falling for me," she thought. "If he, in his physical self, were a bit more of a man, if he were a tough brow-beating man, or big, an athlete or something of that sort ... or if he were rich."

There was something very meek and hopeful and at the same time boyishly sad about Harold. He was always delving about among the poets, finding little verses for her.

Or he read nature books. He was in the philosophy department at the university but said to her that he really had wanted to be a naturalist. He brought her a book by a man named Fabre, something about caterpillars. They, the caterpillars, went creeping along the ground or they ate the leaves of a tree. "Let them," Ethel thought. She grew angry. "Damn. They aren't my trees. Let them strip the trees bare."

For a time she had hung onto the little instructor. He hadn't much money and was working for his Ph.D. She went

for walks with him. He hadn't a car but he took her to several dinners at the houses of professors. She let him hire a
taxi.

He took her, sometimes in the evening, for long drives.
They went west and south. It would be so and so many dollars and dimes for every hour they were out together. "I'm
not giving him much for his money," she thought. "I wonder
if he would have the nerve to try to collect if he knew how
easy I would be for the right sort of man." She made the
drives as long as possible, "Let's go down this road,"
dragging the time out. "He could live a week on what I am
making him blow in," she thought.

She let him buy books for her she did not want to read.
A man, perhaps sitting all day and watching the actions of
caterpillars or ants or even dung beetles, day after day, month
after month—that was what he admired. "If he really wants
me he'd better be up to something. If he'd knock me down.
If he were able. I guess that is what I need."

Ridiculous moments remembered. Once on Sunday she
was with him on a long drive in a hired car. They went to a
place called Palos Park. He needed to do something. It began to bother him. "Really now," she asked herself that day,
"why have I such contempt for him?" He was trying hard
to be nice to her. He was always writing her letters. In the
letters he was much bolder than when he was with her.

He wanted to stop by a wood, at the side of the road.
He needed to. He moved nervously about on the car seat.
"He must really be suffering terribly," she thought. She was
pleased. Maliciousness had taken possession of her. "Why
doesn't he say what he wants?"

If it was a matter of his being too shy to use certain
words surely there was some way he could let her know
what he wanted. "Look here, I've got to go into the woods
alone. Nature calls."

He was so damned hot on nature . . . bringing her books
about caterpillars and dung beetles. Even when he was that

way that day, shifting nervously about on the seat, he tried
to pass it off as enthusiasm for nature. He wiggled and
squirmed. "Look," he cried. He pointed out a tree growing
beside the road. "Isn't it magnificent?"

"You are rather magnificent yourself," she thought. It
was a day of light floating clouds and he called attention to
them. "They look like camels crossing a desert."

"You would like to be alone on a desert yourself," she
thought. All he needed was a lonely desert or a tree between
himself and her.

It was his way, talking as he did about nature, going on
and on about it, about trees and fields and rivers and flowers.

And ants and caterpillars...

And then being so damned modest about a simple matter.

She let him suffer. Two or three times he almost escaped. She got out of the car with him and they walked in
a wood. He pretended to see something at a distance, off
among the trees. "You wait here," he said, but she ran after
him. "I want to see, too," she said. The joke of it was that
the man who was driving the car that day, the chauffeur...
he was rather of the tough city type...he chewed tobacco
and spat....

He had a little snub nose that looked as though it had
been broken in a fight and there was a scar on his cheek,
as though from a knife cut.

He knew what was going on. He knew Ethel knew that
he knew.

Ethel had finally let the instructor get away. She turned
and walked away along a path toward the car, having tired
of the game. Harold would wait a few minutes before joining her. Very likely he would look about, to see if he couldn't
find a flower to pluck....

To pretend that was what he was up to, trying to find
a flower for her. The joke was that the chauffeur knew. He
might have been Irish. When she got to where the car waited
beside the road, he had got out of his driver's seat and was

standing there. "Did you let him get lost?" he asked. He knew she knew what he meant. He spat on the ground and grinned as she got into the car.

*

ETHEL was at the literary party in Chicago. Men and women went about smoking cigarettes. There was a little chattering stream of talk. People disappeared into the kitchen of the apartment. Cocktails were being served out there. Ethel sat in the little room off the hallway and a man came to her. He had spotted her, picked her out. There was an empty chair beside her and he came and sat down. He was direct. "There doesn't seem to be any one doing any introducing here. I'm Fred Wells," he said.

"It doesn't mean anything to you. No, I do not write novels or essays. I don't paint or sculp. I'm no poet." He laughed. He was a new sort to Ethel. He looked at her boldly. His eyes were grayish blue, cold eyes as were her own at times. "At least," she thought, "he's a bold one."

He had marked her down. "You'll do for me," he had perhaps thought. He was looking for a woman to entertain him.

He was at the old game. A man wanted to talk about himself. He wanted a woman to listen, to be impressed, to seem absorbed as he spoke of himself.

It was a man's game but women were no better. The woman wanted to be admired. She wanted beauty of person and she wanted a man aware of her beauty. "I can stand for almost any man if he thinks I'm beautiful," Ethel thought sometimes.

"Look here," the man she saw at the party, the man named Fred Wells said, "you aren't one of these, are you?" He made a quick movement with his hand toward the others sitting in the small room and toward those in the large room near by. "I'll bet you aren't. You don't look like that," he said smiling. "Not that I've anything against these people, particularly the male ones. They are people of distinction, I suppose, at least some of them are."

The man laughed. He was alive like a fox terrier.

"I myself pulled some strings to get here," he said, laughing. "I don't really belong. What about you? Do you sculp? A lot of women do. They take it out that way. I bet you don't." He was a man of perhaps thirty-five, very slender and alive. He kept smiling but his smile did not go very deep. Little smiles chased each other across his sharp face. He had very clear-cut features, such features as might have been seen in a cigarette or clothing advertisement. For some reason he made Ethel think of a fine, highly bred dog. An advertisement ... "the best dressed man at Princeton" ... "the man at Harvard, most likely to succeed in life, selected by his class." He had been to a good tailor. His clothes were not showy. They were without a doubt faultlessly correct.

He leaned over to whisper to Ethel, putting his face quite close to hers. "I didn't think you were one of these," he said. She had told him nothing of herself. It was evident that there was in him a kind of sharp antagonism to the celebrities at the party.

"Look at them. They think they are great shucks, now don't they?

"Damn their eyes. Strutting about here, the men celebrities being fawned on by women, the women celebrities showing off too."

He did not say that at once. It was implied in his manner. He had devoted the evening to her, taking her about and introducing her to the celebrities. He seemed to know them all. He took things for granted. "Here Carl, come here," he commanded. That was a command to Carl Sandburg, a large broad-shouldered man with gray hair. There was something in Fred Wells' manner. He was impressing Ethel. "See, I call him by his first name. I say, 'come here,' and he comes." He called various men to him, Ben and Joe and Frank. "I want you to meet this woman."

"She's Southern," he said. He had caught that from Ethel's speech.

"She's the best-looking woman here. You don't need to worry. She isn't any kind of an artist. She won't be asking any favors of you."

He grew familiar and confidential.

"She won't be asking you to write an introduction to any little book of poems, nothing of that sort."

"I'm not in this game," he said aside to Ethel, "and yet I am too." He had taken her into the kitchen of the apartment and had got her a cocktail. He lit a cigarette for her.

They stood a little to one side, out of the jam of people, Ethel amused. He explained to her what he was, still smiling. "I suppose I'm the lowest of human beings," he said cheerfully, but as he said it he smiled blandly. He wore a tiny little black mustache and, as he talked, kept stroking it. His talk was oddly like the barking of a little dog in a road, a dog barking determinedly at an automobile in a road, at an automobile that has passed around a turn in the road.

He was a man who made his money in the patent-medicine business and explained it all to Ethel at a rush as they stood together. "I dare say you are a woman of family, being Southern. Well, I'm not. I've noticed that almost all Southerners have a family. I'm from Iowa."

He was obviously a man who lived by his contempt. He had spoken of Ethel's being Southern with contempt in his voice, contempt that he was careful to keep controlled, as though to say—laughing—"Don't try to put it over me because you are Southern.

"That game won't go with me.

"But see. I laugh. I am not serious.

"Ta! Ta!"

"I wonder if he is like myself," Ethel thought. "I wonder if I am that way."

There are certain people. You do not really like them.
You stay near them. They teach you things.

It was as though he had come to the party only to find
her and, having found her, was satisfied. At once, having
met her, he wanted to leave. "Come on," he said, "let's get
out of here. Here we shall have to struggle to get drinks.
There's no place to sit. We can't talk. We are of no importance here."

He wanted to be somewhere, in an atmosphere where he
could seem more important to himself.

"Let's go on downtown to one of the big hotels. We
can dine there. I'll manage about the drinks. Watch me." He
kept smiling. Ethel didn't care. She had a queer notion about
the man, had it from the moment when he had first come
to her. There was a touch of Mephistopheles. She was
amus^d. "If that is what he is, I'll find out about him," she
thought. She went with him to get her wraps and getting a
cab they went to a big downtown restaurant where he found
for her a seat in a quiet corner. He did manage about drinks.
A bottle was brought.

He seemed to want to explain himself and began telling
her about his father. "I'm going to talk about myself. Do you
mind?" She said she didn't. He had been born in a county-
seat town in Iowa. His father, he explained, was in politics
out there and had got to be the county treasurer.

After all the man had a story of his own. He was giving Ethel his background.

In Iowa, where he had spent his boyhood, everything
had gone all right for a long time, but then his father had
used county funds for some sort of speculation of his own
and had got caught. There had come a period of depression.
Stocks his father had bought on margin had gone tumbling
down. He was caught short.

That, Ethel gathered, was at about the time Fred Wells
was through high school. "I didn't spend any time moping
about," he said, proudly and quickly. "I came to Chicago."

He explained that he was smart. "I'm a realist," he said. "I don't mince words. I'm smart. I'm as smart as hell.

"I'll bet I'm smart enough to see through you," he said to Ethel. "I know what you are. You are a dissatisfied woman." He smiled saying that.

Ethel hadn't liked him. She had been amused and interested. There was even a way in which she did like him. At least he was a relief after some of the men she had met in Chicago.

They kept drinking as the man talked and as the dinner he had ordered was served, and Ethel liked drinking, although drink did not affect her much. Drinking was a relief. It made her daring, although getting drunk wasn't any fun. She had got drunk just once and when she did it she was alone.

That had been on a night when she was still at the university and just before an examination. Harold Grey had been helping her. He had left her and she went to her room. She had a bottle of whisky there and drank it all. Afterwards she tumbled into bed and was ill. The whisky did not make her drunk. It seemed to excite her nerves, make her mind peculiarly cold and clear. The illness came after that. "I won't do that again," she told herself that time.

In the restaurant Fred Wells continued to explain himself. He seemed to feel it necessary to explain his presence at the literary party, as though to say, "I'm not one of them. I don't want to be."

"There is no danger of my thinking so," Ethel thought. She did not say so.

He had come to Chicago, as a young man just out of school, and, after a time, had begun cultivating the artistic and literary crowd. There was no doubt it gave a man, such a man as himself, a certain standing, knowing such people. He bought them dinners. He went about with them.

Life is a game. Knowing such people is just one hand you hold in the game.

He had become a collector of first editions. "It's a good scheme," he told Ethel. "It seems to put you in a certain class and, besides, if you are shrewd, you can make money at it, that is to say, there's no reason, if you watch your step, why you should lose money."

So he had got in with the literary crowd. They were, he thought, childish, egotistical, sensitive. They amused a man. Most of the women, he thought, were rather soft, they were soft-headed.

He kept smiling and stroking his mustache. He had gone in for first editions and had already a fine collection. "I'll take you to see them," he said.

"They are in my apartment, but my wife is out of town. Of course, I don't expect you to go there with me to-night.

"I know you're not a fool."

"I am not such a fool as to think you can be got so easily, that you can be plucked, like a ripe apple from a tree," was what he had thought.

He proposed a party. Ethel could get another woman and he would get another man. It would make a nice small party. They would have dinner at a restaurant and afterwards go to his apartment to see his books. "You aren't squeamish, are you?" he asked. "You know, there will be another woman and another man there.

"My wife will be out of town for a month yet."

"No," Ethel had said.

He had spent all of that first evening in the restaurant explaining himself. "To certain people, the smartest people, life is just a game," he explained. You get out of it what you can. There were various men who played the game in various ways. Some, he said, went in for being very, very respectable. They were in business, as he was. Well, they didn't sell patent medicines. They sold coal or iron or machinery. Or they ran factories or mines. It was all one game. The money game.

"Do you know," he said to Ethel, "I think you are of the same sort I am.

"Nothing much takes hold of you either.

"We are of the same breed."

Ethel hadn't felt flattered. She was amused, but at the same time a little hurt.

"If it's true I don't want it to be."

Just the same she was interested, perhaps in his assurance, his boldness.

He had lived, as a boy and as a young man, in the town in Iowa. He was the one son in the family and there were three daughters. His father had seemed always to have plenty of money. They had lived well, for that town they had lived rather in the grand manner. There had been automobiles, horses, a big house, money spent right and left. Each child in the family had been given an allowance by the father. He never asked how it was spent.

Then the crash came and the father went to jail. He did not live long. Fortunately there was insurance money. The mother and daughters, by being careful, could get along. "I suppose my sisters will marry. They haven't yet. Not one of them has succeeded in hooking a man," Fred Wells said.

He himself had wanted to be a newspaper man. That had been his passion. He had come to Chicago and had got a job as a reporter on one of the Chicago dailies but presently had given it up. There wasn't, he said, enough money in it.

He was sorry about that. "I would have been a crack newspaper man," he said. "Nothing would have jarred me, nothing would have fazed me." He kept drinking, eating and talking of himself. Perhaps the liquor he drank made him bolder in talk, more reckless. It did not make him drunk. "It affects him as it does me," Ethel thought.

"Suppose there had been a man's or a woman's reputation to be destroyed," he said brightly. "Let's say over a sex scandal, something of that sort... the kind of thing that is so abhorrent to a lot of these literary men I know, to a lot of so-called high-class people. Aren't they a lot of clean ones? The damn children." It had seemed to Ethel that the man before her must hate the people among whom she had found him, the men whose books he collected. There was a tangle of emotions in him as in her. He continued to talk brightly, smilingly, without outward show of emotion.

Writers, he said, the higher-ups among writers were also without scruples. Such a one had a love affair with some woman. What happened? It came to an end after a time. "There is no such thing as love really. It's all a lot of moonshine and bunk," he declared.

"With such a man, a great literary figure, ha! Full of words, as I am.

"But making so many damn pretensions about the words he slings out.

"As though anything in the world really mattered so much. After it is all over with some woman, what does he do? He makes literary material of it.

"He fools no one. Every one knows."

He returned to his talk of being a newspaper man, dwelling on it. "Suppose a woman, married, let's say." He was himself a married man, had married a woman who was the daughter of the man who owned the business he was now in. The man was dead. Now he controlled the business. If his own wife ... "She had better not fool with me ... I certainly wouldn't stand anything like that," he said.

Suppose a woman, married and all that, were to get into an affair with a man not her husband. He imagined himself a newspaper man handling such a story. They were prominent people. He had been a reporter for a time, but no such case had fallen into his hands. He seemed to regret it.

"They are prominent people. They are rich, or in the arts, big people in the arts, or in politics or something of that sort." The man had got himself launched. "And so the woman tries to work me. Let's say I am the managing editor of the paper. She comes to me. She weeps. 'For God's sake, remember I have children.' 'You have, eh? Why didn't you think of that when you got into this?' Little children having their lives ruined. Fudge! Was my own life ruined because my father died in jail? It may have hurt my sisters. I don't know. It may make it hard for them to get respectable husbands. I'd rip her right open. I'd have no mercy."

There was a curious kind of bright shining hatred in the man. "Am I like that? God help me, am I like that?" Ethel thought.

He wanted to hurt some one.

Fred Wells, coming to Chicago, after his father's death, hadn't stayed long in the newspaper game. There hadn't been, for him, enough money to be made. He had got into advertising, into an advertising agency as a copy writer. "I could have been a writer," he declared. He had in fact written several short stories. They were mystery stories. He liked writing them and had no trouble getting them published. He wrote for one of the magazines that print that sort of thing. "I also wrote true confessions," he said. He laughed, telling Ethel about it. He had imagined himself a young wife with a tubercular husband.

She had always been an innocent woman but hadn't specially wanted to be. She took her husband out West, to Arizona. The husband was nearly gone but he hung on for two or three years.

It was during that time the woman, in Fred Wells' story, was unfaithful to him. There was a man there, a young man she wanted, and so she used to creep out with him at night, into the desert.

It had given Fred Wells an opportunity, that story, that confession. The magazine publishers had grabbed at it. He had imagined himself the wife of that sick man. There he lay, slowly dying. He had imagined how the young wife was filled with remorse. Fred Wells sat at the table in the Chicago restaurant with Ethel, stroking his mustache and telling about it all. He described quite perfectly what he said were the feelings of the woman. At night she used to wait until darkness came. There were soft desert moonlit nights. The young man she had taken as a lover came creeping toward the house in which she lived with her sick husband, a house sitting at the edge of a town in the desert and she crept out toward him.

One night she came back and her husband was dead. She never saw the lover again. "I threw in a lot of remorse," Fred Wells said, laughing again. "I made it thick. I fairly wallowed in it. I suppose about all the real fun that imaginary woman of mine ever had was out there with the other man on the moonlit desert, but afterwards I made remorse fairly ooze out of her.

"You see I wanted to sell it. I wanted it published," he said.

Fred Wells got Ethel Long into a mess. It wasn't nice. It was, she knew afterwards, her own fault. One day, a week after she had dined with him, he had called her on the phone. "I've got something swell on," he said. There was a man in town, a famous Englishman, a writer, and Fred had got in with him. He proposed a party. Ethel was to get another woman and Fred would get the Englishman. "He is in America on a lecture tour and all the highbrows have had him in hand," Fred explained. "We'll give him another kind of a party." Did Ethel know of another woman she could get. "Yes," she said.

"Get a live one," he said. "You know."

What did he mean by that? She was sure of herself. "If a man like that . . . if he can put anything over on me."

She was bored. Why not? There was a woman, working in the library with her who might do. She was a year younger than Ethel, a little slip of a woman who had a passion for writers. The idea of meeting a famous man like that Englishman would be exciting to her. She was rather pale, the daughter of a respectable family in one of the Chicago suburbs and had herself a vague desire to be a writer.

"Yes, I'll go," she said, when Ethel spoke to her. She was one of the kind of women that always had admired Ethel. The women out at the university that had got crushes on her had been of this sort. She admired Ethel's style and what she thought her boldness.

"Do you want to go?"

"O, yeees." The woman's voice trembled with excitement.

"The men are married. You understand that?"

The woman, whose name was Helen, hesitated for a moment; this was something new to her. Her lips trembled. Evidently she thought...

Perhaps she thought... "A woman can't always go on, never having adventures." She thought... "One has to accept such things in a sophisticated world."

Fred Wells as an example of the sophisticated man.

Ethel had tried to make it all quite clear. She didn't. The woman was testing her. She was being excited about the idea of meeting a well-known writer, an English one.

There was no way for her to fathom Ethel's real attitude, just at that time, the don't-give-a-damn feeling she had, the desire she had to take risks, test herself perhaps. "We'll dine," she said, "and then we'll go to Mr. Wells' apartment. His wife will not be there. There will be drinks."

"There will be only the two men. You are not afraid?" Helen asked.

"No." Ethel was in an amused cynical mood. "I can take care of myself."

"Very well, I'll go."

Ethel would never forget that evening with the three people. It was one of the adventures in her own life that had made her what she was. "I'm not so damn nice." Thoughts drifting through her head on an afternoon later, when she drove over Georgia roads with her father. He was another one, puzzled by his own life. She was not being frank and open with him, and had not been with that naïve woman Helen she had taken to the party with the two men, that night in Chicago.

The English writer, who had come to the party with Fred Wells was a big-shouldered, rather crumpled man. He seemed curious and interested in what was going on. Such Englishmen coming to America where their books sold in quantities, where they came to lecture and gather in money . . .

There was something in the attitude of such men, toward all Americans. "The Americans are such strange children. My dear fellow, they are amazing."

Something amazing, always a bit patronizing. "The lion's whelps." You felt like saying, "Damn your eyes. You go to hell." With him, that night in Fred Wells' apartment in Chicago, it might just have been a satisfaction of curiosity. "I'll see what this sort of Americans are like."

Fred Wells was a spender. He took the others to an expensive restaurant to dine and then to his apartment. That also was expensive. He was proud of it. The Englishman was very attentive to the woman Helen. Was Ethel jealous? "I wish I had him," Ethel thought. She would have liked the Englishman to pay more attention to her. She fancied herself saying things to him, trying to upset his composure.

Helen was obviously too naïve. She worshipped. When they had all got to Fred's apartment Fred kept serving drinks and almost at once Helen got half drunk and as she got more and more drunk, and, Ethel thought, more and more foolish, the Englishman grew alarmed.

He even got noble . . . the noble Englishman. Blood will tell. "My dear fellow, one has to be a gentleman." Was Ethel sore because the man was linking her, in his mind, with Fred Wells? "To hell with you," she kept wanting to say. He was like a grown man left suddenly in a room with children who were misbehaving . . . "God knows what he expects to happen here," Ethel thought.

Helen had got up out of her chair after several drinks

and had walked uncertainly across a room in which they were all sitting and had thrown herself on a couch. Her dress was disarranged. There was too much leg showing. She kept throwing her legs about and laughing foolishly. Fred Wells kept giving her drinks. "Well, she has good legs, hasn't she?" Fred said. Fred Wells was too coarse. He was really rotten. Ethel knew it. What she resented was the thought that the Englishman did not know she knew.

The Englishman began speaking to Ethel. "What is all this about? Why is he intent on getting this woman drunk?" He was getting nervous and evidently wished he hadn't accepted Fred Wells' invitation. He and Ethel sat for a time by a little table with drinks before them. The Englishman kept asking her questions about herself, what part of the country she had come from and what she was doing in Chicago. He had found out she was a university woman. There was still... in his manner... something... that air of being outside it all... an English gentleman in America... "too damn impersonal," Ethel thought. Ethel was becoming aroused.

"A queer sort, these American university women if this is a sample, if this is the way they spend their evenings," the Englishman was thinking.

He said nothing of the sort. He kept trying to keep the conversation going. He had got into something, into a situation he didn't like. Ethel was glad. "How am I to get gracefully out of this place and away from these people?" He got up, intending no doubt to excuse himself, to leave.

But there was Helen, drunk now. The Englishman's sense of chivalry had been awakened.

At that moment Fred Wells appeared and took the Englishman into his library. After all, Fred was a business man. "I have him here. I have some of his books here. I might as well get him to autograph them," Fred was thinking.

Fred was also thinking of something else. Perhaps the Englishman did not understand what Fred had in mind. Ethel did not hear what was said. The two men went together into the library and there was talk in there. Afterwards, after what happened to herself later that evening, Ethel could pretty well guess what was said.

Fred had simply taken it for granted the Englishman was another like himself.

The whole tone of that evening had suddenly changed. Ethel had become frightened. Because she had been bored and wanting excitement she had got herself into a mess. She imagined the conversation between the two men in the nearby room. Fred Wells speaking . . . he was no such man as Harold Grey, the university instructor . . . "Here I have got this woman for you" . . . meaning the woman Helen. Fred, in there in that room, speaking to the other man. Ethel wasn't thinking of Helen now. She was thinking of herself. There was Helen, lying half helpless on a couch. Would a man want a woman in that state, a woman made half helpless by drink?

It would be an assault. There might be men who liked to get their women in that way. She was trembling with fear now. She had been a fool to allow herself to get into the power of a man like Fred Wells. There were the two men in the nearby room talking. She could hear their voices. Fred Wells had a sharp voice. He said something to his guest, the Englishman, and then there was silence.

Already, without a doubt, he had attended to the matter of having the man sign his books. He would have got them signed. He was making a proposal.

"Well, you see I have got a woman for you. There is one for you and one for me. You may take the one who is lying out there on the couch.

"I have, you see, got her quite helpless. There won't be much of a struggle.

"You may take her into a bedroom. You will not be disturbed. You may leave the other woman to me."

There must have been something of that sort that night.

The Englishman was in the room with Fred Wells and then came suddenly out. He did not look at Fred Wells, did not speak to him again, although he did look sharply at Ethel. He was judging her. "So you are into it, too?" A hot wave of resentment was running through Ethel. The English writer said nothing but went into a hallway where his coat was hanging and getting it and a wrap that had been worn by the woman Helen, came back into the room.

He had gone a little pale. He was trying to be composed. He was angry and excited. Fred Wells had come back into the room and stood in a doorway.

Perhaps the English writer had said something nasty to Fred. "I'll not let him, because he is a fool, spoil my own party," Fred was thinking. Fred's own party was to be Ethel herself. She knew that now. Evidently the Englishman thought Ethel was one of Fred's kind. He wasn't concerned with what happened to her. Ethel's fear was passing and she was growing angry, ready for fight.

It would be amusing, Ethel thought swiftly, if the Englishman had made a mistake. He is going to save the one who does not want to be saved. "She's the easy one to get, not me," she thought proudly. "So he is that sort of a man. He is one of the virtuous ones.

"To hell with him. I have given him this chance. If he doesn't want to take it, it's all right with me." She meant she had given the man the chance to know her, had he really wanted to. "How silly," she thought afterwards. She had given the man no chance at all.

The Englishman evidently felt responsibility for the woman Helen. She wasn't, after all, quite helpless, wasn't quite gone. He got her to her feet and helped her put on her coat. She clung to him. She began to cry. She put up a hand and caressed his cheek. It was evident to Ethel that she was ready to surrender and that the Englishman didn't want her. "It's all right. I'll get a cab and we'll drive. Presently you'll be all right," he said. Earlier in the evening he had found

out certain facts about Helen, as he had about Ethel. He
knew she was an unmarried woman living somewhere in a
suburb with her father and mother. She wasn't so far gone
but that she would know the address of her house. Half
holding the woman in his arms he led her out of the apartment and down a flight of stairs.

*

ETHEL was as a person who had been struck a blow. What
happened in the apartment that evening happened suddenly.
She sat nervously fingering a glass. She was pale. Fred Wells
didn't hesitate. He stood silently, waiting until the other man
with the other woman had gone and then came straight at
her. "And you." Partly now he was taking out his wrath
at the other man on her. Ethel stood up facing him. Now
there was no smile on his face. He was obviously some sort
of perverted man, a sadist perhaps. She faced him. In some
odd way she rather liked the situation she had got herself into.
It was to be a fight. "I'll see that you do not run out on
me," Fred Wells said. "If you go out of here to-night you
will go naked." He put out his hand swiftly and got a grip
on her dress at the neck. With a quick movement he tore
the dress. "You'll have to go naked if you go out of here
before I have what I want."

"You think so?"

Ethel had gone chalky white. There was, as has been
suggested, a way in which she rather liked the situation. In
the struggle that followed she did not cry out. Her dress
got terribly torn. Once during the struggle Fred Wells hit her
in the face with his fist and knocked her down. She sprang
quickly up. Understanding had come to her quickly. The
man before her would not have dared carry on the struggle
had she cried out in a loud voice.

There were other people living in the same apartment
building. He wanted to conquer her. He did not want her as

a normal man wanted a woman. He got them drunk and assaulted them when they were helpless or he got them through terror.

The two people in the apartment struggled silently. Once during the struggle he threw her across a couch in the room in which the four people had been sitting. It hurt her back. She did not feel the hurt much at the moment. That came later. Afterwards for several days, her back was lame.

For just a moment Fred Wells thought he had her. There was a smile of triumph on his face. His eyes were cunning, like the eyes of an animal. She thought—the thought came to her—she was for the moment lying quite passively on the couch his hands holding her there. "I wonder if he got his wife this way," she thought.

Probably not.

He would, such a man would, with the woman he intended to marry, a woman who had money he wanted, her own kind of power, with such a one he would try to create an impression of manliness in himself.

He might even have talked to her of love. Ethel wanted to laugh. "I love you. You are my darling. You are everything to me." She remembered that the man had children, he had a small son and a daughter.

He would have tried to create, in his wife's mind, the impression of being something he knew he couldn't be and perhaps didn't want to be, a man of the type of the Englishman who had just left the apartment, "an honorable man," a man of a sort he was always courting and at the same time despising. He would have tried to create that impression in the one woman's mind, hating her viciously at the same time.

Taking it out on other women. During the early evening, while they were all dining together at a downtown restaurant, he had kept talking to the Englishman about American women. He had been trying subtly to destroy the man's respect for American women. He had kept the conversation on a certain low plane, ready to retreat, smiling as he talked. The Englishman had remained curious and puzzled.

The struggle in the apartment did not last long and Ethel thought it was a good thing it didn't. The man was stronger than she was. At the last perhaps she would have cried out. The man would not have dared hurt her too seriously. He wanted to break her down, to tame her. He was depending on her not wanting it known she was alone with him in his apartment at night.

If he succeeded with her he might even pay her money to keep quiet.

"You are not a fool. You knew what I wanted when you came here."

There was a sense in which it would be quite true. She had been a fool.

She managed by a quick movement to get free. There was a door into a hallway and she ran along the hallway and into the kitchen of the apartment. Earlier in the evening Fred Wells had been slicing oranges to put into drinks. There was a large knife lying on a table. She threw the kitchen door closed behind her, but she herself opened it for Fred Wells' entrance, slashing at his face with the knife, just missing his face.

He backed away. She was backing him down a hallway. The hallway was brightly lighted. He could see the look in her eyes. "You bitch," he said as he backed away from her. "You damn bitch."

He wasn't afraid. He was cautious, watching her. His eyes were shining. "I guess you would, you damn bitch," he said and smiled. He was the sort of man who, if he met her the next week on the street, would raise his hat and smile. "You got the best of me but I may have another chance at you," his smile would say.

She got her coat and got away, going out of the apartment at a back door. There was a door leading out onto a small balcony at the back and she got through that. He did not try to follow. Afterwards she went down a little iron stairway to a small grass plot at the back of the building.

She did not go at once. For a time she sat on the stairs. There were people sitting in the apartment below the one occupied by Fred Wells. Men and women were sitting quietly in there. There was a baby somewhere in that apartment. She heard it cry.

Men and women were sitting at a card table and one of the women got up and went to the baby.

She heard voices and laughter. Fred Wells would not dare follow her there. "It is one kind of man," she told herself that night; "perhaps there are not many of that sort."

She had got out through the yard and a gate and into an alleyway and finally into a street. It was a quiet residential street. She had some money in her coat pocket. The coat partially covered the torn places in her dress. She had lost her hat. There was a car, evidently a private car, with a Negro chauffeur, standing before an apartment building. She went up to the man and thrust a bill into his hand. "I'm in trouble," she said. "Run get me a cab. You may keep that," she said, holding out the bill.

She was amused, angry, hurt. It wasn't the man Fred Wells who had hurt her most.

"I was too sure of myself. I thought the other woman Helen was the naïve one.

"I am myself naïve. I'm a fool."

"Are you hurt?" the Negro had asked. He was a large man of middle age. There was blood on her cheeks and he could see it in the light from the apartment entrance. One of her eyes was swollen. Afterwards it became black.

Already she was thinking of the tale she would tell when she had got to the place where she had a room. An attempt at robbery, two men had attacked her in the street.

Knocking her down, being quite brutal with her. "They snatched my purse and ran. I don't want to report it. I don't want to get my name in the papers." It would be understood and believed in Chicago.

She told the colored man a tale. She had been fighting with her husband. He laughed. He understood that. He left his car and ran to get her a cab. While he was gone Ethel stood with her back against the wall of a building, standing where the heavier shadows were. Fortunately no one passed to see her, battered and bruised, standing and waiting.

4

IT was a summer night and Ethel was lying in bed in her father's house in Langdon. It was late, long past midnight and the night was hot. She could not sleep. There were words in her, little flocks of words, like birds flying ... "a person has to decide, to decide." What? Thoughts became words. Ethel's lips moved. "It hurts. It hurts. What you do hurts. What you don't do hurts." She had come in late and, being tired from much thinking and feeling, had simply slipped off her clothes in the darkness of her room. Her clothes fell from her, leaving her there naked—what she was. She knew that when she had come in, her father's wife Blanche had been awake. Ethel and her father both slept in rooms downstairs but Blanche had moved herself upstairs. It was as though she had wanted to get as far away from her husband as possible. Escape from man ... for the woman ... to escape that.

Ethel had thrown herself, quite naked, on her bed. She felt the house, the room. At times a room in a house becomes a prison. Its walls push against you. Now and then she stirred restlessly. Little waves of feeling ran through her. She had had the feeling, when she had crept into the house, that night, half ashamed, annoyed with herself for what had happened during the evening, that Blanche was awake and had been watching for her return to the house. When Ethel entered, Blanche might even have come softly to the head of the stairs to look down. There was a little light burning in the hallway downstairs and the stairs went up out of the hallway. If Blanche had been up there, looking down, Ethel would have been unable to see her in the darkness above.

Blanche would have waited, perhaps to laugh, and Ethel felt like laughing at herself. It takes a woman to laugh at a woman. Women can really love each other. They dare. Women can hate each other; they can hurt and laugh. They dare. "I might have known it wouldn't do," she kept thinking. She was thinking of her evening. There had been another adventure, with another man. "I have done it again." This had been her third one. Three tries at something with men. Letting them try something—to see if they could. Like the others, it hadn't worked. She didn't quite know why.

"He didn't get me. He didn't get me."

What did she mean by that?

What was it to be got? What was it she wanted?

She had thought she wanted this one. It was the young man, Red Oliver, she had been seeing in the library. She had looked at him in there. He kept coming in. The library was open on three evenings a week and he always appeared.

He spoke to her more and more. The library closed at ten and, after eight they were often alone. People had gone to the movies. He helped close for the night. There were windows to be closed, sometimes books to be put away.

If he had really got her. He hadn't dared. She had got him.

It was because he was too shy, too young, too inexperienced.

She herself hadn't been patient enough. She didn't know him.

She might just have used him to find out whether or not she wanted him.

"It was unfair, unfair."

To find out about another and older man, whether or not she wanted him.

At first the younger one, young Red Oliver, who began coming to the library, looking at her with his young eyes, stirring her, hadn't dared offer to walk home with her but had left her at the library door. Later he grew a little bolder. He wanted to touch her, ached to touch her. She knew that. "May I walk along with you?" he had asked, awkwardly enough. "Yes. Why not? It will be very pleasant." She had been quite formal with him. He began walking home with her sometimes at night. The Georgia summer evenings were long. They were hot. When they got to the house there was the judge, her father, sitting on the porch. Blanche was there. Often the judge had gone to sleep in his chair. The nights were hot. There was a swinging couch and Blanche had curled herself up in that. She lay there wide awake, watching.

When Ethel came in, she spoke, having seen young Oliver leave Ethel at the gate. He lingered there, hating to go. He wanted to be Ethel's lover. She knew that. It was in his eyes now, in his shy hesitating speech ... a young man in love, with an older woman, suddenly, passionately in love. She could do as she pleased with him.

She could open the gates for him, let him into what he thought would be paradise. It was tempting. "I will have to do it if it is done. I will have to say the word, let him know the gates have opened. He is too shy to push forward," Ethel thought.

She didn't think it definitely. She thought it. There was a feeling of being superior to the young man. It was nice. It wasn't so nice.

"Well," Blanche said. Her voice was small, sharp and inquiring. "Well," she said. And "Well," Ethel replied. The two women looked at each other and Blanche laughed. Ethel did not laugh. She smiled. There was love between the two women. There was hatred.

There was something man seldom understands. When the judge was awake, both women remained silent and Ethel went at once to her room. She got a book and, lying in bed, tried to read. The nights that summer were almost too hot for sleep. The judge had got a radio and on some nights he

turned it on. It was in the living-room of the house downstairs. When he had turned it on and had filled the house with
voices, he sat beside it and slept. He snored when he slept.
Presently Blanche arose and went upstairs. The two women
left the judge sitting there, asleep in the chair near the radio.
The noises, coming from distant cities, from Chicago where
Ethel had lived, from Cincinnati, from St. Louis, did not
awaken him. There were men talking about tooth paste, bands
played, men made speeches, Negro voices sang. Northern
white singers were trying hard, valiantly, to sing like Negroes. The noises went on a long time. "WRYK...CK...
coming to you through the courtesy of ... change your underwear ... get some new underwear....

"Brush your teeth. Go to your dentist.

"Courtesy of."

Chicago, St. Louis, New York, Langdon, Georgia.

What do you suppose is going on in Chicago to-night?
Is it hot up there?

"The exact time is now ten-nineteen."

The judge, awakening suddenly, turned off the machine
and stumbled off to bed. Another day had gone.

There were too many days, Ethel thought. There she
was, in that house, in that town. Now her father had become
afraid of her. She knew how he felt.

He had brought her back there. He had schemed and
saved. Her going away to school, staying away for several
years, had cost money. Then, at last this position had come
up. She had become the librarian of the town. Did she owe
something to him, to the town because of him?

To be respectable ... as he was.

"To hell with that."

She had come back there to where she had lived as a
girl, where she had gone to high school. When she had first
come home her father had wanted to talk to her. He had
even looked forward to her coming, thinking they might
be companions.

"He and I pals." Spirit of Rotary. "I make a pal of my son. I make a pal of my daughter. She and I are pals." He was angry and resentful. "She is going to make a fool of me," he thought.

It was because of men. Men were after Ethel. He knew it.

She had begun running about with a mere boy, but that wasn't all. Since she had come home, another man had been attracted to her.

He was an older man, a man much older than herself and his name was Tom Riddle.

He was a lawyer of the town, a criminal lawyer and he had made money. He was an alert scheming man, a Republican and a politician. He handled Federal patronage in that part of the State. He was no gentleman.

And he had been attracted to Ethel. "Yes," her father would be thinking, "she would have to go and attract one of that sort." When she had been in town some weeks he came to see her at the library, coming boldly up to her. There had been none of the shyness of the boy, Red Oliver, in him. "I want to talk with you," he had said to Ethel, looking directly into her eyes. He was a rather tall man of forty-five with thin hair, turning gray, and with a heavy pock-marked face and small bright eyes. He had been married, but his wife was dead, had been dead for ten years. Although he was said to be tricky and was not respected by some of the outstanding men of town—men like Ethel's father, who being Georgians were Democrats and gentlemen—he was the most successful lawyer in town.

He was the most successful criminal lawyer in that part of the State. He was alive, sly and clever in the court room and the other lawyers and the judge were both afraid and envious of him. It was said he made money out of the distribution of Federal patronage. "He consorts with niggers and cheap whites," his enemies said, but Tom Riddle didn't seem to care. He laughed. Since the coming of prohibition his practice had grown enormously. He owned the best hotel in Langdon and had other property scattered about town.

And this man had become enamored of Ethel. "You suit me," he said to her. He invited her to go riding with him in his car and she went. It was another way of annoying her father, being seen in public with that man. She did not want that. That wasn't her purpose. It seemed inevitable.

And there was Blanche. Was she merely malicious? Had she taken some queer perverted kind of fancy to Ethel?

Although she herself seemed to care nothing for clothes, she had a constant interest in Ethel's clothes. "You are going to be with a man. Do put on the red gown." A queer look in her eyes ... hatred ... love. If Judge Long did not know of Ethel's going about with Tom Riddle, being seen with him in public, Blanche would let him know.

Tom Riddle did not attempt to make love to her. He was patient, shrewd, determined. "Why, I do not expect you to fall in love with me," he said one evening, when they were riding over the red Georgia roads past a pine forest. The red road ran up and down over low hills. Tom Riddle stopped the car at the edge of the forest. "You wouldn't expect me to grow sentimental, but I do sometimes," he said laughing. Beyond the forest the sun was going down. He referred to the loveliness of the evening. It was late on a summer evening, one of the evenings when the library was not open. All of the land in that part of Georgia was red and the sun was setting in a red haze. It was hot. Tom had stopped the car and had got out, to stretch. He was clad in a white suit, somewhat soiled. He lighted a cigar and spat on the ground. "Pretty grand, isn't it?" he said to Ethel, who was sitting in the car, a sport roadster painted a bright yellow and with the top down. He walked up and down and then came and stood by the car.

He had, from the beginning, a way of saying ... without saying, without words ... his eyes said it ... his manner said it ... "We understand each other ... we should understand each other."

It was tantalizing. It interested Ethel. He began talking of the Southern country, of his love for it. "I guess you know about me," he said. The man was said to have come from a good Georgia family in a neighboring county. Formerly his people had owned slaves. They had been people of some importance. They had been ruined by the Civil War. By the time Tom had come into the world they had nothing.

He had managed in some way to escape the slavery of the soil in that country and had got himself educated sufficiently to become a lawyer. Now he was a prosperous man. He had been married and his wife had died.

There had been two children, both sons, and they were dead. One had died in infancy and the other, like Ethel's brother, had been killed in the World War.

"I married when I was a mere boy," he said to Ethel. It was queer being with him. In spite of a rather rough exterior, something hard-boiled in his attitude toward life, he had a quick sharp trick of intimacy.

He had got it dealing with many people. There was something in his manner that said ... "I'm not good, not even honest ... I'm a man like you.

"I do things. I pretty much do as I please.

"Don't come to me expecting to find any Southern gentleman ... like Judge Long ... like Clay Barton ... like Tom Shaw." It was a manner he continually used in the court room with juries. Jurymen were, almost always, just common enough, ordinary men. "Well, here we are," he seemed to be saying to the men he addressed. "There are certain legal formalities to be gone through here but we are men together. Life is so and so. So and so has happened. There is a sensible view to be taken of this matter. We common dubs have to stand together." A grin. "Here is how I believe men like you and me feel. We are sensible men. We have to take life as it comes."

He had been married and his wife had died. He told Ethel frankly about it. "I want you for my wife," he said. "You are, of course, not in love with me. I do not expect it. How could you be?" He told her of his marriage. "To be frank with you, it was a shot-gun marriage." He laughed. "I was a boy and had gone to Atlanta where I was trying to work my way through school. I met her.

"I guess I was in love with her. I wanted her. The chance came and I took her."

He knew of the feeling Ethel had got for the young man, Red Oliver. He was the sort of man who would know everything that went on in a town.

He himself had defied the town. He had always done that. "While my wife was alive, I behaved," he said to Ethel. He had become, in that queer way, without her asking it, without her doing anything to lead him on, intimate with her about his own life without asking anything of the sort of her. When they were together he talked while she sat beside him and listened. He had big shoulders that were slightly stooped. Although she was a tall woman, he was nearly a head taller.

"So I married the woman. I thought I ought to marry her. She was in the family way." He said it as one might say ... "She was a blonde, or a brunette." He took it for granted she wouldn't be shocked. She liked that. "I wanted to marry her. I wanted a woman, needed one. Maybe I was in love. I don't know." The man Tom Riddle talked to Ethel in that way. He stood beside the car and spat on the ground. He lit a cigar.

He did not try to touch her. He made her comfortable. He made her want to talk.

"I could tell him everything, all the mean low-down things in myself," she thought sometimes.

"She was the daughter of a man in whose house I had a room. He was a workingman. He fired the boilers in some sort of a manufacturing plant. She helped her mother take care of the rooms in a rooming house.

"I began to want her. There was something in her eyes. She thought she wanted me." Again laughter. Was he laughing at himself or the woman he had married?

"My chance came. One night we were alone together in the house and I got her into my room."

Tom Riddle laughed. He told Ethel as though they had been intimate for a long time. It was odd, amusing . . . it was nice. After all, in Langdon, Georgia, she was the daughter of her father. It would have been impossible for Ethel's father ever in his whole life to have talked so frankly to a woman. He would never, even after long years of living with her, have dared talk so frankly to Ethel's mother or to Blanche, his new wife. It would have been a bit more in the picture of Southern womanhood—after all she was a Southern woman, of a so-called good family—to have been a bit shocked. Ethel wasn't. Tom Riddle had known she wouldn't be. How much did he know about her?

It wasn't as though she wanted him . . . as a woman is presumed to want a man . . . the dream . . . the poetry of existence. To be stirred, aroused, awakened, Ethel could be stirred by the younger man, Red Oliver. She was stirred by him.

Although Tom Riddle took her out in his car a dozen times that summer he never offered to make love to her. He did not attempt to hold her hand or to kiss her. "Why, you are a grown woman. Besides being a woman, you are a person," he seemed to be saying. It was sure she had no physical impulse toward him. He knew that. "Not yet." He could be patient. "It's all right. Perhaps that will come. We'll see." He had told her about life with his first wife. "She had no flair," he said. "She had no flair, no style, there was nothing she could do to my house. She was a good woman, all right. She could not do anything to me or to the children I had by her.

"I began to play about. I have been doing that for a long time. I guess you know I am tired of it."

There were all sorts of stories running about town. Since Tom Riddle had come to Langdon, as a young man, and had set up a law practice there, he had always been in with the rougher elements of the town. He was in thick with them. They were his friends. His cronies from the beginning of his life in Langdon had been gamblers, young Southern men who had taken to drink, politicians.

Formerly, when there were saloons in the town, he was always in the saloons. Respectable men of the town said he conducted his law office from a saloon. At one time he had taken up with a woman, the wife of a railroad conductor. Her husband was much away from town and she rode openly about in Tom Riddle's car. The affair had been conducted with startling boldness. When the husband was in town, Tom Riddle went nevertheless to his house. He drove there and went in. The woman had a child and the town said it was Tom Riddle's child. "It is," they said.

"Tom Riddle has bought her husband off."

It had gone on for a long time, and then, suddenly, the railroad conductor was transferred to another division and he and his wife, with the child, had left town.

So Tom Riddle was that kind of man. Ethel lay in her bed on a hot summer night thinking of him and of things he had said to her. He had made an offer of marriage. "Any time you think well of it, O. K."

A grin. He was tall and stoop-shouldered. He had a queer little trick of occasionally shaking his shoulders—as though to shake off a burden.

"You will not be in love," he said. "I am not the sort that could inspire romantic love in a woman.

"What, with my pock-marked face, my bald head?

"You may get tired of living in that house." He meant her father's house. "You may get tired of that woman your father has married."

Tom Riddle had been frank enough about his reasons for wanting her. "You have style. You would decorate a man's life. It would be worth while making money for you. I like making money. I like the game of it. If you can make up your mind to come live with me, then afterwards, after we begin living together.... Something tells me we are made for each other." He had wanted to say something about Ethel's passion for the younger man, Red Oliver, but had been too shrewd to do so. "He is too young for you, my dear. He is too immature. You have a flair for him now but it will pass.

"If you feel like experimenting with him, go on and do it." Could he have thought that?

He hadn't said so. One day he came for Ethel when there was a ball game to be played between the Langdon mill team, the one on which Red Oliver was playing, and a team from a neighboring town. The Langdon team won and it was largely Red's playing that had made them win. The game was held on one of the long summer evenings and Tom Riddle took Ethel in his car. It wasn't just his interest in the baseball game. She was sure of that. She had begun to like being with him, although she felt in his presence none of the quick physical longings she felt in Red Oliver's presence.

On the very evening before the ball game, Red Oliver had been in the library, sitting at a table in there, and he had run his hand through his thick hair. There had been a quick stab of desire in Ethel. She wanted to run her hand through his hair, hold him close. She took a step toward him. It would be so easy to sweep him away. He was young and sex hungry for her. She knew that.

Tom Riddle did not take Ethel to the grounds where the game was played but stopped his car on a nearby hill. She sat beside him wondering. He seemed for the moment quite lost in admiration of the younger man's playing. Was it a bluff?

It had been a day when Red Oliver had played sensationally. Balls came singing down toward him over the hard clay infield and he fielded them brilliantly. He led his team at bat, once, at a critical moment, knocking out a three base hit, and Tom Riddle squirmed in his car seat. "He's the best player we ever had in this town," Tom said. Could he really be like that, wanting Ethel for himself, knowing of her feeling for Red and, at the time, could he be carried away by Red's playing?

*

HAD he wanted Ethel to experiment? She had done it. On the hot summer night, as she lay, quite naked, on her bed in her room, unable to sleep, nervous and excited, the windows of the room open, hearing from outside the noises of the Southern night, hearing the steady heavy snoring of her father in a neighboring room, herself upset, angry with herself, on that very evening she had carried it through.

She was angry, upset, annoyed. "Why did I do it?" It had been easy enough. There had been the young man, really in her eyes a boy, walking along the street with her. It had been one of the evenings when the library was not officially open but she had gone back there. She was thinking of Tom Riddle and of the proposal he had made to her. Could a woman do that, go to live with a man, lie with him, be his wife . . . as a sort of bargain? He had seemed to think it would be all right.

"I won't crowd you.

"After all, beauty in a man cuts little figure to a woman.

"It is a question of living, of everyday living.

"There is a kind of friendship achieved that is something more than a friendship. It is a kind of partnership.

"It grows into something else."

Tom Riddle talking. It was as though he addressed a jury. He had big lips and his face was heavily pock-marked. Sometimes he leaned toward her, talking earnestly. "A man gets tired going it alone," he said. He had an idea. He had been married. Ethel did not remember his first wife. The Riddle house was in another part of town. It was a fine house on a poor street. There was a large lawn. Tom Riddle had built his house among the houses of the sort of people with whom he associated. They were certainly not the first families of Langdon.

When the wife was alive she seldom left her own house. She must have been one of the meek mouse-like kind who devote themselves to housekeeping. When Tom Riddle had prospered he had built his house on that street. Once it had been a very respectable neighborhood. There had been an old house that had belonged to one of the so-called aristocratic families of the old days, before the Civil War. There had been a big yard going down to a small creek that tumbled down into the river below the town. The whole yard had become overgrown with dense bushes he had cleared away. He always had men working about his place. Often he took the cases of poor whites or Negroes who had got into trouble with the law, and if they couldn't pay him he let them work out the fee on the place.

Tom had said of his first wife, "Well, I married her. I just about had to." After all, and in spite of the life he had led Tom was still, in his own way, an aristocrat at bottom. He had contempt. He didn't care for the respectable standards of others and did not go to church. He laughed at churchgoing people like Ethel's father and when the K.K.K. was strong in Langdon he had laughed at that.

He had got a sense of something that was more Northern than Southern. That was the reason he was a Republican. "There is always some class going to rule," he said once to Ethel, speaking of his Republicanism. "Of course," he said, laughing cynically, "I make money by it."

"Just the same, in our day in America it is money that rules. The big money crowd in the North, in New York, have picked the Republican Party. They are betting on that. I am stringing with them.

"Life is a game," he said.

"There are the poor whites. To a man they are Democrats." He laughed. "Do you remember what happened a few
years ago?" Ethel remembered. He spoke of a particularly
brutal lynching. It had happened in a small town, not far
from Langdon. A lot of people from Langdon had gone there
to take part in it. It had happened at night and people had
gone in cars. The Negro, accused of the rape of a poor
white girl, the daughter of a small farmer, was being
brought to the county seat by the sheriff. The sheriff had two
deputies with him and a string of cars had gone down along
the road to meet him. The cars were filled with young men
from Langdon, merchants and respectables. There were
Fords, filled with poor white employees of the Langdon
cotton mills. It had been a kind of circus, a public entertain-
ment, Tom said. "Nice, eh!"

Not all of the men who went to the lynching had a part
in it. It had happened while Ethel was a student in Chicago.
Afterwards it turned out that the girl, who said she had been
raped, was abnormal. She was of low mentality. A good
many men, whites and blacks, had already been with her.

They took the Negro from the sheriff and his deputies
and strung him up to a tree, riddled his body with bullets.
Then they burned his body. "They seemed unable to let it
alone," Tom said. He laughed, a cynical laugh. Many of the
best people went.

They stood to one side, looking on, seeing the Negro
man . . . he was a huge black. . . . "He would go two hundred
and fifty pounds," Tom said, laughing. He spoke as though
the Negro man were a hog butchered by the crowd, as a kind
of holiday performance . . . respectable men going down to
see it done, standing at the edge of the crowd. Life in Langdon was what it was.

"They look down on me. Let them."

He could put men or women on the witness stand in
court, torture them mentally. It was a game. He liked it. He

could twist what they had said, lead them into saying things they didn't mean.

The law was a game. All of life was a game.

He had got his house. He had made money. He liked to go to New York several times a year.

He wanted a woman who would decorate his life. He wanted Ethel as he might have wanted a fine horse.

"Why not? Life is like that."

Was it a proposal for a kind of whoredom, a kind of high-class whoredom? Ethel was puzzled.

She had resisted. She had left the house that night because she could not bear being either with her father or with Blanche. Blanche also had a kind of talent. She had noted everything about Ethel, what clothes she wore, the mood she was in. Now her father had become afraid of his daughter, of what she might do. He took it out in silence, sitting at table in the Long house, saying nothing. He knew about her going to ride with Tom Riddle and walking through the streets with young Red.

Red Oliver had become a mill hand and Tom Riddle was a shady lawyer.

She was endangering his own position in the town, his own dignity.

And there was Blanche, amused, really pleased because her husband was displeased. It had got to that with Blanche. She lived by the discomfiture of others.

Ethel had left the house in disgust. It was a hot cloudy evening. On that evening her body was tired and she had to make an effort to walk with her accustomed dignity, to keep her feet from dragging. She went through Main Street toward the library, just off Main Street. Black clouds were drifting across an evening sky.

There were people gathered in Main Street. On that evening Ethel saw Tom Shaw, the little man who was president of the cotton mill where Red Oliver worked. He was being driven hurriedly through Main Street. There was a

train going North. Very likely he was off to New York. A
Negro man drove the big car. Ethel thought of something
Tom Riddle had said. "There goes the Prince," Tom had
said. "Hello, there goes the Prince of Langdon." In the new
South Tom Shaw was the sort of man who had become the
prince, the leader.

There was a woman, a young woman, going through
Main Street. Once she had been Ethel's friend. They had
gone to high school together. She had married a young merchant. Now she was hurrying homeward, pushing a baby
carriage. She was round and plump.

She and Ethel had been friends. Now they were ac-
quaintances. They smiled and bowed coldly to each other.

Ethel hurried along the street. In Main Street, near the
court house, she was joined by Red Oliver.

"May I walk with you?"

"Yes."

"Are you going to the library?"

"Yes."

Silence. Thoughts. The young man was hot, like the
night. "He's too young, too young. I don't want him."

She saw Tom Riddle standing with other men before a
store.

He had seen her with the boy. The boy had seen him
standing there. Thoughts in them. Red Oliver was embarrassed by her silence. He was hurt, afraid. He wanted a
woman. He thought he wanted her.

Ethel's thoughts. One night in Chicago. A man ... once
in her rooming-house in Chicago ... just an ordinary man
... a big strong fellow ... he had quarreled with his wife ...
he was living there. "Am I common? Am I just dirt?"

It was on just such a hot rainy night. He had a room on
the same floor of the house on lower Michigan Avenue. He
had been after Ethel. Red Oliver was after her now.

He got her. It happened suddenly, unexpectedly.

And Tom Riddle.

She was alone on that floor of the house that night in Chicago and he ... that other man ... just a man, a male, nothing more ... and he was there.

Ethel had never understood that in herself. She was tired. She had dined that evening in a noisy hot cafeteria, as she thought, among noisy ugly people. Were they ugly or was she? For the time she was disgusted with herself, disgusted with her life in the city.

She had gone to her room and had not locked her door. That man had seen her go in there. He was sitting in his own room with the door open. He was big and strong.

She had gone to her room and had thrown herself on the bed. There were such moments came to her. She did not care what happened. She wanted something to happen. He came boldly in. There had been a short struggle, not at all like the struggle with the advertising man Fred Wells.

She surrendered ... let it happen. Afterwards he wanted to do something for her, take her to a theatre, take her to dine. She could not bear seeing him. It had stopped like that, abruptly as it had begun. "I was such a fool to think anything could be got at in that way, as though I were just an animal, nothing else, as though I wanted just that."

Ethel went to the library and, unlocking the door, went in. She left Red Oliver at the door. "Good night. Thank you," she said. She put up two windows, hoping to get a breath of air and lighted a desk lamp over her desk. She sat there, over the desk, leaning over, her head in her hands.

It went on a long time, thoughts traveling through her. Night came, a hot dark night. She was nervous, as she had been that night in Chicago, on just such another hot tired night, when she had taken that man she did not know ... it was strange she hadn't got into trouble ... got a child ... am I just a whore? ... how many women were as she was, blown about in life as she was ... did a woman need a man, some sort of anchor? There was Tom Riddle.

She thought of life in her father's house. Now her

father was upset and uncomfortable about her. There was
Blanche. Blanche felt actual enmity toward her husband.
There was no frankness. Blanche and her father had both
shot and both missed. "If I take a chance with Tom," Ethel
thought.

Blanche had taken a certain attitude toward herself. She
wanted to give Ethel money for clothes. She dropped little
hints about that, knowing Ethel's love of clothes. Perhaps she
merely let herself go as she did, neglecting her own clothes,
often not even bothering to be clean, to punish her husband.
She would have wormed money out of her husband and
would have given it to Ethel. She wanted to.

She wanted to touch Ethel with her hands, the hands
with dirty fingernails. She approached. "You are lovely,
dear, in that dress." She smiled, a funny cat-like little smile.
She made the house unhealthy. It was an unhealthy house.

"What would I do to Tom's house?"

Ethel was tired thinking. "You think and you think and
then you do something. Very likely you make a fool of yourself." It had grown dark in the street outside the library.
There was an occasional flash of lightning, lighting up the
room in which Ethel sat, the light from the little desk lamp
shining on her head, making her hair red, making it shine.
There came occasional peals of thunder.

*

YOUNG Red Oliver had been watching and waiting. He had
walked restlessly about. He had wanted to follow Ethel into
the library. Once, early in the evening, he opened the street
door softly and looked in. He had seen Ethel Long sitting
in there, her head in her arm, by her desk.

He had become frightened, had gone away, but he had
come back.

He had been thinking of her for days and for many
nights. After all, he was a boy, a nice boy. He was strong

and clean. "If I had seen him when I was myself young, if we had been of the same age." Ethel had thought sometimes.

At night, sometimes, when she could not sleep. She had not slept well since she had come back to the Long house. There was something about such a house. Something gets into the air of the house. It is in the walls, in the wall-paper on the walls, in the furniture, in the carpets on the floor. It is in the bed clothes, on which you are lying.

It hurts. It makes everything gigantic.

It is hatred, alive, watching, eager. It is a living thing. It is alive.

"Love," Ethel thought. Would she ever find that?

Sometimes, when she was alone in her room at night, when she could not sleep . . . she thought of young Red Oliver then. "Do I want him like that, just to have him, perhaps to quiet myself, as I had that man in Chicago?" She was there in her room, lying awake, pitching restlessly about.

She saw young Red Oliver sitting at a table in the library. Sometimes his eyes looked hungrily toward her. She was a woman. She could note what went on in him without letting him see what went on in her. He was trying to read a book.

He had gone to college in the North and had got ideas in his head. She could tell a good deal by the books he read. He had become a workman in the mill at Langdon; perhaps he was trying to get in with other workmen.

He might even want to fight their cause, the cause of working people. There were young men like that. They having a dream of a new world, as Ethel herself had had at moments in her life.

Tom Riddle not having such a dream. He would have laughed at the idea. "It is pure romanticism," he would have said. "People are not born equal. Some men are meant to be slaves, some masters. If they are not slaves in one way they will be in another.

"There are slaves to sex, to what they think is thought, to food, to drink.

"What difference does it make?"

Red Oliver would not have been like that. He was young and eager. Men had put ideas into his head.

He wasn't, however, all mind, all idealism. He wanted a woman, as Tom Riddle did, wanted Ethel; he thought he did. She had got fixed in his mind in that way. She knew it. She could tell it by his eyes, looking at her, by his embarrassments.

He was innocent, glad and ashamed. He came toward her hesitatingly, confused, wanting to touch her, hold her, kiss her. Blanche came toward her sometimes.

Red's coming, his emotions coming toward her, left Ethel feeling rather nice, a little stirred, often a good deal stirred. At night, when she was restless and couldn't sleep, she, in fancy, saw him as she had seen him playing ball.

He was running furiously. He had got the ball. His body fell into balance. He was like an animal, like a cat.

Or he was standing at bat. He stood poised. There was something in him delicately adjusted, delicately timed. "I want that. Am I just greedy, ugly, a greedy woman?" The ball came toward him swiftly. Tom Riddle had explained to Ethel how the ball was made to curve as it approached the batsman.

Ethel sat up in bed. Something within her ached. "Would it do him harm? I wonder." She got a book and tried to read. "No, I will not let it happen."

There were older women, with boys, Ethel had heard. It was odd, the notion many men had, that women were inherently nice. Some of them at least got ugly, were filled with blind desires.

The South, Southern men always being romantic about women . . . never giving them a chance really . . . getting off patter. Tom Riddle was certainly a relief.

in the library that night it had happened, suddenly, quickly as it did that time with the strange man in Chicago. It wasn't like that. Perhaps Red Oliver had been standing for some time just outside the library door.

The library was in an old house, just off Main Street. It had belonged to some old pre-Civil War slave-owning family, or to a rich merchant. There was a little flight of steps.

The rain that had been threatening all evening came. It was a fierce summer rain accompanied by a high wind. It threshed against the walls of the library building. There were loud peals of thunder and sharp flashes of lightning.

It might have been the storm that had affected Ethel that evening. Young Oliver had been waiting for her, just outside the library door. People passing along the street would have seen him standing there. He had thought . . . "I'll walk home with her."

A young man's dreams. Red Oliver was a young idealist; he had in him the making of one.

Men like her father began like that.

More than once, as she sat that night at her desk, her head in her hands, the young man opened the door softly to look in.

He stepped in. The rain drove him in. He had not dared to disturb her.

Afterwards Ethel thought that on that evening she had suddenly become again the young girl—half girl, half tomboy—who had once gone to a tough little boy in a field. When the door opened, admitting young Red Oliver into the large main room of the library, a room that had been made by tearing out walls, there came with him a heavy gust of rain. Already rain was pouring into the room from the two windows Ethel had opened. She looked up and saw him standing there, in the dim light. At first she could not see distinctly, but at that moment there was a flash of lightning.

She got up and walked toward him. "So," she thought. "Shall I? Yes, I will."

She was living again as she had lived that night when her father had come into the field, when he had suspected her, when he had put his hands on her. "He is not here now," she thought. She thought of Tom Riddle. "He isn't here. He wants to conquer me, make something of me I am not." She was in rebellion again now, was doing something, not because it was something she wanted but to defy something.

Her father . . . and perhaps Tom Riddle too.

She walked toward Red Oliver, who stood by the door, a little frightened. "Is there something the matter?" he asked. "Shall I close the windows?" She did not answer. "No," she said. "Am I going to do this?" she asked herself.

"It will be like that man who came to my room in Chicago. No, it will not be like that. I will be the one who does it.

"I want to."

She had got quite close to the young man. A queer weakness came into her body. She fought it. She put her hands on Red Oliver's shoulders and let herself half fall forward. "Please," she said.

She was against him.

"What?"

"You know," she said. It was like that. She could feel the life surging up in him. "Here? Now?" He was trembling.

"Yes." The words weren't said.

"Here? Now?" He understood at last. He could scarcely speak, couldn't believe. He thought, "I'm lucky. How lucky I am!" His voice was husky. "There isn't any place. It can't be here."

"Yes." Again no need of words.

"Shall I close the windows, put out the light? Some one might see." The rain was threshing against the walls of the building. The building shook. "Quick," she said. "I don't care who sees us," she said.

It had been like that, and then afterwards Ethel had

driven young Red Oliver away. "You go now," she said.
She was even gentle, wanting to be motherly with him. "It
wasn't his fault." She half wanted to cry. "I must drive him
away or I will..." There was childish gratitude in him. She
had looked aside once... while it was happening... there
was something in his face... in his eyes... "If I had only
earned this"... it had all happened on a table in the library,
the table at which he was accustomed to sit, reading his books.
He had been there the afternoon before, reading Karl Marx.
She had ordered the book especially for him. "I'll pay for
it out of my own pocket if the library board objects," she had
thought. She had looked aside once and there was a man
passing in the street, his head thrust forward. He did not
look up. "It would be queer," she thought, "if it was Tom
Riddle...

"Or father."

"There is a good deal of Blanche in me," she thought.
"I dare say I could hate well."

She wondered if she could ever love well. "I don't
know," she said to herself as she led Red to the door. She
was at once getting tired of him. He was saying something
about love, protesting awkwardly, persistently, as though not
sure, as though he had been rebuffed. He was queerly
ashamed. She was silently confused.

Already she was sorry for him, for what she had done.
"Well, I did it. I wanted to. I did it." She did not say that
aloud. She kissed Red, a cold forbidding little kiss. A story
popped into her head, a story some one had told her once.

It was about a prostitute who saw somewhere, on a public street, a man who had been with her during the night before. The man bowed and spoke pleasantly to her, and she
was angry, indignant and said to a companion, "Did you see
that? Imagine his speaking to me here. Just because I was
with him at night, what right has he to speak to me in the
daytime and in the public street?"

Ethel smiled thinking of the story. "I may be a pros-

titute myself," she was thinking. "I am." Perhaps all women
had somewhere, hidden away in themselves, like the marbling
in fine meat, a strain of something ... (desire for complete
abandon?)

"I want to be alone," she said. "To-night I want to walk
home alone." He went awkwardly out of the door. He was
confused ... in some queer way his manhood had been assaulted. She knew that.

Now he felt baffled, confused, impotent. How could the
woman, after what had happened ... so suddenly ... after
much thinking and hoping and dreaming on his part ... he
had even thought of marriage, of proposing marriage to her
... if he could get up courage ... what had happened had
been her work ... the boldness had all been hers ... how could
she, after that, dismiss him like that?

The summer storm that had been threatening all afternoon and that had been so violent was passing quickly. It
was perplexing to Ethel but, even at that moment, she knew
that she was going to marry Tom Riddle.

If he would have her.

* * *

ETHEL did not know it definitely at that moment, in the moment, after Red had left her, after she had got him out
through the door and was alone. There was a sharp little reaction, half shame, half remorse ... a little flow of thoughts
she didn't want ... they came singly, then in little clusters
... thoughts can be lovely little winged things ... they can be
sharp little stinging things.

Thoughts ... as though a boy had run along the dark
night street of Langdon, Georgia, with a handful of little
stones. He stopped in the dark street outside the library. The
little stones were thrown. They came rattling sharply against
a window.

Thoughts like that.

She had brought a light rain-coat with her and went and put it on. She was tall. She was slender. She began doing the little trick Tom Riddle did. She straightened her shoulders. Beauty has a queer trick with women. It is a quality. It plays about in the penumbra. It settles suddenly upon them, sometimes when they think they have been most ugly. She turned out the one light, the one over her own desk, and went to stand near the door. "Things pass like that," she thought. There had been for some weeks this desire in her. The young man, Red Oliver, was nice. He had been half frightened, eager. He had kissed her eagerly with half-frightened hunger, her lips, her neck. It had been nice. It had been not-nice. He had been convinced by her. He had not been convinced. "I am a man and have got a woman. I am not a man. I have not got her."

No, it hadn't been nice. There had been no real surrender in her. All the time she had known ... "All the time I knew how it would be after it had happened, if I let it happen," she told herself. Everything had been in her own hands.

"I have done something not nice to him."

People were perpetually doing it to each other. It wasn't just this one thing ... two bodies clasp together trying that.

People did harm to each other. Her father had done it to his second wife, Blanche, and in turn now Blanche was trying to do it to her father. What an ugly jam ... Ethel was mellow now.... There was softness, regret. She wanted to cry.

"I wish I were a little girl." Little memories. She was a little girl again. She saw herself as a little girl.

Her own mother was alive. She was with her mother. They were walking in a street. Her mother held the hand of the girl child that was Ethel. "Was I that child once? Why did life do it to me?"

"Now don't be blaming life. Damn self-pity."

There was a tree, in spring wind, in early April wind. The leaves on the tree played. They danced.

She was standing in the dark large room of the library, near the door, the door through which young Red Oliver had just disappeared. "My lover? No!" Already she had forgotten him. She stood there thinking of something else. It was very quiet in the street outside. After the rain the Georgia night would be cooler, but it would still be hot. Now the heat would be damp and heavy. Although the rain had passed there were still occasional flashes of lightning, faint flashes, coming from far off now, from the receding storm. She had spoiled her relations with the young Langdon man who had been in love with her, who had had a passionate desire for her. She knew that. It might go out of him now. He might not have it any more. No more dreams of her at night—in him . . . hunger . . . wanting . . . for her.

If, for him, in him, for some other woman, now, presently. Had she also spoiled her relations with the room in which she worked? A little shudder ran through her and she went quickly outside.

It was to be an eventful night in Ethel's life. When she got outside she thought at first she was alone. At least the chances were that no one would ever know what had happened. Did she care? She didn't care. She did care.

When you are a mess inside, you don't want any one to know. You straighten your shoulders. Push against it. Push against it. Push. Push.

"Everybody doing it. Everybody doing it.

"For Christ's sweet sake be merciful to me, a sinner." The library building was just off Main Street and at the corner of Main Street there was a tall old brick building with a clothing store on the ground floor and a hall above. The hall was the meeting place of some lodge and there was an open stairway leading up. Ethel walked along the street and when she came to the stairway she saw a man standing there, half hidden in the darkness. He stepped toward her.

It was Tom Riddle.

He was there standing. He was there coming.

"Another?

"I might with him too . . . be a whore, take them all.

"Damn. To hell with all of them.

"So," she thought. "He has been watching." She wondered how much he had seen.

If he had come down past the library, during the storm. If he had looked in. It seemed unlike what she thought of him. "I saw a light in the library and then I saw it go out," he said, simply. He lied. He had seen the younger man, Red Oliver, go into the library.

Then he had seen the light go out. There was a hurt in him.

"I have no rights over her. I want her."

His own life wasn't so nice. He knew. "We might begin. I might learn, even to love."

His own thoughts.

The younger man, leaving the library, had passed quite close to him, but had not seen him standing in a hallway. He had drawn himself back.

"What right have I prying on her? She has promised me nothing."

There had been something. There was a light, a street light. He had seen young Red Oliver's face. It wasn't the face of a satisfied lover.

It was the face of a puzzled boy. Gladness in the man. A queer not understandable sadness in the man, not for himself, but for the other.

"I thought you would be coming along," he said to Ethel. He was walking along beside her now. He was silent. They walked thus through Main Street and got presently into the residential street at the end of which Ethel lived.

There had come a reaction in Ethel now. She was even frightened. "What a fool I was, what a damn fool! I've spoiled everything. I have spoiled things with that boy and with this man."

After all, a woman is a woman. She wants a man.

"She can be such a fool, throwing herself away, throwing herself here and there, so that no man will want her.

"Now don't blame that boy. You did it. You did it."

It might be that Tom Riddle had suspected something. It might have been his test of her. She did not want to believe that. There was a way in which this man, this so-called hard-boiled man, obviously a realist, if there could be such a thing among Southern men . . . there was a way in which he had already won her respect. If she was to lose him. She did not want to lose him, because—out of weariness and perplexity—she had been a fool again.

Tom Riddle walked along beside her in silence. Although she was tall, for a woman, he was taller. In the light of the street lights through which they passed she tried to look at his face without his knowing that she was looking, that she was anxious. Did he know? Was he judging her? Drops of water from the recent heavy rain kept pattering down from the shade trees under which they walked. They had got through Main Street. It was deserted. There were little pools of water on the sidewalks and water, shining and yellow in the lights from corner street lamps, ran in the gutters.

At one place there was no walk. There had been a brick walk but it had been taken up. A new cement walk was to be laid. They had to walk in wet sand. A thing happened. Tom Riddle started to take Ethel's arm and then he didn't take it. There was a little hesitant shy movement. It touched something in her.

There was a moment . . . a little passing thing. "If he, this one, is like that, he can be like that."

It was an idea, faint, drifting across her mind. Some man, older than herself, more mature.

To know that she, like any woman, perhaps like any man, wanted ... wanted nobility, cleanliness.

"If he knew and forgave me, I would hate him.

"There has been too much hatred. I don't want any more."

Could he, this older man ... could he know why she had taken the boy ... he was a boy really ... Red Oliver ... and knowing, could he ... not blame ... not forgive ... not think of himself in the impossibly noble position of being one to forgive?

She grew desperate. "I wish I hadn't done it. I wish I hadn't done it," she thought. She tried something. "Were you ever in a certain position ..." she said to Tom Riddle ... "I mean going ahead and doing something you wanted to do and at the same time didn't want to do ... that you knew you didn't want to do ... and didn't know?"

It was a fool question. She was frightened by her own words. "If he suspects something, if he saw that boy come out of the library, I am only confirming his suspicion."

She was frightened by her own words, but went ahead hurriedly. "There was something you were ashamed of doing, but wanted to do and knew that after you had done it you would be more ashamed."

"Yes," he said quietly, "a thousand times. I'm always doing it." They walked in silence after that until they got to the Long house. He did not try to detain her. She was curious and excited. "If he knows and can take it like this, really wanting me as his wife, as he says, he is something new in my experience of men." There was a little warm feeling. "Is it possible? We are neither of us good people, do not want to be good." Now she was identifying herself with him. At table in the Long house, sometimes nowadays, her father spoke of this man, of Tom Riddle. He did not address his remarks to his daughter, but to Blanche. Blanche encouraged it. She mentioned Tom Riddle. "How many loose women has that man had?" When Blanche asked that she looked up

quickly at Ethel. "I am only goading him on. He's just a
fool man. I want to see him blow himself up—with wind."

Her eyes saying that to Ethel. "We women understand.
Men are only foolish windy children." There would be some
such question thrust out, Blanche wanting to put her husband in a certain position in relation to Ethel, wanting a little
to bother Ethel ... there was the fiction carried on that
Ethel's father did not know of the lawyer's interest in his
daughter....

If the man, Tom Riddle, had known of that, he might
perhaps only have been amused.

"You women settle it ... settle your own goodness, your
own badness."

"A man walking, being, eating, sleeping ... unafraid of
men ... unafraid of women.

"Not having too much bunk in him. Every man would
have to have some. You could forgive some.

"Don't expect too much. Life is full of bunk. We eat it,
sleep it, dream it, breathe it." There was a chance that, for
such men as her father, the good solid men of the town, Tom
Riddle had his own kind of contempt ... "as I have," Ethel
thought.

Stories told about the man, his bold running about with
loose women, his being a Republican, making deals about
Federal patronage, handling Negro delegates at national conventions of the Republican Party, being in with gamblers,
horsy men ... He must have been into all sorts of what
were called, "crooked political deals," fighting all the time a
queer battle in life in that so-smug religious, portentous
Southern community. In the South every man seemed to hold
up as his ideal what he called, "being a gentleman." Tom
Riddle, if he were the Tom Riddle Ethel had now begun to
build up, was suddenly building up that night as he walked
with her, would have laughed at that idea. "Gentleman, hell.
You ought to know what I know." Now suddenly she could

imagine his saying that, without much bitterness, taking a kind of hypocrisy in the others for granted ... not being made too sore, too resentful by it. He had said he wanted her as his wife, and dimly she now understood, or suddenly hoped, she was realizing what he had meant.

He even wanted to be tender with her, surround her with a sort of elegance. If he suspected ... he must at least have seen Red Oliver coming out of the dark library but a few minutes before she came out ... since she had seen him earlier in the evening in the street.

Had he been watching her?

Could he understand something else ... that she had wanted to try something out, find out something?

He had taken her to see that young man play baseball. The name of Red Oliver had never been mentioned between them. Had he taken her there, merely to watch her? ... to find out something about her?

"Maybe you know now."

She was resentful. The feeling passed. She was not resentful.

He had implied, or even said, that, in asking her to marry him, he wanted something definite. He wanted her because he thought she had style. "You are nice. It's nice walking beside a proud fine woman. You say to yourself, 'she's mine.'

"It's nice having her in your house.

"A man feels himself more the man having a fine woman he can call his woman."

He had worked and schemed to get money. Obviously his first wife had been something of a frump, pretty dull. Now he had a fine house and wanted a partner in life who would run his house in a certain style, who knew clothes and could wear clothes. He wanted people to be aware....

"Look. That's Tom Riddle's wife."

"She sure has style, hasn't she? There is some class to that one."

For the same reason perhaps that such a man might like to own a stable of race horses, wanting the best, the fastest. It had been frankly such a proposal. "Let's not be romantic or sentimental. We both want something. I can help you and you can help me." He hadn't used exactly these words. They were implied.

If he could feel now, even if he knew what had happened on that evening, if he could feel.... "I haven't got you yet. You are free yet. If we make a deal I will expect you to stick to your side of the bargain.

"If, knowing what had happened, if he did know, could feel like that."

All of these thoughts running through Ethel's head during the walk homeward with Tom Riddle that evening, he saying nothing. She was nervous and excited. There was a low picket fence before Judge Long's house and he stopped at the gate. It was rather dark. She fancied he was smiling, as though he knew her thoughts. She had made another man feel ineffectual, unsuccessful with her, in spite of what had happened . . . in spite of the thing that was presumed to make a man, any man, feel very manly and strong.

Now she was feeling ineffectual. At the gate that night Tom Riddle said something. She had been wondering how much he knew. He knew nothing. What had happened in the library had happened during a violent rainstorm. To have seen he would have had to creep through the rain to a window. Now suddenly she remembered that, as they had walked through Main Street, some section of her brain had noted that fact, that the rain-coat he had on was not very wet.

He wasn't the sort who would creep to a window. "Now wait," Ethel said to herself that night. "He might even have done that, if he had thought of it, if he had been suspicious, if he had wanted to do it.

"I am not going to begin by setting him up as some sort of nobleman.

"After what has happened it would make him impossible for me."

At that it might have been rather a fine test of a man, of a man with this man's realistic viewpoint on life ... to have seen that ... another man and the woman he wanted. ...

What would he tell himself? How much figure would what he thought her style, her class, how much figure would it cut then?

"It would have been rather too much. He couldn't have stood it. No man could stand it. If I were a man, I wouldn't.

"We go along, hurting, slowly educating ourselves, fighting toward some sort of truth. It seems inevitable."

Tom Riddle was speaking to Ethel. "Good night. I can't help hoping you will decide to do it. I mean ... I'm waiting. I'll be waiting. I hope it won't be long.

"Come any time," he said. "I'm ready."

He leaned a little toward her. Was he going to try to kiss her. She wanted to cry out, "Wait. Not yet. I must have time to think."

He didn't. If he had in mind trying to kiss her, he changed his mind. His body straightened itself. There was that queer little gesture in him, a straightening of stooped shoulders, a pushing ... as though against life itself ... as though to say, "push up ... push up ..." to himself ... talking to himself ... like herself in that. "Good night," he said, and walked rapidly away.

*

"It begins. Will it never end?" Ethel thought that. She went into the house. There was that queer feeling, immediately she had got inside, that Blanche sensed that it had been an upsetting night for her.

Ethel was resentful. "At any rate, she couldn't know anything."

"Good night. What I have said goes." Tom Riddle's words also in Ethel's mind. It sounded as though he did know something, suspected something. . . . "I don't care. I hardly know whether or not I care," Ethel thought.

"Yes, I would care. If he is to know I'd rather tell him.

"But I am not close enough to him to go tell him things. I don't want a father confessor.

"Perhaps I do."

Evidently it was going to be a night of intensive self-consciousness for her. She went into her room, out of the hallway downstairs, where there was a light burning. It was dark upstairs where Blanche now slept. She took off her clothes hurriedly and threw them on a chair. Quite naked, she threw herself on the bed. There was a little light coming into the room, faintly, through a transom. She lit a cigarette but did not smoke. It tasted stale in the darkness and she got out of bed and put it out.

It wasn't quite out. There was a little pale insistent cigarette stink.

"Walk a mile for a Camel."

"Not a cough in a carload." It was to be a dark soft sticky Southern night after rain. She felt exhausted.

"Women. What things they are! What a thing I am!" she thought.

Was it because she was aware of Blanche, the other woman in that house, now perhaps awake in her room, also thinking. Ethel was herself trying to think her way through something. Her mind had got started. It wouldn't quit. She was tired and wanting to sleep, wanting to forget the experiences of the night in sleep, but she knew she couldn't sleep. If her affair with that boy, if it had come off, if it had been what she really had wanted. . . . "I might then have slept. I would have been at least a satisfied animal." Why was she now so suddenly conscious of that other woman in the house, that Blanche? Nothing to her really, her father's wife, "his problem, thank God, not mine," she thought. Why did she have the feeling that Blanche was awake, that she also was thinking, that she had been watching for the homecoming, had seen the man, Tom Riddle, at the gate with Ethel?

Her thoughts . . . "Where have they been in this storm? They aren't driving."

"Damn her and her thoughts," Ethel said to herself.

Blanche would be thinking that Ethel with Tom Riddle might get into some such position, as regards her man, she was herself in.

Was there something to be settled with her, as there had been with the young man, Red Oliver, as there was still something to be settled between herself and Tom Riddle? "Not to-night anyway, I hope. For God's sake not to-night."

"It's the limit. It's enough."

And anyway what was to be settled as between her and Blanche? "She is another woman. I am glad of that." She tried to put Blanche out of her mind.

She thought of the men now concerned in her life, of her father, of the young man Red Oliver, of Tom Riddle.

Of one thing she could be quite sure. Her father would never be much aware of what was going on about him. He was a man for whom life separated itself into broad lines, the good and the bad. He would make quick judgments always, as he decided cases in court. "You are guilty. You are not guilty."

For that reason, life, actual life, would always baffle him. It must always have done that. People wouldn't behave as he thought they should. With Ethel, his daughter, he had got puzzled and confused. He had got personal. "Is she trying to punish me? Is life trying to punish me?"

This because she, the daughter, had problems her father couldn't understand. He had never tried to get understanding. "How the hell does he think it comes to people, if it does come? Does he think certain people, good people, like himself, are born with it?

"What is wrong with my wife, Blanche? Why does she not behave as she should?

"Now there is my daughter, too. Why is she turning out like this?"

There was her father and there was the young man with whom she had suddenly dared be so intimate without really being intimate at all. She had let him make love to her. She had practically compelled him to make love to her.

There was a kind of sweetness in him, even a kind of cleanness. He had not been soiled as she had. . . .

She must have wanted his sweetness, his cleanness, had grabbed at it.

"Did I only succeed in soiling him, too?

"I know this. I grabbed, but I didn't get what I grabbed for."

*

ETHEL was feverish. It was a night. She wasn't through with the night yet.

It never rains but it pours. She was lying on the bed in the dark hot room. Her long slender body was stretched out there. There was a tension, little nerves crying out. The little nerves under her knees were taut. She raised her legs and kicked impatiently. She lay still.

She sat up stiffly in the bed. The door from the hallway had opened softly. Blanche had come into the room. She advanced halfway across the room. She was clad in a white night-gown. She whispered, "Ethel."

"Yes."

Ethel's voice was harsh. She was startled. In all of the communication between the two women, since Ethel had come home to Langdon to live, to be the town librarian, there had been a kind of play. It was half play, half something else. The two women had wanted to help each other. Was something else going to happen to Ethel now? She had a premonition. "Don't. Don't. Go away," she wanted to cry.

"To-night I did something not nice. Now something is going to be done to me." How did she know that?

Blanche was always wanting to touch her. She always got up late in the morning, after Ethel did. She had strange habits. At night, when Ethel was not at home, she went upstairs to her room early. What did she do up there? She did not sleep. Sometimes, at two or three in the morning, Ethel was awakened, hearing Blanche prowling about the house. She went to the kitchen and got food. In the morning she heard Ethel preparing to leave the house and came downstairs.

She looked untidy. Even her night-gown was not very clean. She approached Ethel. "I wanted to see what you were wearing." There was that queer passion, always to know what Ethel was wearing. She wanted to give Ethel money to buy clothes. "You know how I am. I don't care what I wear," she said. She said it with a little fling of her head.

She wanted to approach Ethel, put her hands on her. "That's nice. It's lovely on you," she said. "That cloth is nice." She put her hands on Ethel's dress. "You understand what to wear and how to wear it." When Ethel left the house, Blanche came to the front door. She stood there watching Ethel go off along the street.

Now she was in the room where Ethel was lying naked on the bed. She came softly across the room. She hadn't even put on bedroom slippers. She was in her bare feet and her feet made no sound. She was like a cat. She sat on the edge of the bed.

"Ethel."

"Yes." Ethel wanted to get up quickly and put on her pajamas.

"Lie still, Ethel," Blanche said. "I have been waiting for you, waiting for you to come."

Her voice now was not sharp and harsh. A kind of softness had crept into it. It was a pleading voice. "There has been a misunderstanding. We haven't understood each other,"

Blanche said. There was a faint light in the room. It came
through an open transom from a dim lamp burning in the
hallway outside the door. It was the door by which Blanche
had entered. Ethel could hear her father snoring in his bed
in a nearby room.

"It has been a long time. I have waited a long time,"
Blanche said. It was queer. Tom Riddle had, just an hour
before, said something of the same sort. "I hope it will not
be long now," Tom had said.

"Now," Blanche was saying.

Blanche's hand, her little sharp bony hand touched
Ethel's shoulder.

She had put her hand out, touching Ethel. Ethel had
grown rigid. She said nothing. At the touch of the hand her
body trembled. "I thought to-night I thought ... it is to-night
or never. I thought something was to be decided," Blanche
said.

She spoke in a low soft voice, unlike her voice as Ethel
knew it. She spoke as one in a trance. For just a moment
Ethel was relieved. "She is walking in her sleep. She is not
awake." The conviction passed quickly.

"I have been knowing all evening. 'There are the two
men, the older one and a younger. She will be making up
her mind,' I thought. I wanted to stop it.

"I don't want you to do it. I don't want you to do it."

She was soft and pleading. Now her hand had begun
to caress Ethel. It was creeping down along her body, over
her breasts, over her hips. Ethel remained rigid. She felt cold
and weak. "It's coming," she thought.

What was coming?

"You have to decide sometime. You have to be something.

"You are a whore or you are a woman.

"You have to take responsibility."

There were queer distorted sentences running through
Ethel's mind. It was as though some person, not Blanche,

not young Red Oliver, not Tom Riddle, were whispering to her.

"There is a self and another self.

"A woman is a woman or she is not a woman.

"A man is a man or he is not a man."

More and more sentences running through Ethel's head, apparently disjointed sentences. It was as though some older, some more sophisticated and evil thing, like another person, had come into her, had come in with the touch of Blanche's hand. . . . The hand continued creeping up and down her body, over her breasts, over her hips. . . . "It can be sweet," a voice said. "It can be very very sweet.

"There was a snake in Eden.

"Do you like snakes?"

Thoughts in Ethel, racing thoughts, thoughts she had never had before. "There is this thing we call individuality in us. It is a disease. I have thought, 'I must save myself.' That is what I have been thinking. I have always been thinking that.

"Once I was a young girl," Ethel thought suddenly. "I wonder if I was nice, if I was born nice.

"Was I intended to be something, a woman perhaps?" There was a queer dawning notion of womanhood, something even noble, something patient, something understanding.

What a mess life could get into! Every one saying to some one, "Save me. Save me."

Sex twisting people. It had twisted Ethel. She knew it.

"I am sure you have experimented. You have tried men," Blanche said in her strange new soft voice. "I don't know why but I am sure."

"They won't do. They won't do.

"I hate them.

"I hate them.

"They spoil everything. I hate them."

Now she had put her face down close to Ethel's face.

"We let them. We even go toward them.

"There is something in them we think we want."

"Ethel. Don't you understand? I love you. I have tried to make you know."

Blanche had put her face down close to Ethel's. For a time she was still there. Ethel could feel the woman's breath on her cheek. The minutes passed. There was an interval that, to Ethel, seemed hours. Blanche's lips touched Ethel's shoulders.

*

I⠀ was enough. With a kind of spasmodic movement, a twist of her body, throwing the woman off, Ethel sprang out of bed. A struggle began in the room. Afterwards Ethel never knew how long it went on.

She knew it was the end of something, the beginning of something.

She was fighting for something. When she sprang, twisted herself out of bed, out of Blanche's arms, and stood on her feet, Blanche sprang at her again. Ethel stood erect beside the bed and Blanche threw herself at her feet. She threw her arms about Ethel's body, clung desperately there. Ethel was dragging her across the room.

The two women had begun to wrestle. How strong Blanche was! Now her lips were kissing Ethel's body, her thighs, her legs! The kisses did not touch Ethel. It was as though she were a tree and some strange bird with a long sharp bill was pecking away at her, at some outer part of her. She was not sorry for Blanche now. She herself had become cruel.

She had got one of her hands into Blanche's hair and was pulling the face and lips away from her body. She had become strong, but Blanche was also strong. Slowly she forced Blanche's head away from herself. "Never. Never that," she said.

She did not say the words aloud. Even then, at that moment, she was conscious of the fact that she did not want her father to know what was going on in his house. "I wouldn't want to hurt him like that." Here was something she would never want any man to know. Now it would be comparatively easy for her to tell Tom Riddle about Red Oliver . . . if she decided she wanted Tom Riddle for her man . . . what she had thought she had wanted of the younger man, the experiment she had made, its failure.

"No! No!"

"Blanche! Blanche!"

It was necessary to bring Blanche back out of the place into which she had got. If Blanche had made a mess of her life it was her own mess. She had a desire not to betray Blanche.

She had hold of Blanche's hair and was pulling. With a sudden wrench she turned Blanche's face up to her own and with her free hand struck her in the face.

She kept striking. With all her strength she struck. She remembered something she had heard sometime, somewhere. "If you are a swimmer and have gone to rescue a drowning man or woman if he resists or struggles, strike him. Knock him unconscious."

She struck and struck. Now she was dragging Blanche toward the door of the room. It was odd. Blanche did not seem to mind being struck. She seemed to like it. She did not try to turn her face away from the blows.

Ethel had wrenched the door to the hallway open and had got Blanche outside and into the hallway. With a final effort she freed herself from the body clinging to her body. Blanche fell to the floor. There was a look in her eyes. "Well, I am licked. Anyway I tried."

She had got back the thing by which she lived, her contempt.

*

ETHEL stepped back into her own room and closed and bolted the door. Inside the door she stood with one hand on the knob, the other hand resting on a door panel. She was weak.

She listened. Her father had awakened. She heard him get out of his bed.

He was fumbling for a light. He was getting to be an old man.

He stumbled against a chair. His voice was quavering. "Ethel! Blanche! What has happened?"

"It will go on now like that in this house," thought Ethel. "At least I will not be here."

"Ethel! Blanche! What has happened?" The voice of her father was the voice of a scared child. He was getting old. His voice trembled. He was getting old and he had never grown up. He had always been a child, would be a child to the end.

"It might be why women could so hate and detest men."

There was a moment of intense silence and then Ethel heard Blanche's voice. "Great God," she thought. The voice was as it had always been when Blanche addressed her husband. It was sharp, a little hard, clear. "Nothing has happened, dear," the voice said. "I was in Ethel's room. We were talking in there."

"Go back to sleep," the voice said. There was something terrible in the command.

Ethel heard her father's voice. He was grumbling. "I wish you would not wake me up," the voice said. Ethel heard him getting heavily back into bed.

5

IT was early morning. The room in the Long house in which Ethel lived had a window looking out toward the field her father owned, the field that sloped down to a creek, the field into which she had gone as a young girl to meet a bad little boy. In the hot summer the field got almost bare; it got burned brown. You looked at it and thought . . . "a cow won't get much in that field" . . . you thought. The cow Ethel's father had now had a broken horn.

So! The horn of a cow gets broken.

In the morning, even in the early morning, in Langdon, Georgia, heat. If it has rained, it isn't quite so hot. You have to be born to it. You must not mind.

You can have a lot of things happen to you and then . . . there you are.

You are standing in a room. If you are a woman, you are putting on a dress. You are a man and are putting on a shirt.

It's funny, men and women don't understand each other better. They should.

"I guess they don't care. I guess they don't give a goddamn. They get so they don't give a goddamn.

"Goddamn. Goddamn. Noggle is a nice word. Noggle me. Noggle yourself across a room. Noggle yourself into pants, into a skirt. Noggle yourself into a coat. Noggle yourself downtown. Noggle, noggle.

"It's Sunday. Be a man. Go on, take a walk with your wife."

Ethel tired...a little crazy maybe. Where had she heard, or seen, the word "noggle"?

Once, in Chicago, a man talking. It was strange for him to come back to Ethel, that summer morning in Georgia, after the night, after the sleepless night, after the adventure with Red Oliver, after Blanche. He came into her room and sat down.

How absurd! It was only the memory of him that came. That's nice. If you are a woman, the memory of a man can come right into your room as you sit dressing. You are quite naked. What? What difference does it make! "Come in, sit down. Touch me. Don't touch me. Thoughts, touch me."

Suppose the man is a nut. Suppose he is a middle-aged, bald-headed man. Ethel saw that one once. She heard him talk. She remembered him. She liked him.

He talked crazily. Well. Was he drunk? Could anything be crazier than the Long house in Langdon, Georgia? People might go past the house along a street. How would they know it was a crazy house?

The man in Chicago. Again Ethel was with Harold Grey. You go through life gathering up people. You are a woman and are with a man a good deal. Then you aren't with him any more. So there he is, just the same, a part of you. He touched you. He walked beside you. You liked him or didn't like him. You were cruel to him. You're sorry.

His color in you, a little, your color in him.

In Chicago, at a party, a man talking. It was at another evening party, at the house of one of Harold Grey's friends. This one was a man, a historian, an out-of-doors man, a historian...

A man who gathered people about him. He had a nice wife, a tall handsome dignified wife.

There was a man in his house, sitting with two young women, in a room. Ethel was there, listening. The man was talking of God. Was he drunk? There had been drinks.

"So, every one wants God."

It was a middle-aged, bald-headed man talking.

Who had started that conversation? It had been started at dinner. "So, I guess every one wants God."

Some one at table, at dinner, had spoken of Henry Adams, another historian, *Mont Saint Michel and Chartres*. "White soul of the Middle Ages." Historians talking. Every one wants God.

A man talked to two women. He was eager, nice. "We have been a lot of fools, we men of the Western world.

"So we took our religion from the Jews ... a lot of wanderers ... in a dry barren land.

"I guess they did not like the land.

"So they put God up in the sky ... a mysterious god, far away."

"You read about it ... in the Old Testament," the man said. "They couldn't make it go. The people kept running away. They went off and worshipped a statue of brass, a golden calf. They were right.

"So they got up the story about Christ. Do you want to know why? They had to get it up. All is getting lost. Get up a story. They had to try to get it down to earth where people could get hold of it.

"So. So. So.

"So they got up about Christ. Good.

"They put that in about immaculate conception? Isn't just any ordinary conception nice? I think it is. It's nice."

There were two young women in the room that time, with that man. They blushed. They listened to him. Ethel wasn't in the conversation. She listened. Afterwards she found out that the man at the historian's house that night was a painter, a queer bird. Perhaps he was drunk. There were cocktails, plenty of cocktails.

He was trying to explain something, that he thought the religion the Greeks and Romans had, before Christianity came, was nicer than Christianity because it was more earthy.

He was telling something he himself did. He had taken

a little house out in the country, at a place called Palos Park. It was at the edge of a forest.

> *"When out of Palos came the gold*
> *To storm the gates of Hercules."*

Was that right?

He tried to imagine gods there. He tried to be a Greek. "I fail," he said, "but it's fun trying."

There was a long tale told. The man was describing to two women, trying to describe, how he lived. He painted and then he couldn't paint, he said. He went to walk.

There was a small creek and bushes growing at the edge of the creek. He went there and stood. "I close my eyes," he said. He laughed. "There may be a wind blowing. It blows in bushes.

"I try to convince myself it isn't a wind. It is a god or a goddess.

"It is a goddess. She has come out of the creek. The creek is nice just there. There is a deep hole.

"There is a low hill.

"She comes out of the creek, dripping wet. She comes up out of the creek. I have to imagine it. I stand with my eyes closed. The water makes shining spots on her skin.

"Her skin is lovely. Every painter wants to paint a nude . . . against trees, against bushes, against grass. She comes up and pushes through the bushes. It isn't she. It's a wind blowing.

"It is she. There you are."

That was all Ethel remembered. The man might just have been playing with the two women. He might have been drunk. She went with Harold Grey, that time, to the house of the historian. Some one came and spoke to her and she did not hear any more.

The morning, after the strange mixed-up night in Langdon, Georgia, it might just have come back to her because the man had spoken of bushes. On that morning, **when** she stood by a window and looked out she saw a field. She saw bushes growing by a creek. The rain of the night had made the bushes bright green.

*

Ir was early morning, a hot still morning in Langdon. Already Negro men and women, with their children, were at work in the cotton fields near town. The factory workers of the day shift, in the Langdon cotton mill, had been at work for an hour. A wagon with two mules hitched to it went along the road past Judge Long's house. The wagon creaked dismally. Three Negro men and two women rode a wagon. The street was not paved. The feet of the mules went softly, nicely in the dust.

That morning, at work in the cotton mill, Red Oliver was distraught and upset. Something had happened to him. He had thought he was in love. For many nights he had been lying in his own bed in the Oliver house dreaming of a certain event. "If that would happen, if it could happen. If she . . .

"It won't, it can't happen.

"I am too young for her. She doesn't want me.

"There isn't any use my thinking of it." He had thought of the woman, Ethel Long, as older, wiser, more sophisticated than any woman he had ever seen. She must have liked him. Why had she done what she had done?

She had let it happen there, in the library in the dark. He had never thought it would happen. Even then, at the moment . . . if she had not been bold. It hadn't been anything she said. She had let him know, in some quick subtle way, that it could happen. He had been afraid. "I was awkward. If I hadn't been so damned awkward. I acted as though I didn't believe it, couldn't believe it."

Afterwards he had felt more restless than before. He hadn't been able to sleep. The way in which, after it happened, she had dismissed him. She had made him feel, not like a man but like a boy. He had been angry, hurt, perplexed.

After he had left her he had walked about alone for a long time, wanting to curse. There were the letters he had been receiving from his friend Neil Bradley, the Western farmer's son, who was now in love with a school teacher out there, the things that happened to them. The letters had kept coming that summer. They might have had something to do with the state into which Red had got.

A man tells another man, "I've got me something nice."

He starts thoughts.

Thoughts get started.

Could a woman do such a thing to a man, even to a man so much younger than herself, taking him and not taking him, even using him ...

As though to try out something for herself. "I'll see if this suits me, if this is what I want."

Could a person live like that, thinking only, "Do I want it? Will it be good for me?"

Another person involved in it.

Red Oliver had tramped about alone in the dark of the hot Southern night after the rain. He went out past the Long house. The house was away out, near the edge of town. There were no pavements out there. He had got off the sidewalk, not wanting to make any noise and had walked in the road, in the mud of the road. He had stood before the house. A stray dog came along. The dog approached and then ran away. There was a street light, nearly a block away. The dog ran to the street light and then, turning, stood and barked.

"If a man had guts."

Suppose he could go to the door and knock. "I want to see Ethel Long.

"You come out here. I'm not through with you yet.

"If a man could be a man."

Red had stood there in the road thinking of the woman he had been with, with whom he had been so intimate without being at all intimate. Could it be that the woman had come home and had gone quietly to sleep, after that, after she had dismissed him? The thought had angered him and he walked away swearing. All that night and all the next day as he tried to do his work he swung back and forth. He blamed himself for what had happened and then his mood changed. He blamed the woman. "She is older than I am. She should have known what she wanted." In the early morning, just at daybreak, he had got out of bed. He wrote Ethel a long letter that was never sent and in it he expressed the queer feeling of defeat she had given him. He wrote the letter and then tore it up and wrote another. The second letter expressed nothing but love and longing. He took all the blame on himself. "It was in some way not nice. It was my fault. Please let me come to you again. Please. Please. Let's try once more."

He also tore that letter up.

In the Long house there was no formal breakfast. The judge's new wife had done away with that. In the morning, breakfast was taken about to the rooms on trays. A colored woman, a tall woman with big hands and feet and with thick lips, brought Ethel's breakfast that morning. There was fruit juice in a glass and coffee and toast. Ethel's father would have had hot bread. He would have demanded hot bread. He took a sincere interest in food, was always talking about it, as though to say, "I take my stand. Here I take my stand. I'm Southern. Here I take my stand."

He kept talking about the coffee. "It isn't good. Why can't I have good coffee?" When he went out to dinner, to the Rotary Club, he came home and spoke of it. "We had good coffee," he said. "We had wonderful coffee."

The bathroom in the Long house was on the ground floor, near Ethel's room, and that morning she had been up and in the bath at six. She took it cold. It was nice. She plunged in. It wasn't cold enough.

Her father was already up. He was one of the sort of men who cannot sleep after daylight comes. It comes very early in Georgia in summer. "I have to have the early morning air," he said. "It's the best time of the day to get out and breathe." He got out of bed and tiptoed about the house. He went out of the house. He still kept a cow and went to see the cow milked. A colored man came at an early hour. He got the cow out of the field, the field near the house, the field to which the judge had once gone in anger seeking his daughter Ethel, that time she went there to meet the boy. He hadn't seen the boy but was sure he was there. He had always thought that.

"But what's the use thinking? What's the use trying to make anything out of women?"

He could talk to the man who had brought the cow. A cow he had owned two or three years before had got a disease called "hollow tail." There wasn't any veterinary in Langdon and the colored man said the tail would have to be cut open. He explained. "You cut the tail open lengthwise. Then you put in salt and pepper." Judge Long laughed but he let the man do it. The cow died.

Now he had got another cow, a half Jersey. She had a broken horn. When her time came, would it be better to breed her to a Jersey bull or to some other sort? There was a man, a half mile in the country, who had a fine Holstein bull. The colored man thought he would be a better bull. "The Holsteins give more milk," he said. It made something to talk about. It was homey and nice talking to the colored man about something of the sort in the morning.

A boy came bringing the Atlanta *Constitution* and threw it on the porch. He ran across the judge's lawn, having left his bicycle at the fence, and then he threw the paper. It had been folded and fell with a thump. The judge went to get it and, putting on his glasses, sat on the porch reading.

It was nice in the yard thus, in the early morning, neither of the judge's perplexing women about, only the colored man there. The colored man, who milked and cared for the cow, also did other jobs about the house and yard. In the winter he brought wood for the fireplaces in the house and in the summer he mowed and sprinkled the lawn and the flower beds.

He worked about the flower beds in the yard, the judge watching and giving directions. Judge Long was passionately devoted to flowers and to flowering bushes. He knew about such things. When he had been a younger man he had made a study of birds and knew hundreds of birds by sight and by their songs. Only one of his children had been interested. It was the son who was killed in the World War.

His wife Blanche never seemed to see birds and she did not seem to see flowers. She wouldn't have noticed if they had all been suddenly destroyed.

He had manure brought and put about the roots of the bushes. He got the hose and watered the bushes, the flowers and the grass as the colored man pottered about. They talked. It was nice. The judge had no men friends. If the colored man had not been a colored man . . .

The judge never thought of that. The two men saw and felt things in the same way. To the judge the bushes and flowers and the grass were living things. "He wants a drink, too," the colored man said, pointing at a particular bush. He made some of the bushes masculine, some feminine, as the fancy struck him. "Give her a little drop, Judge." The judge laughed. He liked it. "A little for him now."

The judge's wife, Blanche, never got out of bed before noon. After she had married the judge, she got the habit of lying in bed in the morning and smoking cigarettes. The habit shocked him. She told Ethel that, before she married, she had smoked in secret. "I used to sit in my room smoking late at night and I blew the smoke out the window," she said. "In the winter I blew it into the fireplace. I used to lie

on my belly on the floor smoking. I didn't dare let any one
know, least of all your father, who was on the school board.
Every one thought I was a nice woman then."

Blanche had burned any number of holes in the bed
cover of her bed. She didn't care. "To hell with the bed
covers," she thought. She did not read. In the morning she
stayed in bed, smoking cigarettes and staring out a window
at the sky. After marriage and after her husband found out
about her smoking, she made a concession. She quit smoking in his presence. "I wouldn't do that, Blanche," he had
said, rather pleadingly.

"Why?"

"People will talk. They won't understand."

"Won't understand what?"

"Won't understand that you are a nice woman."

"I'm not," she had said brusquely.

She had enjoyed telling Ethel how she had fooled the
town and her husband, Ethel's father. Ethel tried to think
of her as she must have been then, as a younger woman, or
as a young girl. "It's all a lie, the picture she makes of herself as she was," Ethel thought. She might even have been
nice, quite nice, quite jolly and alive. Ethel saw, in fancy, a
young blonde woman, slender and pretty, alive, rather daring and unscrupulous. "She would have been then terribly
eager, as I was myself, ready to take a chance. Nothing
offered that she wanted." She had got her eye on the judge.
"What am I to do, go on forever being a school teacher?"
she would have asked herself. The judge was on the county
school board. She had met him at some function. Once a
year one of the civic clubs of the town, either the Rotary or
the Kiwanis Club, gave a dinner for all the white school
teachers. She would have got her eye on the judge. His wife
was dead.

After all a man is a man. What works on one will work
on another. You keep telling an older man how young he
looks ... not too often but you slip it in. "You are nothing

but a boy. You need some one to care for you." It works all right.

She had written the judge a very sympathetic letter when his son died. They began seeing each other in secret. He was lonely.

Without a doubt there was something between Ethel and Blanche. It concerned men. It is between all women.

Blanche had gone too far. She had been a fool. Just the same there had been something about the scene in the room, on the night before Ethel left her father's house for good, that was pathetic. It had been Blanche's determination, a kind of insane determination. "I am going to have something. I am not going to be absolutely robbed.

"I am going to have you."

*

If Ethel's father had come into the room at that moment, when Blanche was clinging to Ethel . . . Ethel could imagine the scene. Blanche getting to her feet. She wouldn't have cared. Even though daylight came very early in the summer in Langdon, Ethel had plenty of time to think before daylight came, that night when she decided to leave that house.

Her father, as usual, had got up early. He was sitting on the front porch of his house, reading his newspaper. There was a colored cook in the house, the wife of the yard man. She carried the judge's breakfast around the house and put it on a little table beside him. This was his time of the day. The two colored people hung about. The judge made little comments on the news. It was the year 1930. The paper was full of the industrial depression that had come on during the fall before. "I never bought a share of any kind of stock in my life," Ethel's father said aloud. "Nor I," the Negro yard man said, and the judge laughed. There was that yard man, that Negro, talking about buying stocks. "Nor I." It was a joke. The judge gave the Negro man

advice. "Well, you let it alone." His tone was serious . . .
mockingly serious. "Don't you go buying stocks on margin,
now will you?"

"No sah, no sah, I jes won' do dat, Jedge."

There was the little chuckling laughter of Ethel's father,
playing with the colored man, his friend really. The two old
colored people were sorry for the judge. He had got caught.
There was no way for him to escape. They knew that.
Negroes might be naïve but they weren't fools. The Negro
man knew well enough he was amusing the judge.

Ethel knew something, too. She ate her breakfast slowly
that morning and dressed slowly. There was a huge closet
in the room she occupied, and her trunks were in there. They
had been put in the closet when she came home from Chicago. She packed them. "I'll send for them later in the day,"
she thought.

There was no use saying anything to her father. She
had made up her mind what she was going to do. She was
going to try a marriage with Tom Riddle. "I guess I will.
If he is still willing, I guess I will."

It was a queer comfortable feeling. "I don't care," she
told herself. "I'll even tell him about last night in the library.
I'll see if he'll stand that. If he won't . . . I'll attend to that
when I come to it.

"That's the way. 'Tend to things as you come to them.'

"I may, and I may not."

She went about her room being very particular about
her costume.

"What about this hat? It's a bit out of shape." She
put it on and studied herself in the glass. "I look pretty
good. I don't look very tired." She decided on a red summer
dress. It was rather flaming but it did something nice to her
face. It emphasized the dark olive tones in her skin. "The
cheeks want a bit of color," she thought.

Ordinarily, after such a night as she had been through,
she would have looked worn-out, but that morning she didn't.

The fact surprised her. She kept being surprised at herself.

"What queer moods I have been in," she told herself as she went about her room. After the cook came in with her breakfast on a tray, she bolted the door. Would the woman Blanche be fool enough to come downstairs and say something about the occurrence of the night before, try to explain or apologize? Suppose Blanche should try to do that. It would spoil everything. "No," Ethel told herself. "She has too much sense, too much real nerve for that. She isn't that sort." It was a nice feeling, almost liking Blanche. "She has a right to be what she is," Ethel thought. She elaborated the thought a little. It explained a lot in life. "Let every one be what he is. If a man wants to think he is good (she was thinking of her father), let him think so. People may even think they are Christians, if it does them any good, if it comforts them any."

The thought was a comfort. She arranged and rearranged her hair. There was a little, tight-fitting red hat that went with the dress she had put on. She heightened the color in her cheeks a bit and then her lips.

"If it can't be the feeling I had for that boy, that kind of hungry longing, rather senseless, such as animals have, perhaps it can be something else."

Tom Riddle was a true realist, even a courageous one. "We are a good deal alike at bottom." How nice it had been of him to keep his self-respect all during his courtship! He hadn't tried to touch her, to work on her senses. He had been frank. "We might be able to hit it off," Ethel thought. It would be a gamble. He would know it was a gamble. She remembered with gratitude the older man's words ...

"You may not be able to love me. I don't know what love is. I am no youngster. No one ever called me a handsome man."

"I'll tell him whatever comes into my head to tell, whatever I think he would like to know. If he wants me, he can take me to-day. I don't want to wait. We'll begin."

Was she sure of him? "I'll try to do a good job for him. I think I know what he wants."

She could hear her father's voice, talking to the Negro yard man on the front porch. She felt resentment and at the same time pity.

"If I could say something to him before I leave. I can't."

He would be upset when he heard the news of her sudden marriage ... if Tom Riddle still wanted to marry her. "He will want it. He will. He will."

She thought again of young Oliver and of what she had done to him, trying him out as she had, to see if he, rather than Tom Riddle, was what she wanted. A little vicious thought came. From her bedroom window she could see into the cow pasture where her father had come seeking her that night, when she was a young girl. The pasture went down to a creek and there were bushes growing along the creek. That boy that time had got away into the bushes. It would have been an odd thing if, on the night before, she had taken young Oliver in there, into the pasture. "If the night had been fair, I might have done that," she thought. She smiled, a little revengefully, softly. "He will be all right for some woman. In the end it will not hurt him, what I have done. He may have got educated—a little. Anyway, I did it."

It was queer and baffling, trying to find out what was education, what was good and what was bad. She remembered suddenly a thing that had happened in the town when she was a young girl.

She was on the street with her father. There was a Negro being tried. He had been accused of raping a white woman. The white woman, as it turned out later, was no good. She came into town and accused the Negro. Afterwards he was cleared. He had been with some man at work on a road at the very hour when she said it happened.

That hadn't been known at first. There was excitement and talk of a lynching. Ethel's father was excited. A group of armed deputy sheriffs were standing near the county jail.

There was another group of men in the street, in front of a drug store. Tom Riddle was there. A man spoke to him. The man was a merchant of the town. "Are you going to do it, Tom Riddle, are you going to take that man's case? Are you going to defend him?"

"Yes, and clear him too."

"Well ... You ... You ..." The man was excited.

"He wasn't guilty," Tom Riddle said. "If he was guilty, I would still take his case. I would still defend him.

"As for you ..." Ethel remembered the look on Tom Riddle's face. He had stepped out in front of the man, the merchant. The little group of men standing about, became silent. Had she loved Tom Riddle at that moment? What was love?

"As for you, what I know about you," Tom Riddle said to that man, "if I ever get you into court."

That was all. It had been nice, one man standing out against a group of men, daring them.

When Ethel had completed her packing, she stepped out of her room. All was quiet in the house. Suddenly her heart beat heavily. "So I am leaving this house.

"If Tom Riddle doesn't want me, when he knows all about me, if he doesn't want me ..."

At first she did not see Blanche, who had come downstairs and was in one of the rooms on the ground floor. Blanche stepped forth. She wasn't dressed. She was in a suit of soiled pajamas. She stepped across the little hallway to Ethel.

"You look swell," she said. "I hope it will be a good day for you."

She stood aside as Ethel went out of the house and down the two or three steps from the porch to the walk leading to the gate. Blanche stood just inside the house, looking, and Judge Long, who was still reading his morning paper, put it down and also looked.

"Good morning," he said, and "Good morning," Ethel replied.

She could feel Blanche looking at her. She would go into Ethel's room. She would see Ethel's bags and her trunks. She would understand but would say nothing to the judge, her husband. She would creep back upstairs and get into bed. She would lie in her bed, looking out at a window and smoking cigarettes.

*

TOM RIDDLE was nervous and excited. "She was with that boy last night. They were together there in the library. It was dark in there." He grew a little angry with himself. "Well, I'm not accusing her. Who am I to accuse her?

"If she wants me, I guess she'll tell me. I don't believe she can want him, that boy, not for keeps."

He was nervous and excited as he always was when he thought of Ethel, and went early to his office. He closed his office door and walked up and down. He smoked cigarettes.

Many times that summer, as he stood at his office window, hidden from the street below, Tom had watched Ethel, going to the library. He got excited, seeing her. He became a boy in his eagerness.

On that morning he saw her. She was crossing the street. She was lost from sight. He stood near a window.

There was the sound of feet on the stairs that led up to his office. Could it be Ethel? Had she made up her mind? Was she coming to him?

"Keep still. . . . Don't be a fool," he said to himself. There was the sound of feet on the stairs. They stopped. They came forward again. An outer door to his office opened. Tom Riddle braced himself. He stood there trembling while the door into his inner office opened, and there was Ethel, a little pale, with a queer determined look in her eyes.

Tom Riddle had grown calm. "A woman who is about

to give herself to a man does not come to him like this," he thought. "But why has she come up here?"

"You have come up here?"

"Yes."

There were the two people facing each other. People do not arrange a marriage in that way, in a lawyer's office, in the morning ... the woman coming to the man.

"Can it be like this?" Ethel was asking herself.

"Can it be like this?" Tom Riddle asked himself.

"Not even a kiss. I've never touched her."

The man and woman stood there, facing each other. There were the sounds of a town coming up from the street, a town getting into its daily, rather meaningless, activities. The office was above a store. It was a simple office with one large room, a large flat-topped desk and law books in cases against the walls. There was a bare floor.

There was a sound from below. A clerk in a store dropped a box on the floor.

"Well," Ethel said. She said it with an effort. "You told me last night ... You said you were ready ... any time. You said it was O. K. with you."

She was finding it hard, hard. "I'm going to be a damn fool," she thought. She wanted to cry.

"I'd have to tell you a lot of things ..."

"I bet he won't have me," she thought.

"Wait," she said hurriedly, "I'm not what you think I am. I have to tell you. I must. I must."

"Nonsense," he said, stepping toward her and taking her hand. "Hell," he said, "Let it go. What's the use talking?"

He stood and looked at her. "Dare I, dare I try it, dare I try taking her into my arms?"

Anyway, she knew she liked him, standing there, hesitant and uncertain, like that. "He's going to marry me, all right," she thought. She didn't, at the moment, think beyond that.

BOOK FOUR

BEYOND DESIRE

1

IT was November of 1930.

Red Oliver stirred uneasily in sleep. He awoke and then slept again. There is a land between sleeping and waking—a land filled with grotesque shapes—and he was in that land. Things change swiftly and strangely there. It is a land of peace—and then of terrors. Trees in that land become enlarged. They become shapeless and elongated. They come out of the ground and float away into the air. Desires come into the body of the sleeper.

Now you are yourself, but you are not yourself. You are outside yourself. You see yourself running along a beach ... faster, faster, faster. The land into which you have got has become terrible. There is a black wave coming up out of a black sea to engulf you.

And now, as suddenly, all is again peaceful. You are in a meadow, lying under a tree, in warm sunlight. Cattle are grazing near by. The air is filled with a warm rich milky smell. There is a woman, beautifully gowned, walking toward you.

She is in purple velvet. She is tall.

It was Ethel Long, of Langdon, Georgia, walking toward Red Oliver. Ethel Long had become suddenly gracious. She was in a mood of soft womanhood and was in love with Red.

But no ... it was not Ethel. It was a strange woman, like Ethel Long physically, but at the same time unlike.

It was Ethel Long, beaten by life, defeated by life. See

... she had lost some of her upright proud beauty and had become humble. This woman would be glad for love—any love that came to her. Her eyes were saying that now. It was Ethel Long, no longer fighting against life, not even wanting to be victorious in life.

Look ... even her gown has changed as she walks across the sunlit field toward Red. Dreams. Does a man in dreams always know he is in dreams?

Now the woman in the field was in an old worn calico dress. Her face looked worn. She was a farm woman, a work woman, merely walking across the field to milk a cow.

There were two small boards laid on the ground under some bushes, and Red Oliver was lying on the boards. His body ached and he was cold. It was November and he was in a field covered with bushes near the town of Birchfield, in North Carolina. He had been trying to sleep in his clothes under a bush on the two boards laid on the ground, and the bed he had made for himself with the two boards, found near by, was uncomfortable. It was late at night and he sat up rubbing his eyes. What was the use of trying to sleep?

"Why am I here? Where am I? What am I doing here?" Life is unaccountably strange. Why did a man like himself get into such a place? Why was he always letting himself do unaccountable things?

Red had come out of the half sleep in confusion and so, first of all, when he awoke, he had to gather himself together.

There was the physical fact of himself—a young man strong enough ... a night's sleep did not matter so much to him. He was in this new place. How had he got there?

Memories and impressions came floating back. He sat upright. A woman, older than himself, a tall woman, a working woman, a farm woman, rather slender, not unlike Ethel Long of Langdon, Georgia, had brought him to the spot where he had been lying on the two boards and trying to sleep. He sat up and rubbed his eyes. There was a small tree near by and he crept over sandy ground to it. He sat on the ground with his back against a little tree trunk. It was like the boards on which he had tried to sleep. The trunk of the tree was rough. If there had been but one board, a broad smooth one, he might have gone on sleeping. He had got one of his nether cheeks down between the two boards and had got pinched. He half leaned over and rubbed the hurt place.

He leaned his back against the little tree. The woman with whom he had come to that place had given him a blanket. She had brought it to him from a little tent some distance away and it was worn thin. "I suppose they haven't much bedding, these people," he thought. The woman might have brought him her own blanket from the tent. She was tall like Ethel Long, but wasn't much like her. As a woman she had none of Ethel's style. Red was glad to be awake. "It will be more comfortable sitting here than trying to sleep on such a bed," he thought. He was sitting on the ground and the ground was damp and cold. He crept over and got one of the boards. "Anyway, it will make a seat," he thought. He looked up at the sky. A half moon was out and there were drifting gray clouds.

Red was in a camp of striking workers in a field near the town of Birchfield, North Carolina. It was a moonlit night in November and rather cold. By what a queer chain of circumstances he had got there.

He had come to the camp in the dark on the evening before with a woman who had brought him into the place and had left him. They had arrived afoot, tramping afoot over hills—over half mountains really—coming afoot, not by a road but by paths that climbed up over hills and went along edges of fenced fields. They had come several miles thus in the gray of the evening and in the darkness of early night.

It was for Red Oliver a night when everything about him was unreal. There had been other times like that in his life. Of a sudden he began to remember other unreal times.

To every man and every boy such times come. There

the boy is. He is a boy in a house. The house is suddenly unreal. He is in a room. Everything in the room is unreal. There are, in the room, chairs, a chest of drawers, the bed on which he has been lying. Why do they all seem suddenly strange? Questions asked. "Is this the house in which I have been living? Is this strange room in which I now find myself the room in which I slept last night and the night before?"

Every one knows such times of strangeness. Do we control our own acts, the tone of our own lives? How absurd to ask! We do not. We are all stupid. Will the day ever come when we will shake off this stupidity?

To know even a little of inanimate life, too. There is that chair there . . . that table. The chair is like a woman. Many men have sat in it. They have thrown themselves into it, sat down softly, gently. Men have sat in it thinking and suffering. The chair is old now. There is an aroma of many people hanging over it.

Thoughts coming swift and strange. The imagination of a man or boy must sleep most of the time. It suddenly goes on a spree.

Why, for example, should any man ever want to be a poet? What is gained by that?

It would be best to go through life just being a common man, going along, eating and sleeping. The poet wants to tear things, to tear the veil that separates him from the unknown. He wants to look far out beyond life into dim mysterious places. Why?

There is something out there he would like to understand. Words that men use every day can perhaps be given a new meaning, thoughts given a new meaning. He has let himself run out into the unknown. Now he would like to run back, into a familiar everyday world, carrying back with him into that world something, a sound, a word out of the unknown into the familiar. Why?

Thoughts grouping themselves in the mind of a man or

boy. What is this thing called the mind? It gets out-of-hand, playing the deuce with a man or boy.

Red Oliver, in a strange cold place at night, thought dimly of his own boyhood. When he was a boy he went sometimes with his mother to Sunday school. He thought of that.

He thought of a story heard there. There was a man called Jesus, in a garden with his followers about him, the followers lying on the ground asleep. Perhaps followers always sleep. The man was suffering in the garden. Soldiers were near by, brutal soldiers who wanted to take him and crucify him. Why?

"What have I done that I should be taken to be crucified? Why am I here?" Fear coming. A man, a Sunday-school teacher, was trying to tell the story of the man's night in the garden to the children in a Sunday-school class. Why had memories of that come back to Red Oliver sitting with his back against a tree in a field?

He had come to that place with a woman, a strange woman, met almost casually. They had walked in moonlit places, through upland fields and in and out of dark stretches of forest. The woman Red was with had stopped now and then to speak to him. She had got tired during the walk, not being strong.

She had talked to Red Oliver a little, but there had been a shyness between them. That, as they came along in the darkness, gradually passed off. It hadn't passed completely, Red thought. The conversation between them had been, for the most part, concerned with the path. "Look out. There's a rut there. You will stumble." She called the root of the tree that protruded into the path a "rut." She was taking it for granted that she knew about Red Oliver. He was to her a definite thing she knew about. He was a young communist, a leader of labor, going to a town where there was labor trouble and she was herself one of the laborers in trouble.

Red was ashamed that he had not stopped her along the way, that he hadn't told her—"I'm not what you think I am."

"Perhaps I would like to be the thing you think I am. I don't know. Anyway, I'm not.

"If the thing you think I am is something brave and fine, then I would like to be it.

"I want that: to be something brave and fine. There is too much ugliness in life and people. I don't want to be ugly."

He hadn't told her.

She had thought she knew about him. She had kept asking him, "Are you tired? Are you getting tired?"

"No."

As they had come along, he had pressed close to her. They were going through dark places along the way and she had stopped to breathe. When they had climbed up steep places in the path he had insisted on pushing ahead and had put out a hand to her. There was enough moonlight to see her form dimly below. "She is a good deal like Ethel Long," he kept thinking. She had seemed most like Ethel when he was following her in the paths, she striding along ahead.

Then he ran in front of her to help her up a steep place. "They will never get you coming this way," she said. "They don't know about this path." She thought he was a dangerous man, a communist, come into her country to fight for her people. He went ahead and taking her hand pulled her up the steep place. There was a resting place and they both stopped. He stood looking at her. Now she was thin and pale and worn-looking. "Now you aren't much like Ethel Long," he thought. The darkness of the woods and fields had helped the shyness between them. They had arrived together at the place where Red was now.

Red had got into the camp unnoticed. Although it was late at night, he could hear little sounds. A man or a woman stirred somewhere near by or a child whimpered. There was a particular little sound. Some woman among the striking workers he had got in with had a nursing child. The child had stirred uneasily in sleep and the woman had put it to the breast. He could even hear the baby's lips, sucking and pulling at a woman's paps. A man, some distance away, crawled out through the door of a small shack made of board and, getting to his feet, stood stretching. He seemed huge in the dim light, a young man, a young worker. Red pressed his body against the trunk of the little tree, not wanting to be seen, and the man went softly away. In the distance there was a somewhat larger shack with a light. The sound of voices came from the little building.

The man Red had seen stretching went toward the light.

The camp into which Red had come reminded him of something. It was on a gently sloping hillside that had been covered with bushes, but some of the bushes had been cut away. There was a little open place with shacks, like dog houses stuck up. There were a few tents.

It was like places Red had seen before. In the South, in Red's own country, in Georgia, there were such places set up sometimes in a field at the edge of a town or in the country at the edge of a pine forest.

The places were called camp meetings and people came there to worship. They got religion there. As a young boy Red used to drive sometimes with his father, the country doctor, and once, when they were driving on a country road at night, they had come upon such a place.

There had been something in the air of the place, that night, that Red remembered now. He remembered his own wonder and the contempt of his father. The people were religious enthusiasts, his father had said. His father hadn't explained much, not being a talkative man. Still Red had understood, had sensed what was going on.

Poor people of the South, religious enthusiasts, Methodists and Baptists for the most part, gathered in such places. They were poor whites from nearby farms.

They had put up little tents and shacks as in the camp

of strikers to which Red had now come. Such a religious meeting, in the South, among the poor whites, was carried on sometimes for weeks or even months. People came and went. They brought food from their houses.

There was an in-flocking. The people were ignorant and illiterate and came from the little tenant farms or at night from a mill village. They dressed in their best clothes and came afoot along the red Georgia roads at evening, young men and women walking together, older men with their wives, women with babes in their arms and sometimes men leading children by the hand.

There they were at the camp meeting at night. There was preaching going on day and night. There were long prayers said. There was singing. The poor whites worshipped thus sometimes in the South and so also did the Negroes but they didn't do it together. In the white camps, as in the Negro camps, as the nights grew late, there was intense excitement.

There was preaching going on out of doors under the stars. Quavering voices arose in song. People suddenly got religion. Men and women became excited. Sometimes a woman, often a young woman, began to shout and scream.

"God. God. Give me God," she cried.

Or, "I've got him. He's here. He has hold of me.

"It's Jesus. I can feel his hands touching me.

"I can feel his face touching me."

Women, often young unmarried women, came to such meetings and sometimes grew hysterical. There would be a young white woman, the daughter of some poor white tenant farmer of the South. All of her life she had been shy and afraid of people. She was a little starved thing, physically and emotionally starved, but now at the meeting something happened to her.

She had come with her own people. It was night and she had been working all that day in a cotton field or in the cotton mill in the nearby town. There had been for her that day ten, twelve or even fifteen hours of hard labor in the mill or in a field.

Now there she was at the camp meeting.

She could hear the voice of a man, the preacher, shouting under the stars or under trees. The woman sat, a little thin, half-starved being, looking up occasionally through branches of trees to the sky and the stars.

And even for her, the poor starved one, there was a moment. Her eyes could see the stars and the sky. Red Oliver's own mother had got religion in that way, not at a camp meeting but in a poor little church at the edge of a mill village.

No doubt, Red thought, hers had also been a starved life. He hadn't thought of that when he was a boy with his father and when he had seen the poor whites at a camp meeting. His father had stopped his car in the road. There were voices calling in a little grassy place under trees and he saw men and women kneeling under a torch made from a pine knot. His father had smiled and a look of disdain had flitted across his face.

There was a voice calling to the young woman at the camp meeting. "He's there . . . up there . . . it's Jesus. He wants you." In the young woman a trembling began. There was something going on in her unlike anything she had ever known before. She felt hands touching her body in the night. "Now. Now."

"You. You. I want you."

Could there be some one . . . God . . . a strange being off somewhere in the mysterious distance who wanted her?

"Who wants me, with my thin little body and the tiredness in me?" She would have been like that little girl named Grace who used to work in the cotton mill at Langdon, Georgia, the one Red Oliver had seen the first summer he worked in the mill . . . the one the other mill woman named Doris was always trying to protect.

Doris going to that one at night, caressing her with her

hands, trying to take the tiredness out of her, trying to bring life into her.

But you may be a tired, thin young woman and have no Doris. Dorises are, after all, pretty rare in this world. You are a poor white working girl in a mill or you work all day with your father or mother in a cotton field. You look at your own thin sticks of legs and at your thin arms. You don't even dare say to yourself, "I'd like to be rich, or beautiful. I'd like to have the love of a man." What would be the use?

But at the camp meeting. "It's Jesus."

"White. Wonderful."

"Up there."

"He wants You. He will take you."

It might be just a debauch. Red knew that. He knew his father had felt that way about the camp meeting they had watched when Red was a boy. There was such a young woman letting herself go. She screamed. She fell to the ground. She groaned. People gathered about—her own kind of people.

"Look, she has got it."

She had wanted it so. She hadn't known what she wanted.

It was an experience for that girl, vulgar but certainly strange. Nice people didn't do it. That might be the trouble with nice people. It might be only the poor, the humble, the ignorant, who could let themselves go like that.

*

RED OLIVER sat with his back against the little tree in the camp of workers. There was something in the air of the place, a kind of subdued tenseness that had got into him. That might have been due to the sound of the voices of people coming from the shack where the light was. Voices of people talked low and earnestly in the dark places. There came times of silence, then the talk began again. Red couldn't distinguish words. His nerves were stirred. He had grown wide awake. "Lord," he thought, "I am here, in this place now."

"How did I get here? Why did I let myself get here?"

This wasn't a camp of religious enthusiasts. He knew that. He knew what it was. "Well, I don't know," he thought. He smiled a little sheepishly, sitting under the tree and thinking. "I have got myself into a mess," he thought.

He had wanted to come to the communist camp. No, he hadn't. Yes, he had. He sat quarreling with himself as he had been doing for days. "If I could only be sure of myself," he thought. Again he thought of his mother getting religion in the little church at the edge of the mill village when he was at home, still a high school boy. He had been for a week, for ten days, for perhaps two weeks, coming toward this place into which he had now got. He had wanted to come. He hadn't wanted to come.

He had let himself get excited about something that perhaps didn't concern him at all. He had been reading newspapers, books, thinking, trying to think. The newspapers of the South had been full of strange news. They announced the coming of communism into the South. The newspapers hadn't told Red much.

He and Neil Bradley used to talk about that, about the lying of the newspapers. They didn't lie openly, Neil said. They were clever. They twisted the stories, made things seem as they weren't.

Neil Bradley had wanted a social revolution or had thought he did. "I guess he wants it okay," Red thought that night sitting in the camp.

"But why should I be thinking about Neil?"

It was strange to be sitting there in that place and thinking that only a few months before, that very spring, when he had got out of college, he had been with Neil Bradley on a Kansas farm. Neil had wanted him to stay out there. If he had stayed, how different his summer might have been!

He hadn't stayed. He had felt guilty about his mother, alone after his father's death, and after a few weeks had left the Bradley farm and had gone home.

He had again got a job in the cotton mill at Langdon. The mill people had taken him on again, even though they didn't need him.

That had been strange, too. There were workers in the town that summer, men with families, who had needed any work they could get. The mill people had known that, but they had hired Red.

"I guess they had thought ... they thought I would be all right. I guess they knew labor trouble might come, that it was likely to come. Tom Shaw's pretty slick," Red thought.

The mill at Langdon had kept cutting wages all that summer. The mill people made all the piece-workers do more work for less money. They had cut Red's wages, too. He got less pay than he got the first year he had worked in the mill.

Thump. Thump. Thump. Thoughts kept running through Red Oliver's head. He was excited thinking. He was thinking of his summer in Langdon. Suddenly across his thoughts, as across his dreams when he had tried to sleep, went the figure of Ethel Long. It might have been because he had been with a woman that night that he had suddenly now begun thinking of Ethel. He didn't want to think of her. "She did me dirt," he thought. The other woman, whom he had stumbled upon by accident during the late evening of the day before and who had brought him to the communist camp, was as tall as Ethel. "She's not like Ethel, though. By God, she's not like her," he thought. There was a queer cross-current of thoughts in his head. Thump. Thump. Thump. The thoughts were like little hammers beating in his head. "If I could only let go like that woman at the camp meeting," he thought, "if I could begin, be a communist, fighting the battle of the under-dog, be anything definite." He tried to laugh at himself. "Ethel Long, eh. You thought you had her, didn't you? She played with you. She made a fool of you."

Just the same, Red couldn't help remembering. He was a young man. He had been with Ethel a moment, such a delicious moment.

She was such a woman, so swank. His thoughts had gone flying back to the night in the library. "What does a man want?" he asked himself.

His friend, Neil Bradley, had got himself a woman. It might have been Neil's letters, coming to Red that summer, that had got him stirred up.

Then suddenly had come the chance with Ethel.

Suddenly, unexpectedly, he had her...in the library that night when it stormed. It had taken his breath away.

God, a woman could be strange. She had just wanted to find out whether or not she wanted him. She had found out she didn't.

A man, such a young man as Red, was a queer creature, too. He had wanted a woman—why? Why had he so wanted Ethel Long?

She was older than he was and didn't think the same kind of thoughts he did. She wanted swell clothes—to put on a certain kind of swank in life.

She had wanted a man, too.

She had thought she wanted Red.

"I'll try him out, put him through his paces," she had thought.

"I didn't make good with her." Red felt uncomfortable when the thought came to him. He stirred uneasily. He was a man making himself uncomfortable by his own thoughts. He began trying to justify himself. "She never gave me a fair chance. Just that once. How could she know?

"I was too shy and frightened.

"She let me go—bang. She went and got that other man. Right away—bang—the next day, she did it.

"I wonder if he suspected, if she told him.

"I'll bet she didn't.

"Maybe she did.

"Ah, lay off that."

There was a strike of mill workers in a mill town in North Carolina and it wasn't just an ordinary strike. It was a communist strike and word of it had been running through the South for two or three weeks. "What do you think of it ... it's at Birchfield, North Carolina ... actually. These communists have come into the South now. It's terrible."

A shiver had run through the whole South. It had been a challenge to Red. The strike was in the town named Birchfield, in North Carolina, a town by a river among hills, well down in North Carolina near the South Carolina line. There was a big cotton mill there ... "The Birchfield Mill," it was called ... where the strike had broken out.

Before that there had been a strike in the Langdon mills at Langdon, Georgia, and Red Oliver had been in that one, too. What he had done in it wasn't, he thought, very nice. He was ashamed thinking of it. His thoughts of it were like little pins pricking him. "I was rotten," he muttered to himself, "rotten."

There had been strikes in several Southern cotton-mill towns, strikes breaking out suddenly, upflarings from down below.... Elizabethton, Tennessee, Marion, in North Carolina, Danville, in Virginia.

Then one at Langdon, Georgia.

Red Oliver had been in that strike; he had got into it.

It had come as a sudden outbreak—a strange, unexpected thing.

He had been in it.

He wasn't in it.

He was.

He wasn't.

Now he sat in another place, at the edge of another town, in a camp of strikers, his back against a tree—thinking.

Thoughts. Thoughts.

Thump. Thump. Thump. More thoughts.

"Well, why not let myself think, then? Why not try to face myself? I've got all night. I've got plenty of time to think."

· Red had wished that the woman with whom he had come to the camp—the tall, thin woman, half factory hand, half farm hand—he wished she hadn't left him lying on the boards in the camp and gone off to bed. It would have been nice if she had been one of the sort of women who could talk.

She could have stayed outside the camp with him, anyway for an hour or two. They might have stayed up above the camp in the dark path that came over the hills.

He wished he were himself more of a woman's man, and for a few minutes he sat again lost in woman thoughts. There used to be a fellow in college who said—you met him —he seemed absorbed—he was a wit—he was having wants-woman thoughts—he said, "I was having me a big think time—I was in bed with a woman. Why did you speak to me? You jerked me out of her bed. Boy, she was a hot baby."

Red had begun doing that. For a moment he let his fancy go. He had lost out with the Langdon woman, Ethel Long, but had got him another. In fancy he held her. He began kissing her.

His body was pressed against hers. "Quit it," he said to himself. When he had got to the camp with the new woman he had been with that night, to the edge of the camp ... they were in the path in the woods then, near the field in which the camp had been set up ... they had stopped together in the path at the edge of the field.

She had already told him what she was and she thought she knew what he was. She had made the mistake about him at a place several miles away, over the hills, at the back of a little cabin on a side road, when she had first seen him.

She had thought he was something he wasn't. He had let her thoughts go on. He wished he hadn't.

*

SHE had thought that he, Red Oliver, was a communist going
to Birchfield to help in the strike. Red smiled, thinking that
he had forgotten the chill of the night and the discomfort
of the seat under the tree at the edge of the camp. In front
of the little camp and below it there was a paved road and
just before the camp a bridge crossed a rather wide river.
It was a steel bridge and the paved road crossed the bridge
and went on up into the town of Birchfield.

The Birchfield Mill, in which the strike had been called,
was across the river from the camp of strikers. Evidently
some sympathizer owned the land and had let the communists
set up their camp there. The land, being thin and sandy, was
of no value for farming.

The mill owners were trying to run their mill. Red could
see long rows of lighted windows. His eyes could make out
the outlines of the bridge that had been painted white. Now
and then a loaded truck came along the paved road and
crossed the bridge, making a heavy rumbling sound. The
town itself lay beyond the bridge on rising ground. He could
see the spread of the lights of the town beyond the river.

His mind was on the woman who had brought him to
the camp. She had been working in the cotton mill at Birchfield and was in the habit of going home to her father's farm
for the week-ends. He had found that out. Weary from the
long week of work in the mill she nevertheless started out
on Saturday afternoon to walk home over the hills.

Her people were growing old and feeble. There was a
feeble old man and an old woman back there in a little log
cabin hidden away in one of the hollows in the hills. They
were illiterate hill people. Red had got a glimpse of the old
people after the woman had come upon him in the woods.
He had gone into a little log barn that stood near the mountain house and the old mother had come into the barn while
the daughter was milking a cow. He had seen the father sit-

ting on a little porch before the house. He was a tall old man with a bent form, in figure rather like the daughter.

At home the daughter of the two old people kept busy over the week-end. Red had a sense of her flying about and giving the old people a rest. He imagined that she cooked the food, cleaned the house, milked the cow, worked in the little garden back of the house, made butter and put everything in order for another week away from home. It is true that most of the things that Red had found out about her were imagined. Admiration had been born in him. "There's a woman," he had thought. She was, after all, not much older than he was. Certainly, she was not older than Ethel Long of Langdon.

It had been late on a Sunday afternoon when she had first seen Red. She thought at once that he was something he wasn't.

A communist.

She had gone into a wood above the house late on the Sunday afternoon to get the family cow. To get it she had to go through the wood to where there was an upland pasture. She had gone there. She got the cow and had come out along an over-grown lumber road in the wood to where she saw Red. He must have come into the wood after she passed through the first time and before she returned. He was sitting on a log in a little open place. When he saw her he got up and stood facing her.

She wasn't frightened.

A thought came to her swiftly. "You ain't that fellow they air looking for, air you?" she asked.

"Who?"

"The law—the law was here. You ain't that communist they air looking for?"

She had an instinct which Red had already found out was common to most poor people in America. The law in America was something that could be depended upon to be unfair to the poor. You had to look out for the law. If you were poor, it got you. It lied about you. If you were in trouble, it bullied you. The law was your enemy.

Red hadn't answered the woman for a moment. He had to think fast. What had she meant? "Be you the communist?" she said again, anxiously. "The law's been looking for you."

Why had he answered as he did?

"Communist?" he asked again, looking sharply at her.

And then suddenly—in a flash—he had got it, he understood. He had taken a quick resolution.

"It was that man," he thought. A traveling salesman had given him a lift that afternoon along the road toward Birchfield and something had happened.

There had been talk. The traveling man had begun talking about the communists who were leading the strike at Birchfield and as Red had listened he had suddenly grown angry.

The man in the car was a fat man, a salesman. He had picked Red up in the road. He talked loosely, cursing the communist who had dared to come into a Southern town and lead a strike. They were all of them, he said, dirty snakes who should be hung up to the nearest tree. They wanted to put Negroes on the same basis as the whites. The fat traveling man was such a man, talking loosely, cursing as he talked.

Before he had got onto the subject of the communist, he had been boasting. Perhaps he had picked Red up to have some one to whom to boast. On the night before, on the Saturday night just past, he had been, he said, at another town back along the road, some fifty miles back—another industrial town, a mill town, and he had got drunk with a man there. He and a man of the town had got themselves two women. They were married women, he boasted. The husband of the one he had been with was a clerk in a store. The man had to work late on the Saturday night. He couldn't watch his wife and so the salesman and a man he knew in the town had got her and another woman into a car and had driven into the country. The man he had been with was, he said, a merchant of the town. They had managed to get the women half drunk. The salesman had gone on bragging to Red ... he said he had got the woman ... she had tried to put him off but he had got her into a room and had closed the door ... he had made her come across.... "They can't fool with me," he said ... and then suddenly he had begun cursing the communists who were leading the strike at Birchfield. "They are just cattle," he said. "They've got their nerve coming into the South. We'll fix 'em," he said. He had gone on talking thus, and then suddenly he had grown suspicious of Red. It might have been Red's eyes that had betrayed him. "Say," the man cried suddenly ... they were traveling at that moment on a paved road and were drawing near the town of Birchfield ... the road was deserted ... "say," said the salesman, suddenly stopping the car. Red had begun to hate the man. He didn't care what happened. His eyes had betrayed him. The man in the car had asked the same question later asked by the woman with the cow in the wood.

"You ain't one of them fellows, are you?"

"Ain't what?"

"One of them damn communists."

"Yes." Red had said it calmly, quietly enough.

A sudden impulse had come to him. It would be great fun frightening the fat salesman in the car. In trying to stop the car suddenly he had almost driven it into a ditch. His hands began to tremble violently.

He sat there in the car, his fat hands on the steering wheel, staring at Red.

"What, you ain't one of them ... you're fooling." Red looked hard at him. There were little flecks of white spittle gathering on the man's lips. The lips were thick. Red had an almost uncontrollable desire to hit the man in the face with his fist. The man's fright grew. After all Red was young and strong.

"What? What?" The words came tremblingly and jerkily from the man's lips.

"You air?"

"Yes," Red had said again.

He had got slowly out of the car. The man, he knew, would not dare order him out. He was carrying a small worn hand-bag with a rope to be thrown over his shoulder when he was traveling the road and it had been sitting on his knees. The fat man in the car was pale now. His hands fumbled about, trying to start the car quickly. It started with a jerk, ran two or three feet and then stopped. In his excitement, he had killed the engine. The car hung on the edge of the ditch.

Then he had got the car started and Red, standing at the road's edge . . . an impulse had come to him. He had a passionate desire to frighten the man still more. There was a stone lying beside the road, a rather large stone, and he picked it up and dropping the bag ran toward the man in the car. "Look out," he yelled. His voice rang across the nearby fields and along the empty road. The man had managed to drive off, the car running crazily from one side of the road to the other. It disappeared over a hill.

"And so," Red thought, standing in the woods with a factory woman—"and so, it was him, that fellow." Since he had left the man in the car he had been wandering rather aimlessly for two or three hours along a sandy country road at the foot of a mountain. He had left the main road into Birchfield after the traveling salesman drove away and had gone into the side road. He remembered suddenly that there had been a small unpainted house at the place where the side road he had been following left the main road. A country woman, some poor white tenant farmer's wife, had been sitting barefooted on a little porch before the house. The man he had frightened in the road would have driven on into Birchfield, crossing the bridge before the communist camp. He would have reported the incident to the police. "God only knows what kind of a tale he would tell," Red thought. "I bet he would make himself out some kind of hero. He would brag."

"And so"—as he had been loitering in a country road . . . the road followed the windings of a small stream, crossing and re-crossing it . . . he had been excited by the incident in the road, but the excitement had gradually passed . . . to be sure he had never meant to hit the man in the car with the stone . . . "and so."

Just the same he had hated the man with a sudden furious hatred new to him. He had been exhausted afterwards, a queer kind of emotional cyclone had run through him, leaving him, like the salesman in the car, weak and trembling.

He had left the little road he was following and had gone into a wood, loitering there for perhaps an hour, lying on his back under a tree and afterwards he had found a deep place in the creek, in a field of laurel bushes, and taking off his clothes had bathed in the cold water.

Then he had put on a clean shirt and had gone along the road and had climbed up a hillside into the wood where the woman with the cow had found him. The incident in the road had happened at about three. It might have been five or six when the woman came upon him. It was getting late in the year now and darkness came early, and all that time, while he had been loitering along, going into the woods, finding the place to bathe, officers of the law had been out after him. They would have found out from the woman at the cross-roads which way he had gone. They would have gone inquiring along the way. They would have been inquiring for him—for a crazy communist gone suddenly berserk—a man who attacked respectable citizens on the highway, a man gone suddenly dangerous and like a mad dog. The officers, "the law," as the woman in the woods called them, would have had a story to tell. He, Red, had attacked a man who was giving him a ride. "What do you think of that?" A respectable traveling salesman, who had picked him up in the road. He had tried to kill the man.

Red in his place near the communist camp suddenly remembered standing later with the woman who was driving
the cow in the wood and looking at her in the dim light
of evening. When he had been bathing in the creek he had
heard voices in the nearby road. The place he had found
to bathe was quite near the road, but there was a laurel
thicket between the creek and the road. He was half dressed,
but had dropped to the ground to let the car pass. The men
in the car were talking. "Keep your gun in your hand. He may
be hiding along here. He is a dangerous son-of-a-bitch," he
had heard a man's voice declaring. He hadn't connected the
incident with himself. It was lucky the men hadn't come into
the thicket to search. "They would have shot me like a dog."
It was a new feeling for Red—this being a hunted man.
When the woman with the cow told him that the law had just
been to the house where she lived and had asked whether
such a man as himself had been seen about, Red suddenly
trembled with fright. The officers hadn't known that she was
one of the strikers at the mill at Birchfield, that she was herself now called a communist . . . these poor workers in a cotton mill had suddenly become dangerous people. "The law"
had thought she was a farm woman.

The officers had driven up to the house and had called
in loud voices and the woman was just leaving the house to
go up the hill to get the cow. "Have you seen so and so?"
gruff voices demanded. "There's a red-headed son-of-a-bitch
of a communist loose somewhere around in this country. He
tried to kill a man back on the highway. He wanted to kill
him and get his car, I guess. He's a dangerous man."

The woman to whom they were talking had lost some
of her country-woman's fear and respect for the law. She
had had experience. Since the strike led by the communists
had broken out in Birchfield there had been several riots.
Red had seen accounts of them in the Southern newspapers.
He already knew from his experience at Langdon, Georgia,
during the strike there—the experience that had sent him out

of Langdon, wandering for the time being on the road, upset, really trying to straighten himself out, get his own mind straight as to what he felt about the growing labor difficulties in the South and all over America, ashamed of what had happened to himself during a strike in Langdon... he had already found out something of what workers on strike came to feel about the law and about accounts of strikes published in newspapers.

They felt that, whatever happened, lies would be told. Their own story would not be rightly told. They had learned that they could depend upon the newspapers to give the news a twist in favor of the employers. At Birchfield there had been attempts at parades broken up, attempts to hold meetings broken up. Because the leaders of the strike at Birchfield had been communists, the whole community had been up in arms. The bitter feeling between the people of the town and the strikers had grown as the strike went on.

Crowds of deputy sheriffs, sworn in for the time being, for the most part tough men, some of them imported from the outside, called special detectives, often half drunk, descended upon strike meetings. They bullied and threatened the strikers. Speakers were pulled down from platforms erected for meetings. Men and women were beaten.

"Smash the damn communists if they resist. Kill them." A working woman, an ex-farm woman from the hills... no doubt very like the one who had brought Red Oliver to the communists' camp... had been killed during the strike at Birchfield. The woman Red had got in with had known her, had worked near her in the mill. The newspapers and the citizens of the town of Birchfield hadn't, she knew, told the true story of what had happened.

The newspapers had said simply that there was a strike riot and that the woman had been killed. The ex-farm woman who had become Red's friend knew that. She knew what had happened. There had been no riot.

The woman who had been killed had been one with a

particular talent. She was a song maker. She made up songs
about the life of the poor white people, men, women and
children who worked in Southern cotton mills and in Southern fields. There were songs she had made up about the
machines in cotton mills, about the speed-up in the mills,
about women and children getting tuberculosis working in
cotton mills. She was like the woman named Doris, Red
Oliver had known in the mill at Langdon, and whom he had
once heard singing with other mill girls on a Sunday afternoon as he lay in tall weeds by a railroad track. The song-
making woman in the Birchfield mill had also made up songs
about the girls going to the water closet in the mill.

Or like the women in the Langdon mills they were waiting for the hour to come when they could rest a moment
during the long mornings and afternoons—to drink Coca-
Colas or to eat a kind of candy called "Milky Way." Lives
of such people, caught thus in the trap of life, hung on little
moments like that, a woman cheating a little, going into the
toilet to rest there, the foreman of the room watching her—
trying to catch her cheating.

Or the woman, a mill worker, squeezing out of her
meager pay enough money to buy five cents' worth of cheap
candy.

> *Twicet a day.*
> *Milky Way.*

There were songs like that. No doubt in every mill each
group of workers had its song-maker. Little fragments were
picked up out of the meager hard lives. The lives were made
doubly, a hundred times more pathetic and real, because a
woman, a song-maker, being a kind of genius, could make a
song out of such fragments. It was going on wherever people
were gathered together in groups and were down-trodden.
The factories had their songs and the prisons their songs.

Red had got the story of the death of the song-making
woman at Birchfield, not from the newspapers, but from a

tramp in a place where he had stopped with another young
man near the city of Atlanta. There had been a little grove
of trees out of the edge of a town near some railroad yards
to which he had gone one day with another young man he
had met in a box car. It had happened two or three days
after he had fled from Langdon.

A man there, in that place, a bleary-eyed young man ...
young yet, but with his face all blotched and broken out,
no doubt from drinking cheap moonshine whiskey ... the
man was talking to several others, also tramps and workingmen out of employment.

There had been a discussion going on. "You can't go
work at Birchfield," the bleary-eyed young man said, fiercely.
"Yes, God damn it, I was there. They'll take you on as a scab
if you go there," he said. "I thought I'd do it. By God, I did.
I thought I'd go be a scab."

The man in the tramps' hang-out was a bitter, bitten
man. He was a drunkard. There he sat in the tramps' hang-
out, "the Jungle," they called it. He hadn't minded being a
scab, scabbing on the strikers at Birchfield. There was, with
him, no principle involved. Anyway, he didn't want to work,
he said, laughing unpleasantly. He was simply broke. He
wanted something to drink.

He was describing an experience. "I didn't have a cent
and was dead for the stuff," he said. "Well, you know. I
couldn't stand it." It might not have been liquor the man
wanted. Red had guessed that. He might have been a dope.
The man's hands were twitching as he sat on the ground in
the jungle talking with the other tramps.

Some one had told him that he could get work at Birchfield and he had gone there. He swore violently telling about
it. "Bastard that I am, I couldn't do it," he said. He had told
the story of the singing woman killed at Birchfield. It had
been to Red a simple, a pathetic tale. The woman, the song-
making woman, an ex-farm woman from the hills, now a mill
woman, was like the other woman driving the cow who had

found Red in the wood. The two women had known each other, had worked near each other in the mill. Red didn't know about that when he heard the bleary-eyed young man telling the story in the tramps' jungle.

That one, the singing, ballad-making workwoman, had been sent, with several other women and girls... they were standing together on a truck... they were sent thus through the streets of the town of Birchfield with instructions to stop on crowded street corners and sing their songs. One of the communist leaders had thought out the scheme. He had managed to get for them a truck, a cheap Ford truck owned by one of the men strikers. The communist leaders were alert. They knew the technique of stirring up trouble. The communist leaders thought up schemes to keep the strikers in the strikers' camp busy.

"Beware of the enemy, capitalism. Fight him in every possible way. Keep him worried. Frighten him. Remember that you are fighting for the minds of the people, the imaginations of people."

The communists, from the point of view of fellows like Red Oliver, were unscrupulous, too. They didn't seem to mind sending people out to be killed. They were in the South leading a strike. It was a chance for them. They were snatching at it. There was something in them harder, more unscrupulous, more determined... they were something quite different from the old leaders of labor in America.

Red Oliver had got a look at the old kind of labor leaders. One of them had come to Langdon when the strike had broken out there. He was all for what he called "conferences" with the bosses, talking it over with them. He wanted the strikers to remain peaceful, kept begging them to remain peaceful. He kept talking about labor sitting at the council table with the bosses... "with capitalism," the communists would have said.

Talk. Talk.

Bunk.

Perhaps it was that. Red didn't know. He was a man looking into a new world. The world into which he had got himself suddenly plunged, almost by accident, was new and strange to him. It might be, after all, an actual new world, just coming into being in America.

There were new words, new ideas, striking on the consciousness of people. The words themselves bothered Red. "Communism, socialism, the bourgeoisie, capitalism, Karl Marx." The bitter, long struggle that had to come . . . the war . . . that was what it would be . . . between those who had and those who couldn't get . . . was making for itself new words. Words were flying into America from Europe, from Russia. There would be all sorts of queer new alignments of people in life . . . new alignments made, having to be made. In the end every man and every woman, even the children, would have to line themselves up on the one side or the other.

"I won't. I'll stay standing here to one side. I'll watch, look and listen."

"Ha! You will, will you? Well, you can't."

"The communists are the only people who realize that war is war," Red thought sometimes. "They'll gain by that. Anyway, they'll gain in determination. They'll be the real leaders. It's a soft age. Men must quit being soft." With Red Oliver . . . he was like thousands of young Americans . . . he had got just enough of communism, its philosophy, to make him afraid. He was afraid and at the same time fascinated. He might at any moment surrender, become a communist. He knew that. His going from the strike at Langdon to the strike at Birchfield was like a moth going toward a flame. He wanted to go. He didn't want to go.

He could see it all as pure brutal cruelty . . . a communist leader at Birchfield, for example, sending the singing woman out into the streets of Birchfield, knowing how the town felt, at a time when the town was excited—worked up. . . . People were bound to be most cruel when they were most frightened. Cruelty in man had its roots in that—in fear.

To send the singing women from the strikers' camp out in the town knowing...as the communist leaders did know...that they might be killed...was it brutal, useless cruelty? One of the women was killed, the song-maker. The bleary-eyed young man Red saw in the tramps' jungle, to whom he stood listening, was telling about it.

The truck loaded with the singing women had driven out of the strikers' camp into the town. It was at the noon hour when the streets were full of people. There had been a riot in the town on the day before. Strikers had tried to parade and a crowd of deputy sheriffs had tried to stop them.

Some of the strikers—ex-mountain men—had been armed. There was shooting. The bleary-eyed man said that two or three deputy sheriffs tried to stop the truck loaded with the singing women. Besides their own ballads they were singing another song the communists had taught them. There couldn't have been a chance on earth that the women on the truck knew for themselves what communism was, what communism demanded, what the communists were fighting for. "It might be the great curative philosophy," Red Oliver thought sometimes. He had begun thinking that. He didn't know. He was puzzled and uncertain.

Two or three deputy sheriffs running out into a crowded street to try to stop a truck loaded with singing work women. They had been taught by the communists a new song.

Arise, ye prisoners of starvation,
Arise, ye wretched of the earth,
For justice thunders condemnation.
A better world's in birth.

No more tradition's chains shall bind us.
Arise, ye slaves, no more enthralled.
The world shall rise on new foundations.
Ye have been naught, ye shall be all.

It could not have been that the women singers understood the import of the song they had been taught to sing. There were words in the song they had never heard before —"condemnation"—"traditions"—"tradition's chains"—"enthralled"—"no more enthralled"—but there is something more than exact meaning in words. Words have a life of their own. They have relations to each other. Words are building stones with which dreams may be built. There was dignity in the song the workers sang in the truck. Voices rang out with new courage. They rang through the crowded streets of a North Carolina industrial town. Smell of gasoline— rattle of truck wheels—auto horns—the hurrying, strangely impotent, modern American crowd.

The truck was in the middle of a block, proceeding on its way. The crowd in the streets stared. Lawyers, doctors, merchants, beggarmen, thieves stood silently in the streets with mouths a little open. A deputy sheriff ran out into the street, accompanied by two other deputy sheriffs. A hand went up.

"Stop."

Another deputy sheriff came running.

"Stop."

The man driver of the truck—the mill worker driver of the truck—did not stop. Words flew back and forth. "Go to hell." The truck driver was inspired by a song. He was just a cotton mill worker. The truck was in the middle of a block. Other automobiles and trucks were going forward. "I am an American citizen." It was like St. Paul saying, "I am a Roman." What right had he, the deputy sheriff, the big fathead, to stop an American? "For justice thunders condemnation," the women went on singing.

Some one shot. Afterwards the newspapers said there was a riot. It may have been that a deputy sheriff merely wanted to scare the truck driver. Shot heard around the world. Well, not quite. The leader of the women singers, the ballad-making woman among them, fell down dead in the truck.

> *Twicet a day.*
> *Milky Way.*
> *Twicet a day.*

> *Rest in the water closet.*
> *Rest in the water closet.*

The tramp Red Oliver heard talking in the tramps' jungle was blue with wrath. It may be that, after all, such shots heard here and there, at factory gates, at mine entrances, on picket lines before factories—deputy sheriffs— the law—protection of property . . . it may be they do echo and reëcho.

The tramp did not, after that, take a job at Birchfield. He said he saw the killing. He might have been lying. He said he had been standing in the street, had seen the killing and that it was cold-blooded and deliberate. In him it had produced a sudden hunger for new and more profane words —ugly words that came sputtering through blue, unshaven lips.

A man like that—after a life all ugly and dirty—had he got hold at last of a real feeling? "The bastards, dirty sons-of-bitches," he cried. "Before I'd work for them! The stinking horseflies!"

The tramp in the jungle was even yet, when Red heard him talking, half insanely furious. It might be that you couldn't trust such a man—wrath in such a man. It might be that he only hungered, with a deep, trembling hunger, for liquor or for dope.

2

THE woman with the cow on the hill in the wood in North Carolina on a Sunday evening in November had accepted Red Oliver. He wasn't what "the law," that had just driven up to the house below, had said he was—a dangerous madman, running about the country, wanting to kill people. That afternoon—it was growing dark rapidly on the hill—she took him for what he said he was. He had said he was a communist. It was a lie. She didn't know that. A communist had come to mean a definite thing to her. When the strike had come at Birchfield, there the communists were. They had suddenly appeared. There were two young men from somewhere in the North and a young woman. People in Birchfield said, the newspaper in Birchfield said, that one of them, the young woman among them, was a Jew and that the others were foreigners and Yanks. They weren't foreigners, anyway. The two young men at least were Americans. They had come to Birchfield immediately after the strike had broken out and had at once taken charge.

They knew how. That was something. They had organized the disorganized workers, had taught them to sing songs, had found out the leaders among them, the song-makers, the courageous ones. They had taught them to march shoulder to shoulder. When the strikers had been driven from the houses in the mill village near the mill, the young communist leaders had managed in some way to get permission to set up a camp on a vacant piece of ground near by. The ground belonged to an old man in Birchfield who knew nothing about communism. He was an obstinate old man. People in Birchfield went and threatened him. He grew more obstinate. Going out of Birchfield toward the west you came down a half hill past the mill and then you had to follow the highway across the bridge over the river and there you were at the camp. From the camp, also situated on rising ground, you could see everything going on about the mill and in the mill yard. The young communist leaders had managed in some way to get a few small tents shipped in, and provisions also appeared. Many poor small farmers from the hills about Birchfield, not understanding about communism, came into the camp at night with provisions. They brought beans and pork. They divided what they had. The young communist leaders had managed to organize the strikers into a little army.

There was something else. Many of the workers of the Birchfield mill had been in strikes before. They had belonged to unions organized in the mills. The union grew suddenly strong. A strike broke out and there was an exalted moment. It might last two or three weeks. Then the strike and the union faded away. The workers knew about the old unions. They had talked and the woman Red Oliver had met on the hill on Sunday evening—her name was Molly Seabright—had heard the talk.

It was always the same thing—talk of being sold out. A worker went up and down before a group of other workers. He held his hand behind him with the open palm upward and waved it back and forth. His lips curled unpleasantly. "Unions, unions," he cried, laughing bitterly. That's the way it was. The workers in a mill found life pressing down and down on them. In good times they managed to get along, but then, always, after a few years of good times, the bad times came.

There was a sudden slackening of work in the mills and the workers went about shaking their heads. A worker went home at night to his house. He called his wife aside.

He whispered. "It's coming," he said. What made good
times and bad times? Molly Seabright didn't know. Workers
in the mill began to be laid off. The less strong and alert
ones lost their jobs.

There were cuts in wages and those on piece-work were
speeded up. They were told "hard times had come."

You might have been able to stand that. Most of the
workers in the mill at Birchfield knew about hard times. They
had been born poor. "Hard times," an old woman said to
Molly Seabright, "when'd we ever know any good times?"

You saw men and women in the mill laid off. You knew
what it meant to them. Many of the women workers had
children. A new cruelty seemed to come into the foreman
and into the superintendent. They might be trying to protect
themselves. They had to be cruel. They began speaking to
you in a new way. You were ordered here and there, gruffly,
abruptly. Your work was changed. You weren't consulted
when you were given new work to do. Just a few months
before, when there were good times, you and all the other
workers had been treated differently. Bosses were even more
considerate. There was a different quality in the voices that
addressed you. "Well, we need you. There is money to be
made from your labor now." There were many little things
that Molly Seabright, although she was but twenty-five and
had been in the mill for ten years, had noticed. People of
the town of Birchfield, where she went with the other girls
sometimes at night, to the movies and sometimes just to look
at the shop windows, thought that she and the other girls
like her were stupid, but she wasn't as stupid as they thought.
She had feelings, too, and the feelings got into her brain.
The men in charge of the rooms at the mill, the foremen—
often they were young men who had risen out of the ranks
of the workers—even bothered to find out a workwoman's
name in good times. "Miss Molly," they said. "Miss Molly
do this—or Miss Molly do that." She, being a good worker,
a rapid, efficient worker, was even, at times—in good times

—when workers were scarce—she was even "Miss Seabright." The young foremen smiled when they spoke to her.

There was a story about Miss Molly Seabright, too. Red Oliver never knew her story. Once when she was a young woman of eighteen ... she was a tall slender well-developed young woman then ... once one of the young foremen in the mill ...

She herself hardly knew how it happened. She was working on the night shift in the mill. There was something strange, a bit queer about working on the night shift. You worked as many hours as those of the day shift. You grew more tired and nervous. Molly could never have told any one very clearly about what had happened to her.

She had never had a man, a lover. She didn't know why. There was something in her manner, a kind of reserve, a good deal of quiet dignity. There had been two or three young men in the mill and back in the hills where her father and mother lived who had begun looking at her. They wanted to and didn't dare. Even then, as a young woman just coming out of girlhood, she had felt her responsibility to her father and mother.

There had been a young mountain man, a rough fellow, a fighter, who had been attracted to her. For a time she was herself attracted. He was one of a big family of boys, living in a mountain cabin a mile from her own home, a tall rawboned strong young man with a long jaw.

He didn't like to work much and he got drunk. She knew about that. He also made and sold liquor. Most of the young mountain men did. He was a great hunter and could kill more squirrels and rabbits in a day than any other young man in the hills. He caught woodchuck with his hands. The woodchuck was a coarse-haired fierce little creature as big as a young dog. Woodchucks were eaten by the mountain people. They were looked upon as a delicacy. If you knew how to take out a certain gland in the woodchuck, a gland that, if left in, gave the meat a bitter taste, the meat became sweet. The young mountain man brought such delicacies to Molly Seabright's mother. He killed young coons and rabbits and brought them to her. He always brought them late in the week when he knew Molly would be coming home from the mill.

He hung about, talking to Molly's father, who didn't like him. The father was afraid of the man. Once on a Sunday night Molly went with him to church and on the way home, suddenly, in the dark road, in a dark stretch of road where there were no houses near . . . he had been drinking mountain moonshine . . . he hadn't gone into the mountain church with her but had stayed on the outside with the other young men . . . on the way home in the lonely place in the road he had suddenly attacked her.

There hadn't been any preliminary love making. Perhaps he thought that she . . . he was a great young fellow for animals, both domestic and tame animals . . . he might have thought she was just a little animal too. He had tried to throw her to the ground but he had taken too many drinks. He was strong enough but wasn't quick enough. The drinks confused him. If he hadn't been a little drunk . . . they were walking along the road in silence . . . he wasn't one who could talk much . . . when suddenly he stopped and said to her gruffly, "I'm going to," he said . . . "come on now, I am going to."

He sprang at her, got one of his hands on her shoulder. He tore her dress. He tried to throw her to the ground.

Perhaps he thought she was just another little animal. Molly understood dimly. If he had been a man she cared for enough—if he had gone slowly with her.

He could break a young colt almost by his own strength. He was the best man in the hills for breaking wild young colts. People said, "In a week he can make the wildest colt in the hill follow him like a kitten." Molly had seen his face pressed down close to her own for a moment, the queer determined terrible look in his eyes.

She had managed to get away. She got over a low fence. If he hadn't been a little drunk... When he was getting over the fence he fell. She had to run through a field and through a creek with her best shoes on, with her best Sunday dress on. She couldn't afford it. She had run through bushes—through a strip of wood. She didn't know how she escaped. She never knew she could run so fast. He was there close behind her. He never said a word. He followed her to the very door of her father's house, but she managed to get through the door and into the house and get the door closed again ahead of him.

She told a lie. Her father and mother were in bed. "What is it?" Molly's mother asked that night, sitting up in bed. In the little mountain cabin there was but the one large room downstairs and a little loft upstairs. Molly slept up there. She had to go up a ladder to get to her bed. Her bed was by a little window under the roof. Her father and mother slept in a bed in a corner of the big room downstairs where they all ate and where they sat during the day. Her father also woke up.

"It's nothing, Ma," she said to her mother that night. Her mother was already almost an old woman. The father and mother were both old people who had both been married before, away off somewhere in another mountain community, and they had both lost their first mates. They didn't get married until they were quite old and then they moved to the little cabin and the farm where Molly was born. She had never seen any of their other children. Her father liked to make a joke. He said to people—"my wife has four children and I have five children and together we have ten children. Solve that riddle if you can," he said.

"It's nothing, Ma," Molly Seabright said to her mother that night she was attacked by the young mountain man. "I got scared," she said. "Something in the yard scared me.

I guess it was a strange dog." That was her way. She didn't tell about things that happened to her. She climbed upstairs to her own little half room, her body trembling, and through the window she saw the young man who had tried to attack her standing in the yard. He was standing near her father's bee gums in the yard and looking up at the window of her room. The moon had come out and she could see his face. There was an angry baffled look in his eyes that increased her fright. She might just have imagined that. How could she see his eyes down there? She couldn't understand why she had ever let him walk with her, why she had gone off to church with him. She had wanted to show the other girls in the mountain community that she also could get a man. That must have been why she did it. She would have had trouble with him later—she knew that. Just a week after that happened he got into a fist fight with another young mountain man, a quarrel over the ownership of a mountain still, and he shot the man and had to light out. He couldn't come back, didn't dare. She never saw him again.

3

IN a cotton mill at night. You are working there. There is a
roar of sound—a sustained roar—now low, now high—big
sounds ... little sounds. There is a singing—a shouting—a
talking. There are whispers. There is laughter. Thread laughs.
It whispers. It runs softly and swiftly. It leaps. Thread is
like a young goat on the mountains of the moon. Thread is
like a little hair snake running into a hole. It runs softly
and swiftly. Steel can laugh. It can cry out. Looms in a cotton mill are like baby elephants playing with mother elephants in a forest. Who understands inanimate life? A river
coming down out of a hill, over rocks, through a quiet glade,
can make you love it. Hills and fields can win your love as
can also steel made into a machine. Machines dance. They
dance on their iron legs. They sing, whisper, groan, laugh.
You get woozy-headed sometimes seeing and hearing all the
things going on in a mill. It is worse at night. It is better,
wilder, more exciting at night. It tires you more.

The lights in a cotton mill at night are cold blue. Molly
Seabright worked in the loom room of the mill at Birchfield.
She was a weaver. She had been there a long time and could
just remember when she had not been a worker. She could
remember, sometimes vividly, days with her father and
mother in hillside fields. She remembered little creeping
crawling buzzing things in grass, a squirrel running up the
trunk of a tree. Her father kept gums of bees. She remembered the surprise and pain of a bee stinging her, a ride
her father gave her on a cow's back—he walking beside the

cow holding her on—a quarrel her father had with a man
in the road, a night of wind and heavy rain, her mother ill
and in bed, a calf running suddenly, crazily across a field—
so awkwardly Molly had to laugh.

She had come down to Birchfield with her mother out
of the hills one year when she was little more than a child.
That year her father was half ill and couldn't work much
and there was a drought and a crop failure on the mountain
farm. Just the same that year the mill was booming. It
wanted workers. The mill sent out little printed circulars into
the hills telling the hill people how nice it was in town, in
the mill village. The wages offered seemed high to the mountain people and the Seabrights' cow died. Then the roof of
the house in which they lived began to leak. They had to
have a new roof put on or get the old one fixed.

The mother, already old, went over the hills to Birchfield
that spring and in the fall she put her daughter in the mill.
She didn't want to. Molly was so very young then that she
had to lie about her age. The mill people knew she was lying.
There were many children in the mill who had lied about
their age. It was because of the law. The mother thought,
"I won't let her stay." The mother walked to work past the
offices of the mill. She had a room with a family in the mill
village. She saw stenographers in there. She thought, "I'll
get an education for my daughter. She'll be a stenographer."
The mother thought, "We'll get some money to buy a new
cow and get the roof fixed and then we'll go back home."
The mother did go back to the mountain farm, but Molly
Seabright stayed.

She had got used to being in the mill. A young girl
wants a little money of her own. She wants new dresses and
new shoes. She wants silk stockings. There are movies in
town.

There is a kind of excitement in being in a mill. After
a few years, Molly got put on the night shift. The looms in
the loom-room in the mill were set in long rows. They are

that way in all mills. All mills are pretty much alike. Some are bigger than others and more efficiently run. Molly's mill was a good one.

It was nice to be in the Birchfield mill. Molly thought sometimes ... her thoughts weren't very definite ... she felt sometimes, "It's nice to be here."

There were even thoughts of cloth being made—nice thoughts. Cloth for dresses for many women—shirts for many men. Sheets for beds. Pillow cases for beds. People lying in beds. Lovers lying together in beds. She thought that and blushed thinking it.

Cloth for banners to fly in the sky.

Why can't we, in America—machine people—machine age—why can't we make it a sacred thing—a ceremony—joy in it—laughter in mills—song in mills—new churches—new sacred places—cloth being made for people to wear?

Molly did not think such thoughts definitely. None of the workers in the mill did. Just the same, the thoughts were there, in the rooms in the mill, wanting to fly into people. The thoughts were like birds flying above the rooms waiting to alight in people. "We have to take it away. It's ours. It should belong to us—we the workers. Some day we have to take it away from the little money-changers—the cheaters—the liars. We will do it some day. We'll arise—sing—work—sing with steel—sing with thread—sing and dance with machines—a new day coming—new religion—a new life coming."

Year by year as machines in America had become more and more efficient the number of looms taken care of by one weaver was increased. A weaver had twenty looms, then thirty, the next year forty, then even sixty or seventy looms. The looms were becoming all the time more and more automatic, more and more independent of the weavers. They seemed more and more to have a life of their own. The looms were outside the lives of the weavers, seemed every year more and more outside. It was odd. It gave you, at night sometimes, a queer feeling.

The difficulty was that, after all, the workers—a few workers at least—were necessary to the looms. The difficulty was that thread did break. If it weren't for the inclination of the thread to break no weavers would be necessary at all. All the ingenuity of the smart men who made machines had been used to work out better and better ways of working the thread faster and faster. It was kept slightly damp to make it more flexible. There was a spray—a fine mist—that was blown down from somewhere up above over the flying thread.

It was hot in the mills on the long summer nights in North Carolina. You sweated. Your clothes were wringing wet. Your hair was wet. Fine lint, floating in the air, clung to your hair. In town they called you "lint-head." They did it to insult you. It was said in derision. They hated you in town and you hated them. The nights were long. They seemed endless. The cold blue light, falling down from somewhere up above, came through fine lint floating in the air. You got queer headaches sometimes. The looms you were taking care of danced more and more crazily.

The foreman in the room in which Molly worked had an idea. He put a little colored card attached to a wire on the top of each loom. The cards were blue, yellow, orange, gold, green, red, white and black. Little colored cards danced in the air. That was so you could tell, when you were a long way off, when a thread had broken in one of the looms and it had stopped. The looms stopped automatically when a thread broke. You didn't dare let them stop. You had to run quickly, sometimes a long way. Sometimes several looms stopped at once. Several of the colored cards quit dancing. You had to run swiftly here and there. You had to tie the broken threads in quickly. You can't let your loom stop too long. You'll get fired. You'll lose your job.

There they go—the dancing looms. Watch them closely. Watch. Watch.

Clatter. Clatter. What a racket there is! There is a dancing—crazily, jerkily dancing—the loom dance. At night the lights make your eyes tired. The colored cards dancing made Molly's eyes tired. It's nice in the loom room of the mill at night. It's strange. It makes you feel strange. You are in a world far from any other world. You are in the world of flying lights, flying machines, flying thread, flying colors. It's nice. It's terrible.

The looms in a loom-room had stiff iron legs. Inside each loom the shuttles flew back and forth with flashing speed. You could not follow the flight of the flying shuttles with your eyes. The shuttles were shadowlike things—flying, flying, flying. "What's the matter with me?" Molly Seabright said to herself sometimes. "I got looms in my head, I guess." Everything in the room jerked. It was jerky. You had to be careful or you got the jerks. Molly got the jerks sometimes when she was trying to sleep in the daytime—when she worked at night—after the long night in the mill. She jerked awake when she tried to sleep. The loom room in the mill was still in her head. It stayed there. She could see it. She felt it.

Thread is blood running through cloth. Thread is little nerves running through cloth. Thread is a thin stream of blood running through the body of cloth. It is a little flying stream that makes the cloth. When a thread breaks in a loom the loom is hurt. It stops dancing. It seems to jump off the floor as though hurt, stabbed, shot—as the singing woman was shot in the truck in the street of Birchfield when the strike came. Song, and then suddenly no more song. Looms in a mill at night danced in a cold blue light. In the mill at Birchfield they made many-colored cloth. There were blue threads, red threads and white threads. There was always the endless movement. Little arms and little fingers were at work down inside the looms. Thread was always flying in, flying in. It flew off little bobbins set in cylinders atop the looms. In another big room of the mill they filled bobbins ... they made thread and filled bobbins.

In there the thread came from somewhere up above. It was like a long slender snake. It never quit coming. It came out of tanks, out of tubes, out of steel, out of brass, out of iron.

It wriggled. It leaped. It ran out of a tube onto a bobbin. Women and girls in the spinning-room got thread in the head. In the loom-room there were always the tiny streams of thread-blood running into the body of cloth. Now it was blue, now white, now red again. The eyes got tired watching.

The point was—Molly came to understand it slowly, slowly—that you have to work in a place to know. People on the outside didn't know. They couldn't. You feel things. People from the outside don't know how you feel. You have got to work in a place to know. You have got to be there through long hours, day after day, year after year. You've got to be there at work when you aren't well, when your head aches. A woman who works in a mill gets ... well, you ought to know how she gets. It's monthlies. It comes sometimes suddenly. You can't help it. Some feel like hell when it comes, others don't. Molly did sometimes. Sometimes she didn't.

But she's got to stick.

If you are from the outside, not a worker, you don't know. Bosses don't know how you feel. The superintendent or the president of the mill walks through sometimes. The president of a mill takes visitors through his mill.

The men and women, the children, working in a mill just stand there. Very likely no threads break just then. It's just the luck. "You see, they don't have to work hard," he says. You hear it. You hate him. You hate the visitors in the mill. You know how they are looking at you. You know they have contempt for you.

"Okay, smarty, you don't know...you can't know."
You'd like to throw something. How can they know about
thread always coming and coming, always dancing, looms
always dancing...streaming lights...clatter, clatter?

How can they know? They don't work in there. Your
feet hurt. They hurt all night long. You get a headache. You
get a backache. It's your time again. You look around. Anyway, you know. There's Kate, and Mary, and Grace, and
Winnie. Now it's Winnie's time too. See the dark places
under her eyes. There's Jim, and Fred, and Joe. Joe's going
to pieces—you know that. He's got tuberculosis. You see a
little movement—the hand of a worker is going to her back,
to her head, it is covering her eyes for a moment. You know.
You know how it hurts because it hurts you.

The looms in a loom-room sometimes seem to want to
embrace each other. They get suddenly all alive. A loom
seems to make a queer jerky leap toward another loom.
Molly Seabright thought of the young mountain man who
had once leaped toward her in a road at night.

Molly had her own thoughts working in the weaving
room of the mill at Birchfield through the long years. She
didn't dare do too much thinking. She didn't want to. The
thing was to keep the attention fixed always on the looms,
never to let the attention waver. She had become a mother
and the looms were her children.

But she wasn't a mother. Sometimes at night queer
things happened in her head. Queer things happened in her
body. After a long time, months of nights, even years of
nights, the attention thus fixed hour after hour, the body
gradually becoming synchronized to the movements of the
machines.... There were nights when she got lost. There
were nights when it seemed to her there was no Molly Seabright. Nothing mattered to her. She was in a strange world
of movement. Lights were shining through mist. Colors
danced before her eyes. She tried to sleep during the day

but there was no rest. The dancing machines stayed in her dreams. They went on dancing in her dreams.

If you are a woman and young yet.... But who knows what a woman wants, what a woman is? There are so many smart words written. People say things. You want something alive, leaping toward you, as a loom leaps. You want something determined, coming toward you, outside yourself. You want it.

You don't. You do.

Days, after the long nights in the mill, in the hot summer, become queer days. The days are nightmares. You can't sleep. When you do sleep, you can't rest. The nights when you go back to work again in the mill become just hours spent in a strange unreal world. Both days and nights become unreal to you. "If that young man, in the road that night, if he had come at me more gently, more softly," she thought sometimes. She didn't want to think about him. He didn't come toward her gently. He frightened her horribly. She hated him for it.

4

RED OLIVER had to think. He thought he had to think. He wanted to think—thought he wanted to think. In youth there is a kind of hunger. "I'd like to understand everything —feel everything," youth says to itself. After some months working in the mill at Langdon, Georgia ... being fairly eager-minded ... Red tried to write poetry sometimes ... after the strike among the workers at Langdon, a lost strike ... he hadn't shown up very well in that ... he had thought ... "Now I'll stand by the workers" ... then, at the last, when the pinch came, he didn't ... after the visit in the early summer to the Bradley farm in Kansas ... Neil's talk ... afterwards at home, reading radical books ... he took the *New Republic* and the *Nation* ... then after that Neil sent him the *New Masses* ... he thought ... "It is time to try to think ... we got to do it ... we got to try ... we young American men have got to try to do it ... the old ones won't."

He thought, "We got to begin to show courage, even fight, even be willing to be killed for it ... for what?" ... he wasn't sure ... "Anyway," he thought. ...

"Let me find out.

"Let me find out.

"I'll go this road at any price now. If it's communism, all right. I wonder if the communists would want me," he thought.

"I'm brave now. Forward!"

Maybe he was brave, maybe not.

"Now I'm frightened. There is too much about life to

find out." He didn't know how it would be with him if it came to a test. "Oh, hell, let it go," he thought. What business was it of his? He had read books, had been to college. Shakespeare. Hamlet. "The world is out of joint—wicked spite, that ever I was born to set it right." He laughed . . . "ha . . . Oh, hell . . . I got tried out once and I caved in . . . smarter men and better men than me have caved in . . . but what are you going to do . . . be a professional ball player?" . . . Red could have been that; he had had an offer while he was in college . . . he could have begun in a minor league and worked up . . . he could have gone to New York and become a bond salesman . . . other students in college did that.

"Stay in the mill at Langdon. Be a traitor to the workers in the mill." He had got acquainted with some of the workers in the mill at Langdon, felt close to them. In a queer way he even loved some of them. People, like the new woman he had accidentally stumbled upon in his wanderings . . . wanderings started because of his uncertainty about himself, because of shame of what had happened to him in Langdon, Georgia, during the strike there . . . the new woman he had found and to whom he had told a lie, saying he was a communist, implying that he was something braver and finer than he was . . . he had begun looking upon communists in that way . . . perhaps he was being romantic and sentimental about them . . . there were people just like that woman, Molly Seabright, in the mill at Langdon.

"Get yourself in with the bosses in a mill. Be a suck. Rise. Grow rich maybe some day. Grow fat and old and rich and self-satisfied."

Even a few months spent in the mill at Langdon, Georgia, during that summer and during the summer before, had done something to Red. He had sensed something a little that many Americans do not sense, perhaps never can sense. "Life was an experience full of queer accidents. There was the accident of birth. Who could account for it?

What child could say when or where or how he or she would be born?

"Would the child, to be born, be born in a well-to-do family, or in a middle-class family—lower middle class, upper middle class?... in a big white house on a hill above an American town or in a city tenement or in a coal-mining town... millionaire's son or daughter... Georgia cracker's son or daughter, thief's son, even murderer's son... children are even born in prisons?... Are you legitimate or illegitimate?"

People are always talking. They say, "So and so comes of nice people." They mean that his people or her people are rich or well-to-do.

"By what accident did he or she get born so?"

People are always judging others. There was talk, talk, talk. The children of the rich or well-to-do... Red had seen plenty of that kind in college... they never in a long lifetime really knew anything about hunger and uncertainty, year after year of weariness, helplessness that gets into the very bones, poor food, cheap shoddy clothes. Why?

If the mother of such a one—a worker—got sick or the child of a worker got sick... there was the question of having a doctor too... Red knew about that... his father was a doctor... doctors worked for money too... sometimes the children of workers died like flies. Why not?

"Anyway, it makes more jobs for other workers.

"What difference does it make? Are workers—who are always getting it in the neck—who always in the history of man did get it in the neck—are they, can they be, nice people?"

It was all queer and puzzling to Red Oliver. Having been with the workers a little, having worked with them a little, he thought they were nice. He couldn't help thinking it. There was his own mother—she was also a worker—gone so queerly religious. She was looked down upon by the better-fixed people in his own town of Langdon. He had come to realize that. She was always alone, always silent, always at work or prayer. He hadn't done very well in his efforts to get close to her. He knew that. When the crisis had come in his own life he had run away from her and from his home town. He hadn't talked it over with her. He couldn't. She was too shy and silent and she made him shy and silent. Just the same he knew she was nice, at bottom she was damn nice.

"Oh, hell, it's true. Those who are always getting it in the neck are the nicest people. I wonder why."

ONE summer, when Molly Seabright was working nights in the mill at Birchfield ... she had just passed twenty ... it was a queer summer for her. ... That summer she had an experience. For some reason everything in her body and mind seemed dragged out and slow that summer. There was in her a kind of weariness she couldn't shake off.

Her sick times were harder on her. They hurt her more.

During that summer the machines in the mill seemed to her to become more and more alive. On some days the queer fantastic dreams of her days, when she was trying to sleep, came into the waking working hours at night.

There were queer desires that frightened her. Sometimes she half wanted to throw herself into one of the looms. She wanted to put her hand or her arm into one of the looms ... the blood of her own body woven into the cloth she was making. It was a fantastic notion, a whim. She knew it. She wanted to ask some of the other women and girls, working in the room with her, "Do you ever feel so and so?" She didn't ask. It wasn't her way to talk very much.

There were too many women and girls, she thought. "I wish there were more men." In the house where she had got a room, there were two older women and three younger ones all workers in the mill. They all worked days and she was alone in the house during the day. There had once been a man in the house ... one of the older women had been married but he had died. She wondered sometimes ... did men in the mill die easier than women? There seemed so many old women, unattached workers, who had once had men. Did she herself hunger for a man of her own? She didn't know.

Then her mother grew ill. The days that summer were all hot and dry. The mother had to have the doctor all summer. Every night in the mill she thought about her mother ill at home. The mother had to have the doctor all summer. Doctors cost money.

Molly wanted to quit the mill. She wished she could. She knew she couldn't. She ached to quit. She would have liked to go, as Red Oliver had gone when a crisis had come into his life, to wander in strange places. She didn't want to be herself. "I wish I could get out of my body," she thought. She wished she were more beautiful. She had heard stories about girls . . . they left their families and the places where they worked . . . they went out into the world among men . . . they sold themselves to men. "I don't care. I'd do it too if I had a chance," she thought sometimes. She wasn't beautiful enough. She wondered sometimes, looking at herself in a glass in her room . . . a room she rented in a mill house in the mill village . . . she looked pretty dragged out. . . .

"What's the use," she kept saying to herself. She couldn't quit working. Life would never open out for her. "I'll bet I never can quit working in this place," she thought. She felt dragged out and tired all the time.

At night she kept having queer dreams. She dreamed all the time of looms.

The looms became alive. They leaped at her. They seemed to say, "There you are. We want you."

Everything to her that summer became strange and more strange. She looked at herself in the little glass she had in her room, looking both mornings when she came from work and afternoons when she had got out of bed to prepare her own supper before going to the mill. The days got hot. The house was hot. She stood in her room looking at herself. She was so tired all that summer that she thought she couldn't go on working, but the strange thing was that sometimes . . .

it surprised her . . . she couldn't believe it . . . sometimes she looked all right. She was even beautiful. She was beautiful all that summer, but she didn't know it for sure, couldn't have been sure of it. Now and then she thought, "I'm beautiful." The thought sent a little wave of happiness through her but most of the time she didn't feel it very definitely. She felt it vaguely, knew it vaguely. It gave her a kind of new happiness.

There were men who knew. Every man who saw her that summer might have known. It may be that every woman has a time like that in her life—her own ultimate beauty. Every grass, every bush, every tree in the forest has its time of bloom. Men were better at making Molly know it than the other women were. The men working with her in the loom-room of the Birchfield mill . . . there were a few men in there . . . men weavers . . . the sweepers . . . the men who passed through the room kept looking sharply at her.

There was something in her that made them look. Her time of bloom had come. It hurt. She knew without quite knowing and the men knew without quite knowing.

She knew they knew. It tempted her. It frightened her.

There was one man, a young foreman, in her room, who was married but who had a sick wife. He kept walking near her. He stopped to talk. "Hello," he said. He came near and stood there. He was embarrassed. Sometimes he even touched her body with his body. He didn't do it often. It was always as though it had happened quite accidentally. He stood there. Then he walked past her. His body touched her body.

It was as though she had said to him, "Don't. Be gentle now. Don't. Be gentle now." He was gentle.

She used to say the words sometimes when he wasn't about, when there was no one about. "I guess I'm going a little crazy," she thought. She found herself speaking, not to another human being like herself but to one of her looms.

A thread had broken on one of the looms and she ran

to fix it, to tie it in. The loom was standing silently there.
It was still. It seemed to want to leap at her.

"Be gentle now," she whispered to it. Sometimes she
said the words aloud. There was always a roar in the room.
No one could hear.

It was absurd. It was silly. How could a loom, a thing
of steel and iron, be gentle? A loom couldn't. That was a
human attribute. "Sometimes, maybe ... even machines ...
absurd. Take yourself in hand. ... If I could only run away
from here for a time."

She thought of her childhood on her father's farm.
Scenes of her childhood returned to her. Nature could be
gentle sometimes. There were gentle days, gentle nights, in
nature. Did she think all that? They were feelings, not
thoughts.

It might have been that the young foreman in her room
didn't want to. He was a man who belonged to a church.
He tried not to. There was a small stock room at one corner
of the loom-room in the mill. They kept extra supplies in
there. "Go in there," he said to her one night. His voice was
husky when he said it. His eyes kept seeking her eyes. His
eyes were like the eyes of a hurt animal. "Rest a little," he
said. He used to say that to her sometimes when she wasn't
very tired. "I'm getting woozy-headed," she thought. Such
things happened sometimes in mills, in automobile factories
where modern workmen worked with fast-flying modern machines. A factory workman, suddenly, without warning, went
fantod. He began to yell. It happened to men more often
than to women. When a workman was that way he was
dangerous. He might hit some one with a tool, kill some
one. He might begin to destroy machines. In some factories
and mills they kept special men, big fellows, sworn in as
police, to take care of such cases. It was like shell-shock in
war. The workman had to be knocked out by a strong man;
he had to be carried out of the mill.

At first, when the foreman in the room spoke to Molly

so nicely, so gently ... Molly didn't go to rest in the little room as he told her to but sometimes, later, she did. There were bales and piles of thread and cloth in there. There were spoiled pieces of cloth. She could lie down on a pile of goods and close her eyes.

It was very odd. She could rest in there, even sleep a little sometimes that summer, when she couldn't get any rest or sleep at home in her room. It was odd—so close to the flying machines. It seemed better to be close to them. He put another worker, an extra woman, in her place at her looms and she went in there. The superintendent of the mill didn't know.

The other girls in the room knew. They didn't know. They could guess but they pretended they didn't know. They were pretty decent. They didn't say anything.

He didn't follow her in there. When he sent her in ... it happened a dozen times during that summer ... he stayed in the big loom-room or went away to some other part of the mill, and Molly always thought, afterwards, after what finally happened, that he was off somewhere, after he had sent her into the room, fighting with himself. She knew it. She knew he was fighting with himself. She liked him. "He's my own kind," she thought. She never blamed him.

He was wanting to and not wanting to. He did, finally. You could come into the little stock room through a door from the loom-room or by a narrow stairway from an up-stairs room and once, in half darkness, with the door to the loom-room half open, the other weavers all out there at work ... so near ... the dancing looms in the loom-room so near ... he was silent ... he might have been one of the looms ... leaping thread ... making firm fine cloth ... making fine woven cloth. ... Molly feeling so strangely dragged out. She couldn't have fought anything. She really didn't want to fight. She got pregnant.

Not caring and at the same time caring terribly,

So did he. He was okay, she thought.

If her mother found out. She never did. Molly was grateful for that.

She managed to lose it. No one ever knew. When she went home, over the week-end after that, her mother lying there in bed, she tried everything. She went up into the wood above the house alone where no one could see her and ran hard up and down. That was in the same overgrown woods' road in which she afterwards saw Red Oliver. She leaped and jumped like the looms in the loom-room in the mill. She had heard something. She took great quantities of quinine.

She was ill for a week when she lost it but she didn't have the doctor. She and her mother were ill in the same bed, but when she knew the doctor was coming she crept out of bed and hid in the wood. "He'll only charge it," she said to her mother. "I don't need him," she said. Then she got well and it never happened again. That fall the foreman's wife died and he went away and got another job in another mill in some other town. He was ashamed. After it happened he was ashamed to come near her. She wondered sometimes —would he get married again now? He was nice, she thought. He had never been gruff and hard-boiled with the workers in the loom-room as most of the foremen were and he wasn't a smarty. He never got gay with you. Would he get married again? He never knew what she went through when she was that way. She hadn't told him she was that way at all. She couldn't help wondering if he would get him a new wife in the new place and what his new wife would be like.

6

MOLLY SEABRIGHT, who had found young Red Oliver in the woods above her father's house and who thought he was a young communist going to help the workers in the strike at Birchfield, did not want her father and mother to know about him or his presence on the farm. She had not tried to explain to them the new doctrines that were being taught to her in the strikers' camp. She couldn't. She couldn't herself understand. She was full of admiration for the men and the women who had come among the strikers and were now leading them, but she didn't understand their words or their ideas.

They were always, for one thing, using strange words she had never heard before—the proletariat—the bourgeoisie. There was this or that to be "liquidated." You went to the right or to the left. There was a strange language—big hard words. She had been emotionally aroused. Vague hopes were alive in her. The strike at Birchfield, started over a question of wages and hours, had suddenly become something else. There was talk of a new world to be made, of people like herself lifted out from under the shadow of the mills. There was to be a new world in which the workers were of importance. Those who raised food for others to eat, who made cloth to clothe people, who built houses in which people could live, these people were suddenly to emerge—to stand forth. The future was to be in their hands. The whole thing was to Molly not understandable but the ideas that had been put into her head by the communists, talking in the camp at Birchfield, although perhaps unattainable, were tempting. They made you feel big and real and strong. There was a kind of nobility in the ideas, but you couldn't explain them to your father and mother. Molly wasn't a talker.

And then also there was confusion among the workers. Sometimes, when the communist leaders were not about, they talked among themselves. "It can't be. It can't be. You? Us?" There was amusement. Fear grew. Uncertainty grew. Just the same, the fear and the uncertainty seemed to draw the workers together. They felt themselves isolated—a little island of people separated from the great continent of other people that was America.

"Can there ever be such a world as these men and this woman talk about?" Molly Seabright couldn't quite believe, but at the same time something had happened to her. At times she felt herself willing to die for the men and women who had suddenly brought the new promise into her life and into the lives of the other workers. She tried to think. She was like Red Oliver struggling with himself. The woman communist who had come to Birchfield with the men was small and dark. She could get up before the workers and talk. Molly admired and envied her. She wished she could be such another.... "If I had education and wasn't so shy I'd try," she thought sometimes. The strike at Birchfield, the first strike she had ever been in, had brought her many new and strange emotions she didn't much understand and couldn't explain to others. Listening to the talkers in the camp she had times of feeling suddenly big and strong. She joined in the singing of new songs, full of strange words. She had come to believe in the communist leaders. They were young and full of daring, full of courage, she thought. Sometimes she thought they had too much courage. The town of Birchfield was all alive with threats against them. When the strikers marched singing through the streets of the town, as they sometimes did, the crowds watching scolded at them. There were hisses, oaths, threats shouted. "You sons-of-bitches, we'll get you." The newspaper at Birchfield ran a cartoon on its front page showing a serpent twined about the American flag and it was labeled "Communism." Boys came and threw copies of the paper about the strikers' camp.

"I don't care. They lie."

She felt hatred in the air. It made her afraid for the leaders. It made her tremble. The law had been looking for such a one, she now thought, when she had accidentally come upon Red Oliver in the wood. She wanted to protect him, make him safe but at the same time didn't want her father and mother to know. She did not want them to get into trouble, but, as for herself, she had come to feel that she didn't care. The law had been to the house down below once that evening, and now, after asking questions gruffly—the law was always brutal with the poor—she knew that—now the law had driven away along the mountain road, but any minute the law might return and might begin again asking questions. The law might even find out that she was herself one of the Birchfield strikers. The law hated strikers. There had been several half riots already in Birchfield, the strikers, men and women, on the one side, and the scabs brought in from the outside to take their places and the people of the town and the mill owners on the other. The law was always against the strikers. It always would be. The law would be glad of the chance to hurt any one connected with one of the strikers. She thought that. She believed it. She didn't want her father and mother to know of Red Oliver's presence. Their hard lives might be made harder.

"No use making them tell lies," she thought. Her people were good people. They belonged to a church. They could never be good liars. She didn't want them to be. She told Red Oliver to stay hidden in the wood until darkness came. When she was talking to him in the wood, in the half darkness, looking through trees, they could just see the house down below. There was an opening between trees and she pointed. Molly's mother had lighted a lamp in the kitchen of the house. She would be getting supper. "You stay up here," she said softly and blushed saying it. It was strange to her to be talking thus with a strange man, taking care of him, protecting him. Some of the feeling of love and admiration she had got for the communist leaders of the strike she had at once for Red. He would be as they were—no doubt an educated man. Such men, and such women as the little dark communist woman in the strikers' camp, would have made sacrifices to come to the aid of the strikers, of the poor workers on strike. Already she felt dimly that these men were in some way better, nobler, more courageous, than the kind of men she had always thought of as good. She had always thought that preachers must be the best men in the world but that was strange too. The preachers in the town of Birchfield were against the strikers. They were crying out against the new leaders the strikers had found. Once the woman communist in the camp had talked to the other women. She had pointed out to them how the Christ, the preachers were always talking about, had stood by the poor and lowly. He had stood by people in trouble, by people who were oppressed as the workers were. The woman communist had said that the attitude of the preacher was a betrayal not only of the workers but even of their own Christ and Molly had begun to understand what she meant, what she was talking about. The whole thing was a puzzle and there were other things that also puzzled. One of the women workers, one of the strikers at Birchfield, an old woman, a church woman, a good woman, Molly thought, had wanted to bring a present to one of the communist leaders. She wanted to express her love. She thought the man brave. For the sake of the strikers he was defying the town and the police of the town, and the police had no use for workers on strike. They only liked workers who were always humble, who always submitted. The old workingwoman had thought and thought, wanting to do something for the man she admired. The incident was more amusing, more tragically amusing than Molly knew. One of the communist leaders was standing up before the strikers talking to them and the old woman came up to him. She pushed her way up through the crowd. She had brought him as a present her Bible. It was the only thing she had to give to the man she loved and to whom she wanted to express her love by giving a present.

There was confusion. Molly had gone away from Red that evening, down along the wood road, half overgrown with laurels, driving the cow toward the house. There was a little log barn near the mountain house into which the cow was to be driven to be milked. Both the house and the barn were directly on the road in which earlier Red had been walking. The cow had a young calf that was being kept in a railed enclosure near the barn.

Red Oliver had thought that Molly had nice eyes. When she had been talking to him up there that evening, giving him directions, he had been thinking of another woman, of Ethel Long. It might have been because they were both tall and slender. There had always been something a little tricky about Ethel Long's eyes. They grew warm and then suddenly they were strangely cold. The new woman was like Ethel Long, but at the same time unlike.

"Women. Women," Red thought, a little contemptuously. He wanted to be off women. He didn't want to think of women. The woman in the woods had told him to stay where he was in the woods. "I'll get you some supper after awhile," she said to him, speaking softly, shyly. "Then I'll take you on to Birchfield. I'm going there when it's dark. I'm one of the strikers. I'll take you a safe way."

The cow had a young calf in a fenced-in enclosure near the barn. She ran down the wood road. She bawled loudly. When Molly had let her through an opening in the fence she ran bawling toward the calf and the calf was also ex-

cited. It also bawled. It ran up and down on one side of a
fenced enclosure and the cow ran up and down on the
other and the woman ran to let the cow in to her calf. There
was an impulse in the cow to give and there was crying
hunger in the calf. They both wanted to tear down the fence
that separated them and the woman let the cow in to the
calf and stood watching. Red Oliver saw all of this because
he hadn't listened to the woman's instructions about staying
in the woods, but had followed her closely. There it was.
She was a woman who had looked at him with kindness in
her eyes, and he wanted to be near her. He was like most
American men. There was hidden away in him a hope, half
a conviction, that in some way, some day, he might find a
woman who would save him from himself.

Red Oliver followed the woman and the half-frantic
cow down the hill and through the wood into the farm-
yard. She let the cow into the enclosure with her calf. He
wanted to get near her, to see everything, to be near her.

"She is a woman. Wait. What? She might love me. That
may be all that is the matter with me. After all I may need
only the love of some woman to make my manhood real
to me.

"Live in love—in a woman. Go into her and come out
refreshed. Raise children. Build a home.

"Now you see. There it is. Now you have something to
live for. Now you can cheat, scheme, get on, rise in the
world. Now, you see, you are not doing it for yourself alone.
You are doing it for these others. You are okay."

There was a little stream running along the edge of the
barnyard and bushes grew along the stream. Red went along
the creek stepping on stones dimly seen. It was dark under
the bushes. Occasionally he stepped into the water. His feet
got wet. He didn't mind.

He saw the cow hurry to its calf and had got so close
that he could see the woman standing and watching as the

calf sucked. That, the scene there, the quiet barnyard, the woman standing there watching as a calf sucked a cow—the earth, smell of earth and water and bushes . . . now flaming with fall colors about Red . . . impulses that drove a man in life came and went in a man . . . it would be nice, for example, to be a simple farm man, isolated from others, perhaps not thinking of others . . . even though you were always poor . . . what did poverty matter? . . . Ethel Long . . . something he had wanted from her and hadn't got.

. . . O man, hoping, dreaming.

. . . Always thinking, somewhere there is a golden key . . . "some one has it . . . give it to me. . . ."

When she thought the calf had enough she drove the cow out of the little enclosure and into the barn. The cow was quiet and content now. She fed the cow and went to the house.

Red wanted to get nearer. Already there were vague thoughts in his head. "If this woman . . . perhaps . . . how can a man tell?" The strange woman, Molly, might be the one.

To find love is also a part of youth. Some woman, a strong woman. will suddenly see in me something . . . hidden manhood I can't yet see or feel myself. She will come suddenly toward me. Open arms.

"Something like that might give me courage." Already she thought he was a certain thing. She thought he was a reckless, a daring young communist. Suppose, through her, he suddenly became something. Love with such a one might be the thing he needed, something splendid. She had left the cow and had gone for a moment to the house and he came out of the bushes and ran through the soft darkness into the barn. He looked quickly about. There was a little loft, filled with hay, above the cow and it had an opening through which he could look down. He could stay up there quietly and watch her milk the cow. There was another opening looking out into the yard. The house was near—not more than twenty yards away.

The cow in the barn was content and quiet. The woman had fed her. Although it was late fall, the night was not cold. Red could see through the opening in the loft the stars coming out in the sky. He took a pair of dry stockings out of his bag and put them on. Again he had been visited by the feeling that was always coming to him. It was the feeling that had led him into a confused affair with Ethel Long. It annoyed him. There he was again near a woman and that fact had excited him. "Can't I ever be near a woman without feeling like this?" he asked himself. Little angry thoughts came.

It was always the same thing. He wanted and couldn't get. If he once got, fully, his whole being merged with another... the birth of new life... something to strengthen him... would he be then a man at last? He was lying at that moment quietly in the hayloft remembering sharply other times he had felt as he did then. It had resulted always in his selling himself out.

He was again a boy at home walking on a railroad track. Down along the river, below the town, at Langdon, Georgia, quite removed from the life of the town as was the mill village by the cotton mill, some poor little wooden shacks had been built. Some of the shacks had been made of boards fished out of the stream during floods. They were roofed with tin cans flattened out and made to serve as shingles. Tough people lived down there. The people living down there were outlaws, squatters, tough desperate people out of the poor white class of the South. They were people who made cheap whisky to sell to Negroes. They were chicken thieves. There was a girl who lived down there, red-headed as he was. Red had first seen her one day in town, on the main street of Langdon when he was a schoolboy.

She had looked at him in just a certain way. "What?

Do you mean it?" People of that sort? Young girls coming out of that sort of families. He remembered his surprise at her daring, her boldness. Just the same it was pleasant. It was nice.

There was a hungry look in her eyes. He couldn't have been mistaken. "Hello, come on," the eyes said. He had followed her along the street, a mere boy, afraid, ashamed, keeping far back of her, stopping in doorways, pretending he was not following.

Just the same she had known. She may have wanted to tease him. She played with him. How bold she was. She was a little thing, rather pretty but not very clean-looking. Her dress was dirty and torn and her face covered with freckles. She had on an old pair of shoes, too large for her, and no stockings.

He had spent nights thinking of her and dreaming of her, of that girl. He hadn't wanted to. He went to walk down along the railroad tracks, past where he knew she lived, in one of the poor little shacks. He pretended he was down there to fish in the yellow river that ran below Langdon. He didn't want to fish. He wanted to be near her. He had followed her. That first day he had followed, keeping far back, half hoping she didn't know. He had found out about her and her family. He had heard some men speaking of her father on Main Street. The father had got arrested for stealing chickens. He was one of the men who sold cheap bootleg whisky to Negroes. Such men ought to be wiped out. They and their families ought to be driven out of town. Just the same Red had wanted her, had dreamed of her. He walked down that way, pretending he was going fishing. Was she laughing at him? Anyway he never got a chance at her, never even spoke to her. It might have been that all the time she was just laughing at him. Even little girls were that way sometimes. He had found that out.

And if he had got a chance at her he knew, in his heart, that he wouldn't have had the nerve.

Afterwards, when he was already a young man, when he was in the North at college, there had come another time.

He went with three others—college boys like himself —after a ball game, to a house of prostitution. That was in Boston. They had been playing a game of baseball with another New England college team and returned through Boston. It was the end of the baseball season and they celebrated. They drank and went to the place that one of the young men knew about. He had been there before. The others took women. They went upstairs to the rooms in the house with women. Red didn't go. He pretended he didn't want to and so he sat downstairs in what was called the parlor of the house. It was "a parlor house." They are going out of style. There were several women in there, sitting in there, waiting to serve men. It was their job to serve men.

There was a fat middle-aged man who looked to Red like a business man. That was odd. Had he already, at that time, begun to have contempt for the idea of a man spending his life buying and selling? The man in that house that day was like the traveling salesman he afterwards frightened in the road near Birchfield. The man was half asleep, sitting in a chair in the parlor of the house. Red thought he would never forget the man's face...its ugliness at just that moment.

. He remembered afterwards—thinking...did he have the thoughts at the moment or did they come later?... "Never mind," he thought... "I wouldn't mind seeing a man drunk if I could feel the man drunk as drunk, trying to establish something. There might be drunkenness in a man... a man might get drunk trying to establish a dream in himself. He might even be trying to go toward something thus. If he were drunk that way, I bet I would know it."

There is another sort of drunkenness. "It is disintegration...of personality, I guess. Something slips...falls away ...everything becomes loose. I don't like it. I hate it." Red's own face, sitting in that house that time, might have been ugly too. He bought drinks, spent money he couldn't afford to spend—recklessly.

He lied. "I don't want to," he had said it to the others. It was a lie.

There it is. You dream of a thing as being the most lovely thing that can happen in life. It can be as ugly as hell too. After you do it, you hate the one you did it with. Hate comes flooding in.

Sometimes though you want to be ugly—like a dog rolling in offal... or perhaps like a rich man rolling in his wealth.

The others said to Red, "Don't you want to?" "No," he said. He lied. The others laughed at him a little and he kept on lying to himself. They thought he hadn't the nerve... which was anyway pretty near the truth. They were right. Afterwards, when they had got out of there, when they were outside that house in the street... they had gone to the place in the early evening while it was still daylight... when they came out, the lights in the street were lighted.

Children were playing in the street. Red kept being glad he hadn't but was, at the same time, deep down in what he thought was some ugly corner in himself, sorry he hadn't.

Then he began feeling virtuous. That wasn't a nice feeling either. It was an ugly feeling. "I think I am better than they are." There were so many such women as the ones in that house—the world was teeming with them.

Oldest trade in the world.

Jesus Maria! Red just went along silently with the others through a lighted street. The world in which he walked seemed queer and strange to him. It was as though the houses along the street were not real houses, the people along the street, even some children he saw running and shouting, weren't real. They were figures on a stage—unreal. The houses and buildings he saw were made of cardboard.

*

AND so Red had got a reputation for being a nice boy . . . a clean boy . . . a nice young man.

. . . A good ball player . . . pretty keen in his studies.

"You watch that young man. He's all right. He's clean. He's all right."

Red had liked it. He hated it. "If they only knew the truth," he thought.

For example, in that other place into which he had got, in the barn that night . . . that woman who had found him in the woods . . . an impulse in her to save him . . . to whom he had lied, saying he was a communist.

She came out of the house bringing a lantern with her. She milked the cow. The cow was quiet now. It was eating some sort of soft mash she had put into a box. Red was lying by an opening that looked down and she heard him moving in the hay. "It's all right," he said to her. "I came in here. I'm up here." His voice had got strangely husky. He had to make an effort to control it. "Keep quiet," she said.

She sat by the cow's flanks to milk. She sat on a little stool and as he had got his face to the opening above he could see her, could watch her movements in the light of the lantern. So close to one again. So far from her. He couldn't help making her, in imagination at least, really close to himself. He saw her hands on the udders of the cow. Milk came down, making a sharp sound against the sides of a tin pail held between her knees. Her hands seen thus, in the circle of light down below, made by the lantern . . . they were strong alive workingwoman's hands . . . there was a little circle of light . . . the hands gripping teats—milk coming . . . the strong sweet smell of the milk, of animal life in the barn—barn smells. The hay on which he was lying—

darkness and the circle of light down there... her hands.
Jesus Maria!

Shame too. There it was. There was the little circle of
light in the darkness down below. Once, while she was milking, her mother—a little bent white-haired old woman—
came to the door of the barn and said a few words to her
daughter. She went away. She was speaking of a lunch she
was putting up. It was for Red. He knew that.

He knew the mother didn't know, but just the same
these people were being sweet and kind to him. The daughter was wanting to protect him, to take care of him. She
would have made up some kind of excuse for wanting to
carry the lunch when she left the farm later that evening
to return to Birchfield. The mother wouldn't ask too many
questions. The mother had gone to the house.

A soft circle of light down there in the barn. Circle of
light about a woman's form... her hands... the swelling of
her breast—firm and round... her hands milking the cow...
warm nice milk... swift thoughts in Red....

He was close to her, to a woman. He was very near her.
Once or twice she turned her face up toward him but she
could not see him in the darkness above. When she turned
her face up thus, it—the face—was still in the circle of light
but her hair was in darkness. She had lips like Ethel Long's
lips and more than once he had kissed Ethel's lips. Now Ethel
was another man's woman. "Suppose, after all, that is all I
want... all any man really wants... this restlessness in me
that has driven me from home, made a tramp of me, made a
wanderer of me.

"How do I know that I give a damn for people in general, the generality of people... their suffering... it may be
all bunk?"

She didn't speak to him again until she had finished
milking, when she stood under him, whispering up, giving
him instructions about getting out of the barn. He was to

wait for her by a little corncrib near the road. It was fortunate the family didn't keep a dog.

It was all nothing, except to Red ... his attempt at progress with himself ... to understand something if he could ... an impulse, a feeling, that went on all the time he was walking with her ... behind her ... in front of her, in the narrow path, going up over a mountain, down into a hollow ... now beside a stream, going toward Birchfield in the dark. It was strongest in him when he stopped at one place along the way to eat the food she had brought ... in a little opening near tall trees ... quite dark ... thinking of her just as a woman ... who might possibly have, if he had dared try ... to satisfy something in himself ... as though doing that would give him something he so much wanted ... his manhood ... was that it? He even argued with himself—"What the hell? Suppose, when I was with those other women in that house in Boston ... if I had, would that have given me my manhood?

"Or if I had got that little girl, in Langdon, long ago?"

He had, after all, had a woman once. He had had Ethel Long. "Well!"

He had got nothing very permanent from that.

"It isn't that. I wouldn't do it even if I could," he said to himself. It was time now for men to prove themselves in a new way.

Just the same—all the time he was with the woman—he was as the foreman in the mill had been with Molly Seabright. In the darkness, on the way to Birchfield that night, he had kept wanting to touch her with his hands, touch her body with his body, as the foreman in the mill had done. Perhaps she didn't know. He hoped she didn't. When they had got near the communist camp in the wood—near the clearing where the tents and shacks had been put up—he had asked her not to tell the communist leaders about his presence in the camp.

He had to give her some explanation. They wouldn't

know him. They might even think he was some sort of a spy. "Wait until morning," he had said to her. "You leave me here," he whispered, when they came silently to the place where he afterwards tried to sleep. "I'll go and tell them after awhile." He had thought vaguely, "I'll go to them. I will ask them to give me something dangerous to do here." He felt brave. He wanted to serve or, at least, at the moment when he was with Molly at the edge of the camp, he thought he wanted to serve.

"What?

"Well, maybe."

Something a little vague in him. She had been very, very nice. She went and got him a blanket, perhaps her own blanket, the only one she had. She went away to a little tent where she was to spend the night with some other working-women. "She's nice," he thought, "damn, she's nice.

"I wish I could be something real," he thought.

7

THE night was passing. Red Oliver was alone. He was in a state of feverish uncertainty. He had got to the place toward which he had been going for a long time. It wasn't just a place. Was it a chance, at last, to motivate his own life? Men wanting pregnancy as well as women, eh? Something like that. Since he had left Langdon, Georgia, he had been like a moth flying about a flame. He wanted to approach—what? "This communism—is that the answer?"

Could it be made a kind of religion?

The religion the Western world had given itself to wouldn't do. It had got, in some queer way, corrupt—no good now. Even the preachers knew it. "Look at them—do they walk with fine dignity?

"You can't bargain like that—promise of immortality—after this life you shall live again. The truly religious man wants to throw away everything—he asks no promise from God.

"Wouldn't it be better—if you could do it—if you could find some way to do it, to throw away your life for the sake of a better life here—not over there?" A flourish—a gesture. "Live as a bird flies. Die as a male bee dies—in nuptial flight with life, eh?

"There's something somewhere that's worth living for —dying for. Is it this thing called communism?"

Red wanted to approach, to try giving himself to that. He was afraid to approach. He was there at the edge of the camp. There was still a chance to leave—to light out. He

315

could creep away unobserved. No one but Molly Seabright would know. Even his friend Neil Bradley wouldn't know. He and Neil had talked pretty big sometimes. He wouldn't have to say even to Neil, "I tried but I failed." He could just lie low, keep numb.

Things kept happening, inside himself, outside himself. When he had given up trying to sleep, he sat listening. All his senses on that night seemed extraordinarily alive. He could hear the low voices of people talking in the small rudely constructed hut in the midst of the camp. He knew nothing of what was going on. Now and then he could see shadowy figures in a narrow little street of the camp.

He was alive. The tree against which his back rested was outside the circle of the camp. Within the camp the small trees and bushes had been cut away, but at the camp's edge they began again. He sat on one of the boards he had found and on which earlier he had tried to sleep. The blanket Molly had brought was wrapped about his shoulders.

The seeing of the woman Molly, his being with her, the feelings that had come, being in her woman's presence, all of this was but an incident, but at the same time it was important. He felt the night, still hanging over the camp, pregnant like a woman. A man went toward a certain thing— like communism. He was uncertain. He ran forward a little, stopped, turned back, then went forward again. Until he had crossed a certain line, that committed him, he could always turn back.

"Cæsar crossed the Rubicon.

"O, mighty Cæsar.

"Oh, yeaas!

"I'll be damned. I don't believe there ever was a mighty man.

"By God ... if there ever was one ... world march on ... thump, thump ... world come to your knees now. Here's a man.

"Well, anyway it's not me," Red thought. "Don't begin to think big now," he warned himself.

There was just the trouble—his own boyishness. He was always imagining things—some heroic act he had done or was about to do . . . he saw a woman—he thought, "Suppose she should suddenly—unexpectedly—fall in love with me." He had done it that very night—the workingwoman he had been with. He smiled, a bit sadly, thinking of it.

That was the idea. You thought out certain things. Perhaps you even talked a little to others as Red Oliver had talked to Neil Bradley—the one close man friend he had made . . . as he had tried to talk to the woman with whom he thought he was in love—to Ethel Long.

Red had never been able to talk much to Ethel Long, couldn't get his ideas explained when he was with her. It was partly because they were half formed in his own mind and partly because he was always excited when he was with her . . . wanting, wanting, wanting . . .

"Well . . . she . . . will she let me?" . . .

*

IN the communist camp near Birchfield, across the river from the Birchfield mills, there was an undertone of excitement. Red felt it. Voices kept coming from the rude little hut where, evidently, the leading spirits among the strikers were congregating. Shadowy figures hurried through the camp.

Two men went out of the camp and crossed the bridge that led away into the town. Red saw them go. There was a little light from a waning moon. Daylight would come soon now. He could hear footsteps on the bridge. The two men were going into town. They were scouts sent out by the strike leaders. Red imagined that. He didn't know.

There had been rumors in the camp that day, on the Sunday while Molly Seabright was away, while she was at

home over the week-end with her own people. The struggle
at Birchfield had been carried on between the strikers and
deputy sheriffs appointed by the sheriff of the county of
North Carolina in which Birchfield lay. There had been,
from the local newspaper, the mayor of the town, a call sent
to the Governor of the State for troops but the Governor
was a liberal. He half wanted to stand by labor. There were
liberal newspapers in the State. "Even a communist has some
rights in a free country," they said. "A man or woman has
a right to be a communist if he wants to."

The Governor had wanted to be impartial. He was him-
self a mill owner. He didn't want people to be able to say—
"There, you see." He even wanted secretly to lean far back,
get the name of being the most open-minded and liberal
Governor in the whole Union—"these States," as Walt
Whitman had said.

He had found he couldn't. There was too much pressure.
Now it was said that the State was coming in. Soldiers were
coming. The strikers had even been allowed to picket the
mill. They could picket if they stayed a certain distance from
the mill gate, if they stayed out of the mill village. Now all
was to be stopped. An injunction had been issued. The
soldiers were coming. The strikers were to be hemmed in.
"Stay in your own camp. Rot there." That was the cry now.

But what good is a strike if you can't picket? The new
move meant, if the rumor was true, that the communists
were blocked. There would be a new turn to things now.
That was the trouble with all this business of being a communist. You got blocked.

"I'll tell you what—these poor workers—they are being
led into a trap," the mill owners had begun saying. Com-
mittees of citizens had gone to see the Governor. There were
mill owners among them. "We are not against unions," they
had now begun saying. They even praised unions, the right
kind of unions. "This communism is un-American," they
said. "Its aim is to destroy our institutions, you see." One

of them took the Governor aside. "If anything happens and
it will happen ... already there have been riots, people hurt
... the citizens themselves will not stand for this communism. If a few citizens, upright men and women, are
killed—you know who will be blamed."

It was the trouble with anything in America that had
any kick. Red Oliver had begun to realize that. He was one
of many thousands of young Americans beginning to realize
it a little. "Suppose, for example, you were a man in America who really wanted God—suppose, you wanted to try
really to be a Christian—a God man.

"How could you do that? All society would be against
you. Even the church wouldn't stand that—it couldn't.

"Just the same there must have been—once—when the
world was younger—when men were more naïve—there
must have been godly men, willing and ready enough to die
for God. They might even have wanted to."

*

IN reality Red knew quite a lot. He had got a dose of his
own limitations and that experience had perhaps taught him
something. It had happened at Langdon.

There had come a strike at Langdon and he was in it
and not in it. He tried to get in. It wasn't a communist strike.
There had been a riot in the early morning in front of the
plant at Langdon. They were trying to bring in new workers, "scabs," the strikers called them. They were only poor
people out of work. They had come flocking into Langdon
from the hills. All they knew was that jobs were being
offered. It was a time when jobs were getting scarce. There
had been fighting and Red had fought. The people he had
come to know a little—not very well—men and women in
the plant with whom he had worked—were fighting with
other men and women. There were screams and cries. A
crowd had surged out to the plant from town. They came

racing out in cars. It was early morning and men of the town
jumped out of their beds, sprang into their cars and raced
out there. Deputy sheriffs, appointed to protect the plant,
were in it and Red got in.

That morning he had just gone out there, being curious.
The plant had been closed a week and word had been sent
out that it was to be opened with new workers. The old
workers of the plant were all there. Most of them were pale
and silent. A man stood with his fists in the air, swearing.
Many of the town people did not get out of their cars. They
shouted and cursed the strikers. There were women attacking other women. Dresses were being torn and hair pulled.
There was no shooting, but deputy sheriffs ran about waving
guns and shouting.

Red had got into it. He sprang in. The amazing thing
about it all ... it was amusing really ... it made him want to
cry afterward, when he realized it ... was that, although he
had fought furiously in the midst of a mob of people, fists
flying, himself taking blows, giving blows, women even
attacking men ... no one of the town of Langdon knew and
even the workers did not know that Red Oliver was in there
fighting thus on the side of the strikers.

Things got like that sometimes in life. Life played that
kind of a damned joke on a man.

The point was that afterwards, when the fight was over,
when some of the strikers had been dragged off to the town
jail in Langdon, when the strikers were defeated, dispersed
... some of them fighting furiously to the last and others
caving in ... when it was all over that morning there was
no one, either among the workers or among the town people,
who even suspected that Red Oliver had been fighting so
furiously on the workers' side, and then, when all was quiet,
he had lost his nerve.

There had been a chance. He hadn't left Langdon at
once. After a few days, the strikers, who had been arrested,
were brought up for trial. There they were in court. They

had been kept in the town jail since the riot. The strikers
had formed a union but the union leader had been rather
like Red. When the test came he had thrown up his hands.
He had declared that he hadn't wanted trouble. He had been
advising, begging the strikers to remain quiet. He had been
lecturing them in meetings. He was one of the kind of leaders who wanted to sit at a council table with the employers,
but the strikers had got out of hand. When they saw people
taking their places they couldn't stand it. The union leader
got out of town. The strike was broken.

There remained the people in jail, who were to come up
for trial. Red had been going through a curious struggle
with himself. All the town, the people of the town, took it
for granted he had been in the fight on the town's side, on
the side of property and of the mill owners. He had got a
black eye. Men meeting him on the street laughed and
slapped him on the back. "Good boy," they said, "you got
it, didn't you?"

The men of the town, most of whom had no money
interest in the mill, took the whole thing as an adventure.
There had been a fight and they had won. They felt it their
own victory. As for the people in the jail, who were they,
what were they? They were poor mill hands, no-good poor
whites, lint-heads. They were to be tried in court. No doubt
they would get heavy jail sentences. There were women
workers of the mill, women like the one named Doris who
had attracted Red's attention and the blonde woman named
Nell who had also attracted him who would be sent away
to prison. The woman named Doris had a husband and a
baby and Red wondered about that. If she had to go for a
long term in prison, would she take the baby with her?

For what? For fighting for the right to work, to make
a living. The thought of it sickened Red. The thought of the
position into which he had got himself sickened him. He had
begun keeping off the streets of the town. In the daytime,
during that curious period of his life, he was restless and

went to walk all day alone in the pine forest about Langdon
and at night he could not sleep. A dozen times, during the
week after the strike and before the day came when the
strikers were to be brought to trial, he came to a strong
resolution. He would go into the court. He would even ask
to be arrested and thrown into jail with the strikers. He
would say that he had been fighting on their side. What they
had done he had done. He wouldn't wait until the time for
the trial but would go at once to the judge or to the sheriff
of the county and tell the truth. "Arrest me also," he would
say, "I was on the side of the workers, I fought on their
side." Once or twice Red had even got out of bed at night
and had partially dressed, determined to go down into the
town, to awaken the sheriff, to tell his story.

He didn't. He had caved in. The whole notion had
seemed to him, most of the time, silly. He would only be
playing a heroic rôle, making a silly ass of himself. "Anyway I fought for them. Whether any one knows it or not,
I did," he told himself. In the end, unable longer to bear his
own thoughts, he had left Langdon, hadn't even told his
mother where he was going. He didn't know. It was night
and he had packed a few things in a little bag and had left
the house. He had a little money in his pocket, a few dollars.
He left Langdon.

"Where am I going?" he had kept asking himself. He
bought newspapers and had read about the communist strike
at Birchfield. Was he a complete coward? He didn't know.
He wanted to test himself. There had been moments, since
he had left Langdon, when, if some one had suddenly come
up to him saying—"Who are you? what are you worth?—
he would have answered:

"Nothing—I am worth nothing. I am cheaper than the
cheapest man in the world."

Red had been through another experience that he remembered with shame. It wasn't much of an experience

after all. It was unimportant. It was terribly important.

It had happened in the camp of the tramps, in the place where he had heard the bleary-eyed man talking of the killing of the singing woman on the streets of Birchfield. He had been going toward Birchfield, hitch-hiking his way along and beating his way on freight trains. For the time he lived as tramps lived, as the unemployed live. He had got in with another young fellow of about his own age. He was a pale young man with feverish eyes. Like the bleary-eyed man he was very profane. Oaths fell constantly from his lips, but Red liked him. The two young men had met at the edge of a Georgia town and had climbed aboard a freight train that was crawling slowly toward the city of Atlanta.

Red was curious about his companion. The man looked ill. They got into a box car. There were at least a dozen other men in the car. There were whites and blacks. The blacks stayed in one end of the car and the whites in the other. There was, however, a feeling of friendliness. Jokes and talk went back and forth.

Red still had seven dollars of the money he had brought from home. He had a guilty feeling about it. He was afraid. If this crowd knew it they would rob him, he thought. He had the bills tucked away in his shoes. "I'll keep mum about it," he decided. The train went slowly north and at last stopped at a small town, but a short distance from the city. It was late in the afternoon and the young man, who had attached himself to Red, told him they had better get off there. All the others would be getting off. In Southern towns and cities, tramps and men out of work were often arrested and given jail sentences. They put them to work on the Georgia roads. Red and his companion got out of the car and all along the train—it was a long one—he could see other men, whites and blacks, jumping to the ground.

The young man he was with stuck to Red. When they were in the car he had whispered. "You got any money," he had asked and Red had shaken his head. The moment Red did it he was ashamed. "Still I'd better stick to it now," he thought. A little army of men, the whites in one group and the blacks in another, went along the tracks and turned across a field. They went into a little pine wood. There were evidently veteran tramps among the men and they knew what they were doing. They called to the others, "Come on," they said. There was a tramps' hang-out at that place—a jungle. There was a little stream and inside the woods an open place covered with pine needles. There were no houses near. Some of the men made fires and began to cook food. They took scraps of meat and bread, wrapped in old newspapers, out of their pockets. There were crude cooking utensils lying about, empty vegetable cans blackened by old fires. There were little piles of blackened bricks and stones other wanderers had gathered together.

The man who had attached himself to Red called him aside. "Come on," he said, "let's get out of here. There ain't nothing here for us," he said. He went across the field swearing and Red followed him. "I get tired of these dirty bastards," he declared. They got out on the railroad track quite near the town and the young man told Red to wait. He disappeared along the street. "I'll be right back," he said.

Red sat on the track, waiting, and presently his companion reappeared. He had a loaf of bread and two dried herring. "I got it for fifteen cents. That was my pile. I panhandled it out of a fat son-of-a-bitch in a town back there, before I met up with you." He made a jerking movement with his thumb back along the track. "We had better eat it here," he said. "There's too many in that crowd of dirty bastards." He meant the men in the jungle. The two young men sat on railroad ties and ate. Again shame took possession of Red. The bread was bitter in his mouth.

He kept thinking of the money in his shoes. Suppose they had robbed me. "What of it?" he thought. He wanted to tell the young man, "Look here, I've got seven dollars." His companion would perhaps have wanted to go on a bust.

He would have wanted to get liquor. Red had thought, "I'll make the money go as far as I can." Now it seemed to burn the flesh inside his shoes. His companion kept talking cheerfully, but Red grew silent. When they had finished eating he followed the man back to the camp. Shame had taken complete possession of Red. "We got a hand-out," Red's companion said to the men sitting about the little fires. There might have been fifteen men gathered in the camp. Some of them had food, others didn't. Those who had food divided.

Red could hear the voices of the Negro tramps in another camp near by. There was laughter over there. A Negro's voice began to sing softly, and Red thought sweetly.

One of the men in the white man's camp spoke to Red's companion. He was a tall middle-aged man. "What the hell's the matter with you?" he asked. "You look like hell," he said.

Red's companion grinned. "I got the syph," he said, grinning. "It's eating me up."

There was a general discussion of the disease that had attacked the man and Red drew away to another side and sat listening. Some of the men in the camp began telling of their experiences with the same disease and how they got it. The mind of the tall man took a practical turn. He jumped up. "I'll tell you what," he said, "I'll tell you how to get cured."

"You get into jail," he said. He didn't laugh. He meant it. "Now I'll tell you what to do," he continued, pointing along the railroad track toward the city of Atlanta.

"Well, you go in there. So there you are. You walk along the street." The tall man was something of an actor. He walked up and down. "You have a stone in your pocket—see." There was the half of a burned brick lying near by and he picked it up but the brick was hot and he dropped it quickly. The other men in the camp laughed, but the tall man was absorbed. He got a stone and put it into the side pocket of his torn coat. "You see." he said. Now he took the stone out of his pocket and with a wide movement of his arm threw it aside through bushes into the little stream that ran near the camp. His earnestness made the other men in the camp smile. He ignored them. "So you are walking along a street of stores. You see. You get into a fashionable street. You pick out a street where the best stores are. Then you hurl your brick or stone through the window. You don't run. You stand there. If the store-keeper comes out you tell him to go to hell." The man had been walking up and down. Now he stood as though defying a crowd. "You might as well smash the window of some rich son-of-a-bitch," he said.

"So—you see—you get arrested. They put you in jail ... you see—they cure your syphilis in there. It's the best way," he said. "If you are just broke they won't pay any attention to you. In the jail they got a doctor. A doctor comes in there. It's the best way."

Red had crept away from the camp of tramps and from his companion and after walking a half mile along a road, inquiring his way, he got a street car. The seven dollars in his shoe annoyed and hurt him and he stepped aside behind some bushes and took it out. Some of the men he had been with since he had become a wanderer had laughed at him because of the small bag he carried, but on that day there had been in the crowd a man carrying something even more strange, and the attention of the crowd had been centered upon him. The man said he was a newspaper reporter out of work and was going to try to catch on in Atlanta. He carried a small portable typewriter. "Look at him," the others in the camp shouted. "Ain't we getting swell? We are getting high-brow." Red had wanted to run into the camp that evening and give the men gathered there his seven dollars. "What does it matter to me what they do with it?" he thought. "Suppose they get drunk—what the hell do I care?" When he had got some distance from the camp he went hesitatingly back. It would have been easy enough if he had only told them earlier in the day. For several hours he had been with the men. Some of them were hungry. Just the same if he went back and stood before the men, taking the seven dollars out of his pocket—"Here, you men . . . take this."

How silly!

He would be most ashamed before the young fellow who had spent his last fifteen cents buying the bread and herring. When he got again to the edge of the camp the men gathered there had become quiet. They had built a little fire of sticks and were lying about. Many of them would sleep there on the pine needles. They were gathered in little groups, some talking softly and others stretched out already asleep on the ground. It was then Red heard the story of the death of the singing woman at Birchfield from the lips of the bleary-eyed man. The young man who had syphilis had disappeared. Red wondered if he had already gone off to the city to smash the store window and get himself arrested and put into jail.

No one had spoken to Red when he returned to the edge of the camp. He held the money in his hand. No one looked at him. He stood leaning against a tree holding the money, a little ball of bills, gripped in his fingers. "What'll I do?" he thought. Some of those in the camp were veteran tramps but many of them were men out of work, not young men like himself, adventuring, trying to find out about themselves, seeking something, but just mature men with no work, drifting about the country, seeking work. It would have been something wonderful, Red thought, that night, if there had been something of the actor in himself as in the tall man, if he could have gone to stand before the group at the fire. He might have told a lie, as he did afterwards when he met Molly Seabright. "Look here, I found this money," or "I held up a man." That would have sounded big and fine, being a hold-up man. He would have got admiration. What happened was that he did nothing. He stood leaning against the tree embarrassed, shaking with shame and then, not knowing how to do what he wanted to do, went quietly away. When he got into the city that night he was still ashamed. He wished he had thrown the money in among the men and then run. He got a bed that night in the Y. M. C. A. building in Atlanta, and when he had got into bed he again took the money out of his pocket and held it in his hand looking at it. "Hell," he thought, "men think they want money. It only gets you into trouble. It makes a fool out of you," he decided. Just the same, already, after a week on the road, he had got to the place where seven dollars seemed almost a fortune. "It doesn't take much money to make a man pretty cheap," he had thought.

8

THEY were the same boy—the same young man—that was
the queer part of it. They were American young men and
had read the same magazines and newspapers...heard the
same talks on the radio...political conventions...the man
who...Amos and Andy...Mr. Hoover at Arlington, Mr.
Harding and Mr. Wilson at Arlington...America the hope
of the world...the eyes of the world upon us..."this
rugged individualism." They had seen the same talkies. Life
keeps moving, too. Stand aside and see it move. Stand aside
and see the glory of the Lord.

"Have you seen Ford's new car? Charley Schwab says
we are all poor together now. Oh yeaas!"

Naturally the two young men had gone through many
of the same experiences—boyhood loves—material for later
novels, if they had happened to be novelists—school—baseball—going swimming in the summer—not, of course, in the
same creek, river, lake, pond...the economic urges, drifts,
pushes that make men—that seem so like the accidents of
life—are they accidents? "The next revolution that comes
will be economic, not political." Talk in drug stores, in court
houses, on streets.

A young man gets his dad's car in the evening. Ned
Sawyer had done that more than Red. He was a young man
who felt freer—moved more freely in the atmosphere into
which he was born.

His mother and father felt freer in their atmosphere—
neither of them ever having been poor or having been of

working people like Red Oliver's mother. They were respected, looked up to. They subscribed. Ned's father was
never a drunkard. He had never been a chaser of loose
women. The mother was soft speaking and gentle. She was
a good church member.

If you are a young man like Ned Sawyer, nowadays,
you get the family car in the evening and drive out into the
country. You pick up a girl. The automobile has certainly
changed life. With some girls you can go in for big petting.
With some you can't.

It's a problem for the girls, too—to pet or not to pet.
How far is it safe to go? What is the best line?

If you are a young man you pass through times of depression. Some young men like to read books. They go in
for being intellectuals. They like to get into a room with
books and read and then later they go out and talk bookish
talk while other young men are all for action. They have
got to be doing something or they'll bust. Extraverts and
introverts, hello.

Some young men go big with women while others do
not. You can never tell what will get a woman.

The two young men who met so strangely, tragically,
one morning in a town called Birchfield, in North Carolina,
didn't know they were so much alike. They had never before
seen each other or heard of each other. How were they to
know they were so much alike?

Were they both just ordinary young American middle-
class men? Well, you can't blame yourself, being middle-
class, if you are an American. Isn't America the greatest
middle-class country on earth? Haven't its people more middle-class comforts than any other people on earth?

"Sure."

The one young man was named Ned Sawyer and the
other Red Oliver. One was the son of a North Carolina small-
town lawyer and the other the son of a Georgia small-town

doctor. One was rather stockily built, a broad-shouldered young man with thick, rather stiff red hair and with troubled questioning gray-blue eyes, while the other was tall and slender. He had yellow hair and gray eyes that also occasionally grew questioning and troubled.

With Ned Sawyer it wasn't a question of communism. It wasn't that definite with him. "Damn communism," he would have said. He didn't know about it and didn't want to know about it. He thought of it as something un-American—strange and ugly. However, there were disturbing things in his life, too. There was something going on in America in his day, an under-current of questionings pretty much voiceless yet, that disturbed him. He didn't want to be disturbed. "Why can't we, in America, go on just as we have always gone on?" was about what he thought. He had heard of communism and thought of it as something strange and foreign to American life. He even talked about it now and then to other young men he knew. He made pronouncements. "It's foreign to our way of thought," he said. "So? You think? Yes, we believe in individualism here in America. Give every man a chance and let the devil take the hindmost. That's our way. If, in America, we don't like a law we break it and have a good laugh. That's our way." Ned was himself half intellectual. He had read Ralph Waldo Emerson. "Self-reliance, that's what I stand for."

"But," a young man friend said to him. "But?"

One of the two young men, mentioned above, shot the other. He killed him. It all happened in this way....

The one young man—the one named Ned Sawyer—had joined up with the military company of his town. He had been too young to get into the World War, just as had Red Oliver. It wasn't that he thought of war-wanting—wanting killing and all that. He didn't. There wasn't anything cruel or savage about Ned. He liked the idea...a company of men swinging along a street or along a road, all in uniform, himself one of them—himself in command.

Wouldn't it be strange if this individualism we Americans so love to talk about was something we don't want after all?

There is a gang spirit in America, too—

Ned Sawyer had gone to college as Red Oliver had. He also played baseball in college. He was a pitcher while Red played shortstop and sometimes second base. Ned was a pretty good pitcher. He had a fast ball with a little hop on it and a tantalizing slow ball. He was a rather nice, steady curve-ball pitcher.

One summer, while he was still in college, he went to an officers' training camp. He liked it. He liked commanding men and later, when he was back again in his own home town, he got elected, or appointed, first lieutenant of the military company of his town.

It was nice. He liked it.

"Fours-right into line."

"Present arms!" Ned had a good voice for it. He could bark it out—sharp and nice-like.

It was a nice feeling. You took the young men, your company, awkward fellows—white men from the farms near the town and young fellows from town—and you drilled them up by the schoolhouse, in the vacant lot up there. You took them swinging down Cherry Street into Main.

They were awkward and you made them not awkward. "Come on, now! Try that again! Catch it! Catch it!

"One, two, three, four! Count it off in your own minds like that! Make it snappy, now! One, two, three, four!"

It was nice, nice—in the evening in the summer, taking the men thus out into the street. Up in the hall, in the big town hall in the winter, it wasn't quite so gaudy. You felt shut in up there. You got tired of it. There wasn't any one watching as you drilled the men.

There you were. You had a nice uniform to wear. An officer bought his own uniform. He wore a sword and at night it glistened in the town lights. After all, you know— being an officer, it was—every one admitted that—it was being a gentleman. In the summer young women of the town were sitting in cars parked along the streets, the streets down which you swung your men. The daughters of the best people in town were looking at you. The captain of the company was in politics. He was getting rather fat. He hardly ever came out.

"Shoulder arms!"

"Mark time!"

"Company, halt!"

There was the rattle of gun butts hitting the pavement in the main street of a town. Ned halted his men before the drug store where there was a crowd loitering about. The men wore uniforms furnished them by the State or by the national government. "Be ready! Be prepared!"

"For what?"

"My country, right or wrong, but always my country!"

It wasn't likely that Ned Sawyer ever thought . . . surely no one ever mentioned it when he went to the officers' training camp . . . he didn't think about taking his men out and facing other Americans. There was a cotton mill in his home town and some of the fellows in his company were cotton-mill hands. It was nice for them, he thought, being in the company. After all, they were cotton-mill hands. They were mostly unmarried cotton-mill hands. They lived up there in the mill village at the edge of town.

It was true, you had to admit it, that such young fellows were rather separated from the life of the town. It was nice for them, getting a chance like that—joining up with a military company. Once a year, in the summer, the men went to a camp. They got a fine vacation, costing them nothing.

Some of the cotton-mill hands were great joiners and a lot of them, only a few years earlier, had joined up with the Ku Klux Klan. The military company was a lot better than that.

In the South—you understand—it isn't the tradition for the first-class white men to work with their hands. First-class white men don't work with their hands.

"I mean—you understand—the kind of men who have made the South and the traditions of the South."

Ned Sawyer never made any such pronouncement, not even to himself. He had been for two years up North in college. The traditions of the old South were being broken down. He knew that. He would have laughed at the idea of himself having contempt for a white man who had to work in a factory or on a farm. He often said so. He said there were Negroes and Jews who were okay. "I like some of them fine," he said. Ned always wanted to be broad-minded and liberal.

His home town in North Carolina was called Syntax, and the Syntax mills were there. His father was the leading attorney of the town. He was an attorney for the mills and Ned intended to be an attorney. He was three or four years older than Red Oliver and that year—the year he went with his military company to the town of Birchfield—he had already been graduated from college, from the North Carolina State University at Chapel Hill, and after Christmas that year he had planned to go to law school.

But things in his family had got a little tightened up. His father had lost a good deal of money in the stock market. It was the year 1930. His father said, "Ned," he said—"I'm a little tight just now." Ned had one sister in school yet, taking post-graduate work in Columbia University in New York, and she was a bright woman. She was as bright as hell. Ned would have said it himself. She was several years older than Ned and had got her M.A. and was now working for her Ph.D. She was a lot more radical than Ned and hated his going to the officers' training camp and later she hated his taking the lieutenancy in the local military company. When she came home she said, "Look out, Ned." She was going to take her Ph.D. in economics. Women like that get notions in their heads. "There's going to be trouble," she said to Ned.

"What do you mean?"

They were at home, in the summer, and were sitting on the front porch of their house. Ned's sister—named Louise— would sometimes, suddenly, break out at him like that.

She foretold the struggle coming in America—a real struggle, she said. She didn't look like Ned, but was small like the mother. Like the mother, her hair was inclined to turn prematurely gray.

Sometimes, when she was at home, she jumped out at Ned like that and sometimes at her father. The mother sat listening. The mother was the kind of woman who never offered an opinion when men were about. Louise said, either to Ned or to the father, "It can't go on," she said. The father was a Jeffersonian Democrat. He was counted a keen man in his North Carolina county and was even well known in the State. Once he had served a term in the State Senate. She said, "Father—or Ned—unless all the men under whom I am studying—unless the professors, men who ought to know, the men who have spent their lives studying such things— unless they are all wrong, something is going to happen in America—one of these days—perhaps soon—it may, for that matter, happen all over the Western world. Something is cracking. . . . Something going."

"Cracking?" Ned had a queer feeling. It was almost as though something, perhaps the chair in which he was sitting, was going to give way. "Cracking?" He looked sharply around. Louise had such a damn way.

"It's capitalism," she said.

Once, she said, in an earlier day, what her father believed might have been all right. Thomas Jefferson, she thought, might have been all right in his day only, "You see, Dad—or Ned—he didn't count on something.

"He didn't count on modern machinery," she said.

Louise had in her a lot of talk like that. She disturbed the family. There was a kind of tradition ... the position of women and girls in America and particularly in the South ... but it also was cracking up. When the father lost most of his money in the stock market he didn't tell his daughter or his wife and when Louise came home she kept talking. She didn't know how it hurt. "It's opening out, you see," she said, seeming pleased. "We're going to get it. Middle-class people like us are going to get it now." The father and the son didn't much like being called middle-class. They winced. They both loved and admired Louise.

There was so much that was fine and even splendid in her, they both thought.

Neither Ned nor the father could quite understand why Louise hadn't married. They both thought—"God, but she would make some man a good wife." She was a passionate little thing. To be sure, neither Ned nor the father let that thought quite come up into words. A Southerner—a gentleman—didn't think—of a sister or of a daughter—"she's a passionate one—she's a live one. If you could have such a one as your own, what a beautiful lover she might be!" They didn't think that. But ...

Sometimes in the evening when the members of the family were sitting on the porch of their house ... it was a big old brick house with a wide brick terrace across the front ... you could sit there on the summer evenings looking at pine forests on low hills in the distance ... the house was almost in the center of town but was on high ground ... Ned Sawyer's grandfather and great-grandfather had lived there. You could look over roofs of other houses into distant hills ... neighbors liked to drop in there in the evenings. ...

Louise would sit on the edge of her father's chair with her soft bare arms about his shoulders or she would sit like that on the edge of her brother Ned's chair. On the summer evenings when he had put on his uniform and was later going down into town to drill his men, she looked at him and laughed at him. "You do look grand in it," she said, touching his uniform. "If you weren't my brother I'd fall for you, I swear I would."

The trouble with Louise, Ned said sometimes, was that she was always analyzing things. He didn't like it. He wished she wouldn't. "I guess," she said, "it's us women, falling for you men in your uniforms ... you men going out to kill other men ... there's something savage and ugly in us too.

"There must be something brutal in us too."

Louise thought ... she spoke out sometimes ... she didn't want to ... she hated to disturb her father and mother ... she thought and said that unless things changed rapidly in America, "new dreams," she said, "growing up to take the place of old hurtful individualistic dreams ... dreams become utterly corrupted now—by money," she said. She grew suddenly serious. "The South will have to pay bitterly," she said. Sometimes when Louise talked to her father and brother in the evening like that they were both glad there weren't any others present ... people of the town who might have heard her going on. . . .

It wasn't any wonder that men, Southern men, the kind you would have expected to be courting such a woman as Louise were a little afraid of her. "Men don't like an intellectual woman. That's the truth ... only with Louise—if the men had only known—but never mind that—"

She had queer notions. She had got that way. Sometimes the father answered her almost sharply. He was half angry. "Louise, you're a damn little red," he said. He laughed. Just the same—his own daughter—he loved her.

"The South," she said, seriously to Ned or the father, "it'll have to pay and pay bitterly.

"This old gentleman idea you men down here have built

up—the statesman, the soldiers—the man who never works with his own hands—all that sort of thing. . . .

"Robert E. Lee. An attempt at kindness built into it. It's sheer patronage. It's a feeling built on slavery. You know it, Ned—or Father. . . .

"It's an idea in us, ingrained in us—sons of good Southern families like Ned here." She looked sharply at Ned. "Isn't he perfect in his uniform?" she said. "Such men couldn't work with their hands—they wouldn't dare work with their hands. It would be a disgrace, wouldn't it, Ned?

"It's going to come," she said, and the others grew serious. She was speaking now outside her own class. She was trying to explain to them. "There's this new thing in the world now. It's machinery. Your Thomas Jefferson, in his thinking, didn't count on that, did he, Father? If he were alive to-day perhaps he would say—I've a notion—quickly enough—now machinery has thrown all his thoughts into the scrap heap.

"It'll begin slowly," Louise said, "consciousness in labor. They'll begin more and more to realize that there is no hope for them—looking to people like us."

"To us?" the father asked sharply.

"You mean us?"

"Yes. We are middle-class, you see. You hate the word, don't you, Father?"

The father was annoyed, as Ned was. "Middle-class," he said contemptuously—"if we're not first-class, who is?"

"Just the same, Father—and Ned . . . you, Father, are a lawyer and Ned's going to be one. You are the lawyer for the mill people here in this town. Ned hopes to be."

There had been, a short time before, a strike in a mill town in the South, in a town in Virginia. Louise Sawyer had gone there.

She had gone as a student of economics to study what

was going on. She had seen something. It concerned a newspaper of the town.

She had gone with a newspaper man to a strike meeting.
Louise moved about among the men freely ... they had con-
fidence in her ... as she and the newspaper man were leaving
a hall, where a strike meeting had been held, a small excited
fat little workingwoman had rushed up to the newspaper
man.

The workingwoman was almost tearful, Louise said later,
telling her father and brother about it. She had clung to the
newspaper man and Louise had stood a little to one side,
listening. She had a sharp mind—that Louise. She was a new
kind of woman to her father and brother. "The future, God
knows, may after all lie with our women," the father sometimes said to himself. The thought forced itself upon him.
He didn't want to think that. The women had—some of them
at least—a way of facing facts.

The workingwoman in the Virginia town had pleaded
with the newspaper man. "Why, oh, why, don't you give us a
fair break? You're on the *Eagle* here?" The *Eagle* was the
only daily paper in the Virginia town. "Why don't you give
us a square deal?

"We're humans even if we are workers." The newspaper man had tried to reassure her. "That's what we want
to do—it's all we want to do," he said brusquely. He had
edged away from the excited little fat woman but afterwards
when he was in the street with Louise and Louise had asked
him, directly, frankly, in a way she had, "Well, are you giving them a square deal?"

"Hell, no," he said, and laughed.

"What the hell," he said. "The lawyer for the mill company writes the editorials for our paper and we slaves have
to sign them." He was an embittered man too.

"Now," he said to Louise, "don't squeal on me. I'm
telling you. I'd lose my job."

*

"AND so you see," Louise said afterwards, talking of the incident to her father and Ned.

"You mean that we?" That was her father speaking. Ned was listening. The father was hurt. There had been in that tale—told by Louise—something—it had cut in close to the father. You could tell it by looking into his face while Louise was talking.

Ned Sawyer knew. He knew that his sister Louise—in bringing up such things—he knew she didn't want to hurt him or his father. Sometimes, when she was at home, she would begin talking thus and then stop. The family might be sitting on the porch of the house on a hot summer evening and birds were chirping in the trees in the yard. You could see over roofs of other houses into distant hills—pine-clad. The country roads in that section of North Carolina were red and yellow as in Red Oliver's Georgia country. There was the low night call of bird to bird. Louise would begin to talk and then stop. It happened once on an evening when Ned had on his uniform. The uniform always seemed to excite Louise, to make her want to talk. She was frightened. "Some day, perhaps soon," she thought, "people like us—middle-class, nice people in America—plunged perhaps into something new and terrible . . . what fools we are not to see it . . . why can't we see?

"We may be shooting down the workers on whom everything rests. Because they are workers who produce everything and who begin to want—out of all this richness that is American—a new, a stronger, perhaps even a dominant voice . . . upsetting in the process all American thought —all American ideals. . . .

"I guess we thought—we Americans really believed—that every one had an equal opportunity here.

"You go on saying, thinking that to yourself—year after year—and of course you come to believe it.

"It makes you comfortable—believing.

"It's a lie, though." A queer look came into Louise's eyes. "The machine has made a joke of it," she thought.

These thoughts in the mind of Louise Sawyer, Ned Sawyer's sister. Sometimes, when she was at home with the family, she began talking and then suddenly stopped. She got up from her chair and went into the house. Once Ned followed her. He also was disturbed. She was standing by a wall, crying softly, and he went and took her in his arms. He didn't tell the father.

He said to himself, "After all—a woman." Perhaps the father said the same thing to himself. They both loved Louise. That year—the year 1930—when Ned Sawyer put off going to law school until after Christmas—his father had said to him—he laughed saying it—"Ned," he said, "I'm in a tight fix. I put a lot of money into stocks," he said. "I think we're all right. I think they'll come back.

"You're bound to be safe betting on America," he said, trying to be cheerful.

"I'll stay on here in your office for a time if you don't mind," Ned said, "I can study here." He was thinking of Louise. She was to try for her Ph.D. that year and he didn't want her to stop. "I don't agree with anything she thinks but she's got the brains of the family," he thought.

"That's it," the father said to Ned. "If you don't mind waiting, Ned, I can see Louise through all right."

"I don't see why she need know anything about it," and "Of course not," Ned Sawyer replied.

9

MARCHING with soldiers in the darkness before dawn through the streets of Birchfield was exciting to Ned Sawyer.

"Atten-shun."

"Forward—guide right."

Tramp. Tramp. Tramp. There was the shuffle of heavy uncertain feet on pavement. Listen to the sound of feet on pavements—the feet of soldiers.

Do the feet like it—this taking of the bodies of men—Americans—to where they must put down other Americans?

Common soldiers are common men. This may happen more and more often. Come on, feet, hit the pavements firmly! My Country 'Tis of Thee.

The dawn was coming. Three or four companies of soldiers had been ordered to Birchfield but Ned Sawyer's company was the first to arrive. His captain being ill, being indisposed, hadn't come and so Ned was in command. The company detrained at a railroad station across the town from the Birchfield mill and the camp of the strikers, at a station quite far out at the edge of town, and at that hour just before dawn the streets of the town were deserted.

There are always in every town a few men who will be abroad before the dawn. "You miss the best part of the day if you sleep late," they say, but no one listens. They are annoyed that others will not listen. They speak of the air in the early morning. "It's good," they say. They tell how, in the early morning, just at dawn in the summer, the birds sing. "The air is so good," they keep saying. Virtue is virtue. A

342

man wants credit for what he does. He even wants credit
for his habits. "They are good habits, they are mine," he
says to himself. "You see, I'm continually smoking these
cigarettes. I do it to give people employment in cigarette
factories."

In the town of Birchfield a citizen saw the arrival of the
soldiers. There was a little thin man who ran a stationery
store on a side street in Birchfield. He was on his feet all day
every day and his feet were tender. At night they hurt him
so that for a long time he could not sleep. He was unmarried, a bachelor, and slept on a cot in a little room at the back
of his shop. He wore heavy glasses of a sort that magnified
his eyes in the eyes of others. They looked like owl's eyes.
In the morning, before dawn and after he had slept a little,
his feet began to hurt again so he got up and dressed. He
went along the main street of Birchfield and sat on the steps
of the court house. Birchfield was a county-seat town and the
jail was immediately back of the court house. The jailer was
also an early riser. He was an old man with a little stubby
gray beard and sometimes he came out of the jail to sit with
the stationer on the court-house steps. The stationer told him
about his feet. He liked talking of his feet and liked people
who would listen. There was some kind of growth. It was unusual. No other man in town had such feet. He was always
saving up money to have operations, and during his life had
read a good deal about feet. He had studied them. "They are
the most delicate part of the body," he said to the jailer.
"There are so and so many small delicate bones in the feet."
He knew how many. There was a thing he liked to speak
about. "You know, soldiers now," he said. "Well, you take
a soldier. He wants to get out of war or out of a battle so
he shoots himself in the foot. He's a damn fool. He doesn't
realize what he is doing. The damn fool, he couldn't shoot
himself in a worse place." The jailer thought so too, although
his own feet were all right. "You know," he said, "you know
what . . . if I was a young man and a soldier and wanted to

get out of war or a battle I'd say I was a conscientious objector." That was his idea. It was the best way, he thought. They might throw you into jail but what of it? He thought jails were all right, pretty good places to live. He spoke of the men held in the Birchfield jail as "my boys." He wanted to talk about jails, not about feet.

There was this man, the stationer, awake and abroad in the early morning when Ned Sawyer took his soldiers to Birchfield to put down the communists there—to hem them in in their camp—to make them quit trying to picket the Birchfield mills . . . to make them quit trying to parade . . . no more singing in the public streets . . . no more public meetings.

There was the stationer awake on the streets of Birchfield, and his friend the jailer hadn't come out of the jail yet. The sheriff of the county was awake. He was at the railroad station with two deputy sheriffs to meet the soldiers. The town had heard rumors that the soldiers were coming, but there wasn't anything definite. The time set for their coming hadn't been given out. The sheriff and his deputies had kept mum. The owners of the mill at Birchfield had issued an ultimatum. There was the one company that owned mills in several North Carolina towns. The president of the company had told the manager at Birchfield to speak sharply to some of the prominent citizens of Birchfield . . . to the three bankers in town, to the mayor of the town and a few others . . . some of the more influential merchants had been told . . . "We don't care whether we run our Birchfield mill or not. We want protection. We don't care. We'll close the mill.

"We don't want any more trouble. We can close the mill and keep it closed for five years. We've got other mills. You know how business is in these times."

There was the stationer of Birchfield awake when the soldiers arrived, and the sheriff and his two deputies were at the station, and there was another man. He was a tall old man, a retired farmer, who had moved into town and who also got up before dawn. When there was no work to be done in his garden ... it was late fall now ... gardening for the year was at an end ... this one took a walk before breakfast. He walked through the main street of Birchfield and past the court house, but he would not stop to talk to the stationer.

He just wouldn't. He wasn't a talker. He wasn't very sociable. "Good morning," he said to the stationer sitting on the court-house steps and without stopping went on his way. There was a kind of dignity in the man striding along thus in the empty street in the early morning. Rugged individuality! You couldn't approach such a man, sit with him, talk with him about the pleasure of getting up early, speak to him about how good the air is—what fools others are to lie abed. You couldn't speak with him about your feet, about operations on your feet and what delicate things the feet are. The stationer hated the man. He was a man filled with many little obscure hatreds. His feet did hurt. They hurt all the time.

Ned Sawyer liked it. He didn't like it. He had his orders. The only reason the sheriff met him at the railroad station at Birchfield that morning was to show him the way to the Birchfield mill and to the communist camp. The Governor of the State had come to a decision regarding the communists. "We'll hem them in," he thought.

"We'll let them fry there in their own fat," he thought ... "the fat won't last long" ... and Ned Sawyer commanding the company of soldiers that morning also had thoughts. He thought of his sister Louise and wished he hadn't gone into the military service of his State. "Still," he thought, "these soldiers are only boys." Soldiers, the kind of soldiers who belonged to a military company, at a time like that, when they are called out—they whisper to each other. Rumors run through the ranks. "Silence in the ranks." Ned Sawyer called to his company. He barked the words out—barked them out harshly. At the moment he almost hated the men of his company. When he had got them off the train and had made them fall into company formation, all of them a little sleepy-eyed, all a little worried and perhaps a little frightened, dawn was coming.

Ned saw something. There was an old warehouse near the railroad station at Birchfield and he saw two men come out from under the shadow of the warehouse. They had bicycles and, getting on them, they rode rapidly away. The sheriff hadn't seen that. Ned thought of speaking to him about it but didn't. "You drive on slowly to this camp of communists," he said to the sheriff who had come in his car. "Drive slowly and we'll follow you," he said. "We'll surround the camp.

"We'll hem them in," he said. At the moment he also hated the sheriff, a man he didn't know, a rather fat man in a broad-brimmed black hat.

He swung his soldiers off along the street. They were heavily accoutered. They had their blanket rolls. They had belts filled with loaded cartridges. On Main Street before the court house, Ned halted his men and made them fix bayonets. Some of the soldiers—after all they were mostly raw boys —kept on whispering in the ranks. Their words were little bombs. They were frightening each other. "This communism. These communists, they carry bombs. A bomb can blow up a whole company of men like us. A man doesn't get a chance." They saw their young bodies torn by a terrible explosion in their midst. Communism was something strange. It was un-American. It was foreign.

"These communists kill every one. They are foreigners. They make women public property. You ought to see what they do to women."

"They are against religion. They will kill a man for worshipping God."

"Silence in the ranks," Ned Sawyer cried again. In Main Street, when he had halted his men to have them fix bayonets, he saw the little stationer sitting on the court-house steps and waiting for his friend the jailer, who hadn't yet appeared.

The stationer sprang to his feet and when the soldiers had moved on he also got into the street and limped along behind. He was also a communist hater. "They ought to be wiped out, every one of them. They are against God. They are against America," he thought. Since the communists had come to Birchfield it had been good to have something to hate in the early morning before he got out of bed when his feet hurt. Communism was some vague foreign idea. He didn't understand it, said he didn't, said he didn't want to understand, but he hated it and hated the communists. Now the communists, who had so disturbed things in Birchfield, were going to get it. "God, it's good, it's good, it's good. God, it's good," he muttered to himself limping along behind the soldiers. He was the only man in Birchfield, besides the sheriff and his two deputies, who saw what happened that morning and all the rest of his life he was to be made happy by that fact. He became an admirer of Ned Sawyer. "He was as cool as a cucumber," he said afterwards. It gave him something to think about, something to talk about. "I saw it. I saw it. He was as cool as a cucumber," he cried.

The two men on bicycles who had ridden out from under the shadow of the warehouse near the railroad station were scouts from the communist camp. They rode off to the camp, driving their bicycles at a furious pace through the main street and down the sloping road past the mill and over the bridge to the camp. There were several deputy sheriffs on guard about the mill gate and one of them shouted. "Halt," he shouted but the two men did not stop. The deputy took out his revolver and shot into the air. He laughed. The two men rode quickly over the bridge and into the camp.

In the camp all was excitement. Dawn was breaking. Leaders of the communists, suspecting what was coming, had been awake all night. Rumors of the coming of the soldiers had also reached them. They had kept their scouts out. It was to be a test. "It has come," they said to themselves, when the bicycle riders, leaving their wheels in the road below, ran up through the camp. Red Oliver saw them arrive. He heard the shot from the revolver of the deputy sheriff. Men and women were now running through the street of the camp. "The soldiers. The soldiers are coming." The strike at Birchfield was to come to something definite now. This was the critical moment, the test. What would the communist leaders, the two young men, both pale now, and the little Jewish woman Molly Seabright so admired, who had come with them from New York—what would they think now? What would they do?

It was all right to fight deputy sheriffs and citizens of the town—a few men, for the most part excited and untrained as they were—but what of the soldiers? The soldiers are the strong arm of the state. Afterwards it was said of the communist leaders at Birchfield, "Well, you see," people said, "they got what they wanted. They only wanted to use these poor mill people at Birchfield for propaganda. That's what they were up to."

The hatred of the communist leaders grew after the affair at Birchfield. In America, the liberals, the broad-minded people, the intellectuals of America, also accused the communists of this cruelty.

The intellectuals do not like bloodshed. They hate it.

"The communists," they said, "will sacrifice any one. They get these poor people killed. They get them thrown out of work. They stand aside and push the others in. They get their orders from Russia. They get money from Russia.

"I'll tell you what—it's true. The people are starving. So these communists get in money. Tender-hearted people give money. Do communists feed the starving? No, you see they do not. They will sacrifice any one. They are insane egotists. They use any money they get for their propaganda."

As for the matter of some one getting killed—there was Red Oliver waiting at the edge of the communist camp. What would he do now? What of him?

During the strike at Langdon he had fought, as he
thought, for labor, and then, when it came to the test afterward—it would have meant going to jail—it would have
meant facing down the public opinion of his own town—when
the test had come, he had drawn back.

"If it were just a question of death—a question of walking up to it—of just taking it—taking death," he had said to
himself. He remembered with shame the incident of the
seven dollars hidden in his shoe in the tramps' jungle, his
lying about the money to the companion picked up on the
road. Thoughts of that moment, or his failure in that moment, clung to him. His thoughts were like wasps flying
about his head, stinging him.

In the camp as the dawn came there was a hum of voices,
a rush of people. Strikers, men and women, were running
excitedly about. There was a little open place in the midst
of the camp and the woman among the communist leaders, the
little Jewish woman, her hair hanging down about her eyes,
her eyes shining, was trying to harangue the people. Her voice
was shrill. It rang through the camp. "Men and women. Men
and women. Now. Now."

Red Oliver heard her voice. He started to creep away
from the camp and then stopped. He turned back.

"Now. Now."

What a fool a man is!

At any rate, no one but Molly Seabright knew of Red's
presence in the camp. "A man talks and talks. He listens to
talk. He reads books. He gets himself into a position like
this."

The voice of the woman in the camp went on. Voice
heard round the world. Shot heard round the world.

Bunker Hill. Lexington.

Bunk. Bunker Hill.

"Now. Now."

Gastonia, North Carolina. Marion, North Carolina. Paterson, New Jersey. Remember Ludlow, Colorado.

Is there a George Washington among the communists? No. They are rag-tag people. The rag-tag people of the earth—the workers—who knows anything about them?

"I wonder if I am a coward. I wonder if I am a fool."

Talk. Shots. On the morning when the soldiers came to Birchfield there was a gray fog lying low down over the bridge—the yellow Southern river down below.

Hill and streams and fields in America. Millions of acres of fat rich land.

The communists had said, "There is enough here to make every one comfortable ... all of this talk of no work for men—it's nonsense ... give us a chance ... start building ... build for the new manhood—build houses—build new cities ... use all of this new machinery the brain of man has invented for the benefit of all. Every one can be employed here for a hundred years making rich free living for all ... the end of the old greedy individualism now."

It was true. It was all true.

The communists were cruelly logical. They said, "The way to do it is to begin doing it. Strike down whoever stands in the way."

A little group of crazy rag-tag people.

The floor of the bridge at Birchfield just emerged out of the fog. It may have been that the communist leaders had a plan. The woman with the disheveled hair and the shining eyes stopped trying to harangue the people and the three leaders began to herd them, men and women, down out of the camp and onto the bridge. Perhaps they thought, "We'll get over there before the soldiers come." There was one of the communist leaders, a thin tall young man with a large nose—very pale and that morning without a hat—he was almost bald—who had taken command. He thought, "We'll get over there. We'll begin to picket." It was still too early for the new workers—the ones called "scabs," who had taken the strikers' places in the mill, to come to the mill gate. The leader of the communists thought, "We'll get over there and get into position."

Like a general. He was trying to be like a general.

"Blood?

"You have to throw blood into the faces of people."

It was an old saying. A Southerner had once said it in Charleston, South Carolina, and had got a civil war started. "Throw some blood into the faces of the people." The communist leader had also read history. "Things like this will happen again and again."

"Hands of workers take hold now." There were, among the strikers at Birchfield, women with babes in their arms. Already that other woman—the singing woman, the ballad-maker, had been killed at Birchfield. "Suppose now they killed a woman with a child in her arms."

Had the communist leaders thought that out—a bullet passing through the body of an infant babe and then on through the body of a mother? It would serve. It would educate. It could be used.

The leader may have thought that out. No one knew. He had got the strikers down on the bridge—Red Oliver following at their heels . . . fascinated by what was going on— when the soldiers appeared. They were marching down the road, Ned Sawyer at their head. The strikers stopped and stood huddled on the bridge and the soldiers came on.

It was light now. There was silence among the strikers. Even the leader had grown silent. Ned Sawyer deployed his men across the road near the entrance to the bridge on the town side. "Halt."

Was there something wrong with Ned Sawyer's voice? He was a young man. He was a brother of Louise Sawyer. When, a year or two before, he had gone to the officers' training camp and then when, later, he became an officer of local militia, he hadn't counted on this. At the moment he was self-conscious and nervous. He did not want his voice to give way—to tremble. He was afraid it would.

He was growing angry. That would be a help. "These communists. Damn such crazy people." He thought of something. He also had heard talk of the communists. They were like the anarchists. They threw bombs. It was queer; he half wished it would happen.

He wanted to be angry, to hate. "They are against religion." In spite of himself he kept thinking of his sister Louise. "Well, she's all right but she's a woman. You can't get at things like this in a woman's way." His own notion of communism was vague and cloudy. Workers, dreaming of taking actual power into their own hands. He had been thinking all night on the train, coming to Birchfield. Suppose it were true, as his sister Louise said, that everything in the end rested on the workers and the farmers, that all true values in society rested on them.

"You can't upset things by violence."

"Let it come slowly. Let the people be educated to it."

Ned had said once to his sister . . . he sometimes argued with her . . . "Louise," he said, "if it's socialism you people are after, come at it slowly. I'd almost be with you if you'd come at it slowly."

In the road by the bridge that morning Ned's anger grew. He liked having it grow. He wanted to be angry. Anger steadied him. If he grew angry enough, he would also grow cool. His voice would be steady. It wouldn't tremble. He had heard, somewhere, had read, that always when a mob gathered . . . one cool-headed man facing a mob . . . there was a figure like that in Mark Twain's *Huckleberry Finn*—a Southern gentleman . . . a mob, a man. "I'll do it myself." He had halted his men in the road facing the bridge, had thrown them across the road facing the entrance to the bridge. His plan was to drive the communists and the strikers back into their camp, to surround the camp, to hem them in. He gave a command to his men.

"Ready."

"Load."

Already he had seen to it that the bayonets were fixed on the soldiers' guns. That had been done on the way out to the camp. The sheriff and his deputies, who had met him at the railroad station, had drawn back away from the affair at the bridge. The mob on the bridge was pressing forward now. "Don't come any farther," he said sharply. He was pleased. His voice was all right. He stepped out in front of his men. "You will have to go back into your camp," he said sternly. A thought came to him. "I'll bluff them," he thought. "The first one who tries to come out of the bridge—

... "I'll shoot him like a dog," he said. He took out his loaded revolver and held it in his hand.

There it was. It was the test. Was it the test for Red Oliver?

As for the communist leaders, one of them, the younger of the two men leaders, would have gone forward to meet the challenge of Ned Sawyer that morning but he was prevented. He had started to step forward, thinking, "I'll call his bluff. I won't let him get away with it," when hands grabbed him, women's hands clutched at him. One of the women whose hands had gone out—clutching at him was the Molly Seabright, who on the evening before had found Red Oliver in the wood back in the hills. The younger leader of the communists was pulled back again into the mass of the strikers.

There was a moment of silence. Was Ned Sawyer bluffing?

The one strong man against the multitude. It worked in books and stories. Would it work in life?

Was it a bluff? Now another man stepped forward from among the strikers. It was Red Oliver. He also was angry.

He also was saying to himself, "I won't let him get away with it."

*

AND so—for Red Oliver—the moment. Had he lived for that?

The little stationer of Birchfield, the man with the bad feet had followed the soldiers to the bridge. He had come limping along the road. Red Oliver saw him. He was dancing in the road beyond the soldiers. He was excited, filled with hatred. He danced in the road, throwing his arms above his head. He clenched his fists. "Shoot. Shoot. Shoot. Shoot the son-of-a-bitch." The road sloped down sharply to the bridge. Red Oliver could see the little figure above the heads of the soldiers. It seemed dancing in the air over their heads.

If Red hadn't gone back on the workers that time at Langdon... if he hadn't grown weak-kneed then, at what he thought a vital moment in his life... then later when he was with the young man who had syphilis—the man he had met on the road... his keeping quiet about the seven dollars that time—his lying about it.

He had tried to creep away from the communist camp earlier that morning. He had folded the blanket Molly Seabright had given him and put it neatly on the ground by the tree—

And then—

There had come the excitement in the camp. "It's none of my business," he had said to himself. He had tried to go away. He hadn't succeeded.

He couldn't.

When the mob of strikers had surged down to the bridge he had followed. There was that queer feeling again—"I am of them and not of them...."

...as during the struggle at Langdon.

...a man is such a damn fool...

"...it isn't my struggle...it isn't my funeral...

"...it is...it's the struggle of all men...it has come ...it is inevitable."

"...it is...

"...it isn't...."

*

At the bridge, when the younger communist leader had been pulled back in among the strikers, Red Oliver had pushed his way forward. He had worked his way through the crowd. Facing him was another young man. It was Ned Sawyer.

"...What right had he...the son-of-a-bitch."

It may be a man has to do it—at such a time he has to hate before he can act. There was in Red at the moment also a flame. There was a sudden little burning feeling inside. He saw the absurd little stationer dancing in the road beyond the soldiers. Did he also represent something?

At Langdon there had been the people of his own town, his fellow-townsmen. It might have been thinking of them that made him step forward.

He thought—

Ned Sawyer thought—"They aren't going to do it," Ned Sawyer had thought just before Red had stepped forward. "I've got them," he had thought. "I've got their nerve. I've got it on them. I've got their goat."

He had got himself into an absurd position. He knew that. If one of the strikers came forward now, out of the bridge, he would have to shoot him. Not very nice business, this shooting another man, perhaps an unarmed man. Well, a soldier's a soldier. He had made a threat and the men of his company had heard the threat. A commander of soldiers cannot weaken. If one of the strikers did not come forward soon, did not call his bluff...if it was just a bluff...he would be all right. There was a little prayer in Ned. He wanted to call out to the strikers. "Don't. Don't do it," he wanted to cry. He had begun to tremble a little. Was he growing ashamed?

It could last only a minute. If he won they would go back into their camp.

None of the strikers except the woman, Molly Seabright, knew Red Oliver. He had not seen her that morning in the mass of strikers but he had consciousness of her. "I'll bet she's here—looking." She was standing in the crowd among the strikers, her hand gripping the coat of the communist leader who had wanted to do what Red was now doing. When Red Oliver stepped forward her hands dropped to her side. "God! Look!" she cried.

Red Oliver had stepped out from among the strikers. "Well, hell," he thought. "What the hell," he thought.

"I'm a silly ass," he thought.

Ned Sawyer also thought. "What the hell," he thought. "I'm a silly ass," he thought.

"Why'd I want to get myself into such a hole? I've made an ass of myself.

"No brains. No brains." He could have made his men rush forward—with fixed bayonets rushing the strikers. He could have overwhelmed them. They would have had to give way, go back to their camp. "A damn fool, that's what I am," he thought. He wanted to cry. He became furiously angry. His anger steadied him.

"The hell," he thought, raising his revolver. The revolver spoke and Red Oliver pitched forward. Ned Sawyer appeared cool now. Afterwards, the little stationer of Birchfield said of him, "I'll tell you what," he said, "he was as cool as a cucumber." Red Oliver had been killed at once. There was a moment of silence....

*

THERE was a cry from the lips of a woman. It came from Molly Seabright's lips. The man shot and killed was that young communist she had, only a few hours before, found sitting quietly in a quiet wood far from this spot. She with a crowd of other men and women from among the workers surged forward. Ned Sawyer was knocked down. He was kicked. He was beaten. Afterwards it was said—it was sworn to by the stationer of Birchfield and by two deputy sheriffs—that the commander of the soldiers did not shoot on that morning until after the communists had attacked. There were other shots fired ... some of the shots coming from among the strikers ... many of the strikers were mountain men ... they also carried guns. ...

The soldiers did not shoot. Ned Sawyer had kept his head. Although he had been knocked down and kicked he got to his feet. He made the soldiers club their guns. Many of the strikers were knocked down in the forward rush of the soldiers. Some were beaten and bruised. The strikers were driven back across the bridge and across the road to the camp and, later on that same morning, all three of the leaders, with several of the strikers, all those who had been beaten ... who showed bruises and who had been such fools as to remain in the camp ... many had fled into the hills back of the camp ... were taken from the camp and thrown into the Birchfield jail and later they were given prison sentences. The body of Red Oliver was shipped home to his mother. He had a letter in his pocket, a letter from his friend Neil Bradley. It was a letter about Neil and his school-teacher love—an immoral letter. It was the end of the communist strike. A week later the mill at Birchfield was running again. There was no trouble getting plenty of workers.

*

RED OLIVER was buried in Langdon, Georgia. His mother had his body shipped home from Birchfield and many people of Langdon went to the funeral. The boy—the young man—remembered there as such a nice boy—a bright boy—a crack ball player—he, killed in a communist riot? "Why? What?"

Curiosity had taken the people of Langdon to Red's funeral. They were puzzled.

"What, young Red Oliver a communist? I don't believe it."

Ethel Long, of Langdon, now Mrs. Tom Riddle, did not go to see Red buried. She sat at home. After her marriage she and her husband did not speak of Red and they did not speak of what had happened to him at Birchfield, in North Carolina, but one night, during the summer of 1931, a year after Red's burial, when there was a sudden violent thunderstorm—just such a storm as the one on the night Red went to Ethel in the Langdon library—on that night Ethel took a drive. It was late at night and Tom Riddle had been at his office. When he came home the rain was beating against the walls of his house. He sat down to read his newspaper. No use turning on the radio. The radio is no good on such a night—too much static.

This happened—his wife was sitting near him and reading a book, but suddenly she got up. She went and got a raincoat. She had her own car now. When she had reached the door, Tom Riddle looked up and spoke. "What the hell, Ethel," he said. She had gone pale and did not answer. Tom followed her to the door of the house and saw her run across the yard to the Riddle garage. The wind was threshing the branches of the trees overhead. It was raining violently. There was a sudden flare of lightning and the crash of thunder. Ethel backed her car out of the garage and drove away. The day had been fair. The top of the car had been put down. It was a sport model car.

Tom Riddle never did speak to his wife of what happened that night. Nothing much happened. Ethel drove her car at a furious speed out of the town and into the country.

The roads about Langdon, Georgia, are sand-clay roads. In fair weather they are smooth fine roads but in wet weather they are treacherous and uncertain. It was a wonder Ethel didn't get killed. She drove her car furiously for miles along country roads. The storm continued. The car skidded in and out of the road. It was in the ditch. It leaped out. Once she just missed going over a bridge.

A kind of fury had seized her, as though she hated the car. She was soaking wet and her hair was in disorder. Was she trying to get killed? She did not know where she was. Once during the drive that night she saw a man walking in the road and carrying a lantern. He shouted at her. "Go to hell," she screamed. It is a country of many poor little farm houses, shacks really, and now and then, when the lightning came, she could see a house close to the road. In the darkness there were a few distant lights, like stars fallen to earth. In one house, near a town ten miles from Langdon, she heard a woman singing.

She grew quiet and returned to her husband's house at three in the morning. Tom Riddle had gone to bed. He was a shrewd capable man. He was awake but he said nothing. He and his wife slept in separate rooms. On that night he did not speak to her of her drive and afterwards he did not ask her where she had been.

THE END